BEYOND THE GLOOM

BLOOD SINGS

DENISA MIH

Developmental editing by Lauren Carpenter at www.lmcarpenter.com

Copy/line editing by Ellie Race at www.raceediting.wordpress.com

Formatting by Denisa Mih

Map by Denisa Mih

Interior Graphics by AnesayArt, PaperHareDesign, and RomannaBoch

Table of contents

Author's Note

Dear reader,

Before you dive into Blood Sings, a word of caution: this tale doesn't shy away from the darker aspects of existence. It contains scenes of violence, gore, and torture. There are instances of sexual assault, including flashbacks. Emotional abuse, racism, and sexual content are also present.

To those who've faced trauma, please tread carefully. While I've strived to address mental health topics with sensitivity, I acknowledge that every person's experience is unique. This narrative touches on anxiety, depression, and PTSD.

A specific note about Chapter 8: this chapter contains explicit scenes of sexual abuse. If you feel the need to protect your mental health, you may choose to skip this chapter. Doing so will not impact your understanding of the overall story.

Remember, your mental well-being is paramount. If at any point you feel overwhelmed, please don't hesitate to step away or seek support.

Some of what you'll read comes from research, some from the insights of those who've lived through similar experiences, and some from my own battles with emotional trauma. If you've lost someone, if you struggle with depression or anxiety, if you've felt misunderstood or wanted to disappear—I see you. I've been there.

Aurora's story is for those who aren't okay, for those wondering if it ever gets better. My hope is that it serves as a small beacon in the darkness, a reminder that you're not invisible, not unloved, not alone.

Your story matters. Mine does too. We're all an essential and irreplaceable part of this vast, complex tapestry of life.

With love,
Denisa Mih

Dedication

To my husband,

For the countless meals, the quiet support,
and the love that fueled every word.
This book exists because you do.
Thank you for making my dreams ours.

All my love,
Denisa

Glossary

GODS

Bendis *(BEN-DEES)* - The Mother Goddess. Ruler of the earth and magic.

Zalmoxis *(ZAL-MOX-IS)* - Firstborn. Demi-god.

Sabazios *(SAH-BAH-ZEE-OS)* - Secondborn. A thunderbird. God of the Sky.

Kotys *(KO-TIS)* - Secondborn. A hydra. Goddess of the Sea.

Gebeleizis *(GEH-BEL-AY-ZIS)* - Secondborn. A dragon. God of Fire.

Derzelas *(DER-ZEL-AS)* - Secondborn. A demon. God of the Underworld.

The Great White - A wolf. Zalmoxis becomes a god.

CREATORS

Derzelas' Enforcers on earth. Vampires.

Dracula *(DRA-KU-LAH)* - Creator of the Tepes Coven.

Lucian *(LOO-CHEE-AHN)* - Creator of the Wurdulak Coven.

Marcus *(MAR-CUS)* - Creator of the Hansen Coven.

NATIONS

Crowned Republic of Transylvania - Founded by the three Creators.

Tsardom of Russkaya *(ROOS-KA-YA)* - Founded by the Great White. Rival nation to the Republic.

Aerothria (A-EH-RO-THRI-A) - Iele Kingdom. Founded by Sabazios.

Solanthia (SO-LAN-THI-A) - Human Kingdom. Founded by Bendis. Zalmoxis/Great White as Protector.

RACES

Pureblood - Plural is purebloods. Immortals. Citizens of the Republic. Blood Magic.

Original - Plural is originals. Immortals. Purebloods. Citizens of the Republic. Wield the Darklings. Blood Magic.

Halfblood - Plural is halfbloods. Mortals. Former citizens of the Republic. Ieles, varvas, balaurs, or humans. Magic specific to their races.

Varcolac (VUR-CO-LAK) - Plural is varcolacs. Mortals. Citizens of Russkaya. Great White's children. Werewolves. Magic unknown.

Iele (YEH-LEH) - Plural is iele. Mortals. Citizens of Aerothria. Sabazios' children. Air Nymphs. Air Magic.

Varva (VUR-VAH) - Plural is varvas. Mortals. Unknown location. Kotys' children. Water Nymphs. Water Magic.

Balaur (BAH-LAU-R) - Plural is balaurs. Mortals. Unknown location. Gebeleizis' children. Half-dragons. Fire Magic.

Humans - Mortals. Solanthia. Bendis' children. Thirdborns. Earth Magic.

STALKERS

Russkaya's creations to defeat the Republic.

Limus (LEE-MUS) - Plural is Limuses. Sand Manipulation.

Glacie (GLAY-CHEE) - Plural is Glacies. Ice Manipulation.

Nebula (NEB-YU-LA) - Plural is Nebulas. Pressure Manipulation.

Ignis (IG-NIS) - Plural is Ignises. Magma Manipulation.

OTHER

Zmeu *(Z-MEH-OO)* - Plural is Zmei (z-may). Dragons dwelling high up in the Carpathian Mountains.

Palinka *(PAH-LEEN-KAH)* - Hard liquor made by the Wurdulaks.

Kafea *(KAH-FAY-AH)* - Homemade blend of roasted dandelion root and ground chickpeas.

Pronunciation Guide

LOCATIONS

Sibiu - *SEE-BYOO*

Sighisoara - *SEE-GYSH-OH-AH-RAH*

Brasov - *BRAH-SHOV*

Bethlen Fortress - *BETH-LEN FORTRESS*

PERSONAE DRAMATIS

Characters in order of appearance or mention:

Aurora Rada Tepes - *AW-ROH-RAH RAH-DAH TSEH-PESH*

Vlad Tepes - *VLAHD TSEH-PESH*

Lev Wurdulak - *LEHV WUR-DOO-LAHK*

Matei Covacs - *MAH-TEH-EE KOH-VAHCH*

Selena Popescu - *SEH-LEH-NAH POH-PES-KOO*

Elena Tepes - *EH-LEH-NAH TSEH-PESH*

Harambea - *HAH-RAHM-BEH-AH*

Andrei Stoica - *AHN-DRAY STOY-KAH*

Petru Tepes - *PEH-TROO TSEH-PESH*

Bodgan Enescu - *BOHG-DAHN EH-NES-KOO*

Sonya - *SOH-NYAH*

Azalea - *AH-ZAH-LEE-AH*

Tiberius - *TEE-BEH-REE-OOS*

Victoria - *VEEK-TOH-REE-AH*

Katerina - KAH-TEH-REE-NAH

Lucius - LOO-CHEE-OOS

Sevastyan - SEH-VAHST-YAHN

Alexandru Wurdulak - AH-LEK-SAHN-DROO
  WUR-DOO-LAHK

Anastasia Hansen - AH-NAH-STAH-SEE-AH HAHN-SEN

Olaru - OH-LAH-ROO

Ivan - EE-VAHN

Gregor - GREH-GOR

Traian - TRAH-HYAHN

Aurelius - AW-REH-LEE-OOS

Luminita - LOO-MEE-NEET-SAH

Constantin Noica - KOHN-STAN-TEEN NOY-KAH

Stefan Luchian - SHTEH-FAHN LOO-KEE-AHN

Ditoa Firestarter - DEE-TOH-AH FIRESTARTER

Burebista - BOO-REH-BEES-TAH

Radu Lowe - RAH-DOO LOH

Horia Bratu - HOR-YAH BRAH-TOO

Sabin Cantemir - SAH-BEEN KAHN-TEH-MEER

Alina Wyrm - AH-LEE-NAH WERM

Karina Bulwark - KAH-REE-NAH BUL-WAHRK

Tudor Steros - TOO-DOR STEH-ROS

Lena Longtail - LEH-NAH LONGTAIL

THE GLOOM
THE CARPATHIANS
DRACULA
BRASOV
SIGHISOARA
BLACK GUILD
SIBIU
10TH WARD
9TH WARD
8TH WARD
N
S
E
W
CROWNED
REPUBLIC OF
TRANSYLVANIA

Aurora

The world was ending, and we had no idea.

A cool breeze kissed the back of my neck, and I paused, inhaling deeply as the metallic door sealed shut behind me, confining me in the command room. The space stretched out before me—a perfect square, fifteen feet in each direction, with a high ceiling looming overhead.

My skin prickled as I took in the vast emptiness.

Invisible fingers seemed to tighten around my throat, squeezing in tandem with the room's oppressive silence.

Far beneath Corvin Palace, I had nothing to fear. But I tugged at my collar, exhaling sharply. This was my domain, my sanctuary. The fortress, once my coven's stronghold during Father's reign, now buzzed as the nerve center for the Crowned Republic of Transylvania's military might.

I was safe. The Sparrows were not.

The lives of my outliers hung in the balance of tonight's mission.

My heels echoed against the concrete slab as I moved further into the room. Light from six overhead tubes reflected on the white-tiled walls, which were veined with whispers of green and black, lending the room an almost—but not quite—austere elegance.

A cloying scent of cherry and almond assaulted my senses, my nose wrinkling in disgust. I rolled my eyes without Mother here to scold me. That was when I noticed it.

There, perched on the glossy corner of my desk, sat another 'gift' from Lev Wurdulak.

Fury and agony built at the sight. I screamed into the walls.

The box, decorated with intricate chip carvings, dredged up memories I'd fought to bury.

Lev and I had been groomed to rule together since our fangs first broke through. That future had shattered the day his family orchestrated my coven's downfall, while my father's ashes still smoldered on the battlefield.

He'd stolen *my* crown, *my* birthright—and one day, I would challenge him for my throne, when I was ready, when I grew into my power. One day, it would all be mine to set right.

Acid burned in my throat as I pried open the box. A vial of his blood glimmered like liquid rubies, taunting me. My fingers curled around it, arm tensed and ready to shatter the glass... but I hesitated.

The satisfaction wasn't worth the mess.

When would he understand I wanted nothing to do with him? Five decades of silence, and still he persisted. Even Mother's meddling couldn't excuse his obsession.

We had both changed. Those childhood promises of 'forever'?

They were nothing but fading echoes now.

With a flick of my wrist, I sent the box tumbling into the waste bin. The vial clattered after it, unbroken and dulled in the shadows of the bin.

Good riddance.

Closing my eyes, I willed my racing heart to slow and took my seat. One... two... three...

The reclining chair cradled me as I shifted my focus to what truly mattered.

The mission was routine, simple: keep the Ninth Ward safe, improve attack strategies, gather Stalker intel, alert the captain of incoming strikes. Nothing new, nothing shocking. Just the backdrop to every breath I'd ever taken.

War wasn't just what I did. It was who I was. It was woven into the fabric of my existence, as constant as my heartbeat. Peace? That was the fairy tale. This endless cycle of strategy, combat, and survival? That was my reality.

So yes, today was just another Tuesday. Because in my world, every day was a battle, and that was how it had always been.

I twisted my mane of thick, jet-black waves over my shoulder, breathing in the sharp tang of chemicals and disinfectants, and activated the Bloodthorn Nexus at my nape. It unfurled like a blossoming flower, ready to bridge my mind with the outliers on the front lines.

The needle's sting made me grit my teeth.

Underworld's balls. I hated this part.

A few agonizing seconds passed as microscopic tendrils burrowed into my cerebellum. Then, blessed relief. Tiny electric tingles danced across my skin, followed by a surge of clarity that sharpened the world to a razor's edge.

Now, this? Worth every second.

I flexed my fingers and spoke into the hushed room. "Initiate Harmonization. Projector Aurora Tepes, Commanding Control Officer, Western Front's Ninth Ward, Third Defensive Guild. Set Harmonization target, Outlier Stoneheart."

The Nexus hummed against my skin as Stoneheart's consciousness flooded my mind—crisp and clean. It tasted just like his blood sample at the Initiation eight years ago, like mint leaves and green tea.

With a sudden, violent jolt that resonated through my skull and made my teeth ache, our mental link snapped into place. Screens flickered to life around me, pouring a stream of battlefield data: colorful maps, frenzied movement charts, and scrolling environmental readings.

• Ninety neon green stars winked on the central display—my Sparrows and two other guilds. The Stalkers' red dots swarmed like angry fireflies, far too abundant for comfort.

My pulse quickened despite my best efforts to regain control.

"Projector Tepes to Stoneheart. Confirm Harmonization," I said, proud of how steady I kept my voice.

"Stoneheart to Projector Tepes. Harmonization complete. I read you loud and clear." His voice, cool and composed, carried that sharp edge typical of mature young men.

The captain, bearing the title in name only, was two decades my senior. Originally human, he endured the Change in his early twenties, well before the war. He had also forgone the mortal world for night and blood—and the benefits of becoming a mixed-breed citizen. Now, his service was part of an agreement to reclaim civil rights for himself and his family.

"Good evening, Stoneheart," I said. "I look forward to working with you today."

"Your enthusiasm warms my halfblooded *heart, Projector."*

His words sliced through me, pouring acid over old wounds.

Guilt crashed into me. Hot. Suffocating.

I stiffened, fighting to keep my resolve and not say something that would trigger his ire again. Our discussions seldom ended on a friendly tone.

The Republic's views on mixed-breeds were archaic, plain and simple. I'd seen their potential firsthand, worked alongside them for almost my entire life. They were anything but inferior. But nothing I said erased what we did to them.

With effort, I pushed his casual cruelty aside and tapped into my magic. Our shared consciousness expanded, mapping Stoneheart's surroundings. Through him, my Blood Manipulation stretched over a mile in every direction, particularly adept at sniffing out mortals, especially Stalkers.

It didn't take long to find them.

The Stalkers stood out like oil slicks on water, their dark, viscous outlines unmistakable blots of corruption among the outliers' soft blue auras.

A century of war, and I still couldn't believe Russkaya had stooped so low. It was a nation without a moral compass. Inoculating allies with immortal blood, forcing the Change upon them—it turned my stomach. Our tests had found traces of human, iele, varva, and balaur DNA in Stalker blood, but never varcolac. Never their own.

Cowards.

They disregarded the sanctity of life so casually. Not that we hadn't wronged in the past—forefather Aurelius's transgression against Solanthia millennia ago was a dark stain on our history. But the varcolacs had crossed a line.

Using innocent people as pawns in their war...

The irony twisted like a knife in my gut. Weren't *we* doing the same? Exiling mixed-breeds beyond our borders to fight our battles?

Releasing a strangled breath, I opened the Harmonization link with the whole guild, only to slam into a wall of anxiety. "I've intercepted the enemy forces half a mile to the east," I reported. "Confirming a mixed battalion-size of Limuses and Glacies. At least eighty each."

Silence stretched, thick and heavy.

"Acknowledged, Projector Tepes," Stoneheart's voice crackled through, taut as a bowstring. *"I can see them from here. Stand by."*

Gunfire erupted; thunderous, even through our linked-hearing sense. I sensed projectiles whizzing past him, fear and desperation flooding my mind. One stray bullet could end him—mixed-breed or not, he wasn't truly immortal.

"Stoneheart to the Sparrows! Quiet your movements." His orders rang sharp and clear. *"Remember, the Limuses detect vibrations through the ground. Engage from a distance!"*

"Enemy to your right! In the mist!" Blaze's foghorn voice pierced my skull. *"Fire now!"* The vice-captain, a balaur female, was only a few months away from finishing her conscription.

"Blaze! Use your flames! I'll cover you," Stoneheart commanded. *"Everyone else, stick to rifles. No magic—I won't have you collapsing in battle."*

The ground rumbled as Stoneheart's magic surged.

Limuses snarled and clawed against his bulwark, their fury reverberating in my head. I couldn't see them now, but their razor-sharp claws and needle-like teeth had plagued my nightmares for years.

His breathing grew ragged with the effort of maintaining the shield. *"We need to move,"* he gasped. *"Blaze, can you clear a path?"*

"On it. But run like hell. I'm running on fumes here."

Footsteps crunched as Blaze approached. With a roar, she unleashed a jet of fire that lived up to her name, engulfing the Limuses until their howls dissolved into the night.

But more were coming. Fast.

Stoneheart dropped the wall and bolted for the forest, the Sparrows on his heels. The other guilds held positions and engaged the enemy.

"Projector," Stoneheart panted, jolting me. *"Didn't you say mixed battalion?"*

My eyes snapped to the screen. The Glacies blips hadn't moved.

Why aren't they attacking?

A bone-chilling growl ripped through the link. Blaze's cry for help twisted my insides. Limuses had cut her off, herding outliers from the other guilds toward her like cattle to slaughter.

My heart slammed against my ribs, the room tilting. This was all wrong.

"Blaze down!" a desperate voice cut through the chaos. *"Captain, I can use my water magic. I can save her!"* Ripple, a varva with unreliable power, was already racing to Blaze's aid.

Stoneheart's command thundered through my skull. *"Ripple, stand down! You're outmatched!"*

I agreed. He wasn't wrong. A dozen more red blips converged on the vice-captain's position, with more in pursuit. It was the right tactical move.

"No. I can save her. I can save her."

Stoneheart demanded, *"Stand down!"*

Ripple's blood-curdling scream tore through my mind. White-hot agony lanced through our blood connection, followed immediately by Blaze's anguished cry. "I'm sorry, guys... This is it for me. It's been an honor—"

I hissed through pursed lips, desperately trying to maintain our links.

"Stoneheart to Blaze! Hold—hold on! I'm coming!" The captain's voice broke with desperation. *"Cyclone, with me!"*

Darting my eyes on the screen, I searched for Ripple's location. His silence was deafening.

The ground roared and cracked open with Stoneheart's effort to keep the Limuses away from his guildmates, but too many had joined the horde.

Blaze and Ripple's signals winked out, followed by half a dozen more from the other guilds.

Gunfire faded to silence. Deathly silence. The type only heard on battlefields and the land where life was laid to rest for eternity.

In the distance, Limuses howled, drunk on bloodlust. Even in my room's safety, fear slammed into me, locking my knees and straining my muscles.

Stoneheart tumbled to the ground, a string of curses spilling out of his mouth. The sound freed me from the silence as he scrambled to his feet and bolted for the treeline.

An alarm blared, and only by the mercy of Mighty Derzelas, our Dark Father and God of the Underworld, did I not crash to the floor. I spun back to the screens and gasped.

Eight neon green stars streaked in from the north, a perfect V formation.

Is t-that... Another guild coming to our aid?

The irregular angle of their approach signaled tactical strike—not rescue, but ambush. Every instinct told me they were hunting, their formation designed to hem in and trap the Stalkers from multiple angles. These weren't reinforcements. Their stars on the map moved with a cold, calculated precision that suggested this wasn't their first raid.

No one in their right mind would stroll on Stalker-infested land, let alone join a battle without their commanding officer to oversee their perimeter and strategy.

On the other half of the screen, the once-static enemy blips stirred to life. The idle Glacies shuffled, reorganizing into neat rows. But they held position, as if waiting for... something.

What in the Underworld is going on?

"Stoneheart, friendlies should enter your line of sight in three, two—"

"Well, I'll be damned!" He huffed. *"Projector Tepes, that's Captain Harbinger from the Tenth Ward. On patrol."*

Some patrol. But Stoneheart's relief was palpable, and we needed all the help we could get.

"Regroup. Focus on the Limuses," I ordered. "Harbinger's team is moving to engage the Glacies. Provide support when you can."

"Copy that, Projector. Stand by."

My heart sped as I yanked open my desk drawer, eyeing the silver box within. I needed eyes on the battlefield. No time for hesitation. I pressed my thumb to the lock.

The lid sprung open with a quiet electronic hiss. The Astral Visor lay nestled on black velvet, my fingertips tingling with anticipation as I lifted it.

"Stoneheart, status report," I commanded, securing the device around my head. In the screen's reflection, I glimpsed neon blue lights flickering along the band's edges. A soft beat pulsed through it as it sought connection to my Nexus.

"Visibility zero, Projector," Stoneheart's voice buzzed in my ear. *"Mist's thicker than pea soup. We've lost visual on friendlies and hostiles alike."*

The holographic screen dropped over my right eye, battlefield data materializing even as adrenaline flooded my system. *"Open Transpectre via Stoneheart,"* I projected to the Visor, my mind already racing through strategy. We needed to coordinate our forces—fast.

The ticking ceased, and in an instant, I was there. Thrust into the nightmare, hundreds of miles away.

Moonlight bathed the battlefield in silver, casting an eerie glow over the blood-soaked grass. Wisps of ivory mist—no, sand particles—swirled skyward, forming a thick curtain that obscured the combat going on in the background. Blood pooled among eviscerated bodies, a crimson tide.

I pushed past the vomit bubbling in my throat. "Sweet Derzelas!" I gasped.

Stoneheart's gaze snapped to the right, scanning over the charred Limuses. Something more sinister stirred within the mist.

My breath stuck in my windpipe and remained there, heavy as a rock.

From the swirling, opaque fog, monstrous creatures emerged, their gray skin stretched taut over bone crests that jutted sharply from their spines. They charged the First Defensive Guild, magic cranked to maximum as sand exploded from the earth, muffling their thunderous approach. Gaunt and sinewy as hellhounds, they leaped, tearing through the outliers with savage glee.

Rifles choked. Elemental magic fizzled and died. A jet of water hung suspended before gravity reclaimed it, splattering into crimson puddles.

The hellhounds emerged from all sides, encircling the Second Defensive Guild.

Arterial spray painted the air red.

Terror clawed at me, begging me to sever the connection and flee. But I couldn't look away.

I had to see. To witness.

Stoneheart drew a ragged breath, summoning the dregs of his magic. His heart stuttered, a desperate rhythm pumping life into his exhausted muscles. The earth trembled beneath his command, a six-foot shield rising to guard the survivors.

Battle cries echoed like distant thunder beyond the sandy veil.

I glanced at my desktop screen, seeking Harbinger's guild. Eight green stars in a sea of scarlet, they looked like a tiny boat struggling against raging waves as they engaged the Glacies on the hill.

Stoneheart's pulse spiked, and I refocused on the Astral Visor's holo-screen.

A creature stared back at me, its bloodshot eyes glowing in the moonlight.

The captain bit down hard, a curse escaping his lips. The hellhound dropped to the ground, then rose on its hind legs. Another emerged from the mist. Then another. And another. Stoneheart stood a hundred yards away.

That meant that the Limuses were... the size of a large technical supply crate.

"Stoneheart to Cyclone," he barked. *"Take flight and blast them with a Shockwave!"*

"On my way, Cap!" the iele replied.

"Cyclone, halt! Hold your ground!" the words exploded from me, frantic.

Cyclone froze mid-crouch, my command halting him like a statue. The iele's lithe frame tensed, dark hair whipping about his shoulders. His midnight-black wings, now fully extended, cast imposing shadows across the battlefield. Every muscle tensed, each fiber coiled tight, as if poised to unleash a burst of powerful movement with the slightest provocation.

All children of Sabazios, God of the Sky, bore the gift of flight and the magic of zephyrs. But Cyclone's powers were limited.

"Stoneheart," I addressed the captain. "A Shockwave will drain him. I can't let you sacrifice him. Turn back, regroup."

"Easy for you to give orders from your cozy little room, Projector." His response rumbled with defiance. *"But I'm the one with boots on the ground, and I'm calling the shots here. Cyclone, await my signal."*

Remorse and anger warred for first place inside my body. "Cyclone, I'm your commanding officer. Stand down!"

The image bobbed with Stoneheart's curt nod, and Cyclone vanished in a blur of beating wings.

My throat tightened. "Goddammit, Stoneheart!" I slammed my fist against the armrest, frustration boiling over. *Not again.*

"Now!" Stoneheart's command thundered, and the sky answered with a deafening roar.

Trees splintered as a massive fist of air dropped from the heavens, shattering the earth and hurling Limuses skyward. Their bodies disintegrated on impact and rained gore across the field.

In the blast's wake, Cyclone's limp silhouette plummeted like a dark arrow.

My heart leaped to my throat. I'd told him this would happen.

"Stoneheart!" I cried out, silently counting the seconds until impact.

My stomach cramped, as if someone was wringing the blood out of me. The room spun, my suit suddenly too tight, suffocating. A migraine burst behind my eyes, and I rubbed at my temples, willing it to go away.

I should never have opened that damn drawer.

"I've got him!" Stoneheart snapped, barking orders to the remaining Sparrows. *"Aqua and Inferno, split into teams, secure the flanks. Breeze, handle the remaining vanguard!"*

Dropping to his knee, he slammed his palms into the earth, fingers spread wide, nails digging in. A pillar of compressed soil shot up, nine feet high. It broke Cyclone's fall, but the ghastly crunch of bone made me wince.

At least his unconsciousness had spared him.

Stoneheart collapsed, staring at the star-strewn sky with half-lidded eyes.

I sank into my chair, sighing heavily. Past battles had taught me that although he wasn't knocked out, he wouldn't make it back to base without help.

Assessing the enemy numbers, I checked the main screen.

Then my breath caught, and my spine straightened.

"Stoneheart, do you read?" I gasped, double-checking the stats to make sure I wasn't hallucinating. The crimson blips representing the Glacies had dropped to less than half. "Harbinger did it. The Stalkers are retreating north."

His eyelids drooped, and I was selfish enough to wish they hadn't so I could have another glimpse at the unspoiled night sky above him.

"Acknowledged," he rasped. *"That's Harbinger for you. He comes in, gets the job done, and disappears. Without him, you'd have no guild left to see us squabble through your little mind trick."*

Tears stung my eyes, and a sob escaped despite my clenched jaw. Stoneheart was right. I was immortal, safe, while they bled and died.

"Projector Tepes to the Sparrows. The enemy has retreated. Second Guild will take over patrol duties. Please... return to base." My voice cracked. I dug my nails into my palm, letting the pain wash away my guilt. "You did well today. For those we lost... I'm so, so sorry."

Silence filled the Harmonization, broken by Stoneheart's icy contempt. *"We're ever so grateful for your kind words, Projector Tepes."*

With a final exertion of strength, he pushed himself upright, taking one last, lingering look at the carnage that lay before him. Moonlight glinted off spilled entrails and mangled corpses. Sand had settled but still swarmed the air.

He spat, and I could almost taste his disgust.

Unable to withstand the sight any longer, I severed the link and ripped the Astral Visor from my head. Tears streamed down my face, haunted by Blaze's last words replaying in my thoughts.

'I'm sorry, guys... This is it for me. It's been an honor—'

Aurora

Fighting a pounding headache and roiling nausea, I elbowed my way through the throng of projectors crammed into the palace's bustling foyer. The white marble walls glared under crystal chandeliers, each sparkle a dagger to my eyes.

Oomph.

"Watch it!" A woman in a white coat—from the Healing Corps, no doubt—stumbled as I collided with her. She landed hard, letting loose a torrent of curses.

Hundreds of curious glares bore into me, twisting my insides into knots. Fire licked at my cheeks as I raised a hand to shield my face, mumbling "Sorry!" and hurrying past Derzelas' alabaster statue toward the exit.

My pulse pounded as I pushed through the heavy doors, desperate for escape.

Finally breaking free of the stifling foyer, I gulped in the cool night air, hoping for relief—only to gag on the rotten stench of dead animals wafting from the Eternal Blood National Park.

My insides revolted.

The taste of decay and copper filled my mouth as I doubled over, losing the battle with my insides. Visions of crushed corpses and vile ichor flooded my mind, forcing a violent heave.

My stomach emptied onto the pristine steps, a scarlet stream trickling down toward the stone fountain below. I swiped at my mouth and droplets coated the back of my hand.

Water jets hissed and danced in front of me, reaching for the sky between three ivory busts—our revered Creators, Derzelas' sons: Dracula, Lucian, and Marcus.

The squeak of boots had me tensing like a drawn bowstring. Dammit. The last thing I needed was an audience.

"Well, well. Ain't this a pretty picture?" a harsh male voice grated against my ears like nails on rusted metal. Three others chimed in with discordant laughter.

Just what I needed. *Perfect.*

I wiped my mouth once more and spun around, dismissing Matei's lackeys with a scathing glance before locking eyes with their ringleader. That gaunt face, those beady eyes... and dear god, that hair. Cropped short on the sides and back, but sprouting a good two inches on top like some demented yellow shrub.

Matei Covacs. Wurdulak loyalist with an over-inflated ego—and a bad dye job. My unfortunate *colleague.*

As the Ninth Ward First Defensive Guild's commanding officer, we were forced to work together more often than I cared for. Like today's nightmare of a mission. And with each encounter, I became increasingly convinced that evolution had taken a wrong turn with this one.

"Come on, boys," he drawled, flashing crooked teeth. "Let's give the halfblood-loving princess a proper greeting."

On cue, the four of them executed the most ludicrous bows I'd ever seen. The reek of antiseptic and sickly sweet liquor wafted over me. *Palinka.* That piss-poor excuse for booze the Wurdulaks peddled.

White-hot anger sparked within me, burning the nausea into something more violent. This idiot had just lost a quarter of his outliers, and he was in the mood for jokes?

"Tell me you weren't playing cards in your control room while the Stalkers nearly wiped out your guild," I hissed, grinding my teeth.

Matei shrugged, and something in me snapped.

"You bastard!" I lunged forward, seizing the lapels of his leather coat. Tears of fury streaked down my cheeks. "You could have helped! Why? So many lives... we could have *saved* them!"

He pouted. Onyx eyes danced with cruel amusement as he cocked his head. "Aw, don't cry, little Tepes. Filth breeds like rabbits. Plenty more where they came from." His thumb swiped at one of my tears.

Red crept into my vision.

Still gripping him tightly, I swung my fist. Etiquette be damned.

It connected with a satisfying crack, but he shifted at the last second. My knuckles met teeth instead of jaw, pain shooting through my hand as the skin ripped against bone.

"You're repulsive," I spat, rising on my toes to get in his face. "I hope you choke on your own ignorance!"

I shoved him hard.

He staggered back, spitting blood. The amusement on his face vanished, replaced by murderous rage.

I bared my fangs and hissed, beyond caring that he towered over me like a muscle-bound mountain. "Scram, you worthless maggots!"

Like a force of nature, Selena materialized beside me, her elegant blood-red pantsuit screaming 'hot date.' A restless energy crackled from her, making me giddy. At five-foot-three, my best friend packed enough venom in her voice to corrode stone and more courage than half the army combined.

Raven-black hair slipped over her pointed ears as she fixed Matei with a glare that could wilt flowers at fifty paces.

Without missing a beat, her lip curled with the same disdain one might reserve for week-old roadkill.

His pulse quickened, a vein throbbing in his neck, and I suppressed a triumphant smirk. Selena had a way of making even the toughest men simultaneously fear and crave her approval.

Her obsidian eyes flicked to his lackeys, and they froze like deer in headlights. "Are you deaf? Or simply stupid?" she snarled. "Walk away before I code your Nexuses to self-destruct on your next activation."

Matei hesitated, ping-ponging his gaze between us as blood trickled down his sharp chin.

Selena's eyes narrowed to deadly slits. "Hey!" She snapped her fingers. "Did I stutter? Beat it!"

With a final sneer in my direction, Matei signaled his goons. "Let's go."

They skulked away, and a Cheshire cat grin spread across my face. "Can you really do that?" I muttered, half-hoping to see them slip and break their necks. They'd heal in minutes, but their egos wouldn't.

"Of course," Selena drawled, rolling her eyes. "But I wouldn't risk my job on those morons."

Fair point.

Selena held the same rank as me, but as head of R&D in the Healing Corps, she had a code to uphold. As a medical lieutenant, she'd gone for the big brain career—and the fat paycheck that came with it. Every Nexus in the past decade had passed through her brilliant hands in one form or another.

"I knew you weren't just a pretty face," I teased, nudging her shoulder.

She smirked. "Don't you forget it."

I looped my arm through hers, and we sank onto the top stair. Away from my vomit. Exhaustion hit me, weighing down my shoulders. The night had caught up to me, and it wasn't even close to being over.

"A?" Sel asked after a brief pause.

"Hmm?"

Her thousand-watt smile lit up the darkness. "Did you really punch Matei Covacs in the face?"

I shrugged, unable to hide my satisfied grin. "Guess I did. Bastard had it coming."

"They always do," she said sagely. Then her head tipped back, and that infectious laugh of hers spilled into the night. I couldn't resist joining in, my shoulders shaking.

"Oh man," she wheezed, "if Elena finds out, you'll never hear the end of it."

Sel always had an off, kind of brutal, way of lightening my heart.

I groaned, jabbing a finger at my face. "Take a good look. If she does, I'll be Miss Harambea's prisoner for the next decade."

"The manners teacher?" She chuckled.

"Shh!" I hissed, glancing around in jest. "Don't let her hear you call her that. But yeah, who else?"

Sel's body went rigid, her brows knitting together. She leaned in close, rudely pinching the skin under my eyes. "Wait a minute... Is that...?" Her voice turned to ice. "Did you Transpect again?"

Shame burned my cheeks as I averted my gaze to the pocket of her jacket. The last time I'd admitted to using the Astral Visor was three years ago, and she'd nearly lost her mind. So I'd kept it to myself.

What she didn't know couldn't hurt us, right?

Selena pulled back, and we both turned to stare at the sprawling park. A wall of uncomfortable silence rose between us as she fixed her gaze on the busy street below, while I focused on the distant aerodrome nestled among the trees.

It was still early for takeoff, but the pilot flying today's zeppelin into the combat zone had agreed to overlook the extra supply crates I'd snuck into the cargo. At least my Sparrows would have warm clothes and new mattresses to stave off the biting cold.

Unable to bear her cold shoulder any longer, I met Sel's eyes. "I had to," I admitted, my voice meek. "The Limuses were tearing through them. Sharing their pain... it was the least I could do." Fresh tears stung my eyes as Blaze's strained farewell echoed in my mind.

She sighed, raking a hand through her hair. Her heart raced like a galloping horse, but her face could have been carved in stone from all the emotions she let show.

"What happened today?" she asked flatly.

Huh. Looks like I'm not the only one keeping secrets.

Deciding to let it slide, for now, I dove into rehashing the mission. By the time I reached Harbinger's guild engaging the Glacies, her pulse had settled.

Interesting.

"A," Sel said, her voice carefully neutral, "in nine decades of war, the Stalkers have never shown signs of intelligence. Are you sure you didn't imagine it? Maybe the stress—"

I shot her a look. "The scanners don't lie." Clasping my hands behind my neck, I exhaled and stared at the clear sky. "You should have seen them, Sel. Their reaction was instantaneous. They moved like a single unit, coordinating perfectly to intercept the outliers' advance." My voice faltered, a shudder running through me. "It was almost like... a hive mind."

If I was right, if the Stalkers were evolving, things could get a whole lot worse. An intelligent enemy with seemingly endless beasts to replace the ones we felled. The consequences were horrific.

Sel's heart rate spiked again, and I lowered my arms, studying her closely. It wasn't the Stalkers' potential evolution that had her on edge. She'd been calm throughout that part of my story. No, this was something else entirely.

I cut straight to the chase. "What aren't you telling me?"

Sel's pupils dilated. She hugged herself, mouth opening and closing like a fish out of water.

"I don't want you using the Astral Visor again," she finally said. "It's not good for your... your mental health. It affects you."

A snort escaped my lips. "Come on, Sel. We both lied tonight. Be honest with me."

The vein in her neck had a pulse on its own now. It had always been her tell. "You're too involved," she blurted out. "Outliers are expendable. They don't last long on the battlefield."

My heart clenched, an iron anchor dragging me down. I swallowed hard, willing the night to hide the tears pooling in my eyes. "I know that," I muttered.

Hundreds of notebooks, filled with the names of the fallen, lined my bookshelves and the space beneath my bed. If the Republic wouldn't honor their memory, I would. I had to.

Selena pulled me close, her cheek resting on my shoulder. "I'm sorry," she murmured. "I shouldn't have snapped. I just... don't want you getting hurt. The Republic sees them as resources, A. Resources to be used up."

I tried to pull away, but she held tight.

Then she continued, "You can't afford to get attached. Promise me you'll be careful."

Words failed me, so I settled for a nod. It must have convinced her, because she hauled me to my feet. "Come on. Let's grab a drink. A Blood Pact and a few pints of blood will fix that broken heart of yours."

I grimaced inwardly. The thought of another meaningless one-night stand made my stomach churn. I hadn't shared this with her yet, but lately, I'd craved more—someone who understood duty came first and would be there to hold me after a long night. But what my heart desired wasn't easily attainable. Few purebloods would accept playing second fiddle, and I couldn't blame them.

"Can't," I managed, my voice thick. "Mother summoned me to dinner."

"Want me to swoop in for a rescue?"

That forced a smile out of me. "Now that would start a war we couldn't win."

She grinned, winking. "That's my girl."

Just like always, she'd pulled me back from the edge.

A waft of jasmine trailed behind her as she sashayed back toward the palace entrance, her stilettos tapping sharply. "You know where to find me," she called, flashing a final smile before vanishing through the towering doors.

My smile evaporated. The leaden weight in my stomach refused to budge, and I realized I hadn't even asked about her date. Some friend I was.

THE IRON HANDS OF the tower clock crept toward three, each tick bringing me closer to the inevitable: starched napkins, stilted conversation, and Mother's disapproving gaze.

But first, I needed to see the zeppelin off. The distant roar of engines thrummed through my chest as I stood on Aviators Boulevard, fingers curled inside my pockets.

A sharp hiss sliced the night air as the aircraft detached from its mooring tower. I watched the zeppelin ascend, its golden hull gleaming in the moonlight like a delicate film of water catching the glow of distant flames. My lips moved in a silent prayer to our Dark Father, begging for protection on its journey.

The Stalkers were nothing if not unpredictable.

Tearing my eyes from the sky, I spun on my heel and strode down the bustling avenue toward the din of laughter. Near the palace, blood dens thrived, their red-and-white tablecloths and glowing string lights stretching across the road.

I ducked between a gnarled trunk and an old street sign pointing to Liberty Street in faded letters and caught a whiff of HemaTech-9—my favorite blend of synthetic blood—above the sweet perfume of jacaranda blooms.

My mouth watered, fangs itching beneath my gums.

Right on cue, the giant screen across the intersection crackled to life, static giving way to Andrei Stoica's chiseled features. The Republic's official newscaster smiled with perfect, gleaming teeth, his burgundy eyes a shade too dark for an original. Somewhere along his line, an ancestor had strayed from the conjugal bed and sought pleasure in the arms of a pureblood.

Behind him, the Republic's five-blazoned flag glowed in the spotlight, its bold colors overshadowing the unconvincing bookshelf backdrop.

"We have news from the front," he announced, his syrupy voice drawing people like moths to flame.

An excited murmur rippled through the crowd. I gripped Father's pocket watch, my collar feeling too restrictive suddenly.

"Today, a group of Stalkers known as Limuses and Glacies infiltrated the Ninth Ward," Andrei intoned, his face a mask of rehearsed concern. "Our brave projectors, the pride of the Crowned Republic, intercepted and forced the enemy to retreat. Once again, we emerged unscathed, reporting no casualties."

I ran a hand over my face and glowered at the moon, frustration burning in my chest. My superiors had ignored my reports yet again—

"Did you hear that, Mommy? We won," a young girl chirped from nearby.

I snapped my eyes to her, all corduroy and innocence, strolling hand-in-hand with picture-perfect parents.

The mother crouched, tapping her daughter's tiny nose. "Yes, my love. The heroes of this country, the projectors, are protecting us. We have nothing to fear."

Nothing to fear.

A groan clawed up my throat, but I swallowed it down. Only the fear of Mother's wrath kept me from hurling a rock at Andrei's smug face.

Unable to bear the spectacle any longer, I turned my gaze to the monolith at the end of Aviators Boulevard. Corvin Palace loomed over the First Ward, a colossal white structure stretching two-hundred-and-seventy-six feet into the sky. The sheer number of windows could keep you counting for an entire night.

On the rooftop, the Republic's flag fluttered in the wind, its stripes bearing witness to our fractured nation. Red and gold—the colors of the purebloods—dominated the fabric, but thin ribbons of blue, green, yellow, and brown wove through the design, a fading reminder of our mixed-breed citizens.

The sight tugged at my heart.

When had we abandoned our values? Was it when we cast them aside? Or when the government imposed Total Rendition, branding them enemies of the state? Their national colors still threaded into our very standard—prominent enough to be seen, but too thin to truly matter.

Andrei Stoica's voice boomed over the crowd, "Our skilled projectors efficiently vanquish the Stalkers, guarding our nation and sparing precious pureblood lives!" His arms rose in a rallying cry. "The Tsardom of Russkaya's downfall draws near. Hail the Crowned Republic of Transylvania! Long live our nation! Glory to the five-blazoned flag!"

"Long live the Republic! Glory to the five-blazoned flag!" they echoed.

I watched the crowd, torn between contempt and pity.

Except for Bogdan Enescu, my godfather and commander, no purebloods in the military had seen actual combat. We hid behind fortified walls while outliers faced death. We weren't heroes—just cowards in sanitized chambers.

Our Republic, once a sanctuary where mortals found strength and longevity—living up to five hundred years—was crumbling. We'd strayed from our original role as advocates for democracy, seduced by greed and power, aided by technology.

This wasn't the Republic of my childhood.

My superiors deemed the outliers unworthy of the ink needed to fill up the reports. In their eyes, there were no casualties on the battlefield today.

No official records of their sacrifice. No witnesses to their bravery. And my own accounting felt even more necessary now.

A searing agony shot through my chest, and haunting images of the battlefront flashed through my mind—crimson-eyed Limuses tearing into fallen outliers with yellowed, sharp fangs. Shredded clothes and viscera littered the ground, punctuated by desperate, gurgling screams.

I rubbed my knuckles over my heart, trying to ease the ache.

Fourteen...

Fourteen people died today on the Ninth Ward's front.

AURORA

Growing up without Father was tough.

I had fond memories of us playing hide-and-seek in the echoing halls of Corvin Palace. I'd dart away, hoping to outwit him, while he made it his mission to find me. Despite my best hiding spots, he always tracked me down. It wasn't until years later that he shared his secret with me: the moonstone sugar from my Red Brownies was a dead giveaway every time.

Then the war came, taking him away and leaving Mother to manage our coven and the monarchy alone. She fought valiantly against the Wurdulaks, but their growing influence and cunning schemes had out-maneuvered her.

She had to give up the throne.

My throne.

Dracula had marked me as his next heir to inherit his magic instead of my older brother. The crown belonged to our coven, and though she yielded it to the Wurdulaks, it was my birthright to wear it once I came into my power.

All the rage she felt against the usurpers, she'd channeled into molding me into a capable ruler. I underwent intensive training in etiquette, dance, seduction, as well as politics, history, and the science of genetically modified hemoglobin and blood plants.

A queen could never be too prepared.

Sometimes, I wondered if life would've been simpler, maybe even happier, had Derzelas chosen to deposit me down the chimney of a modest, low-ranking family. Would I have been like that crowd, feeling safe and ignorant of the world we lived in?

A sudden thud, reminiscent of a heel clicking, brought me back to the present.

I turned my eyes on Petru, my brother, seated at the head of the long dining table, poring over a stack of reports. His duties as the Governor of the Crowned Republic of Transylvania always trailed after him like an eager pup.

At two-hundred-and-ten, he had a certain charm of people in power. We'd never been close. The gulf between our ages was too vast to bridge for a more affectionate relationship.

Unlike me, who bore a striking resemblance to Elena with her softer features—a gently upturned nose, heart-shaped lips, fuller cheeks, and an hourglass figure—he took after Father, inheriting his tall, lean frame. Dark hair framed his strong, angular face and cascaded past his shoulders. It was the type of face that would inspire you to follow him into battle. But few knew that beneath his amiable exterior lay a fierce determination, perhaps surpassing even our mother's, to restore the Tepes name to its former glory, whatever the cost.

"You haven't touched your dinner, Aurora," Mother's voice cut through the silence. Disapproval. Judgement.

Wearing a simple black dress that hugged her form, she looked every bit like an exiled queen on the five-thousand-acre family estate Father had built for us.

I lifted the silver cup and took a healthy sip of synthetic blood, humming in pleasure as the bouquet of flavors exploded in my mouth—bittersweet with hints of cantaloupe, orange, and a faint trace of honey.

My favorite.

Her rouged lips curved into a cryptic smile, then dropped as she exchanged a conspiratorial glance with Petru.

I maintained my mask of indifference, but internally, my heart rate ticked up, betraying my impatience. Whenever she smiled like that, trouble usually followed.

"Dear, your brother and I have decided it's time for you to leave the army,"—*ah, there it is*—she said with genuine concern. "We fear Prince Lev will not appreciate you wasting your time with your halfblood *pets.*"

I suppressed a sigh, clutching my drink like a lifeline in a storm. Her persistent harping on the Wurdulak heir and my repeated refusal to marry him had tested my fortitude over the years. My military service was a thorn in her side, but what she deemed unsuitable for a queen, I found most fitting.

What better way to demonstrate my dedication to the citizens of our nation than by serving in its defense?

"I understand your point, Mother," I replied, willing my pulse to remain steady. "But my loyalty lies with the Republic. I cannot shirk my duties simply because the prince *desires* it. I will not abandon my post."

The corset cinched around my waist with merciless force, yet I found myself fond of the dress. Its color straddled the line between dusk and darkness, a reflection of the duality of my existence: between day and night, battles and ballrooms.

Mother narrowed her scarlet eyes. "Halfbloods fighting Stalkers shouldn't be your concern, Aurora. You're an original. Your undiluted blood draws from Dracula himself. Sure, your father, Derzelas rest his soul, was a soldier, but let others deal with the battle. We must focus on the future."

I moved my lips for a retort, then smacked them together. Arguing with her felt futile, like shouting into the wind.

Good God. What was even going on inside her head? Did she think I would just ignore the war and pretend the Stalkers weren't a threat anymore?

Petru rarely intervened in our disagreements, so when he spoke up, I couldn't help but arch my brows. "In fifty years, our Creators will awaken. They'll send the hybrids to their graves and put an end to this war. Nothing can stand up to their blood magic, sister."

A glimmer of hope sparked within me, shadowed by a persistent question, almost like an itch. How many more lives had to die before that day finally came?

"However," he continued, "we can no longer ignore the growing civilian demand for a shift in priorities—a cut in the exorbitant war budget for vital welfare and public works. In response, the government has decided to reduce military spending gradually and discharge thirty percent of the outliers."

"But weakening their ranks would jeopardize our defense," I blurted. *Not to mention endanger their lives.* Mother was already too worked up for it to be worth mentioning, so I kept my mouth shut. "We've already filled their properties, and the Seventh Ward is at full capacity. Where will they go?"

"Solutions exist. For now, our focus is to hold the line," he muttered, returning to his documents.

He was the Governor, damn it. Didn't he see how catastrophic this decision was?

My stomach hollowed, and the sensation of falling had me locking my knees together. I drew strength from the tightness of the corset encasing me, keeping my form from withering under his words.

Whether Dracula's Blood Aura, which I'd inherit after my birthday, would be enough to compensate for the reduction in ranks, I had no idea. Lev had already absorbed Lucian's power. Our best shot was to work together and slow the Stalkers down, but pigs would fly before he agreed to help the outliers—even if it meant ensuring our survival.

He was too proud to see beneath his nose.

"The more reason for me to keep protecting the motherland," I retorted. "Projectors need to stand united and hold the front lines until the end. And Mother," I directed my words at her, "please, enough with the name-calling. They are citizens of the Republic too, and deserve respect—they've earned it."

"Respect?" she hissed. "For those blood-tainted aberrations? When will you learn, child? You treat animals like animals. Those *savages* will never understand us. They will never be civilized like us. We must confine them to their cages and control their lives."

My grip on the goblet tightened, and the metal bent inwards, spilling blood onto the table. "Do you hear yourself? If it weren't for them, Russkaya would have knocked at our doors long ago!"

Elena sneered, settling her gaze on my brother. The hatred emanating from her was so clear it tasted like bile on my tongue. "What is the government thinking, allowing these savages to return to Republic soil?"

"It's a right they should never have lost," I countered. "We cannot exploit their strengths when convenient, only to discard them when it suits us. True strength lies in unity, not manipulation."

"No, my dear." She waved a dismissive hand. "You're missing the bigger picture. The Wurdulaks are the ruling royals now. We need their alliance before the Hansens take advantage. Don't let sentimentality cloud your judgment."

Lifting my gaze to the arched ceiling, I silently begged the heavens for patience. Sabazios was a merciful god. Surely, he would accept my prayer for restraint.

"Equality is more than sentiment. It's a basic right. And there are other ways to secure the alliance than me marrying Lev." I slumped back in my chair. "Once I master the Blood Aura, we won't need them. Dracula's magic is more potent than his brothers'. I'll *make* them give my crown back."

"You mean well, dear," she said, cynical yet proud. "But you have much to learn about ruling. The Hansens have always lusted for power. If they marry Anastasia to the prince, not even the Blood Aura could win against the magic of Lucian and Marcus. Don't underestimate them. Because they *will* fight you for the throne. And if you keep up these childish and misguided loyalties, you *will* lose."

"Anastasia is hardly ready for marriage," I scoffed. The princess had at least eighty more years to grow into her power. She studied psychology, not how to rule over the Republic. "Your concern is unnecessary. The worst that could happen is the Wurdulaks surrendering the monarchy when Dracula awakens."

"If only your father were alive..." she lamented, splaying her fingers over her chest. "If only Russkaya's monsters hadn't taken him from us."

And we are back to square one.

"To imagine those halfbloods inside our borders again... How far must their corrupted blood taint our Republic's principles? Aurora, you must sever any ties with those filths!"

Derzelas, give me strength. Would I be a terrible daughter if I strangled her?

I couldn't take it anymore. Tonight... had officially caught up to me. "If anything soils those ideals, Mother, it's you," I snapped.

Her neck stiffened. "I beg your pardon?"

I lowered my eyes to my lap, remorse eating at my anger. She had raised me better than this.

Petru stayed quiet, his face betraying nothing. I knew not to expect his support. He always let Elena have the last word.

"Your father took pity on those savages, and now you're taking after him. Is that it?" she asked.

Trust Mother to drive the blade straight into my heart. Father's resistance to the Total Rendition was a defining part of my childhood—his courage, his sacrifice.

But I didn't want to follow in his footsteps. Even if I did, times had changed, and the outliers resented us more than ever.

"It's not about pity," I said. "It's about doing what's right. Protecting *all* people of the Republic, just as he taught me."

And figuring out why a varcolac saved my life instead of leaving me to face my father's killer alone.

But I kept that to myself.

Mother's gaze assessed me before she sighed—a dramatic, long-suffering sound that pressed around my throat like a vice. I needed to get away from her.

Pushing my chair back, I dabbed my mouth with a cotton napkin. "Thank you for dinner, Mother. Brother, I will see you next week," I dismissed myself, rising to leave.

AURORA

"I'm in the middle of my lesson!" Aunt Sonya's voice rang out from beyond the maze of bookshelves.

I grimaced. The youngest of the three sisters, Sonya had a voice like a foghorn and a flair for the dramatic—exactly what I *didn't* need right now.

Three weeks had passed since that dreadful mission with the Sparrows. We'd completed three more sorties since then, but none dragged like today's patrol. Hunger gnawed at me, my head throbbed, and exhaustion clung like morning dew. I longed to be anywhere but here. To listen to anyone but her.

But did we always get what we wanted? *No.* We did not. And every day I was reminded that others had it worse than me.

"Why are you here? Answer me," she persisted. Then, lowering her tone to a gentle tambourine, added, "Back straight, Azalea. Don't hunch, or you'll develop a hump. Tiberius, stop gawking. It's rude."

A chuckle escaped me despite my irritation. Three hundred years old, and she hadn't changed a bit since I sat where my twin cousins now stood.

"Mother sent word to meet her here after your class," I replied, tracing the initials I'd carved into the wood ages ago. I stepped out into the study area, eyeing the towering bookshelves and the dust-covered antique globe on the corner of her desk. "Work kept me longer than I thought. Mind if I stay?"

Sonya glanced at her children, then fixed her crimson gaze on me. "Only if you don't interrupt."

"You won't even know I'm here," I promised, zipping my lips.

She clicked her tongue. "I've heard that before."

Ignoring her remark, I slipped into the empty seat beside Tiberius and nudged his bony shoulder. "Hey, Ty. What's today's lesson?"

His grin revealed sharp milk fangs that hadn't fallen out yet. "We're diving into the war."

"The war," I echoed, leaning in conspiratorially. "I slept through that one."

He stifled a giggle under Sonya's sharp glare.

"And you got in trouble for it," she interjected and turned to her daughter. "Azalea, in which year did our northern neighbor, the Tsardom of Russkaya, declare war and send the first wave of hybrids?"

I leaned back, glancing at Azalea over Tiberius' sable curls. Though born minutes apart, her shoulder-length hair was the only thing setting them apart. Both had the typical look of kids in puberty: pale, nearly translucent skin, vivid red eyes, and slender frames.

Azalea straightened up. "The Nightwatch first spotted the Stalkers ninety-four years ago, in nineteen thirty-five of the Republic Calendar and thirty-seven in Solanthia."

That's right. I'd been six years old when the deafening alarms blared across the Republic.

"Well done," Sonya commended. "What actions did the government take after Russkaya breached our walls, Tiberius?"

He shot me a wary look. Was he afraid his response might upset me? *That's why he's my favorite cousin.* "They evacuated all pureblood citizens beyond the Seventh Ward and enacted the Total Rendition law."

Sonya nodded, prompting further. "And what did this law entail?"

"It took away the *halfbloods'* civil rights and labeled them as Russkaya's supporters," he said, forehead wrinkling. "By then, our soldiers had pushed the hybrids up north, but we lost the last three wards. The government decided to put the *criminals* in detention camps between the ruins and reinstated mandatory conscription."

The way his voice dropped each time he spoke those words told me he didn't agree with the historians' chosen labels. Hope bloomed inside my chest as I shifted to the edge of the chair, the leather suit creaking like an old saddle.

Change in the younger generation's view about the injustice of the Total Rendition could start here, right now, with my two young cousins. What my father had taught me could be passed down.

Sonya exhaled in frustration. "Do you have something to add, Aurora? Your fidgeting is distracting."

"If you don't mind," I said, rising to crouch between the twins. "Lea, Ty, do you like playing goblin-gobble-bean-bag-toss with your friends?"

They nodded eagerly, welcoming the break from their lesson.

"It's a great game, isn't it? Sonya, remember Mother's freak-out during the Fateless Festival in nineteen forty-one?"

Her face softened, but her terse reply urged me to get to the point. "She searched everywhere for you. You're lucky she didn't send the entire Nightwatch on your trail."

I smiled and turned back to the twins. "That night, I discovered the magic of goblin-gobble-bean-bag-toss. Do you know what made me fall so in love with it that I forgot about my curfew?"

"Was it the losers' chant at the end?" Azalea chirped.

My grin widened. "That too, but mostly it was the company. I met kids who made me feel accepted, regardless of our differences. Do you feel the same about your friends? I've noticed half your group are the servants' children."

"With some of them, yes," Tiberius replied.

"Now, what if at your next playdate, your pureblood friends introduce a new rule? One that bans original players because they say the Creators' blood makes them more powerful?"

"That's not true!" Azalea protested, her voice rising to a shrill. "Purebloods and originals have the same blood magic."

"Yeah, and they're just as strong," Ty chimed in. "The only difference is our Darklings, but they don't help us in the game anyway."

I nodded. "I agree with you, but they don't see it that way. They think you're cheating. You argue, and they find new excuses to exclude you. This time"—I traced a finger up Azalea's slender neck—"it's the shape of your ears. They say they're not pointed enough to match theirs."

"But that's not fair!" they exclaimed in unison.

Pride swelled within me. "No, it's not," I agreed.

I met Sonya's gaze, a silent plea for her approval to continue. Teaching was her domain, and I didn't want to overstep. My lengthy experience with outliers made me biased, and I preferred letting the twins form their own conclusions.

Her response was a slow, deliberate blink. *Alright then*.

"Think about what happened to the mixed-breed citizens," I began. "Even now, we lack evidence to prove they collaborated with Russkaya. You're too young to know this, and the books documenting how the

Republic once welcomed other races have been banned. But before the war, mixed-breeds and purebloods were inseparable." I hooked my index fingers together to illustrate.

Tiberius's eyes widened. "They were?"

"Oh, yes. Good friends," I said. "After the Stalkers breached the walls, the government created this *rule* to banish them based on nothing concrete—"

"The Total Rendition," he murmured, deep in thought.

I nodded, my heart swelling. He'd drawn the conclusion himself. I'd known his intonation on those words had been more than a dislike for the subject matter.

"We hate the mixed-breeds and call them names because they look different from us. Do you think it's fair to judge people on their physical and social differences?"

They both shook their heads, but only Azalea spoke up. "No, it's not," she muttered. "But how can we be sure they didn't betray us?"

Sonya closed the history book and pushed it away. "We can't," she said. "Not until a thorough investigation proves their innocence, which is impossible while the war rages. Perhaps after Dracula awakens and ends it, we'll be able to shed some light on this puzzle."

Guilt and confusion battled across my cousin's face.

"Lea," I said softly, "it's okay to have doubts, as long as you remember that just because something *could* have happened, it doesn't mean it's true."

She nodded, a thoughtful hum escaping her throat.

Ty's gaze darted between me and his mother, building courage. Finally, he asked, "Do you think they'll come back if the government revokes the Total Rendition?"

"With how things are now, I don't believe they would," I replied honestly.

No matter how much I wanted to believe otherwise, I couldn't envision Stoneheart and the Sparrows living peacefully in the Republic after all they'd endured. Gripping the high backrest of Tiberius' seat, I rose to my feet, searching for the right words to explain without sounding prejudiced.

"Hate can only sow more hate," I said at last. "The mixed-breeds don't like us very much"—*understatement of the year*—"for forcing them into conscription. They and their loved ones suffered too much to trust that we'd welcome them back after what we did. For many, that trust is lost forever."

Ty's expression fell, and my heart ached for him.

I met his dull, wet gaze. "It's our job to rebuild that trust, so *if* they choose to return, they find a home where they feel safe and wanted. We can start by seeing them as our equals," I said, smiling as color returned to his cheeks. "They might not have any blood magic or Darklings, but their control over the elements is incredible. You'll like them." I stroked Azalea's head, and she looked up at me with large, hopeful eyes. "Both of you."

The air rustled with the *whoosh* of shadows, and the cloying scent of stale caramel and toffee hit my nostrils. Victoria. Everyone's smell was unique, but when their magic emerged, it became a hundred times more potent. Even if two people shared an element—like vanilla or roses—the balance differed from person to person. A person's magic was a glimpse into their soul, and my older cousin's was rotten to the core.

"Your compassion for those low-lives sickens me," she snarled, her caustic tone striking my back like a whip.

Hot fury boiled inside me as I turned, flicking her off with a saccharine smile. "Like you're one to talk. What use do you have besides casting a shadow?"

Victoria hissed like a viper, her Darklings flaring with her rising temper.

Sonya's scent spiked. "Enough! Both of you!" She slammed her hand on the table and stood. "Twice my lesson was interrupted today. What business do you have here?" Lavender and moonflowers wafted after her as she rounded the corner, her light purple gown billowing in the thick shadows pooling at her feet.

I glanced at the twins. Their lips twitched as they watched the spectacle.

They enjoy this, the little rascals.

"I'm meeting Aunt Elena for her big announcement," Victoria said, her nasally voice grating. "Didn't she say anything to you?"

I snapped my head toward her. This was news to me, and from Sonya's dumbfounded look, she didn't know either.

"No, she did not," Sonya muttered.

Victoria shrugged, her hideous frilly gown riding up around her ankles. "I suppose there was no need since you were already here." She focused on me, a cruel smirk curling her thin lips. "Cousin, erase that pathetic look on your face. If Derzelas thought you worthy, he would have gifted the shadows to you a long time ago. It's not like they'll come if you stare hard enough."

"Azalea, Tiberius, lesson's over. Gather your things and go to your rooms," Sonya ordered, her tone turning icy.

Though the twins were old enough to understand right from wrong, I agreed with her decision to keep them out of family politics. They had an eternity ahead to witness our squabbles.

I was so used to Victoria's barbs that her comment bounced right off me. But I couldn't deny the burning desire to best her and strip her of her Darklings.

The shadows set us apart from the purebloods, alongside our eye color and ear shape. A gift from our Dark Father, they helped originals—even young ones like my twin cousins—escape sunlight and preserve our bloodline. But with technological advances making them obsolete, they'd been repurposed for transportation, moving us a thousand times faster than our natural ability.

I let out an ironic laugh. My ancestors were the first originals on this continent, yet I couldn't even ride my own 'shadowmobile.' Royal status or not, I was the only original in history who couldn't summon the Darklings at my age.

It was a shame—a weakness in the Tepes coven. A... lack of discipline, as my mother might say.

Rejecting her presence from my eyeline, I stared out the floor-to-ceiling windows, waiting for the twins to leave. Adrenaline surged in my veins and urged me to strike back.

"Oh, *cousin,*" I spat the toxic word as if it pained me to speak it, "you should really work on your motivational speeches—they're almost as uplifting as your bland personality."

Her frustrated groan filled me with petty pride. Victoria had a knack for bringing out the worst in me, and while I usually resisted, today, I welcomed it.

"Keep talking like that," she retorted, absorbing the shadows back into herself, "and someone will backhand the wits out of you."

I placed my palm on my heart. "Your concern is touching. Are you offering, or is this just more worthless yapping?"

An explosion of amber and spices filled the air. "AURORA!" Mother thundered, her steely voice settling like lead in my bones.

Her Darklings had moved silently, depositing her near the crackling hearth.

Forcing a smile, I made to greet her, but she silenced me with a scathing glare.

"Since when do you speak like that, arguing like a lowly commoner?" she seethed, dispersing the shadows with an elegant flick of her wrist. "It's unacceptable. This is not how a queen behaves."

The train of her dress swished softly as she glided over to Sonya's chair. I lowered my head, focusing on the rubies embroidered into the corset of her midnight gown.

With her, it was better to yield than to butt heads. "I apologize, Mother. It won't happen again."

Victoria snickered, drawing Elena's ire upon herself.

"You petulant child," Mother snapped. "Don't think for a second I don't know you're the one who foments trouble."

My cousin choked, and I swallowed a snort.

Sonya discharged her Darklings, her gilded bracelets chiming. "Alright, sister. We're all here. What's so important that you need to tell us?" she asked.

"The guest list for next week has had last-minute changes," Mother announced, casting another withering glare at Victoria. "The Wurdulaks will join us for Aurora's birthday dinner."

My stomach plummeted.

Without sparing me a glance, even though it was *my* anniversary she was talking about, she continued. "I expect both of you to make the necessary arrangements to welcome the prince and his family into our house. Derzelas knows I can't rely on anyone else to do things right."

The ringing in my ears drowned out their replies. "Why are they coming?" I croaked.

Finally, she deigned to look at me, and I found the answer in her eyes. "Why, for your hundredth birthday, of course. Lev is coming to make an official claim on you now that you're eligible to inherit Dracula's magic."

The world tilted, acid rising in my throat.

Underworld's tits.

My mind raced, searching for an escape, a loophole, anything. But Mother's resolve was clear in the set of her jaw, the steel in her eyes. This wasn't a request or a suggestion—it was a decree.

"You can't be serious," I drawled, fear twisting in my gut. "You'll hand me over to the people who trampled Father's name and usurped my throne? I won't accept him!"

I had assumed her encouragement of Lev was just another one of her games, a way to exact her revenge, but now I wasn't so sure.

"Don't be immature! This is politics. You'll leave the army and secure this alliance I've worked so hard to maintain. This is your purpose. This is who you were always meant to be, not running off playing war games."

A growl left my lips, a bastard child between a roar and a whine.

The idea of marrying Lev without love felt like a plastic bag over my head—I could endure it for a while, but I still needed a breath of fresh air when there was none left.

"If Father were alive, he would never have agreed to this," I muttered and immediately regretted it.

Mother had many faults, but no one could deny her love for him. Her gaze softened, and hope flickered in my heart.

Then she spoke.

"Until you come into your power, focus on making the prince fall in love with you," she hissed.

Like that's what Lev wants. Love.

Dracula's magic wasn't just the most powerful—it controlled both immortal and mortal blood. Lucian's power to conjure blood and shape it into physical objects, or Marcus' ability to reanimate mortal bodies, paled in comparison to their oldest brother's ability to compel them to do his bidding.

The Wurdulaks coveted the Blood Aura. Mother either couldn't see it, or didn't care, as long as the Tepes name stood at the head of the monarchy again. I leaned toward the latter.

She spun on her heels, shadows leaking from her palms.

"Duty and honor come first. I won't leave my post," I yelled, fighting back tears. "We're still at war. People rely on me. Russkaya took Father away from us! Or have you conveniently forgotten that, too?"

Her body stiffened. "Your duty is to our coven alone. Honor your birthright, then you're free to do as you please. This discussion is over," she retorted before vanishing in black smoke.

"No one ever wins with her," Sonya added oh-so-helpfully and disappeared with her Darklings.

I stared into the flickering fire, nails biting into my palms. *This can't be happening.* The pressure behind my eyes reached unbearable heights, and the need to cry, to release this pent-up energy, made me sick to my stomach.

A shadow stirred in the moonlight filtering through the windows, and I jerked my head to find Victoria sneering at me.

"Don't let us *all* down, cousin," she snarled.

That was all it took.

I snapped.

My body lunged at her, but her Darklings whisked her away before I had a chance to grab her hair. Peals of laughter trailed after her, echoing down the corridor like foxes in heat.

"I hope the Stalkers tear you apart, bitch!" I screamed at the slamming doors and collapsed in tears as our family motto sealed together.

Semper Fidelis: *Always faithful.*

How did my life end up like this?

Aurora

"Aurora! Aurora!" Mother's voice bulldozed through the fog of slumber.

The wardrobe doors screeched open, and I jolted awake. Damn those squeaky hinges.

"Get up this instant!"

I forced my eyes open, each blink feeling like sandpaper scraping across my corneas. The harsh light stabbed at my senses, sending shards of pain lancing through my skull.

"Please... could you keep it down?" I groaned, massaging my temples.

She paused, her heels going silent on the hardwood. "You don't sound well, child."

Understatement of the century, Mother.

Sleep had been a stranger this past week, especially after losing three more Sparrows on our last mission. We were down to two-thirds of our capacity now. I hadn't eaten properly, couldn't focus, and had barely left my room.

A cramp knifed through my abdomen, and I hissed out a groan. Anxiety and hunger jarred inside me, but until Stoneheart confirmed the reinforcements I'd requested, the ball of dread wouldn't stop playing catch with my organs.

Mother swept aside my canopy curtains, tossing a wispy silver dress onto the bed. Her sharp intake of breath told me I looked as awesome as I felt. "Dark Lord help us, Aurora. When did you last feed?"

"Not hungry," I lied, even as my body cried out for sustenance.

"Don't be ridiculous. We can't have you fainting at tonight's dinner."

If my brain hadn't been swimming in molasses, that little tidbit would've set off all kinds of alarms. Of course she cared more about the dinner than my welfare.

I hauled myself upright, fighting a wave of dizziness. "I said I'm fine," I snapped. And, oh boy, how my body protested.

The mere thought of blood set my insides on fire, a primal hunger clawing at me with razor-sharp talons. I gritted my teeth, forcing it down. Later. I'd feed later, when she was gone.

Flopping onto the edge of the mattress, I eyed the offending dress like it might bite. "What exactly is this?" I asked, dangling it from my fingertips. "A dress or a window curtain?"

Mother's lips curled into an infuriating smile. "Not to your taste, dear?"

Oh, Elena is a comedian today.

The rich scent of synthetic blood from her cup made my stomach growl like a beast. *Traitor.*

I watched her drift to my desk, her fingers hovering over the notebook where three names stood out in bold letters against the ivory paper. Pyro. Torrent. Clay. My chest tightened, their loss still raw and hemorrhaging.

Her presence suddenly felt invasive, almost profane. My spacious bedroom shrank around me. The light oak furniture, the plush rug, even my beloved floor-to-ceiling bookshelf—all of it pressed closer, choking me with a suffocating mix of guilt, sorrow, and rising unease. Something was very wrong. I could feel it in my bones.

Taking a steadying breath, I steeled myself. "Alright, Mother. What's going on?"

The window latch shrieked, and a gust of night air swept in.

My fangs extended, my starved body honing in on a decadent sweetness that made me forget about the ridiculous dress. I drifted to the window, pulled by an aroma so intoxicating it made my head swim.

This was no ordinary scent. It was spring's first bloom, a bath of milk and honey. My nostrils flared, drinking it in. Mighty Derzelas, I hadn't smelled anything this exquisite since Stoneheart's blood sample.

Nothing smelled this good.

Except fresh blood.

My blissful trance cracked as brutal reality seeped in like venom through my veins. Beneath that sweetness lurked something darker—bitter, familiar, whispering of old grudges and deceit. Ice-cold dread slithered down my back.

The Wurdulaks.

"They are here, aren't they?" I choked out, stumbling back to the bed and clutching the bedpost for dear life.

Elena shadowed to my side, her face a mask of calm. "Yes, dear. And we're already running late."

This wasn't a nightmare. She *really* planned to marry me off to Lev. I squeezed my eyes shut, wishing I could vanish, melt into the walls, anything to disappear.

"I can't do this," I whispered.

She cupped my cheek, her gaze unusually tender. "You can and will, my dear. It's for our coven's future."

"Please, there must be another way." I shook my head, desperation hollowing out my chest. "I'll do anything."

Mother sighed, genuine sorrow darkening her ruby-red eyes. "I'm sorry, Aurora, but there's no turning back now. Lev will be here soon." She tucked a wayward strand behind my ear. "Breathe. You are ready."

"Ready?" The word tasted like ash.

This wasn't just a marriage. It was a blood union under the sacred moon, binding us for eternity. I didn't love Lev. I barely knew him.

"Arms up." Mother's tone brooked no argument.

I complied mechanically as she slipped the gossamer shroud over my head. Her icy fingers skimmed my nape, fastening the ruffled collar, and a shudder rippled across my skin. Panic writhed inside me like a nest of vipers, but I forced it down.

What choice did I have?

This was the beginning of my end. And my own mother had instigated it.

If she noticed my discomfort, she didn't acknowledge it. Instead, she grasped my hands, tugging me toward the dressing table. "Come, Aurora."

I followed on leaden feet, my reflection growing clearer with each step. The dress shimmered over my skin, morphing from soft lavender to a faint blush under the warm glow of the crystal chandelier. A white leather under-bust, sewn with mother-of-pearl beads, cinched my waist before tapering into a narrow triangle that skimmed my thighs.

Bile burned the back of my throat. The thought of parading before the Wurdulaks in this barely-there outfit made me want to scream.

Elena's sharp nails dug into my shoulders, urging me to sink onto the cushioned seat. "Don't look so terrified, dear. It's just a birthday dinner," she drawled, but the trashing of my heart swallowed her words.

I scoffed. "A dinner where I'm the main course."

"Don't be dramatic. Alliances have always been forged through marriage." She picked up the hairbrush and began working through the knots in my hair. Her voice softened, taking on an almost wistful quality. "When did it grow so long? You were so eager for it to reach your lower back."

The abrupt change of subject threw me. "I was fifteen, Mother," I retorted and avoided her gaze in the mirror.

At fifteen, I'd have given anything to look like her. Now, save for my father's round eyes, I was her mirror image. So alike, yet worlds apart.

The lack of blood had turned my white, smooth skin ashen and drawn. I traced a finger along my cheekbone, wondering when I'd started to look so... haunted. Dark-purple crescents shadowed my bloodshot eyes, while black veins crept from my hairline like spidery cracks in a ceramic set.

I looked as dead as I felt inside. But perhaps that was the only way to survive it—become numb.

"You might feel helpless now, but it shall pass," she said, stroking my hair. "Forever is a long time to grow feelings for your husband. And the prince is... pleasing to look at. You can't argue with that."

I whipped my gaze to her. If Elena could describe Lev as 'pleasing' in the same breath, the world must be ending. I snatched her goblet, taking a long sip to wet my throat—and steel myself for this conversation.

"He's not right for me," I murmured. "I want what you and Father had—real love, not a political transaction."

Elena's shoulders sagged, and I instantly regretted bringing him up. She missed him, I knew that much. Six centuries together was a long time for anyone, even for purebloods. But then she met my gaze, her lips curving into a smile that revealed her familiar dimples.

"It wasn't always a fairy tale, you know." Her eyes gleamed with long-buried memories. "I was quite the rebel in my day. Your father pursued me for a century before I finally yielded." She chuckled, and a bittersweet sorrow gripped my heart. "I came to see how our union could benefit the coven. Love, my dear, isn't always a lightning strike. Sometimes it's a slow burn that grows stronger with time."

"Could Lev and I really work?" I murmured, my voice almost lost in the rustling fabric.

She paused, considering my question. "He's a capable ruler, already leading his coven in all but name. His qualities, I'm certain, extend beyond what you see on the surface."

"What about his harem?" I asked. "The rumors about how he treats his concubines?"

"You of all people should know rumors can be misleading. And you, my dear, are not like his mistresses." She gave my shoulder a gentle pat. "You'll wield your own power soon."

Am I seriously contemplating this? If Dracula granted me the Blood Aura before the Red Moon, I could escape this sham of a marriage. But until then, I was trapped.

I'd *have* to marry him. For the coven.

Still, Lev having a harem bothered me. Whoever he bedded mattered little to me, but as his bride, I refused to accept him with other women. I wouldn't compromise my pride.

"I have no desire to be another one of his conquests," I said, straightening my spine. "And I doubt he'd give up his concubines for me."

"That, my dear," she mused, parting my hair with practiced fingers, "depends on how much you wish them gone. You possess all the weapons necessary to captivate and hold his attention." Her words hung in the air, heavy with implication.

I caught my reflection in the mirror, seeing myself through her eyes for a moment. The gossamer dress, my pale skin, the subtle curve of my neck—were these the weapons she meant? My lessons in seduction had only gone so far. Could I really go through with this? The previous Blood Pacts hadn't necessitated *that* much planning. Our bloodlust didn't care as long as our hunger was satiated.

I took a deep breath, trying to quell the storm in my chest. If only I could borrow some of her confidence to wear like armor against the night ahead.

Elena didn't need a crown to look regal. Her emerald dress hugged her curves like a mermaid's tail, a chain of black diamonds drawing attention to her ample bosom. She was positively stunning. My childhood jealousy of my mother raised its beastly head.

"And what if I fail?" I asked, fiddling with my cuff buttons. God, I hated how insecure I sounded about something I didn't even want.

"You won't fail," Mother assured me. "But if he keeps his harem, what stops you from having your own? Long-lasting partnerships aren't built overnight. They grow from seeds. Even a grapevine needs support to stand tall." She lifted my chin, our eyes meeting in the mirror. "Such matters shouldn't prevent you from ruling together, nor would you be the first to seek pleasure outside the royal chambers."

Another chasm between us. Elena commanded respect like a seasoned general, while I was just a hopeless romantic. She'd been holding our coven together since Father passed, and here I was, too selfish to sacrifice my happiness for the family's greater good. If not for the constant threat of Stalkers looming over the Republic, I might have fled from Prince Lev as far as my feet could carry me.

"What about my Darklings?" I asked, worrying my lip. "Won't he reject me because of them?"

"You are Dracula's chosen, Aurora!" she snapped, her sharp tone slicing through my doubts. "A Tepes never shows weakness. Once you grow into your power, you'll be the most feared original in the Republic.

Darklings or not, you'll wield the most coveted magic in existence. Don't lose your dignity over frivolities, you're much too important."

She set down the brush and vanished in a whirlpool of Darklings, reappearing beside my four-poster bed with silver high-heeled sandals dangling from her finger. "It's time. We should go greet our future allies."

I released a weary exhale, crossing to her and grasping her arm. My stomach stirred as I muttered, "I'm ready," before the shadows enveloped us, whisking us away.

Aurora

Elena's Darklings escorted us to the grand foyer, our heels echoing like gunshots in the cavernous space. Automated blinds covered the windows, sealed out the night, and plunged us into near-darkness. A streak of moonlight filtered through the stained-glass dome high above, painting colorful shadows across the black Venetian plaster and ivory marble.

Ahead, a double staircase wrapped around Dracula's polished bust, one side leading up to the family quarters, currently cordoned off. The other sloped underground.

Five doorways awaited below: three on the left to guest bedrooms and the cellar, one straight ahead to the dining hall, and the last to the right, leading to a hallway that ended in Father's office.

We descended in uneasy silence. At the bottom, two purebloods stood guard—Ivan, with a cleanly shaven face and defined jaw, and Gregor, whose scruffy beard seemed to defy the very concept of grooming.

"Mistress, Princess," they chorused, bowing their heads in reverence.

I acknowledged them with the smallest lift of my chin.

The ancient doors creaked open, their hinges groaning in protest. Great-grandfather Traian's coven crest—twin silver fangs swimming in a sea of crimson—flashed in the flickering light as we stepped through.

Then it hit me.

Fresh blood.

The scent slammed into my chest like a blow, making my head spin. "Underworld's tits," I hissed, feeling my fangs extend in my mouth.

My throat burned. Every instinct screamed at me to hunt, to feed. I squeezed my fists, nails piercing into my palms as I fought for control. Hunger roared through my veins.

Not here. Not now. I couldn't embarrass myself in front of the Wurdulaks.

Mother, ever the picture of poise, glided forward, the very air seeming to part before her.

No mortals bled in sight, thank Derzelas. So, taking a shaky breath, I forced my features into a mask of calm and trailed after her, drinking in the feast hall.

Mahogany shelves laden with ancient tomes and glittering trinkets lined the walls, interrupted by oil paintings of our ancestors. Above the crackling hearth, a portrait of my infant self, cradled in my parents' arms, sat atop the mantle.

Sonya and her lovers lounged on dark velvet settees by the fire, silver goblets glinting in their hands. I acknowledged their silent nods but quickened my pace to catch up with Elena. A queen did not linger.

"The lady of the house has arrived!" a boisterous, gruff voice echoed off the walls.

A chair scraped against the floor. Lord Sevastyan, Lev's rabid dog, rose from the end of the ebony table, his rat-gray leather coat creaking as he straightened to his full height. At nearly six-three, he towered over most in the room.

"Elena, you've found her!" His lips twisted into a sneer. "I feared you'd abandoned us."

His voice was the auditory equivalent of stale blood and spilled rotten guts. An icy tremor ran through my body in revulsion, so I darted my gaze to the lit eastern façade of the Corvin Palace beyond the windows, seeking a distraction.

Snorts and chuckles rippled through the room.

A dozen pairs of crimson eyes fixed their gaze on me from towering wingback chairs. Lev's inner circle mingled with my family members.

Heat crept up my neck, flushing my cheeks. I scanned their faces, Lev's absence standing out like a raw diamond in coal. The knot between my shoulder blades loosened, and I exhaled. I still had time to collect myself.

"Beauty takes time, Sevastyan," Mother drawled, smooth as silk and sharp as a blade. "Perhaps you should give it a try sometime."

Another round of chuckles erupted from our guests.

"As sharp-tongued as ever," the lord sneered. "You never fail to impress."

Katerina's ruby-red eyes narrowed, boring into me with an intensity that made my skin crawl. Something unsettling churned within her gaze, betraying cunning intelligence, a quick temper, and deep-seated vanity. Every instinct demanded I retreat from Lev's younger sister, but I stood my ground. This was my house, and I was older than she was. Slowly, intentionally, I raised my chin and met her stare head-on.

"Princess Aurora," Sevastyan called out, his tone sharp with false politeness. "What an honor to have you grace us with your presence! How busy the filth must be keeping you." He bent forward in a grotesque parody of a curtsy, his leather creaking obscenely once more.

I suppressed a sneer. What was it with idiots and their awkward, constipated bows?

Mother's grip on her chair tightened, her knuckles whitening as she offered Sevastyan a smile that could freeze hellfire. "Lord Sevastyan," she chided, her melodic voice carrying an icy edge that pebbled my flesh. "It's rare to have so many guests in our home. You'll have to forgive her. Aurora is a shy child. She's honored to spend her first century among family. Isn't that right, dear?"

I nearly choked. *What game are you playing now, Mother?*

Sevastyan's gaze raked over me, lingering on my chest with blatant lust. I usually had no qualms about my nakedness, but the hunger in his gaze felt like sizzling oil on my skin. I'd never felt so exposed, so... violated.

"Of course," I managed, forcing myself to bow low despite the revulsion curling in my stomach. His sharp inhale nauseated me. "I hope you find our home to your liking, my lord."

I wish you'd choke on that quail egg wobbling in your throat, you leering bastard.

"Elena and Vlad did well downgrading from the old palace," Sevastyan purred, his voice thick with desire. "Prince Lev will be *most* pleased. Please, sit with us, princess."

Rage bubbled within me, pounding in my ears. *How dare he speak my parents' names so casually?* As if he had any right—

"Join us, Aurora," Mother commanded, her tone final.

I complied, my anger simmering like banked embers as I slid into the vacant seat between Victoria and Petru.

Victoria's face twitched with triumphant glee. The bitch was clearly enjoying the show, her maroon vest with its plunging neckline and exaggerated shoulder pads screaming for attention. Black kohl rimmed her eyes, completing the gothic ensemble designed to lure unsuspecting Wurdulaks into her bed.

Ignoring her, I focused on Petru. My brother was deep in conversation with a mountain of a man I recognized as the head of Lev's personal guard. Their attire spoke volumes: Petru's dark-blue suit befitting his governmental role, the Wurdulak's leather waistcoat proudly displaying coal-black tattoos, suitable for his coven's barbaric reputation.

"How considerate of His Highness to send another member of the royal family to our humble abode," Lucius, my other insufferable cousin, drawled from across the table. "You grace us with your presence, princess."

Katerina sighed wearily. And, for a fleeting moment, I almost sympathized with her—my cousin was gross. Until she opened her mouth...

"You're always so generous with your compliments, Lucius," she sneered. "Perhaps a ball gag would prevent any further flattery from escaping your lips... and rescue my ears. Do be a darling and give it some thought."

"One cannot fault me for trying," he purred, running his fingers through his four-inch electric-blue mohawk and flopping it to the other side of his head.

As I said, gross.

Katerina waved him off. "Your attempts didn't get me into your bed fifty years ago, and they certainly won't help you now."

"You cruel, cruel creature—"

I tuned him out as he began nipping at his lower lip, his face contorting in arousal. If I could gouge out my eyes to unsee this, I would. In a heartbeat.

Lucius, for all his foolishness, had a knack for charming attractive women. Katerina's resistance only seemed to fuel his obsession, blinding him to her many faces—each more dangerous than the last. You never knew which one would plunge the dagger into your back, but you could be sure of its arrival.

Katerina was every pureblood's wet dream. A thick leather belt cinched her waist, emphasizing a bosom that strained against her black strapless corset. I often marveled at how her slender frame didn't simply snap under all that weight.

Victoria laced her fingers together, forming a bridge, and rested her chin on it. Her gaze locked onto Katerina, a cynical smile twisting her violet-stained lips. "What a… pleasant surprise to have you with us, princess," she said as her upper lip twitched as if the word 'pleasant' was poison. "Aurora is positively thrilled to celebrate her anniversary with her future sister-in-law." She cast a sidelong glance at me, eyes glinting with malice. "Do tell her, dear cousin. Tell her how you count the days until the Red Moon. You'll be besties in that big ol' palace."

The bitch knew exactly how much I loathed Katerina. She never missed a chance to twist the knife. Gritting my teeth so hard I thought they might crack, I muttered, "Yes, what she said," and put on a bright, false smile.

Katerina's eyebrow arched, clearly seeing I was full of it, but she remained silent.

Ever since the last Fateless Festival, where we honor the Arrival of our Creators, Victoria's hatred for both the princess and me had grown to volcanic proportions. I wasn't sure who she despised more: me, for being Dracula's chosen, or Katerina, for crushing her dreams of a more advantageous marriage.

Katerina's gaze never wavered from me, her pupils constricting to pinpricks. She raised her goblet, took a long, satisfying sip, and said, "I wouldn't be here if I could help it." She dabbed a droplet of blood from her lip with her pinkie. "But my brother asked me to attend his betrothed's celebration. I couldn't refuse him." Then her tongue snaked out as she licked the blood from her fingertip.

"And when will the prince be joining us?" Victoria, the oblivious fool, persisted.

A muscle drew taunt at Katerina's jaw. "His duties kept him longer than expected. He sends his sincerest apologies," she hissed, her words clipped and frosty.

The lingering anxiety about Lev's possible last-minute appearance slid off my shoulders and fell to the floor. It would have sunk to the depths of the Underworld if it had any substance. Whatever kept him away, I was grateful. I'd take his sister's company over his any day. However, neither was ideal for a lifetime, for marriage.

Victoria's face lit up like a lighthouse. "What could be more important than celebrating the first century of his future bride?" She gasped, her elbow digging into my ribs. "See, Aurora? I knew he'd grow tired of you. Not even Derzelas can make you worthy of Prince Lev—"

"VICTORIA!" Mother's voice cracked like thunder, silencing everyone.

Fury radiated off her like electricity in a storm, matching the inferno raging inside me. Darkness crept into the edges of my vision as I resisted the temptation to stake my cousin in the back. It was one thing to attack me in private, but to do it in public, in front of the royal family no less, was a betrayal of our coven and her future ruler. I couldn't believe she had allowed herself to give in to her disdain.

"Know your place, *commoner*," Katerina snarled, her tone chilling, cooling even my boiling blood.

That stopped me from clawing the bitch's eyes out.

An eerie hush fell over the table as the Wurdulak princess leaned forward, a predatory grin spreading across her face. "You may be promised to the Obayifo, but there is no Blood Pact to seal the betrothal yet." Her eyes hardened to crimson ice. "You wouldn't want him to receive you in... parts, would you?"

Every part of my being roared to run away from Katerina's unhinged mania. My cousin was far from a commoner, but I'd be damned if I defended her after the way she spoke to me.

Victoria's face flushed like a tomato, her eyes bulging in shock. Her lips moved as if she would speak, but nothing came out.

"It's alright, Katerina," I intervened before they started a catfight. "Victoria sometimes speaks before she thinks. I'm sure she didn't mean—"

The heavy doors screeched open, flooding the room with that tantalizing scent once more. My nostrils flared, fangs threatening to drop as my gaze darted around the room. Nothing.

Frustrated, I turned to the newcomers.

Selena glided in on Commander Enescu's arm, a vision in a cherry-red mermaid gown that clung to her curves like a second skin. She moved with grace—round hips swaying, drawing attention to her slim waist and voluptuous bosom. Her hair flipped outward at the ends, framing a face that could launch a thousand ships. Shimmering gold eyeshadow made her eyes smolder, while lips painted the same vibrant red as her dress pouted slightly.

She didn't just turn heads; she broke necks and held them broken.

But beneath her perfect facade, I sensed a tension that sent my knees bouncing beneath my dress.

They halted by the entrance, Selena executing a perfect curtsy while the Commander gave a solemn nod. Tall and dapper in a sleek dark suit, Bogdan Enescu exuded power and authority from every pore.

"Princess, I hope we are not too late," she said, her tone heavy.

I glanced at my godfather, but he avoided my eyes.

"Not at all," I replied, following them to the fireplace, where four members of our coven and Academy instructors stood with grim expressions. An unsettling flutter seized my chest.

"Sel, what's wrong?" I whispered, just above a breath. Not that anyone curious couldn't hear me.

Her throat bobbed, her galloping heart thrumming like a racehorse. Commander Enescu's lion-headed cane struck the floor, and our gazes collided.

"They are here," he announced, his voice cold and disdainful.

A storm erupted in the foyer, doors rattling violently. My pulse thundered as panicked cries filtered in from outside. I struggled to breathe, struggled to speak or think or compose myself.

Because if I hadn't just imagined that scent, if there wasn't even the tiniest hint of spilled blood somewhere in the room, there could only be one logical source.

Mortal blood.

It saturated the air, sweet and tangy, like a ripe plum oozing with juice. I licked my lips, tasting it on my tongue. Almost feeling it drip down my throat.

I wondered if it went down as smoothly as I remembered, dense but not too thick, with a silky, sweet flavor, maybe a hint of fruit—

A tremor ran through me, and I ripped my eyes open. Tears stung my waterline as I silently pleaded, *Derzelas, give me strength. Please God, don't let it be what I think it is.*

"Our prince got carried away," a harsh voice boomed behind me, jolting me in my seat. "Fresh batch for you, princess."

AURORA

IN ANCIENT TIMES, THE concept of blood factories existed only in the minds of hopeless dreamers. Feeding was easy then. Humans were plentiful and easily controlled, lost in their wars and lust for power. But the Empire of Transylvania, led by my forefather Aurelius, made a crucial error—it neglected to enforce feeding regulations.

A human *Changed*, then a hundred, then a thousand more. Millions succumbed to bloodlust without proper guidance. Entire cities were abandoned overnight. Kings and their subjects vanished without a trace. Dynasties disappeared forever.

Chaos plagued my great-great-great-grandfather's rule. The only silver lining that saved Solanthia from complete annihilation was that mixed-breeds couldn't perform the Change. Still, with so many blood-thirsty killers on the loose, the outlook remained grim.

Aurelius, sick with remorse, took action to eradicate the hybrids. He imposed strict prohibitions against purebloods feeding on human blood, urging brilliant minds to find a more sustainable solution. Over time, other mortal races multiplied—ieles, varvas, balaurs—establishing dominions and competing for territory. Solanthia had other enemies to worry about.

The first blood bank appeared on Republic soil in the year 658, and not a single drop of mortal blood had been drawn by fang since then.

The doors burst open, and Ivan and Gregor stormed in, herding five terrified mixed- breeds. Primal fear permeated the air. An undercurrent of terror that only enhanced the swirling scent of their blood as their hearts pounded more and more of the delicious substance around their bodies.

It was intoxicating. Their heightened emotions only synthesized the aroma for my fangs to—

No.

I will not.

Saliva flooded my mouth, my fangs aching. I swallowed thickly, disgusted at my own reaction warring with predatory hunger.

Shock soon gave way to fury.

I launched to my feet, wood splintering under my grip. "What's the meaning of this?" I demanded, the sound of my voice muffled over the roaring in my ears.

Silence.

Blood from shallow cuts tainted the mortals' rags. A visceral pain seared through me, as if someone had plunged a hand into my chest and squeezed my heart.

"Explain yourselves!" I roared.

The guards exchanged nervous glances, eyes darting toward the exit. In the corner, three women huddled together, sobbing, their clasped hands a pitiful defense against a room of hunters.

Petru seized my elbow, forcing me back into my seat. "Sit down!" he hissed.

I reacted on pure instinct.

The crack of my hand against his cheek echoed off the vaulted ceiling. Petru's head snapped to the side, loose strands of ebony hair falling free from his hair tie.

Shadows writhed beneath the table as his eyes, blazing scarlet, locked onto mine.

I staggered, one hand clamped over my mouth, the other still gripping the mangled backrest. Splinters bit deep, drawing blood that soaked into my sleeve.

The air *hrked* with Mother's Darklings, plumes of dark smoke billowing on the outskirts of my vision. "Aurora, be careful or you'll ruin your dress," she said, her voice deceptively calm. I knew that tone—it was the devil's whisper before hell broke loose.

She seized my wrist, her grip like iron as she wrenched my hand free.

I swallowed a cry of pain, silently pleading with her to spare the mortals. Her eyes flashed, irises shifting through shades of crimson. The vein on the side of her neck throbbed with repressed fury.

"Petru, dear," she told my brother, her voice honey-sweet and just as deadly, "there's no need to overreact." But her false calm fooled no one.

I'd never seen Elena so livid. Public humiliation was her greatest pet peeve—whether personal or against the Tepes name. My loss of control didn't just embarrass her. It dishonored our entire coven. For the heir to attack family... It was unthinkable.

Family drama stayed private. We didn't air our dirty laundry in public. First Victoria and now this; it was shameful.

I lowered my gaze to the dark blooms on the table—dahlias, marigolds, roses—feeling the blush spread to the roots of my hair.

"Brother, please forgive me," I murmured. Then, louder, "I apologize for my behavior. I don't know what came over me."

Elena's smile was as false as the Great White the varcolacs worshipped. At her summons, a servant waltzed in with a new chair, ignoring the whimpering mortals as if this were just another day at the Tepes household.

"Everyone remembers their first time, dear. Isn't that right, Alexandru?" she drawled, her nails biting into my shoulders as she steered me to my new seat—close enough to control any further... outbursts.

Alexandru's gaze fastened on me and wouldn't let go. "I can't fathom how you kept her away from fresh blood this long." He huffed. "Lev selected them on his last expedition beyond the walls. He wanted the best for his betrothed."

The. Best. For. His. Betrothed.

Ice spread through my chest, my breath shuddering high in my throat. I felt so livid, I no longer cared if my composure revealed my weakness. That *bastard*. He did this to infuriate me, to flaunt his reach and influence over the Republic. Lev Wurdulak was above the law, and he wanted to ensure I knew it.

This was no courting gift—it was a power play, another damn twisted game.

Lev knew I wouldn't harm the mixed-breeds. He wanted me to witness their suffering, to break me, make me compliant. Mother's words had nearly blinded me to my hatred, and I had been close to caving in and going through with this alliance. But now? My loathing for him blazed with supernova intensity.

If he thought killing five souls would win me over and make me accept his hand, he could kiss this farce of a marriage goodbye. I would never be ready to tie myself to a man like him.

Over my dead body.

"Princess?" Alexandru's voice cut through my seething thoughts. "Hopefully, you won't keep us waiting too long? I believe I speak for everyone when I say we're... ravenous." His playful smile faltered at my glare.

"I'm not planning to," I replied, frost dripping from every syllable.

Alexandru Wurdulak, Lev's right hand, was a master of court politics. Though he seemed friendly, there was something about him that communicated incredible violence, as if he knew he was the most powerful person in the room and didn't need to prove it. I had no doubt he could single-handedly annihilate everyone at the table.

It spoke volumes about my state of mind that, at that moment, I almost wished he would.

Alexandru rose, his Darklings swirling impatiently around him, and extended a hand. "How gracious of you, princess."

Victoria folded her arms, pushing her breasts higher. *The harlot.* "Save your efforts, Alex. You'd wither away long before Aurora would harm her little pets," she sneered.

Oh, how I longed to snap her neck, just to silence her for a moment.

Alexandru appraised me with sharp eyes, his smile as dangerous as a stray sunbeam—alluring, yet lethal. With an exaggerated bow, he offered his arm to Katerina, and they vanished in an instant.

I should have fled, but paralyzing terror rooted me to my chair. Without Elena's support, I was powerless to save them. The mortals' fate sealed.

Agonized screams shattered the air, each cry a dagger to my soul.

Katerina stalked toward the iele male cowering behind an armchair, his ivory wings jutting out like a neon sign. He scrambled back, sweat-slicking hair plastered to his face, and crumpled to the floor. The sickening crack of fragile bones snapping turned my stomach, and I stifled a sob. Blood and feathers trailed in his wake as he tried to get away from her.

Katerina blurred, seizing him by the collar, her razor-sharp fangs bared. "Look what you've done!" she snarled, tearing into his neck.

I watched, transfixed with horror, as pure anguish contorted the iele's face, his body convulsing while Katerina drank greedily. His eyes, wide with terror, met mine for a fleeting moment. I witnessed the light in them flicker and fade, like a candle guttering out. All that he was and could have been was gone in an instant.

Sated, Katerina let out a satisfied sigh and discarded him like a ragdoll. His lifeless form collapsed to the floor with a muffled thump.

My stomach heaved. I tore my gaze away, only to see Alexandru tormenting another victim—a varva desperately summoning his magic. A water globe swelled between his trembling hands, twirling on its axis, growing bigger and bigger and—

The original melted into his Darklings, becoming one with the shadows. They expelled Alexandru behind the mortal.

His lips nearly touched the man's ear. "Boo!" he whispered, shattering the varva's concentration.

The globe burst, sloshing on the hard floor. Aquamarine eyes glazed with dread, silently begging for mercy.

But the Wurdulak wouldn't have it. Alexandru gripped his neck, and the crunch of vertebrae echoed like breaking glass.

I stifled a scream, my hand firmly pressed against my mouth.

One by one, the Wurdulaks and my family disappeared into swirling darkness, leaving me alone at the table. The remaining women wailed as my 'guests' drained them dry, not even bothering to ease their suffering with blood magic.

My eyes burned, but I had no tears left. I wanted to vanish into the night, to unleash this sickness festering inside me at the uncaring stars. But it wouldn't go away. It coiled tighter around my heart, its claws raking against my ribs—a reminder of the monster I was born to be. Horror, grief, and outrage tore me apart. I was drowning in a sea of red, suffocating. And still, that primal part of me hungered, filling me with self-loathing.

So, yes, I was beyond tears. Almost beyond sanity.

By Derzelas' eternal fires, the sounds of our bloodlust were awful. I could hear them ripping flesh. It wasn't quiet, elegant, or graceful. It was noisy, animalistic, and unbearable.

The reality of our violent nature crashed into me like a battering ram. For a century, I'd lived in denial. Without synthetic blood, I would become this—a bloodthirsty beast preying on the weak for a quick fix. The thought made me shudder. I'd sooner face the sun than turn into a cold-blooded killer.

Elena shadowed back to her chair, blood sloshing over the rim of her goblet. "You'll have to get used to this, dear," she said coldly. "Animals are for slaughter. Otherwise, it's just a waste of good land."

The discharged outliers... who will return to the Republic...

Nausea roiled within me. If I didn't leave—now—I'd vomit right here at the table. I stood, chair scraping against the floor.

"I can't—" I choked out. "This isn't who I am."

Elena set down her cup, fixing her gaze on me. "I'm sorry you had to find out like this, dear. The Red Moon is approaching. It's best to acclimate to Lev's way of feeding. Who knows, you might even enjoy it."

Her betrayal cut so deep it stole my breath. I lifted my eyes to the ceiling, unable to look at her anymore. She had ambushed me—and lied about the fate of the outliers. My heart bled, shattering into jagged shards. I should've known by now that I could not escape her manipulation, no matter how far it pushed me.

Clinging to the last threads of my self-control, I navigated the sprawl of lifeless bodies. My fists clenched, the pain of the splinters grounding me. I knew losing my temper now would change nothing. It wouldn't bring them back.

A human girl, not Changed yet, lay curled up on the floor. Her neck bent at an unnatural angle, bite marks marring her pale skin. Blood seeped into her clothes, her face frozen in an expression of utter terror.

This night had carved a wound so deep it would never fully heal. There was no reality where I could forgive Elena for this.

She was dead to me.

The pain seared like the inferno that had followed Father's passing. Only, I knew, with time, it would dull to an ache—something I could learn to live with.

As the doors closed, Elena's final, twisted barb slipped through the narrowing gap, "Happy Birthday, my dear!"

Aurora

I stepped into Father's office, and his scent—labdanum and cedarwood—crashed over me like a giant wave. Nine decades, and it still clung to every surface. In the stacks of books on his desk, which Elena insisted be dusted but not disturbed. In the half-closed tome on top with his silver-and-black fountain pen peeking out from the yellowed pages.

My gaze drifted to the ripped armchair, angled just as he'd left it. The Persian rug beneath my feet whispered tales of his Solanthian expedition. Every shelf, every corner, held a piece of him.

I hugged my waist, trying to hold myself together as his scent tore through my shattered nerves. Tears burst from my eyes with a vengeance. I thought I was done crying. That I'd reached my limit for the century after tonight's cursed dinner.

But never when I came here. Never when I thought about him.

I missed him. Sweet Dark Father, I missed him like a drowning woman misses air. And it was at times like this that I truly *needed* him, his guidance.

Stumbling to his desk, I glared up at his oil portrait. "Why?" I croaked. "Why did you leave me?"

His fierce eyes, rimmed with bright vermillion, bore into me with solemn intensity. Father had always possessed the vigilance of a lion, and missed nothing. If he were still with us, those five poor mortals would still be breathing. The Wurdulaks wouldn't have dared defy Aurelius' decree under his watch. Father would've snapped their necks before they could even think of spilling innocent blood in his house.

At his daughter's birthday, no less. *Bastards.*

He was supposed to be untouchable. Invincible. Vlad 'the Impaler' Tepes, felled in some pissant ambush like a mere foot soldier. It wasn't right. It wasn't fair.

I swiped at my face, willing the tears to stop as I shuffled to the window. One tug on the lamp cord, and soft light flooded the room. How many nights had I curled up in his lap right here, on this armchair, listening to stories of far-off lands while the weight of the Republic waited outside?

"Come back," I whispered to the emptiness. "Save Elena from her darkness. Save me from this plagued alliance. Please. I need you to fix this."

But only silence answered, heavy with his absence.

"Happy Centenary, my betrothed," Lev's gravelly voice slithered through the room like tar. *Speak of the devil, and the bastard appears.*

I swallowed the vomit welling up inside me and turned to face the man I despised with every fiber of my being.

There he stood on the doorstep, tall, four inches over six feet, with a swimmer's build: narrow waist, wide shoulders, long legs. His features were sharp with high cheekbones and a firm jawline, his brow strong, and his nose slightly upturned, more pronounced since he had shaved off one side of his head. Onyx hair flowed down his back like a horse's mane. He only needed a bone throne and a horde of sycophants, and he'd be the spitting image of Derzelas ruling over the Underworld.

"Get out," I snarled, fists clenching in my skirts.

The haughty smirk died on his lips. Arrogance and ancient power emanated from him in spades. Gone was the boy who'd smelled like ripe cherries, who'd chased me through moonlit orchards and shared laughter.

Lev Wurdulak was pure poison now.

"I gather you didn't like my present." He sauntered in, defiling Father's sanctuary. Darklings writhed around him, lashing out, blending with his pretentious black suit.

Rage set my blood on fire.

"Stay back, or so help me—"

"Rory, Rory," he sneered, brushing off my threat like lint. "My patience is running dry. Fifty years I've waited for you to see the halfbloods for the vermin they are."

Icy shadows slithered up my bare legs. I refused to shiver.

He cocked his head, as if truly trying to understand. "Why this obsession with them? Trying to get under my skin?"

I backed up, bumping my leg into the armchair. He lunged, arm clamping around my waist like a vise. Air fled my lungs as he spun and slammed me against the bookshelf.

Lev leaned in close, his breath hot against my ear. "Soon, you'll be mine, little Rory," he purred. "I'll make you forget all about your pathetic pets."

The world narrowed to a single point. I thrashed, fists pummeling his chest. "Let go, you monster! I'll never marry you, not after what you've done. Never!"

Darklings swarmed around him, slowing my blows as if I were hitting through molasses. A scream tore from my throat as I channeled all my anger and fear into a single strike, my palm cracking against his chin with a satisfying crunch.

Lev's head snapped back, shock flashing in his eyes as he staggered backward, his grip on me loosening. But the victory was fleeting. In an instant, he reclaimed control, forcing me against the shelves. My spine cracked, and the breath vanished from my lungs, stars bursting across my vision.

"You think you have a choice?" he snarled, his face mere inches from mine. Fetid breath washed over me, reeking of cyanide and blood. "I'll break you, mind, body, and soul. You'll be my perfect little bride, obedient and eager to please. With Dracula's magic, we'll take over the continent. Together. And you'll relish every single death I'll lay at your feet." Lower, he whispered, "Including your precious animals you love so much."

Revulsion churned in my gut. "Go to hell."

I raked my nails down his face, splitting skin, drawing blood.

Lev roared, recoiling just enough for me to bring my knee up to his groin. He doubled over with a strangled grunt.

Seizing my chance, I bolted for the door, my heart jackhammering against my ribs. I had never wished for my Darklings like I did at this moment. The air grew dense with his cloying scent, sickly sweet, choking.

Lucian's ancient magic, the Blood Link, responded to Lev's summons and came rushing like a gale, a wave of power that nearly tripped me. Glancing back, I saw the red haze shimmering around him, like heat above a fire, and gasped when chains of hardened blood shot from his palms. They coiled around my ankles, and I crashed to the floor, pain exploding through my body.

Lev stalked toward me, fury burning in his gaze, blood dripping from the closed gouges on his cheek. "You'll regret that, bitch," he spat.

Two more crimson links whipped forward, binding my wrists and throat and lifting me into the air. The door slammed shut, its hard wood pressing into my back.

I bucked and writhed, fighting to break free, but the restraints squeezed tighter, cutting off my airflow. Black mist crept in on the fringes of my vision.

"No one defies me," Lev bellowed, spittle flying from his lips. "I'll drench the Republic in the blood of halfblood scum, starting with the wretch in your command."

Asphyxiation clearly clouded my judgment, because the next thing I knew, I spat in his face, managing a weak, "Harm them, and I'll kill you," despite the frantic pounding of my heart. A promise I would be more than happy to fulfill.

He wiped his cheek with the back of his hand, his gaze darkening. "Good. Then you won't mind if I have a little taste now, before you hate me for eternity."

Panic seized me as he closed the gap between us, his heated breath scorching my skin. The noose around my neck loosened and dropped to my collarbones.

"You're curious, too, aren't you?" he murmured, tracing his nose along my pulse, sniffling my scent, my fear. "A small preview might be just what you need to change your perspective about our union."

He wanted to share blood, to take advantage while I was defenseless. Lev Wurdulak was the last person on the continent I'd trust with my body and thoughts during a Blood Pact—let alone one under the Red Moon that would bind our souls for all time.

"Get off me, you sick bastard!" My fury crumbled, replaced by a stark terror that paralyzed my mind. I released the shriek building up in my throat, "Help! Someone, help me!"

Lev snarled, fangs bared. The blood chains shot upward, stretching my wrists above my head. They chafed my skin, but he pressed closer, pinning me with his body. "No one's coming," he growled. "Don't fight it. It will only make it worse."

"Lev, please don't." I panted, desperate. "I will never forgive you if you do this."

His lips peeled back in a feral grin, eyes blazing with a wild, unquenchable thirst. With a vicious yank, Lev tore at my dress collar, exposing my neck and chest to his rapacious gaze.

I screamed, the sound raw and feral, but his Darklings devoured it, trapping my cries within the room.

He struck like a viper, fangs puncturing my jugular.

No!

White-hot agony ripped through me, my vision blurring, warping. Tears poured down my face, turning to blood as liquid fire flooded my veins. My head pounded, razors shredding my mind to ribbons.

"Stop, it-it hurts..." I slurred.

Lev wrenched away, blood splattering his face. "Stop crying and bite me back, you whore! Complete the bond," he roared, eyes wild with bloodlust. He rutted against my hip, his arousal turning my stomach. "It's your fault it hurts."

"Please... stop..."

Speaking took monumental effort, and I gave up. *He'll tire eventually,* I told myself through the haze of torment. *He'll leave me alone.*

He sank his fangs in again, deeper, more brutally.

Agony annihilated every nerve, every thought. My blood turned to lava, scorching my insides and charring my bones as he stole my essence. Copper flooded my mouth, mingling with the salt of my tears. A blinding light exploded behind my eyes, and I sagged against him.

Beyond the door, distant footsteps echoed like a dying heartbeat, but I was drowning, sinking, the glimmering surface slipping further and further away. I tumbled through the darkness.

Lev's final savage thrust tore a ragged cry from my throat, my jugular snapping as he pulled back. "Fuck!" He groaned, licking around the weeping wound. "I've wanted to taste you since your magic matured—"

The approaching steps sounded louder, closer, mercifully dragging his focus away.

Lev dissolved the blood links into crimson smoke and grasped my chin, forcing me to meet his rabid gaze. "We're far from finished," he promised before melting into the shadows.

They whirled him out of the room, and I swayed, my mind fracturing, thoughts scattering like ashes on the wind. The floor lurched beneath me, and I dropped, darkness rising to claim me.

"Aurora? Derzelas, protect us!" Selena's voice shook as she caught me in her arms. "What happened? Are you alright?"

My vocal cords failed, replaced by uncontrollable sobs. She smelled of jasmine, familiar and comforting, and it broke through my defenses. I clung to her, weeping, releasing the torrent of emotions and aches that wrecked me inside.

"Shh, don't worry. I'm here now," she murmured, wiping the blood from my face with gentle fingers. Her hand froze briefly as it grazed the scars below my jaw. "I've got you, my darling. I'll protect you."

The wound had closed, but the pain didn't lessen. It lingered, sharp as a thousand burning needles piercing my skin. Shivers ran through me, making my teeth chatter. I couldn't make sense of what I was feeling. Everything hurt. My insides were on fire, while my skin was freezing cold.

I felt... lost. In the sensations, in the fear.

"Who did this to you?" she asked, her dark eyes glossy with tears. "This... this is unforgivable. You must report it. It's against our laws. Your brother—"

I shook my head, ignoring the stabbing pain in my temples. "No, Sel, you don't understand. He won't—he won't intervene." My voice broke as fresh tears spilled down my cheeks. "Petru believes I belong to *him*."

Selena's brows furrowed. "What are you saying?" Then understanding flashed across her face, and her curses filled the room. "That bastard! How dare he lay a hand on you? We have to tell someone—your mother, the Council, anyone!" Without a word, Selena adjusted her strapless corset and marched toward the door. "That damn coward!" she growled. "I'm going to tear him apart!"

I caught her wrist before she could storm out. "Sel, wait," I implored. "Lev has too much power, too much influence. It's my word against his. We can't accuse him without proof." Another sob racked my body. "Please, don't go. I couldn't bear it if you got hurt because of me."

She glanced at the door, conflicted, but pulled me into her arms, stroking my hair as I wept into her shoulder. "Nothing will happen to me. I swear it by Derzelas' fangs. We'll find a way to bring that bastard down, together, okay?"

I nodded, clinging to her. She was right—I couldn't let Lev win, couldn't let him get away with this. For the innocent lives he'd taken, for the outliers whose futures he threatened, for *me*, I had to stop him, make him pay.

This wasn't a game of politics anymore; it was war.

Taking a deep breath, I pulled back, meeting her gaze. "We'll need allies," I said, my voice steadier now, "people we can trust. And a plan."

A glint of mischief sparkled in her eyes. "Well then, it's a good thing you have me. I'm excellent at scheming." She tilted her head toward the exit, a soft smile playing on her lips. "What do you say, birthday girl? Want me to whip you up some Red Brownies?"

"With extra icing and blood flakes?" I sniffled.

Selena's grin stretched to her ears. "Enough to clog your arteries and mend your soul. Just how you like them."

Her attempt at humor didn't quite land, but the promise of sweets dulled the storm raging within me.

"I need to scrub him off me," I whispered, shuddering.

Selena squeezed my shoulder, then, leading us out of the office, she said, "Lavender bath first. Then, we indulge."

AURORA

I STORMED INTO GODFATHER'S office, the reassignment notice crumpled in my fist. "You're assigning me to another guild?" Fury and disbelief choked me. I was shaking. The Sparrows wouldn't survive under a projector like Matei, or worse, if I left them vulnerable to Lev Wurdulak. "No. I will not accept this."

The room, like much of Corvin Palace, walked the line between tasteful and pretentious. A massive desk dominated the right, a seating area the left, and at the far end, before velvet-curtained windows, stood a conference table fit for a war council. Towering oak shelves dominated the walls, showcasing antiques and mementos from Bogdan Enescu's eight-hundred-and-seventy-three years of existence.

He sat behind his desk, eyes fixed on a spread of reports. There always seemed to be papers around people in charge. It reminded me of how my reports had always gone unacknowledged and unanswered.

"Projector Tepes. Have a seat." He raised his head, pinning me with his 'commander' gaze, his power leaking in waves.

My cheeks flushed hotly as I bowed, a touch deeper than usual, and lowered myself into the nearest armchair. The leather exhaled a mix of tobacco and wine, making my nose wrinkle.

"I'm sorry, sir. I spoke out of turn—"

He raised a hand, then pushed a strand of salt-and-pepper hair behind his ear. "It's alright, Aurora. I understand your concern."

I tried to return his smile, but it felt hollow, echoing the pain in my heart. Bogdan Enescu had been my father's brother-in-arms long before earning his general's epaulets. He was all I had left of a father figure.

Which made this reassignment order hurt even more.

"The Sparrows haven't suffered enough losses to warrant a new projector," I said, my gaze fixed on the red line on the map behind him, marking the 'Active War Zone' where the eighth ward once stood.

For a heartbeat, chaos engulfed the room, and I was back there—the explosion, sulfurous fumes burning my nostrils, the roar of twisting metal drowning out my own screams, and my father's vibrant eyes dimming before me. The memory tore through me like jagged shrapnel, leaving me breathless.

I blinked hard and forced myself to the present. Now wasn't the time to fall apart. "I don't understand," I croaked. "I've requested reinforcements for our losses. Why reassign me now?"

For forty-two years, I'd led the Sparrows. Sixty-seven outliers, five captains—we'd endured countless missions together. Shared sacrifices, shared triumphs. How could I just walk away?

The realization struck like lightning, and I shot to my feet, heart thumping against my ribs like a caged beast. "You're disbanding them? Without even consulting me?"

He sighed heavily. "You're overthinking this. I'm not abolishing the Sparrows—"

"You're taking away everything I have left," I murmured.

I'd already lost so much—my trust, my safety, my pride and dignity. The joy and intimacy I had looked forward to in a Blood Pact. I couldn't lose my guild too.

A sharp knock shattered the silence. The door creaked open, a wave of jasmine drifting in.

"Lieutenant Popescu. Join us," Commander Enescu said, gravel coating his voice.

Selena snapped a salute—fist to heart, heels clicking—before sliding into the vacant chair beside me. Her tight smile mirrored mine, though confusion creased my brow. The black turtleneck, gadot skirt, and thick-soled Mary Janes she had on were jarringly casual for this setting. I loosened my collar, unease coiling my limbs. What was she doing here on her day off?

The Commander's eyes hardened to chips of ice. "Aurora, listen. Your father would've challenged that bastard prince publicly. I'm bound by rank and can't break Lucian's magic." A muscle feathered in his jaw, his hands clenching into fists. "Only you can match the Blood Link. When your power manifests, you'll be Lev's equal. For now, I've taken this to the Council."

Selena scoffed. "The Council? Sir, with all due respect, they're useless. We know where their loyalties lie." Her dark eyes flashed as she darted a glance at me. "They won't care what that monster did."

I gaped at her, heat rushing to my head, my molars grinding. "I thought *we* agreed to keep this quiet," I hissed, gesturing between us.

My scars twinged. They rarely hurt now, but my mind hadn't been right since Lev bit me. Every attempt to harmonize with the Sparrows left me out cold, bleeding from my eyes and ears. At least the Stalkers had been quiet these past few weeks.

"You said we needed allies." Selena shrugged. "The Commander's with us."

I readied my voice to argue, then decided against it. She had a point. The Commander was one of the few people we could trust. Still, a flicker of betrayal ignited in my chest, smoldering like an ember. This was *my* story to tell, my pain. I wished she'd let me choose when to share it—or to share it at all.

"I would have preferred if you'd come to me sooner," the Commander said. "But I understand it's sensitive, and you'd rather confide in your—"

"Sir," I interrupted, taking a deep breath and steadying myself, "I appreciate your concern, but please, don't mention Elena. I'm done with her. For good."

Godfather's face was a mask of concern and smoldering anger—not at me, I realized, but at the situation. At Lev. At Elena. At a world that had failed to protect me.

He held my gaze, then nodded slowly. "Fair enough. Well, my door is always open. No matter what."

I swallowed around the lump in my throat. "Thank you. I... I'll remember that." The words came out clipped, tension threading through my voice despite my efforts to keep it neutral.

Turning to Selena, I locked eyes with her. "Sel, I know you mean well, but..." I paused, jaw clenching briefly. "Some things are hard to talk about, even indirectly. Maybe next time, give me a heads up before my personal *affairs* become a topic of discussion, yes?"

I left the rest unsaid—how each mention of the attack made my skin crawl, forcing me to relive the fear, confusion, dread, guilt, and shame of that day. How desperately I wanted to move on, to forget. But I could see the realization dawning in Selena's eyes. She meant well, but now she also understood.

Selena nodded and reached out with her hand hovering near mine, not quite touching. "I'm sorry, A," she whispered. "I just... I wanted to help. I'm here for you, however you need."

I took it, giving it a quick squeeze. "I know." Eager to change the subject, I squared my shoulders and met the Commander's gaze. "Alright, let's get back on track. Sir, I need an explanation. Why am I being reassigned?"

The warmth in his eyes cooled, his demeanor shifting to that of the Guild Division Commander. "I need a new projector for the Black Guild," he said. "It's a restructured unit—the best of the best. Former captains and vice-captains, the elite of our defense."

Darting my eyes at Selena and then back to him, I couldn't shake the feeling that her presence here was tied to more than what Lev Wurdulak had done to me. "I'm assuming there's more to this reassignment than just me commanding an elite guild?"

"It is," he admitted. "It will keep you safe until Dracula awakens or you inherit your magic. You can plead your case to our Creator then, or be strong enough to challenge the prince yourself."

I raised two fingers. "Two problems with that plan. He's scheduled to awake in fifty years"—I dropped the middle finger—"and there's no telling when I'll get the Blood Aura. How is that supposed to keep me safe? I-I can't marry *him*."

His voice lowered to a growl, dark and dangerous. "Aurora, I won't let you proceed with the Blood Pact, even if it's the last thing I do."

"Count me in on that," Selena added firmly.

"Then how?" I pressed. "How exactly will changing guilds help me?"

"It's the Black Guild's captain," he explained. "There was an... incident a while ago. The investigation is long overdue."

I glanced between them, disbelief quickly giving way to disappointment, then indignation. My stomach hollowed. "This is your grand plan? Hide me away between the outliers like some dirty secret?"

Deflating back into my seat, I continued, "Don't misunderstand me. If I see Lev in a thousand years, it would be too soon. But I can't abandon my duties out of fear. What kind of queen runs at the first sign of trouble? How can I earn my people's trust and loyalty if I run like a coward?"

Selena surged to her feet, her cheeks flushed. "You'd rather look over your shoulder every moment? Lev assaulted you in your own house, A! What's stopping him from cornering you in the palace hallway—or on your way home? Nowhere inside the walls is safe anymore. He's grown too brazen."

The Commander leaned forward, the wood creaking softly as he steepled his hands. His weary, ancient eyes pierced into mine. "You speak of duty, Aurora. But your primary duty right now is to survive, to become strong enough to take back your throne. A dead queen serves no one. This isn't retreat, it's strategic withdrawal."

His voice dropped an octave lower, a rumble that I felt vibrating in my bones. "With the Stalkers roaming freely, accidents happen. You'll disappear in a patrol gone awry, have a martyr's death. Meanwhile, you'll lead the Black Guild, gather intelligence, build strength, all while out of Lev's reach. When you return, you will be more powerful than ever."

"The Sparrows," I choked out. "If Lev hurts them because of me..." I couldn't finish, the fear for my guild squeezing my chest.

Underworld's balls, am I really considering leaving them? Faking my own death?

"I'll erase any trace linking them to you. There's no existing paperwork about them... except your reports."

The Commander opened a drawer, retrieved a bundle of creased documents, and tossed them onto his desk. The thud echoed in the silence.

"These are the outlier casualties you sent in the last six months. I don't have to tell you how dangerous it is if the prince finds out about them. Stop documenting them. The Republic no longer recognizes them as citizens. We can't accept death records of those who don't officially exist." In a softer tone, he added, "I can't assist your efforts. No one takes this matter to heart anymore."

"After everything they sacrifice—"

"Aurora, your ideals are admirable, but sometimes their value lies in their very unattainability. You, as future queen, can make real change. But first, you need to be alive and safe."

I clasped my hands behind my neck, sighing heavily as I stared at the ceiling. "So I'll trade one monster for another?" I muttered.

"A conniving sonofabitch for bloodthirsty Stalkers," Selena hummed, her tone sardonic as she slouched back into her seat. "Pick your poison. At least your magic works on the hybrids."

Supposedly.

Thousands of reports from the initial attack on the Republic claimed Blood Manipulation could control Stalkers. But no projector today had tested this beyond the preserved blood samples at the Academy. Separation, coagulation, tracking, altering its dynamics—it was easy to manipulate when it didn't fight back.

The thought of flying over the contested zones and facing live Stalkers made the fine hairs at my nape stand on end, and I shuddered with a mix of terror and exhilaration.

I dropped my hands to my lap, worrying the button on my leather coat until it nearly came loose. "And the Sparrows' new projector?" I asked, my voice tight. "They need someone competent, someone who'll protect them." Stoneheart was strong and opinionated. He would disregard his projector, just as he had me, if it meant the survival of his guildmates.

The Commander's eyes turned to steel. "Aurora, you know as well as I do that on the battlefield, safety is never guaranteed." His jaw locked briefly, but his tone lost its edge. "I promise you, I'll personally select and oversee their new projector. If you accept the Black Guild position."

I nodded, pressing my lips into a thin line as I stared at my boots. His words, though I knew them to be true, hit me like a punch to the gut. A projector could only do so much against Russkaya's hybrids. Those monsters never tired, never followed a logical plan. For every one we cut down, two more took its place. It was an endless, nightmarish cycle.

Pain shot through my temples.

I pressed my fingers against my forehead, trying to ease the building pressure. The weight of abandoning my guild settled an even heavier weight on my shoulders. But staying... staying could mean condemning them all.

"I..." My voice faltered. I forced down a swallow, once, twice, before the words finally came. "I'll do it. For their sake—and mine." Raising my chin, I steadied my voice. "I'll take command of the Black Guild and defend the Tenth Ward."

The decision was simple in the end. Step into the unknown or live a lifetime of regret. I chose the unknown. I had too many regrets as it was.

A tight, almost sad smile pulled at his lips. "About the Black Guild's captain... Harbinger has quite a complex history."

Recognition jolted through me. Stoneheart had mentioned Harbinger when his mysterious guild had swooped in to aid us. He had claimed they were on patrol, but even then, I found it hard to believe they had detoured almost a hundred miles to the ninth ward.

Leaning forward, I gripped the edge of my seat, curiosity and dread wrestling in my tone. "Harbinger? I've heard about him, but—"

"*The* Harbinger?" Selena yelped, clawing her nails into my arm. Her scent shifted, floral notes giving way to bitter grass.

Trying to lighten the mood—and save my arm—I quipped, "What, was the Lord of the Underworld unavailable?"

"Don't joke about him," she snapped, her face draining of color. "He's—"

"The longest-lived outlier," the Commander interjected. "Over five decades on the front lines. We know little about him or his team, except they're seasoned warriors with complete control over their elemental powers. Harbinger's magic remains a mystery."

My mind reeled, blood rushing to my head. Fifty years of service? Most outliers didn't survive their first year outside the detention camps. "How? Shouldn't he have earned his civil rights by now? Why hasn't he returned?"

Commander Enescu's features tightened as he rubbed his chin, his fingers brushing through the coarse hairs of his goatee. "None of them want to return. No living family, as far as we know."

"Then why keep fighting?" Selena asked.

"If I could read minds, Miss Popescu, we might have won this war decades ago," he huffed. "What matters is Harbinger is our best frontline fighter, and he's doing a hell of a great job at keeping the Stalkers at bay. But..." his voice dropped, a scowl pulling at his brows, "the manner in which he damages his projectors... is unprecedented."

I blinked, stifling a laugh. "Damages projectors? Sounds like a bad ghost story to me. Surely it's more likely for a projector to harm an outlier?" I shook my head. "I'm sorry, but that's hard to believe."

"I'd hoped your brother would bring the captain in for questioning, but he dismissed the reports as manipulation tactics." He sighed, long and low. "Whether it's true or not, projectors who've worked with Harbinger in the past requested reassignment or early discharge."

"But why would Harbinger do that? He'd be signing his own death sentence."

"That's what we need to find out," he said, flattening his lips.

"Sir," Selena cut in, her voice bitter as wormwood, "you forgot about the projector who took his life. After one mission with Harbinger, he walked into the sun—"

"Suicide?" I all but shrieked. "That's extreme."

Talk about stating the obvious.

Purebloods were too proud for that, our survival instinct too deeply ingrained. And to go by way of sunlight...

Commander Enescu nodded grimly, his eyes darkening to a burnished sienna. "Projector Olaru, during your Academy days. Left no explanation. His death shocked us all." His teeth locked. "I would've investigated sooner, but no one volunteered for the job. Sending someone onto the battlefront isn't a decision I take lightly. This is our best chance to uncover the truth and keep you away from the prince. You're our best hope, Aurora."

"If Harbinger's endangering projectors, he's putting us all at risk," I agreed, then frowned as it dawned on me. "Wait, you said Academy? That means Harbinger's served for eight decades."

"There are no records, but you're right."

Eight decades fighting Stalkers? Even our army of two hundred thousand purebloods couldn't stop Russkaya's advance. Yet one man held out for years?

Like I said—a ghost story.

"The Black Guild can keep you safe, but be cautious," he said. "Avoid harmonizing during sorties. Limit your interactions with Harbinger and the others. Remember why you're there."

"Sir, it's my duty to know my outliers. If they accept me as their projector, I'm committed to fostering connections."

Selena's fist hit the armrest with a crack that made me wince. "She never learns," she muttered.

"No, she doesn't. Good grief. You really do take after Vlad..." He sighed, matching the exasperation in her voice. "Now then, Projector Aurora Tepes, I appoint you Commanding Officer for the northern front's Tenth Ward's first defensive guild, effective immediately. I expect your finest."

I stood, anxious excitement fluttering in my chest. "Thank you, sir," I said, pride burning in my eyes as I executed the Republic's traditional salute, fist over my heart. Like our flag, it represented the unity of the five races that once thrived in our nation—a symbol I carried with honor. The world could forget how we had once co-existed as equals, but I would not.

Commander Enescu nodded, shifting his gaze to Selena, who stood by my side, mirroring my salute. "Pack your things, soldiers," his voice thundered. "I'll inform the Black Guild's captain of your arrival. The first supply zeppelin departs tomorrow after dusk. Extra supplies of synthetic blood—"

"But, sir! Selena isn't even on active duty!"

"Oh, hush!" she scoffed, digging her elbow into my ribs. "We had the same training. I'm as skilled in combat as you." She stepped closer, her head barely passing my shoulder. "I'm coming with you."

The Commander studied us, his lips twitching in what I could only read as amusement. "You didn't think I'd send you out there alone, did you? Besides, she's a medical lieutenant. Who better to accompany you?"

Selena planted a fist on her hip, one brow arching high. "Exactly."

Relief and dread warred. My protective instincts flared up at the thought of putting Selena in danger. Yet facing half a century alone was equally daunting.

"You have a life here, Sel," I whispered, my voice almost inaudible even to my own sensitive ears. "Fifty years is a long time."

"Nah," she said, waving dismissively. "The Healing Corps will still be here when we get back, and I'll have more field experience than the lot of them combined." Her voice hardened slightly, a trace of venom creeping in. "Besides, I'm already dead to my parents since I refused that fossil they picked for a husband. They won't even notice I'm gone."

I inhaled her scent—jasmine, vetiver, and Red Brownies. Home. She wasn't blood, but she was my safe space. I liked to pretend I didn't need anyone until I did. I couldn't do this alone.

"Sel, if you're sure..." I half-smiled, still worried for her. "I won't stop you. I'm too selfish for that."

"You could have just accepted from the beginning." She slipped her arm around my waist, and I draped mine over her shoulders. We held each other close.

Looking at the Commander over her head, I asked the question weighing on my mind, "What will you tell Elena and Petru?"

He tutted, rapping a knuckle on his desk. "Whatever's necessary to prevent them from raising alarm. They need to believe you've died in action. The simpler your deaths, the easier for them to accept."

"A patrol gone wrong..." I murmured, and he responded with a brief nod.

Nausea rose in my throat. Elena's lies were a betrayal, sure, but Petru? He'd known *everything* from the start. He'd watched those mortals march to their deaths without a word. Not a gesture, not even a flicker of remorse. Nothing.

My brother wasn't just complicit—his hands were as bloody as Lev Wurdulak's. He'd looked me in the eyes and lied straight to my face when I'd asked about the fate of the discharged outliers. He knew, and he'd done nothing.

"I feel guilty deceiving them, but after what they did at that dinner..." I muttered, my fingers curling into fists. "Sweet Derzelas, how could I ever trust them again?"

"Your father was exceptional," Commander Enescu said. "Life was easier for them when he was alive, especially for Elena as a consort, not leading a ruined coven." He offered a sorrowful smile that didn't quite reach his eyes. "Petru may not show it, but he has the Republic's interests at heart. Elena... she strayed from Vlad's path. She'll live with her choices. But you, Aurora, must prioritize what's right for you and the Republic."

"Be selfish. Live a little," Sel added, giving me a light shove.

I groaned. "Easier said than done when the whole coven expects me to secure the crown—"

"You mean Elena expects you to marry that asshole and save the Tepes name," she snarled.

"It's more than her. *I* inherited Dracula's marks," I said, rubbing my nape. "Petru can't ascend because of his governor's oath. He needs to uphold democracy, serve the people. Our coven's only path to monarchy is through me."

The Commander's voice swelled with pride. "Words of a future queen! I have complete faith in your reign."

Selena squeezed my hand, her eyes bright with an intensity that compelled me to look away. "You've got this, A. I know you do."

Their confidence left me lightheaded. How could they believe in me so much when I felt like I was on the edge of falling apart? Like I was one step away from making the worst decision of my life?

I'd never be my father. But maybe I could be something else, something our people needed. Returning to the old, savage ways wouldn't move us forward. We couldn't give in to the monster inside us. I could bridge the gap between mixed-breeds and purebloods, and mend our fractured homeland though.

I wouldn't—couldn't—accept anything less.

If healing our nation meant risking everything, then so be it. I'd walk through fire, fight from the shadows, stand on the front lines—I would die trying. We wouldn't win this war from behind our desks or locked away in our command rooms.

My heart drummed, the sound thundering in my ears, but I held my salute. When I spoke, my voice was steadier than I felt. "Do what you have to do, sir. I'm ready."

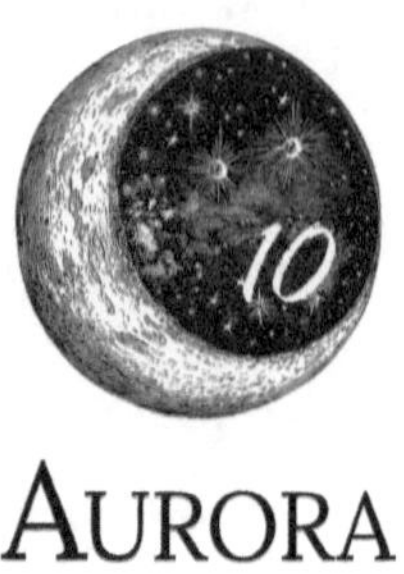

AURORA

THE ROBOTIC ARM GLIDED over my body like a satin sheet, leaving a track of goosebumps. It tickled in places I'd rather not discuss, especially with Selena attacking the keyboard as if it had personally insulted her entire bloodline. I kept a straight face, curious about what had crawled up her ass this time. A bad date, or perhaps a stale bottle of blood?

"You're done," she snapped.

Oh, the joy of being around her in her work mode—about as pleasant as a stake through the heart.

The machine slunk back into the ceiling with a soft whir, and I hopped off the examination table, my gown fluttering like gossamer wings. I was about to make a quip about feeling like a half-wrapped birthday present when her voice carved through the silence, thick with worry and something darker.

"A, Harbinger isn't a joke."

Here we go again.

"Seriously, you're caught up in this, too?" I shot her a pointed look over my shoulder. "It's just a silly ghost story. Probably concocted by projectors looking to dodge their duties. What's next, the boogeyman hiding under our beds? I didn't take you as one for conspiracy."

The reinforced glass door hissed shut behind me, sealing me—and my decidedly un-queenly posterior—in the changing room. The sudden shift in air pressure made my ears pop, and I wiggled a finger inside to ease the discomfort.

Her voice crackled over the intercom, the static failing to mask the tremor in her words. "Someone died, Aurora. I knew him. Projector Olaru and I had a brief fling back in our third year at the Academy."

A chill raced down my spine, as if Death himself had traced a finger along my back. "And why am I finding out about this now?" I demanded, popping the last button of my medical robe.

"Didn't think it was relevant. We barely knew each other—"

The intercom buzzed and hummed as Selena fed the Bloodthorn Nexus with new settings and guild information. Without access to real-time sensor data, every detail mattered. Slipping into my leather suit, I zipped it halfway when her voice broke through the static again.

"You're probably right." She huffed. "Damaging projectors? I mean, come on. I know how rumors work, but Projector Olaru—Pfft, what's this doing here? Hang on." A flurry of keystrokes later, she continued as if nothing had happened. "He walked into broad daylight, A. One day, everything was fine, and then—POOF! He was gone."

"It's true then? He chose death by sunlight? I thought the Commander was pulling my leg," I blurted and stooped to lace my knee-high boots.

"Dead serious. Hey, want me to upload a scan of the archived map? You never know, it might prove useful."

"Yes, please," I responded, eager for any information that might give us an edge.

Unhooking my coat, I draped it over my shoulders and stepped back into the room. Selena's lab straddled the line between sterile modernity and a mad scientist's lair. A state-of-the-art medical bay lurked behind a privacy screen on the right, a bank of monitors hummed on the left, and sleek metal counters cluttered with vials of eerily glowing liquids and half-dissected Nexuses hid the rest of the space.

"Anyway," she said, "the healers received orders to use the Blood Transcendence to get the truth from him. Resignations aside, word gets out when someone kills themselves."

I perched on the edge of her desk, swinging my legs. "And what were the results?" I asked.

She shrugged. "Who knows?"

"What do you mean, 'who knows'?"

Selena extracted the needle from the Bloodthorn Nexus, disposed of it in the bin, and returned it to its stand. Her chair creaked loudly as she turned to face me.

"They couldn't bring him back," she admitted, raising her 'life's-too-short-for-bad-blood' mug to her lips. The liquid sloshed, muffling her words. "No abnormalities registered in his Nexus. That's it."

But that surely couldn't be the whole truth. The Blood Transcendence was the most powerful and complex, arcane spell, a gift from Derzelas himself. Even Selena, who had trained for decades, acknowledged that taming immortal blood might mean sacrificing her firstborn's soul.

She took another sip, and I waited, anxiety knotting in my stomach.

Selena's mind worked like a meticulous filing system, each piece of information carefully categorized and linked. Asking her a question was like pulling a thread—you had to wait for the whole tapestry to unravel before you got to the part you wanted. Rushing her wasn't just ineffective, it was counterproductive. Interruptions threw her off course.

She'd start all over again, oblivious to your mounting frustration, as she methodically worked her way back to the point.

So I swallowed my irritation, reminding myself that good things come to those who don't strangle their best friends.

"But the Blood Transcendence can bring any immortal back, right?" I eventually pressed.

Selena clenched her jaw. "Theoretically, yes. Every time. But only if there's blood left."

A wheel squeaked.

She shifted, investigating briefly before continuing in a clinically detached tone, "They couldn't find a single drop to harmonize with his brain. The reports state he was completely exsanguinated."

I recoiled. Projector Olaru had defied every survival instinct to let the sun reduce him to ash.

"God, he didn't just want to die," I gasped. "He made damn sure of it."

Commander Enescu's warning rang in my thoughts, chilling me to the bone. *'The manner in which he damages his projectors...'*

But that was impossible. No outlier could harm their commanding officer. A pureblood sleepwalking into sunlight was more likely than a mixed-breed overpowering an immortal.

We are invincible.

Aren't we?

The implications squeezed the breath out of me. If Black Guild's outliers turned on us, and we couldn't control their minds fast enough... They could tear us apart. Leave us to the sun's mercy. My knees locked, muscles seizing.

"They should've brought Harbinger in and looked deeper," Selena hissed, oblivious to my mounting panic. "Picked his brain apart and investigated."

I shuddered internally. Without a doubt, were she in the healers' ranks at the time, she would have eagerly volunteered for the task herself.

A heavy silence enveloped us, broken only by the soft hum of machinery. Selena's upper lip curled into a sneer, her voice dripping with malice. "You know what Harbinger said when they told him his projector died?"

A lump formed in my throat, dread seeping into my bones.

"*'Good riddance. Next time, send someone who can keep up.'*" Selena's face contorted with rage, her fist slamming onto the desk with such force that metal and glassware rattled. "That heartless bastard! The halfbloods don't give a shit about us, A. Not one fucking bit. Remember that whenever you're tempted to take their side."

"Don't worry," I rasped. "No one understands their hostility better than I do. You forget, I've spent my entire life working with them."

With my hands supporting me on the table, I stared at the iron-rimmed ceiling squares. "The Sparrows trusted me to lead in our fight against a common enemy. I'm not naïve—I don't expect the Black Guild to be as cooperative, but I won't submit to them, either," I said, trying to muster conviction I didn't truly feel.

A vision of Olaru's surely excruciating final moments flashed in my mind, and I couldn't shake the image of my own ashes scattered by the wind. My pulse quickened. The prospect of meeting Harbinger wasn't as exhilarating anymore.

Selena sighed, running a hand through her raven hair, her golden earcuffs catching the light. "Harbinger isn't just dangerous, A," she muttered. "He's unpredictable. And that makes him lethal."

A gulp echoed in my throat. "We have fifty years to figure him out," I said, more to reassure myself than her. "That should be enough time."

Sel's shoulders slumped as she wheeled herself to her desk, her fingers shaking over a stack of papers. "A, there's something I need to tell you," she murmured, eyes fixed on the dark screen before her. "I kept quiet because you were always within reach of emergency care. But now that we're venturing beyond the walls..."

The unspoken 'with no prospect of return' hung heavily in the air.

"Damnit, Selena! Spit it out!" I snapped, clenching my fists in frustration.

She turned to me, a deep furrow etched into her forehead. "The Bloodthorn Nexus..." Her words softened to a murmur. "It's not safe. If you ask me, it's a ticking time bomb."

My hand shot to the back of my neck, fingers tracing the familiar spot where the needle had pierced my skin countless times. "What? But they said... They promised it was safe!"

Selena's laugh was bitter, hollow. "The studies are 'open to interpretation,'" she said, air quoting with her fingers. "You know how it is. The reports say one thing, but the reality?" She shook her head, irritation written on her face.

Raging fury poured through me. I jumped to my feet, sending papers fluttering to the floor. "Those lying bastards! They're risking our lives to save face?"

"Even if the Nexus has flaws, the Republic would never admit it."

"To hell with their pride!" I snarled, pacing the lab. "The real danger isn't the Stalkers, it's our own damn arrogance!"

Selena flinched, worrying her lower lip with her teeth. "They made me take an oath, A," she whispered. "I wanted to tell you, but I... I couldn't."

The room felt suffocating, closing in around me. I remembered her reaction when I first told her about my Transpection with the Sparrows—the panic in her eyes, the tremor in her voice. How had I missed it?

"Hey," I said, squeezing her shoulder, my anger still simmering beneath the surface. "It's not your fault. I should have seen how worried you were for me. But damn it, Sel, I wish you had found a way to tell me sooner."

Then again, who would I be now without my time spent with the Sparrows? Would I have *chosen* the risk of serving with them?

She covered my hand and gave it a gentle pat, folding her lips into a taut line. Then, like a switch flipping inside her, her expression shifted. Selena wasn't one to dwell in self-pity. "You know," she said, her voice taking on that familiar clinical tone, "it was actually a halfblood who pioneered the Bloodthorn Nexus. Found the exact spot in the brain to stimulate."

My eyebrows shot up. "A halfblood? How on earth did that happen?"

Selena wheeled herself to the small device on its stand. The Nexus, connected by a web of wires to an information terminal, looked ominous despite its innocuous appearance. "Like any mad scientist pushing boundaries," she explained, amusement slipping into her voice. "He believed linking his consciousness to the world's collective void could grant him immortality."

"Derzelas Almighty," I breathed. "Did he succeed?"

Sel barked out a laugh. "God, no. Can you imagine trying to harmonize with every mortal across the world, all at once, at a rate pushed to the theoretical maximum?" She made a dry clicking noise with her tongue. "His brain ended up so fried that even the Blood Transcendence couldn't keep him conscious for more than a few minutes each hour."

The imagined pain made me wince. Sometimes, just having the Sparrows in my head gave me a monstrous headache. "So that's how they found out about his research?"

"Bingo," she confirmed, spinning her chair to face me. "You can call him a madman if you want. Adds a bit of flair to the story."

"Selena," I chided, though a small smile pulled at my lips.

She rolled her eyes dramatically. "Fine, fine. No more name-calling. Want the gritty details, or should I spare you the nightmares?"

I set my shoulders straight. "Tell me everything. If I'm going to be using this thing again, I need to know what I'm getting into."

Selena's eyes gleamed with the usual scientific fascination she wore whenever she had a breakthrough. "Alright, but don't say I didn't warn you. In theory, Blood Manipulation gives us complete control over a mortal's mind, like a simple seize-and-grab move," she explained, mimicking the action with her hands. "They're aware of our intrusion, yet powerless against it. Remember seeing the guards use it on the half-bloods when you were a kid?"

"Vaguely," I admitted, a memory surfacing of me sneaking into the Eternal Blood National Park, despite Father's warnings. I'd seen officers forcing mixed-breeds into military trucks, their faces blank and compliant.

"The Bloodthorn Nexus is a whole new ballgame. When you harmonize, you're not just controlling—you're accessing their consciousness, opening up their minds. It's more... subtle. They don't even realize you're there."

Her jeweled black irises caught the light as she cast a sidelong glance my way. "Of course, you don't have to take over if you don't want to. This is where frequency comes into play," she continued. "You can discreetly tune into one of their senses, and their awareness sort of fades into the background. But you're familiar with this, aren't you?"

I couldn't help but laugh, the sound surprisingly cathartic. "Come on, Sel. I've Transpected, what, a dozen times? Plus, you gave me hell every time I mentioned it."

Her smirk expanded into a primal grin, all teeth. "I should have told Elena. Let her knock some sense into you."

"You wouldn't dare!" I mock gasped.

"Keep testing me, and I might. No matter how much we hate her," she parried, her narrowed eyes daring me to push back.

If Elena ever discovered I was risking my life for the outliers, she'd pull me from the army faster than I could say 'blood.'

I raised my right hand in surrender. "Truce, okay?"

She snorted, dismissing me with a hiss—rude, but comfortingly familiar.

"Anyway," she continued, "we still don't fully understand the complexity behind the Nexus. We speculate. The gap between 'safe' and 'probably safe' is as deep as a tunnel to the Underworld."

She paused, threatening me with her index finger. "The Blood-thorn Nexus has a protective feature now. It should be secure as is. However," her voice sank to a grumble, "if you try to bypass it to fully take over a mortal's conscience, you could overload your brain. Harmonizing at the maximum synchronization rate might 'stimulate' you beyond return."

My breath hitched.

By Derzelas' eternal fires, trust Selena to soften the blow.

A strange, almost liquid-like feeling washed over me, and I gripped her desk to keep from melting into a puddle on the floor.

How many times had I skirted death when Transpecting?

Anger flared inside me, boiling my blood and making my heart gallop. Was the Republic's 'advanced technology' built on such shaky ground? Did our government even realize how vulnerable we were? We hid behind a false sense of invincibility, wrongly accusing those who shielded us from the Stalkers, when we didn't even have a safe means of defending ourselves. And now, the Republic aimed to cut the warfare budget—the very lifeline protecting our nation?

What in the Underworld was wrong with them?

Selena's impatient taps on my thigh snapped me out of my spiraling thoughts. "A, you need to calm down," she croaked, concern furrowing her brows. "You look like you're about to set the lab on fire."

I took a slow, measured breath, trying to rein myself in. "Sorry, it's just... How can the Republic be so *reckless*?"

"I know," she said. "But losing our heads won't help. Remember Luminita?"

Despite my anger, I snorted. "What, when she snatched my crush during sophomore year?"

"Yeah, and remember how worked up you got? It almost got us expelled," she muttered, a grin stretching her lips. "In hindsight, you dodged a bullet. That guy turned out to be a total jerk."

"True," I conceded, feeling some tension leave my body. No one liked being wronged, but I had a tendency to take things too far when pursuing justice.

"So, back to the Nexus," I said and refocused on the matter at hand. "Wasn't this your father's research? "

"Not exactly," she replied, opening the top drawer and clearing away odds and ends. "He continued the work the halfblood started. It became a team effort. The basic ideas and theories came from other researchers, his colleagues."

The screen flickered to life, and I found myself transfixed by the neon-green loading bar. It had almost finished overwriting the Bloodthorn Nexus.

"Any idea who the mixed-breed researcher was?" I asked.

A soft beep announced the task was done.

Selena unplugged the Nexus, wound the cable around her fingers, and tossed it into a nearby wired basket. "The Republic wiped his records. We don't even know which camp they sent him to, let alone who he was."

"Then ask your father," I said flatly.

Her head shot up, her eyebrows arching toward her hairline. "Ask him what, exactly? 'Daddy, we're joining the halfbloods on the battlefront to save Aurora from a crappy marriage. Can you guarantee the Bloodthorn Nexus won't scramble her brain?'"

"Valid point." I smirked.

"They're ready," she said, placing the harmonization device in the silver container alongside the Astral Visor.

The box's interior was soft and padded, with a thumbprint lock matching the Nexus's black crystal. It smelled faintly of jasmine mixed with Selena's favorite synthetic blood, which I'd spilled in my haste to join the Sparrows on patrol.

"Listen," she said, her voice wavering slightly as she closed the lid and pushed the box toward me. "We don't know the long-term side effects. I couldn't care less about the halfbloods, but if something happens to you, I..." Her voice caught.

Before she could finish, I sprang to my feet, nearly toppling her desk as I wrapped my arms around her neck.

"I promise not to fry my brain." I chuckled, planting kisses on her cheeks. "Not now, not ever. There's no one else I'd rather annoy for the next half-century. Thank you." I wanted to add 'my confidante, sister, better half,' but held back, knowing Selena's gag reflex was sensitive to too much sugar.

Trying to break free, she grimaced like a blood store vendor disapproving of kids touching her goods. "Yeah, yeah. Just remember, I warned you," she retorted, fighting a smile that was slowly winning. "More than once."

With Selena by my side, I could face anything—and felt invincible.

I tightened my hold, sensing her resistance crumble. "I hear you, Sel. Loud and clear," I murmured into her hair.

FROM THE SANCTUARY OF my room, I pushed open the arched window, inhaling the crisp dawn air. Eastward, the sky bled pink and purple, casting a silvery glow over the quiet streets. Nightingales and corncrakes sang their farewell from the palace gardens, their melodies twisting like daggers in my chest. Tonight, under the cover of darkness, Selena and I would break free from our pasts—and my dictated future—and leave behind everything we'd ever known.

"I will return," I whispered just before the shutter slammed shut and plunged me into darkness.

Crossing to the other side of the room, I switched on Father's Solanthian lamp. Painted crystals hummed and flickered, sending shadows chasing each other on the walls.

This time, the face staring back from the three-panel mirror of my vanity was strong and resolute, a blade forged in fire.

Except for the silk scarf wrapped around my neck—a flimsy attempt to hide Lev's bite from prying eyes. The scars throbbed beneath, but I refused to acknowledge them, refused to give them power over me.

"One day," I vowed, settling onto the ottoman. "I'll see Solanthia with my own eyes."

Yet another reason to stay alive.

With shaky hands, I unwound the scarf and lifted the Bloodthorn Nexus from its box. It looked like a blooming rose with the Tepes crest carved into one petal. A deadly weapon in disguise.

Outrage and fear roared inside me as I hesitated. Had I really been flirting with death since my Academy days? If news of this new threat spread, it could ignite a civil revolution. Our situation was dire enough. The Republic wouldn't survive another internal conflict.

I exhaled and attached the Nexus to my nape. The needle prickled with the usual sting, soothing the fire in my veins. I rose, the short legs of my chair scraping on the floor. The closet doors squeaked as I swung them open, grabbed an armful of clothes, and tossed them on the bed.

That's when I saw it.

The black envelope on the nightstand. Commander Enescu's unique scent—aged whiskey and resin—wafted from the paper as I reached for it with trembling fingers. He must have left it while I was with Selena.

Heart pounding, I tore through the Republic's seal. An unexpected fragrance of freshly ground coffee and sweet roses greeted me, so at odds with the image of a hardened Stalker fighter. Unfolding the letter, I gulped as Harbinger's elegant cursive danced across the page.

Congratulations on your promotion, Projector. We'll prepare the base for your arrival.

Harbinger

The words, seemingly innocent, made my heart skip a beat.

I read the line over and over, searching for hidden meanings or veiled threats. His penmanship was exquisite, hinting at a refined background that contradicted the monster Selena and the Commander had described.

A ghost story. I scoffed.

"Well, Harbinger..." whispering, I traced the elegant script with my fingertip, "you're quite the puzzle, aren't you?" A spectral breeze brushed my spine. "I guess I've got fifty years to figure you out."

HARBINGER

THE NIGHT WAS QUIET. Too quiet. The Stalkers were lying low, giving us a rare moment of peace before dawn. I'd sent out the usual bullshit reports—claiming we were patrolling like good little soldiers.

As if.

Why pursue ghosts when there were none to chase?

Fuck them. The new projector was on his way, and if he thought I'd break my back for him on day one, he'd better think again.

A projector actually coming to the frontlines—haven't seen that in a while. Most of them preferred to stay behind the walls, safe in their command posts while barking orders through the Harmonization and pretending they hadn't sent us to die. Either this one was crazy brave or had something to prove.

I breathed in the crisp spring air, my eyes drawn to the sky. Stars blazed across the darkness, Orion and his cosmic buddies—Sirius and Pleiades—putting on a show. The air was thick with the heady mimosa scent of starneedle blooms, their bell-shaped flowers glowing like tiny lanterns.

Book in hand, I strode through the iron gate, following the commotion at the front of the house. We'd finished dinner in the backyard. Our little fortress of trees and ivy-choked walls wrapped around us like nature's own bulletproof vest. Not that it'd protect us from Stalkers. Those bastards could sniff out a paper cut from the next ward over.

Five shots splintered the night's quiet, sending nightjars into a panicked flurry. Our pet *zmeu* erupted from a patch of white blooms with a yelp that could wake the dead. The thing was a walking weapon—charcoal hide bristling with ridges and spikes sharp enough to gut a man. It took to the air for a hot second before crash-landing in a tangle of limbs and wings. Yellow eyes, glowing like hellfire, locked onto mine before it scuttled off into the shadows of an evergreen. The little beast could never sit still for more than a heartbeat.

I picked up my pace, eager to see what kind of mess my guild was making.

The grand portico echoed with gunshots and laughter—their own little sharpshooting tournament in full swing. Just another night of draining the Republic's coffers nice and empty. After all, what else were those deep pockets good for?

"That's one shot on His High-*ass*, Prince Lev, and two on Wimpy Princess Anastasia!" Gale's voice boomed. "Quakelord's racking up seven points!"

I rounded the corner just as Quakelord dropped to his knees, his straight alder-wood hair dancing in the breeze. He threw his arms up like some tragic hero in a terrible play.

"Ah, shit! Two misses!" he groaned, fingers flying over his firearm and stripping it down. "Bullets, man. Like writing poetry with a sledgehammer."

I bit back a grin. *Fucking drama queen.*

"Stop whining!" Gale snapped, rushing to pick up the fallen cans Hummingbird had scribbled caricature portraits of the key originals on with a marker. "Phoenix! You're up!"

Phoenix sprawled on the grass, fanning her freckled face. "Come on, give me a break! Next! Who's next?"

A smile spread across my face. Watching my friends cut loose was a rare treat. We didn't get many nights like this—just us, no projector breathing down our necks, no Stalkers. I melted into the shadows, leaning against a column propping up the balcony. From here, I had a perfect view of the circus.

And if I was being honest? It felt damn good to see them like this. Alive. Happy. Even if it was just for one night.

Pearl stepped up, peeling back her knitted scarf to reveal a grin that spelled trouble. Three rapid-fire shots, three cans down.

"Ten points!" Gale hollered, scrambling to reset the tins, this time in a tower.

Terraknight clapped Pearl on the shoulder as he took his stance. A mountain of a man, his midnight skin and raven hair melded with the darkness. My right hand, my vice-captain, my brother in all but blood. A sharp click punctuated the silence as he loaded his pistol.

"Raising the stakes, Gale?" he asked, eyes narrowing on the targets.

As he aimed, I scanned the eerie silence beyond our little sanctuary. Nothing but the usual whispers, voices just out of earshot. To the west, something growled and bolted, wings flapping in panic. Closer, a breeze whispered through dry leaves and stubborn grass, carrying the scent of nicotiana, gunpowder, and our recent feast.

I snorted, recalling Hummingbird and Quakelord's sorry state after yesterday's hunt. They'd blamed the Limuses, but we'd all heard the wild boar that sent them ass-over-teakettle into a ravine. Their misfortune, our luck.

Tonight's dinner had started with friendly jabs and ended with every-one gorging like bears prepping for hibernation. When Terraknight worked his magic in the kitchen, even fresh blood couldn't compete.

More shots cracked the air. Cans pinged and clattered, tumbling down the slope.

"Holy shit," Gale whistled, tossing her damp hair over her shoulder. "Five for five, dead center. You're on fire, Terraknight!"

Hummingbird's dove-gray wings stirred up a mini-cyclone. "No way," he groaned, tugging at his honey-brown curls. "That's insane."

At seventy-five, the kid still looked like he was fresh out of puberty. I'd known him long enough to know that his lanky frame wasn't filling out anytime soon.

Gale lunged for a runaway can, flaring her bronze wings as she hissed, "You little shit—"

"Ember!" Phoenix bounced up, scooping up cans from the grass. "Show 'em how it's really done!"

Ember snatched a rifle from the rack, golden hair whipping in the wind. She strode back fifty yards, her white dress billowing, and dropped to the ground in one fluid motion. "Watch this," she called, squinting through the scope. "Phoenix, forget stacking. Throw 'em!"

I left my shadowy perch, silent steps carrying me behind Gale, who had Hummingbird by the ankle and was threatening to introduce him to gravity if he didn't quit hovering.

Phoenix started juggling cans, all fumbling hands and determination. One sailed wide, smacking Hummingbird square in the forehead with a dull *thunk*.

He staggered, wings tucking in reflexively. "Hey!" he yelped, just as another can hit his chest.

"Nice catch, birdbrain!" Quakelord's laugh boomed across the yard.

The third can clattered at my feet, betraying my presence.

Gale's head swiveled, fixing me with a glare that could freeze hell over. Despite her youthful appearance, she was only a decade my junior. She should know better.

I wagged my head, warning her off, but she couldn't resist.

"Captain's sneaking around again!" she hollered.

Snitch.

I pulled up my hood and slipped between the two winged trouble-makers. Crossing the lawn, I thumbed open my book to the dog-eared page. The outdated text was riddled with errors, but it was the only one I hadn't memorized yet.

"Your turn, Harbinger!" Ember called out from the clamor of swords, crossbows, and rusty gun barrels as she stowed her rifle. "Phoenix, hustle those cans before he bails!"

I turned the page, only to find the text cut off mid-sentence. It made no sense.

"Fuck!" I snarled, clenching my jaw.

Few things got under my skin these days, but I'd trade a chunk of my soul to find the bastard who'd cut out that page and introduce their face to my fist. You'd think I'd be used to it by now. Half my books were incomplete. Still, I lugged them everywhere, like a drowning man clinging to driftwood. That old library I'd stumbled on two decades back had been my salvation.

I slammed the book shut, drew my gun, and fired without looking. Didn't bother to check if I'd hit anything. That missing page was driving me insane.

"Holy shit," Quakelord whined. "He just cleared them all. It's no fun when you don't even try!"

Gale emerged from the house, carrying two chipped mugs of *kafea*. It wasn't real coffee, but we made do with our brew of roasted dandelion root and ground chickpeas.

"Let it go," she said, her dark waves now dry and flowing.

Petite but commanding, Gale was everyone's big sister. Those copper wings set her apart, but even without them, she'd turn heads in any crowd. Nut-brown eyes, golden skin, and cheekbones sharp enough to draw blood. If there were any sculptors left in this world, they'd kill for the chance to carve her likeness.

She circled the fountain, set down the mugs, and scooped up the baby zmeu from the basin. It chirped and squirmed in her arms, so she let it loose.

"How're you gonna explain this?" she asked, yanking back my hood.

I shrugged, brushing off the hard clench in my abdomen. If the Republic found out about me, we were all dead. I wasn't only an enemy, I was *the* enemy, and with the new projector on his way, I was running out of options.

"I'll cover it up for as long as I can," I said, watching our pet paw at the laces of my boot. "I'd rather die than let Pearl near me with that stinking dye again. Never lasts anyway."

Gale sipped her kafea. "Any good?" She eyed my book.

"Not really," I grunted. "Quiets the noise though."

She nodded, a flicker of concern flashing in her eyes before she masked it with a tight smile. That was what I appreciated about Gale—no pity, just quiet understanding.

"Holy hell," she gasped, her pupils dilating in shock. Her grip on my arm was like a vise. "Is that vanilla pudding? I haven't smelled anything that sweet since…" Her voice dropped to a whisper. "Since Aerothria."

I took in a long breath. "Peaches, too. And… leather?"

"Weird dessert, but I'll take it any time." She chuckled, flaring her nostrils. "Is that jasmine, or am I going crazy?"

"You're not crazy," I muttered. The scents grew stronger by the second.

I cocked my head, listening to the faint stirrings from the woods. The trees had devoured the Tenth Ward, swallowing the residential complex and stretching all the way to the National Library in the Eighth.

Dawn Park used to be all manicured lawns and cookie-cutter brick houses. Now it was a proper parkland where white picket fences died and vegetation reclaimed everything in sight. Dense underbrush choked the eroded roads, oaks and poplars towering over blue-green pines and cypresses. Pre-war maps claimed forty acres, but the reality was closer to triple that. A hell of a lot of ground for trouble to hide in.

A crack echoed from the forest, followed by tumbling rocks and a whoop of laughter. A carefree sound I hadn't heard since the world went to shit nearly a century ago. Someone was coming, and they were in a hurry.

"What in the—" Hummingbird tensed, ready to launch skyward. His wings snapped open with a soft whoosh and spanned the width of the driveway. He and Gale were our eyes in the sky.

But this wasn't a Stalker attack. This was something *far* worse.

HARBINGER

TIME SLOWED AS I sprang into action, my hand slamming into Hummingbird's chest before my brain caught up.

Fuck. This was bad. My body hummed with sudden energy, fight-or-flight kicking into high gear.

A shadow burst from the treeline, landing with the litheness of a cat. The air filled with her floral scent, so potent it clogged my nose. She moved, impossibly balanced on high-heeled boots that could double as weapons. Her sharp-tipped ears warned of danger, but she wasn't what had my stomach in knots.

A second blur shot past, trailing sweetness that made my mouth water. She landed in a crouch, gravel crunching beneath her feet. My senses zeroed in on her, drowning out everything else.

Every tiny detail called out to me—the shift of stones under her boots, the soft hitch in her breath, the relentless drum of her pulse. It was like someone had cranked up the volume on her and muted the rest of the world.

Our pet zmeu let out a startled squeak, claws scrabbling against stone as it scurried for cover. My pulse raced, blood rushing in my ears. The usual self-control I boasted fled.

Then she rose, unfurling like a goddamn unholy bloom.

Hummingbird's heart pounded under my palm, and I got it. I really did. She tossed her head, midnight curls catching moonlight as they framed the perfect curve of her butt. That catsuit left nothing to the imagination, and my starved body noticed.

When her god sculpted those legs, it was to tempt men. Perhaps even to tempt me.

I wrenched my gaze away, throat suddenly bone-dry.

Hotness, for me, was more than just looks. It was a complex equation involving brains, humor, and a distinct lack of immortal blood. But fuck me if she wasn't a masterpiece. Especially with that zipper teasing just low enough to—

Zalmoxis. Get it together, man.

"Good morning, Black Guild," her voice rang out like silver bells. "I am Projector Tep—"

I let out a sharp whistle, and my team scattered across the lawn, snatching up spent casings faster than roaches fleeing light. Dealing with an original was a nightmare on its own. No need to add 'wasting ammo' to our list of sins.

Metal clanged as someone chucked the targets onto the balcony and they bounced across the cracked tiles.

I winced. So much for subtlety.

"Well, fuck me sideways. It's Princess Aurora Tepes in the flesh," Terraknight rumbled, striding over as if meeting royalty was an everyday occurrence. He ghosted a hand over his chest, smoothing nonexistent wrinkles—right where his holster strapped over his left pec. "Harbinger," he muttered under his breath, "you knew about this?"

I shook my head, then made the mistake of looking at her again. Those deep claret eyes pinned me like a bug under a magnifying glass. My mouth dried, tongue glued to the roof.

Fuck.

I'd faced down Stalkers, stared death in the eye more times than I could count. But this woman? She made my heart hammer like a damn teenager's.

The moon chose that moment to break through the clouds, and my breath snagged. Her skin... Gods. It was like someone had taken the finest ivory, melted gold into it, and sculpted her into perfection.

My fingers twitched, aching to reach out and touch her. To trace that jawline, to feel if her skin was as impossibly smooth as it looked. I needed to know she was real, not some fever dream conjured by my sleep-deprived brain.

A gust stirred her silk scarf, a darker hue than those hypnotic eyes. How had I missed that? Hell, I might've overlooked an elephant perched on her shoulder at this point.

"Hey, dipshit," her companion called out, blowing a stray hair from her face. "That's not how you address your superior." Black gloves, melding into her coat sleeves, creaked as her hands moved.

Terraknight froze, his jaw hanging slack. His forest-green eyes widened, zeroing in on her like she was some kind of apparition. *Well, I'll be damned. Zalmoxis had finally answered my prayers and served up his match.*

She barely topped Gale in height, but what she lacked in stature, she made up for in presence. Heart-shaped face, all angles and attitude, and eyes... Razor-sharp didn't do them justice. They could flay a man's soul with a glance, dissect his deepest secrets without breaking a sweat.

For once in his life, the unflappable Terraknight looked like a freight train had hit him. And I was savoring every damn second of it. At least I wasn't the only one our guests had knocked sideways tonight.

I sauntered back to the fountain, picked up my book, and sat with a propped ankle on my knee—the picture of nonchalance. "Welcome, ladies. We're *honored*." The word went like gravel down my throat.

Gale's head whipped around, her glare hot enough to melt steel. Yeah, we all hated immortals with the fire of a thousand suns, but sometimes you just had to clench your ass and put on a good front.

I forced my face into a neutral mask as the projector smiled. Fuck me, it was like staring into the sun—beautiful and likely to burn your eyes out.

"Apologies for crashing your little... party," she purred, amusement dancing in her crimson gaze. Shit. She knew exactly what we'd been up to.

"I'm Projector Aurora Tepes, your new commanding officer." She nodded toward her stone-faced friend. "Lieutenant Selena Popescu from the Healing Corps. She's here for the outlier Initiation."

The way 'Initiation' rolled off her tongue made the hair at my nape rise. Like we should be grateful for the chance to be poked and prodded. Or was she... going to bite us?

Fucking immortals. Always playing games, always dangerous. Everything about them was designed to lure in prey. They were the perfect predators. But damn if part of me didn't want to bare my throat anyway.

I sized up the lieutenant and saw a hard-ass staring back. Now *there* was a proper projector—all ice and steel. Made the princess look like a kitten who'd stumbled into a wolf's den. Maybe I could have some fun with this.

"So, Projector," I drawled, not bothering to hide my smirk. "Are we lining up like good little lab rats, or have you got something extra special planned for tapping our veins? Don't hold back on the gory bits."

Snickers and muttered curses rippled through my team. Gale jabbed an elbow into my ribs and nearly cracked my carefully constructed poker face.

Hummingbird's wings folded with a whisper, and he flashed a grin that was all teeth, like a catapulted missile. "My room's always open, Projector," he purred. "I'll let you suck on me all night long." Light-brown eyes turned molten.

The floodgates burst. Ember doubled over, tears streaming down her face as she fought for breath between laughs. Quakelord leaned in, whispering something that set off another round of hysterics.

I should've shut them down. Should've been the responsible leader. But watching my team, my family, facing down Republic brass with nothing but balls and bad jokes... fuck it. Let them have this moment.

My chest swelled with pride. Immature bastards, the lot of them, but they were *my* immature bastards. And I wouldn't trade them for all the sanity in the world.

"You feather-brained pest," the lieutenant snarled, her arctic tone capable of chilling the sun.

I stole a quick glance at the princess, expecting retaliation.

Nothing. Just a blank stare and the occasional swallow. Almost felt sorry for her. Then I caught the pureblood's eyes, endless pools of obsidian, and every alarm in my head went off. Crap. That look promised murder.

Her wrists rolled at her sides, precise, deliberately slow for a simple stretch.

I narrowed my eyes. *No way she's stupid enough to try something here—*

Hummingbird's gasp sent ice down my spine, but it was Pearl's scream that had me on my feet, heart plummeting.

The kid hit the ground, clawing at his throat, fear and sweat stinking up the air. Pearl was there in a flash, her scarf whipping as she batted his hands away, searching for wounds.

"I can't find anything!" she yelled and fought to keep him from shredding his own skin. "Someone, hold him!"

Terraknight locked Hummingbird's arms behind his back before the kid could do more damage. Pearl conjured a trickle of water, wetted the hem of her cotton blouse, and dabbed at the blood with a mother's touch. But the iele kept getting worse, going purple, gasping like a landed fish.

My eyes ping-ponged between Hummingbird and the lieutenant. Was this her doing?

Every instinct said yes. But how? I thought their magic worked only if they drank the blood first. Those wrist movements, though...

Fuck, no time to figure it out now.

"Gale!" I roared, panic choking my words.

"On it!"

The air shimmered as Gale's power took hold, forming an invisible bubble around Hummingbird's head. But it didn't help. His breaths still came in ragged, high-pitched whistles, like something was strangling him from the inside.

Mixed-breeds healed fast, but they weren't invincible. They could even go a few hours without air. So why the hell was he suffocating? My mind raced a hundred miles a minute. A new magic targeting us? Some new weapon we'd never seen before? Or was it the lieutenant, somehow?

I shot her a glare, but her face gave nothing away.

Nothing made sense. We were trained to face any threat, but how do you fight an enemy you can't see—or understand? I gritted my teeth, fighting back the urge to lash out blindly.

"SELENA, STOP THIS INSTANT!" the projector's voice exploded like a stun grenade. "What in Derzelas' name do you think you're doing?"

Her eyes glowed with fury. Any trace of the demure kitten gone. And that scent—sweet and peachy—filled the air, so thick you could cut it with a knife.

"Teaching them respect," the lieutenant snarled back. "You can't let them talk to you like that."

"Enough! We're here to work with them, not terrorize. Stand. Down. Now. That's an order."

Well, well. Looks like there's some fire in her, after all. But it didn't change a damn thing. Her psycho friend had just attacked one of mine, and that wasn't something I'd forgive or forget. If she couldn't keep the pureblood on a leash, I'd do it for her. Nobody, nobody touched my people and walked away unscathed.

Blood roared in my ears. *So they don't need blood to use their magic after all.*

Good to know.

My vision tinged red, hands curling into fists. Knuckles cracked. I'd tear them both apart, immortal or not.

"I'm fine," Hummingbird croaked. His voice was raw, but it was the lifeline I needed to keep from losing it completely.

Orange and blue-green fires flickered at the edge of my vision. Phoenix and Ember were powering up, ready to turn the immortals to ash. Part of me wanted to let them. Hell, I'd even help—maybe stitch what was left of their bones to a tree, make sure they didn't heal before the sun came up. The thought was damn tempting.

Quakelord struck first.

The earth rumbled, cracks spiderwebbing across the driveway.

The projector's eyes went wide, fear finally breaking through that perfect mask. They reminded me of the poppy buds Pearl had planted around the house. We'd never seen them bloom—we were always out before sunrise. But I bet when they opened their petals, they were just as startling to gaze at as the blood-red panic in the projector's eyes right now.

"Wait!" she yelped as debris soared around them. "Please, just wait!"

I raised a hand, signaling Quakelord to hold. The fury inside me was a living thing now, clawing to get out.

"Speak," I growled.

Quakelord grumbled a string of curses that would make a pirate proud, but he finally got the message. The earth stopped its tantrum, dust settled, and silence reigned.

For about two seconds.

The projector coughed, brushing dirt from her leather suit. Crimson eyes swept over my guild before locking onto mine. For a flash, I saw something there. Regret? Shame?

"I... I'm sorry," she said, voice soft but steady. "This is my fault. I should have prepared Selena better. We're not here to fight you—"

"Are you fucking kidding me?" the lieutenant spun around, face twisted in disbelief.

"Enough, Selena!" There was steel behind that silk, and even the pureblood's death glare wilted under it. "We are here now, so get with the program. The Black Guild has been battling Stalkers for decades. They're not just our best chance," she lowered her voice, "—they're our only chance. So you will show them the respect they've earned, or I'll ship you back to the Republic myself. Am I clear?"

Didn't make it right, but hell if it wasn't refreshing to hear an immortal admit they had screwed up. I didn't like to admit it, but this projector was full of surprises, and it unsettled me.

"Best chance at what, exactly?" I arched an eyebrow.

The projector gave me a hesitant glance before her companion muttered, "I'll behave." It sounded like the words physically pained her.

Gale's fingers dug into my side. "She *behaves*," she whispered, struggling to restrain her snicker.

I masked my smirk. Yeah, this ought to be interesting.

My team was a mixed bag of emotions. Hummingbird, still rubbing his throat, eyed the immortals like they might pounce any second. Ember's hands glowed faintly, ready to turn them into a barbecue. Quakelord's scowl could've curdled milk.

Whatever brought the purebloods here, they were in for a rude awakening. First line of defense wasn't just a fancy title—we'd seen shit that'd turn their perfect hair white. Might as well enjoy the show while it lasted.

I got to my feet and stepped forward, boots crunching on the debris-strewn lawn. Time to play nice, at least for now.

"We started on the wrong foot," I said, forcing the words past the fury still burning in my throat. "I'm Harbinger, captain of the Black Guild. Pleasure to meet you, Projector Tepes." I nodded to her friend, teeth clenching. "Lieutenant Popescu."

Projector's shoulders relaxed a fraction; relief flickered across her face. "Likewise, Captain. I've heard good things about you," she replied, taking my hand in a light, but sure grip.

Her fruity scent hit me like one of Terraknight's punches during morning sparring, setting every nerve in my body on fire. Her hand was ridiculously small, but it fit perfectly in mine. It was almost comical how delicate she seemed. Because she wasn't fragile like a flower. She was fragile like a meteor.

Lieutenant Popescu, on the other hand, looked like she'd rather swallow sunbeams than shake my hand. Her eyes darted between Aurora and me, a mix of resentment and resignation in her gaze. She gave a curt nod, lips pressed into a thin line.

I dropped the projector's hand, ignoring the lingering chill. Time to get this circus on the road.

"So, ladies. How do you want to do this?" I looked at the lieutenant, my insides cramping. "I don't see you carrying the usual... *medical instrument.*"

More like device of torture.

Projector Tepes began to speak, but her friend cut her off. "The lab caught fire, and we couldn't retrieve the pincher. We'll have to perform the Initiation the old way."

What a load of bullshit.

I didn't miss the blood draining from the princess' face—or the rapid flutter of her pulse. "D-do you mind?" she stammered, eyes wide. "I promise to be quick and gentle."

Do I mind?

A device that feels like it's sucking out your brain, or an immortal latched onto my vein? Neither option appealed. Zalmoxis, I hated this part. I'd been through more Initiations than I could count, but this... this was new territory. *She* was new territory.

I'd never had an original as projector.

I adjusted my stance, trying to ignore the way her fear mixed with her natural perfume. It was doing things to my head that I couldn't afford right now.

A shudder ran through my entire body. "Alright, boys and girls," I barked, all business. "Let's get this over with. Line up behind me and follow my lead."

To her, because there was no way in hell she couldn't hear my thundering heartbeat, I said, "You know, Projector, there are easier ways to get a man's blood pumping. A bed or a secluded meadow usually do the trick."

Surprise flickered in those scarlet eyes, a delicious blush creeping up her neck. Good. If we were gonna dance this dance, might as well not look like a complete fool. My stomach turned, but hell if I'd let her see me sweat.

Of course, my guildmates didn't miss the opportunity to pile on.

"He's a big boy, Projector," Terraknight boomed. "He can take it."

"Show no mercy!" Quakelord chimed in, the little shit.

I tugged my hood lower, my ears burning. But I laughed it off, rolling with the punches.

"Don't worry, boys, your turn will come," I shot back. "And when it does, I'll show you the meaning of 'gentle.'"

The projector rose on her toes, her hands burning ice-cold through my shirt. "Don't be afraid," she murmured, her voice almost a purr. "I promise not to bite too hard."

Her smile was pure temptation. It stirred things in me I shouldn't be feeling. Not for *her*. Not for an immortal.

Her fangs slid past her full upper lip, and the world turned to white noise. I pulled my hood back just enough to expose a sliver of neck, careful to keep my hair hidden.

My skin felt like it was on fire, her soft breath on my chin sending jolts straight to my groin. Any fear of discovery evaporated as she dragged her teeth along the exposed patch of my jugular.

I went instantly, painfully hard, my pants suddenly way too tight.

When she finally pierced the skin, pressing against me, it was like fireworks exploded in my veins. I couldn't hold back a groan, our connection electric, a live wire of pure sensation. I knew this could get awkward if I resisted, so I went all in. Projectors only needed a taste for Harmonization, after all.

But this? This was *different*.

I could hear her blood singing, luring me like a siren, encouraging me to let loose. I did, forgetting that she wasn't just any projector. That she was Aurora fucking Tepes, the last woman in the world I should want to fuck. And yet here I was, battling the impulse to grind against her, to take this further than it ever should go, all while praying she wouldn't notice what I desperately tried to hide beneath my hood.

"That's enough," I rasped, my voice too rough. *Goddammit, my body shouldn't be this responsive to her.*

Then I felt her in my mind, a rush of power and pleasure that sent panic coursing through me. She had no fucking business being in my head.

I shoved her away, hands shaking with the effort, torn between wanting more and needing her to get the hell away from me.

We stood there, panting, my grip firm on her arms as we shared the same heated air.

Her eyes welled up, glistening with pain, and she stumbled back, baring her bloodstained teeth. The sight should've disgusted me. Instead, it sent another jolt of want through me.

The tendons in her neck stood out; her breathing turned ragged.

Boots crunched around us, and she went rigid, her pulse hammering so hard I could practically see it jumping. Tears streamed down her cheeks in tiny rivers. Her trembling distracted me, caught in a tug-of-war between shielding her from my approaching guildmates and pushing her away, so much so that I missed her strike.

A sharp burn on my cheek snapped me back to reality.

I released her just as the lieutenant and Terraknight reached us, their worried shouts drowned out by her primal scream.

"Don't ever touch me again!" she cried, clawing at her scarf like it choked her.

AURORA

CHILDHOOD MEMORIES FLICKERED LIKE candlelight in my mind: sneaking out my window, heart drumming with delicious rebellion, the Eternal Blood National Park.

It had been my kingdom, a silver-dappled wonderland where I reigned as the hero princess. Woodland creatures bowed before me, while guards melted into shadows, their orders to watch but not interfere unknown to my younger self.

Then came the nightmare that shattered everything.

I remembered jolting awake in Father's lap, his bedtime story dying on his lips. His scent—smoky and sweet—enveloped me as I burrowed into his chest.

"What's wrong, little bug?" His gruff voice rumbled through me, soothing me.

"Daddy," I choked out, "the park... it swallowed me alive."

In my dream, I'd wandered deeper than ever before. The familiar path narrowed, trees looming closer, their branches reaching out like gnarled fingers. A miasma of decay oozed over twisted roots, and then—

The ground had given way.

I'd plummeted into an endless abyss, the stench of rot filling my lungs. Wind whipped past as I clawed at nothing, my stomach lurching with each second of freefall. Alone. Powerless. A harrowing certainty had sunk into my very core that no one would find me at the bottom of that pit.

If there even was a bottom.

Ninety-two years later, I could still taste that putrid air. Father's kisses never scrubbed away the phantom stench that clung to my skin.

The world had changed. I had changed. But that primal fear, that sense of falling into an inescapable darkness—it lingered, lurking just beyond my consciousness, ready to leap forth at the slightest provocation.

And now, it surged with a vengeance.

The captain's fury rolled off him like a scorching heatwave, igniting every dormant terror I locked away. My subconscious recognized him as a greater threat, and I stumbled back, my heart racing so fast it felt like it might burst from my chest.

The silk of my scarf chaffed like sandpaper against my skin. I brought my hand to my neck, trying to calm the burning scars. The world around me began to blur, reality slipping away like sand through an hourglass. Deeper and deeper.

Then I wasn't there anymore. I was falling again, tumbling into that nightmarish pit from my childhood. That familiar, paralyzing fear gripped me, depriving me of oxygen. An endless agony awaited me.

"Aurora? Sweetie, can you hear me?" Sel's worried voice pierced through the darkness. Her hand brushed my arm, gentle and grounding, her familiar jasmine scent wrapping around me. "I'm right here, A. You're safe."

I squeezed my eyes shut, focusing on her touch. But even as I clung desperately to her presence, Lev's phantom weight crushed me. Her hands were his hands. His fangs buried in my throat, my ragged screams echoing in the void. His scent surrounded me. Shame and hopelessness flooded my mind, as suffocating as they'd been that awful night.

"You bit me, remember?" Harbinger's growl hammered in my head, making me flinch. His hand caressed his reddening cheek, golden eyes narrowing with a mix of rage and... was that concern?

I blinked, my surroundings snapping back into focus. The sting in my palm registered belatedly. Oh, Sweet Dark Father, I'd hit him.

Pebbles crunched under his boots as he stalked toward me, each step calculated and menacing. His broad chest heaved with angry breaths, shoulders bunched tight beneath his cowl.

I willed my legs to move, to put distance between us, but the lingering torment kept me rooted.

"What the hell was that?" he snarled, looming over me. The scent of freshly brewed coffee and blooming roses on his breath was intoxicating, terrifying. "I've had dozens of projectors bite me. But none made me feel that way. What's different about you?"

A ring of crimson flickered around his irises, tiny red flecks dancing in liquid gold. My heart fluttered, then raced. No. It couldn't be.

"Who are you?" I gasped, my voice muffled by the roar in my ears.

But I already knew. I recognized the color that ran in the eyes of our Creators. A hue I'd seen in my own eyes every time I looked in the mirror. My stomach roiled, vomit rising in my throat.

I covered my mouth, choking back a sob. It burned like acid, but I couldn't let it out. Because if Harbinger was a direct descendant of Derzelas, then I had just forced a Blood Pact on him. Just like Lev did to me.

I was no better than him. A monster of my own making.

The awful truth slammed into me with crushing force. Guilt and self-loathing consumed me, turning my blood to ice. How could I have been so reckless? How could I do this to him?

My legs finally remembered how to move, but instead of fleeing, they buckled beneath me. Before I could hit the ground, Harbinger's muscular arms caught me, his touch sending a jolt through my body.

"Answer me," he insisted. "What did you do to me?"

I looked up into his turbulent eyes, seeing his frustration reflected there. Didn't he already know?

A feminine voice, touched with a tinge of fear, called out, "Captain? Are you alright?"

Her scent reached me first—rosemary and honey, like summer distilled. She materialized at my side, a petite figure grasping Harbinger's forearm. The wind caught her white dress, sending it dancing around her ankles, revealing soft curves and generous proportions. Her body was a far cry from my own. Not that I was jealous. My body served me just fine—it was strong, quick, resilient.

But her hair... that I envied. It cascaded down her back in gentle curls, a shade of gold that defied classification. Not ash, not strawberry, not platinum—but true, molten gold. She fixed me with vivid green eyes, peering down a delicate, upturned nose.

"What did she do to you?" she demanded, her face contorting into a vicious glare.

That look, coupled with her rich contralto voice and its soft, exotic lilt, seared me to my core. I looked away, unable to withstand the intensity of her hatred.

Selena's whisper sent a shiver through me. It surged hot and cold down my spine. "That," she hissed, nostrils flaring as she leaned toward Harbinger, "looked too much like a Blood Pact." Her eyes turned to slits. "You're not even an immortal. How is that possible?"

Harbinger's jaw flexed, a muscle twitching beneath his bronze skin. Heat radiated from him like a blazing hearth as his peculiar eyes darted between Sel and me, brows furrowing in a deep slope. Pulling his hood lower, he ran a hand down his head.

"Fuck. I forgot about it," he growled, the sound a deep hum in his throat. He pivoted toward a man I assumed—from the little information the Commander provided—was Terraknight, folding his arms. "They're red again, aren't they?"

Terraknight moved with the same confidence as a seasoned performer or elite warrior and positioned himself behind Harbinger. "Like a decoy flare," he confirmed.

Selena's fingers twitched at her sides, her shoulders tensing. I followed her captured gaze to Terraknight, and couldn't fault her for being this startled. Something about him drew the eye like a magnet—the rich chocolate of his skin, his short-cropped hair, and his rugged handsomeness created a perfect harmony. It wasn't his individual features that made him attractive, but how everything about him fit together. Especially the way he looked at you, his focus seeming to pierce right through to your core. He wasn't even my type, and it stirred thoughts of every hot desire I wouldn't admit out loud.

Harbinger's gaze held enough contempt to drown me. "Well... damn. Ma's legacy always comes back and bites me in the ass," he muttered, his upper lip curling to reveal the tip of his fangs. "But don't worry, *Projector*, I have nothing in common with the pigs in your beloved Republic."

"Thank Goddess for that!" a masculine voice said.

Ignoring the barb, I raised my voice over the ensuing laughter. "What do you mean?"

For a second, I got no reaction.

Then he smiled—a quirky half-smile that tipped up only the right corner of his mouth and revealed a sultry dimple. That sinful, irresistible smile had me clenching all over, a burst of attraction so strong it nearly brought tears to my eyes.

I swallowed it down like a bad gulp of stale blood and looked away, hating myself for my lack of restraint and professionalism. Biting Harbinger had been like the strongest wine in Elena's cellar while it was on fire. It was pure hunger. Ravenousness. I should have stopped at the first signs of the Blood Pact. I should've known, recognized the lust it sparked in me.

But mortal blood wasn't strong enough to subdue our minds, our bodies. I hadn't even thought it was even possible.

My breath hiccupped; my windpipe closed in.

His smirk stretched into a full grin, golden-scarlet eyes glinting dangerously. "I mean, I'm special, Projector. Just. Like. You." He paused, pulled his elbows inwards, and raised his arms, flexing his fingers. "*Precious* original blood flows through these veins." The way he spat out 'precious' betrayed a loathing so deep, it seesawed through my thoughts.

"You're... you're half-original?" I blurted out the answer my mind refused to accept. "That's not—how is this possible?" My eyes shifted to Selena. "How is this possible?"

I staggered back, my legs suddenly boneless beneath me. The sky fractured like a broken mirror, and reality fell apart. It shattered into tiny pieces that rained down around me. Even though I'd seen his eyes, hearing him say it aloud made it absolute. Unmistakable.

An original, here? Fighting among the outliers as if he were just another mixed-breed? It erased every truth I'd been taught, every pillar of my understanding. Purebloods weren't made. We were born immortal. For Harbinger to exist, one of his parents had to be mortal. But that defied everything I knew about our biology—cross-species procreation was supposed to be impossible. Had it been another lie?

132

My gaze locked onto his eyes again—those impossible, beautiful dual-colored eyes that held the unmistakable mark of our Creators. They were the proof my rational mind needed, yet my heart still rebelled against the truth they revealed.

"How?" I whispered, feeling a little light-headed from the rush of blood to my head.

Jasmine and vetiver filled the air like a dark cloud foreboding a catastrophic storm. Dirt crunched, and before I could react, Selena lunged at Harbinger.

"And you let her bite you?" Her voice rose to a shriek, her eyes wild with panic. "You sonofabitch! She's been through enough already!"

Terraknight intercepted, grasping her wrists. "What in all the Gods out there is your problem?" he growled.

Clad in midnight black and towering over her by at least a foot, the vice-captain looked like he could chew concrete and spit out gravel. His muscles rippled beneath his tight shirt like steel cords. But with Selena this far gone, she'd face down a raging bull. Height and muscle be damned.

"Let go of me, you bastard!" She thrashed against his grip.

"Sel... It's not what you think," I said, trying to calm her down.

The beginnings of a migraine bloomed between my eyes. Harbinger's revelation had turned our world upside down, but starting a fight wouldn't solve anything. Underworld's balls, we probably wouldn't survive them all. And even if we did, where would that leave our plan?

Sel's fury was born of love, and I appreciated her fierce loyalty. But in her blind panic to shield me, she'd missed the heart of the issue. The real victim here wasn't me; it was Harbinger, bound by my reckless actions.

Writhing like a fly caught in a web, she slammed her head back, connecting with Terraknight's chin. An awful crack echoed above the din.

The vice-captain recoiled, surprise and frustration battling on his face as he released her.

Selena whirled on me, seemingly unfazed by the fact she'd just head-butted a man who could snap her like a twig.

"He let you bite him this close to the Red Moon, A," she snarled, jabbing a finger at Harbinger. Her glare blazed like the pits of the Underworld. "This close!" She held her thumb and forefinger a hair's breadth apart, her hand trembling with the intensity of her rage.

I became acutely aware of everyone watching. This was not how I'd planned our first meeting to go.

"The Red Moon is months away," I said, running a hand through my hair. Then lower, "And, in case you forgot, it takes two to seal the bond."

"It's still too dangerous," she conceded with a frustrated sigh.

Harbinger's gaze seared into me like morning sun rays, and I forced myself to meet his eyes. The intoxicating scent of him, his blood... I could still taste him on my tongue.

My cheeks flared like embers as I fought to keep my fangs from descending, struggling against the monster inside me that craved more. By some miracle, I kept my voice even.

"I'm sorry for hurting you. I didn't know..." The words felt inadequate even as they left my lips. Guilt rolled in my gut, warring with the shameful desire for another taste. I straightened my shoulders, ready to face the consequences. "If you want to make a formal complaint, I understand. I'll take full responsibility."

Harbinger's brow furrowed, confusion flickering across his face before he let his stern mask slip back on. A feather twitched in his jaw. He looked at me for a long time, long enough that crickets began to chirp around us.

The silence stretched, growing uncomfortable.

I almost begged him to end it.

Then he blinked, breaking the trance he'd drawn me into. "Projector, let's just... finish the Initiation," he said. His voice was gruff but lacked its earlier edge of contempt. Or at least he muted it down. "Everyone, get back in line. Terraknight, you're next!"

The outliers shuffled into position, footfalls scuffing against the ground. Terraknight stepped forward, halting an inch from my boots. His presence felt as commanding as the captain's. I looked up, meeting hazel eyes that glimmered like polished agates. No crimson. No sign of immortality.

The thought struck me like a bolt of lightning.

Was Harbinger an immortal? The notion seemed absurd, yet... No. He smelled mortal. Tasted like one too, if I ignored the side of me that wanted to worship his blood. To drop to my knees and beg him to feed me for the rest of my existence.

Derzelas' fangs. *What is wrong with me?*

Terraknight cleared his throat, snapping me out of my thoughts. I blinked and focused on his face. His lips quirked, as if he could see the hunger in my eyes. *Great.*

"May I?" I asked, gesturing to his neck.

He nodded, a hint of a smile playing at the corners of his mouth. "Go ahead, Projector. I promise I won't bite back."

Rising on my toes, I gripped his broad shoulders for balance. His scent was earthy and rich, like sun-warmed soil after rain. As my fangs sank into his flesh, I braced myself, half-expecting the same overwhelming rush I'd experienced with Harbinger. But there was nothing beyond the usual exhilaration of fresh blood.

No otherworldly connection, no burning desire.

It didn't sing to me. Or attempt to lure me into his thrall.

Relief surfaced as I pulled back, watching the punctures close before my eyes. I'd gotten through it without incident, thank God. Maybe Harbinger had been a fluke, a one-time anomaly.

Terraknight stepped back and winked—not at me, but at Selena, who scoffed, unimpressed. He laughed it off and walked away, blending into the night.

An iele with silvery-white wings glided into Terraknight's place, bringing with him the crisp scent of a storm. Hummingbird was... pretty. There was no other word for it. Though not as tall as the others, he still stood half a head above me, lithe and graceful. Eyes of pure marigold peered from beneath waves of chestnut hair, set in a face of perfect symmetry. His smile, framed by a hint of stubble, was all teeth and shone brighter than the moon.

A breeze ruffled the immaculate feathers, and my gaze strayed to his wings. Tucked close to his back, they summoned unwanted memories—ivory feathers torn and scattered, bones crushed beneath Katerina's savage bloodlust. Too much innocent blood had spilled at my family's whim on my hundredth birthday. Because even though the Wurdulaks had instigated it, Mother and Brother had to have known about it.

Now, the fresh tang of blood on my tongue felt like tar, turning my insides.

Hummingbird shuffled in place, silver filaments in his feathers catching moonlight. My fingers itched to feel their softness, to reassure myself they remained whole, unharmed.

"Do you mind?" I asked, raising a hand to touch and pulling it back at the last minute.

Hummingbird's lips curved into a sly grin, his eyes twinkling with mischief. His voice was pure velvet. It promised a messy tumble in black satin sheets and an inevitable broken heart. "Oh, sweetheart, you're not quite ready for that yet."

I bristled at the endearment, memories of Elena's condescending 'dear' flashing through my mind. "I don't do pet names," I retorted, my tone sharper than intended.

He leaned in, close enough that I could feel the body heat emanating from him, but not quite touching. His words ghosted across my face as he whispered, a hint of challenge in his voice, "Tell me, then... do you *do* ieles?"

I felt my cheeks flush. Despite myself, I found his boldness oddly refreshing. "Okay, that's it. I'm done talking to you," I said, unable to keep the smile from my voice.

"Finish your work, Projector," Harbinger's growl cleaved the air. "Dawn's approaching. Play and flirt as much as you like, but do not endanger my team."

HARBINGER

Fangs sank into the iele's flesh, and my middle twisted like I'd been fucking sucker-punched. Couldn't look away if I tried, and I tried. What kind of twisted game was this turning into?

Hummingbird, the brat, was putting on a show that would make the characters in Pearl's trashy romance novels blush. Head thrown back, curls bouncing, moaning like the Goddess herself had touched him.

My fists clenched at my sides. A growl ripped from my throat, urging me to yank her away and end this whole fucked-up Initiation. I wanted to punch myself in the face for even caring, but I didn't want them to share what she and I had. Not that we had anything. By the Moon, was I envious of the kid?

Seconds. That's all it took until the projector pulled back. But watching it stretched into an eternity in hell. The kid was floating on cloud nine while I felt like... what? Cheated? Hollow?

Zalmoxis, I needed to get laid.

It'd been too long since we hit up the lower ward guilds. Maybe that's exactly what we all needed—a good old-fashioned stress release. But even as the thought crossed my mind, I knew it was bullshit. The princess had royally fucked that up for me. Comparing what I'd felt when she drank from me to some quick tumble was like putting a candle next to the damn sun.

She'd slipped past my defenses, eroding at the cracks like invasive roots, and messed with my head. I hated her for it. Hated how she dredged up things I'd buried so deep I thought they were fossilized. It wasn't loneliness—I had my team, my family. This was... different. Unsettling. But I couldn't bring myself to take it back either.

She'd shown me a glimpse of something I'd convinced myself I didn't need. Now I was itching for another hit of whatever the hell had happened between us. Pissed me off that I even gave a damn. I was doing fine before her, never wasted a thought on living any other way. *She had to come and stir up this shit, didn't she?*

It gnawed at me, made me feel deprived and furious. Deprived because a fragment of me craved to feel that rush again, and furious because she was a goddamn immortal. I shouldn't want anything from her. Shouldn't need it.

This clusterfuck of desire and rage simmered in my chest. No way was I letting her throw me off balance, electric connection or not.

Gale stepped up next, brushing her chocolate hair aside like it was no big deal.

The original cupped her neck and sank her teeth into her vein, drawing a gasp out of Gale that sent my blood rushing south. Fuck me, the image my twisted brain cooked up of them together was going to haunt my dreams for weeks.

I really did need to get laid. Soon.

Scrubbing a hand over my face, I ground my teeth together and stalked back to the fountain, the old mansion lurking in the shadows. I couldn't watch anymore. Had to remind myself that Gale was my friend and the immortal was the enemy. They weren't just any women I could fantasize about. But try telling that to my backstabbing body. Might as well try to reason with a Stalker.

The house was a classic Victorian relic with a sandstone veranda, slightly crooked from Quakelord's last temper tantrum. A gale breezed past, carrying the scent of damp pine and wildflowers and drowning out the voices in my head. Small mercies.

I snatched up my book and planted my ass on the concrete edge as moss squelched beneath me. The shower curtain Rosebud had tied against the rusty latticework flapped in the wind, his message still clear as day: 'TWENTY DOWN, TEN MORE TO GO. GLORY TO THE FUCKIN' REPUBLIC!'

My insides clenched. Rosebud had been dead three months now, Terraknight taking up the upkeep of the tally. Our most recent loss happened last week—Mandrake, a balaur with only five years left on his conscription. Two lines crossed out the words 'twenty' and 'ten,' the new numbers were partially visible, but we all knew what they meant.

I white-knuckled the book, trying to focus on the title instead of the red haze edging into my vision. Reading usually helped, but right now all I wanted was to rip the Republic apart with my bare hands and piss on the ashes.

"What was that bull about?" Gale landed in front of me, her raspy voice drowned out by the rustle of feathers. Her scent—citrus and hon-ey—clung to her like a hot cup of tea by the fire.

I took a big sniff. She was my comfort smell.

"Any idea why the lieutenant freaked out like we kicked her puppy?" she asked.

"Hell, if I know. You never know with *them*," I grunted.

Living for too long wasn't healthy. Immortals were too bored for their own good. They'd make up shit just to keep themselves entertained.

Gale flared her copper-brown wings to her side, momentarily eclipsing the moon and casting me in shadow. She folded them close to her back with a quiet swish. Her look said she knew exactly what I meant. "Ever heard of the Red Moon?" she asked.

"Nope, but Miss Psycho dropped something about a Blood Pact." I pinched my nose, the projector's fruity scent still clinging to me like a bad hangover. "Got a pretty good idea what that means now."

Her eyes widened, the amber flecks in them catching the moonlight. "Oh shit, you don't mean—"

"Yep." I arched an eyebrow at the blush spreading across her neck. "Since when did you turn into a blushing schoolgirl?"

"Shut up," she mumbled, hitting my arm as the blush spread to her cheeks. The impact almost sent me flying on my back—damn, she packed a hell of a punch.

A hiss from Ember caught our attention. We both turned to watch just as the original sank her fangs into her neck. Fire lit up her veins, casting a golden glow across the yard.

Gale's tentative smile bloomed into a cheeky grin. "So, they feed and fuck like the rest of us. Big whoop."

"Ever seen fireworks, Gale?"

"Yeah, but what's that got to—"

"It's like that. Times a thousand."

She snorted, slapping my shoulder. "Fireworks? Seriously?"

I nodded, grateful my hood hid my burning ears. "Honest to God."

"Holy shit, you actually enjoyed it!" Gale's giggles turned into full-blown laughter. "Boy, you're in big shit."

No point lying. She could read me like a damn book. "Didn't even touch her. Still better than any sex I've had."

She crossed her arms, giving the projector a once-over. I forced myself not to look. "Must be your special blood or something. For me, it was just like a feed. Bit tingly, if that."

"That's not what's got me worried. This Red Moon thing... I'd bet my ass it's tied to the Blood Pact somehow." I leaned back, staring at the sky like it might actually give me answers.

Fat chance. The Great White was a god of few words. With a heavy sigh, I focused back on Gale.

"She said 'it takes two to seal the bond.' There's more to it, and now we're all neck-deep in it, so I'm gonna find out what."

"What do you want me to do?"

Commotion sparked on the driveway. The original had wrapped up the Initiation. I turned at the sound of boots on gravel, scanning the approaching crowd for our 'guests.' The air felt charged, like the moment before a lightning strike, setting my teeth on edge.

"For now, we wait," I said, eyes narrowing on the lieutenant as she fell behind. "That one's up to something. I can smell it."

No sooner had the words left my mouth than the pureblood frowned, digging deep into her coat pockets. Metal clinked, and with a triumphant cry, she scooped out a pile of silver disks.

My stomach bottomed out. Whatever those things were, they looked about as friendly as a Limus' teeth.

"Transmitters," she announced, picking one up and jiggling it in the air before she vanished into the crowd.

She weaved between bodies in a blur of motion, almost invisible to the naked eye. One moment she was at the back, the next she reappeared at the front, leaving only a gust of displaced air in her wake.

Rolling a disk between her knuckles, she spoke slowly, her tone dripping with condescension. It was clear she wouldn't repeat herself. "The Bloodthorn Nexus hasn't been tested on short distances. It's safer if your commanding officer refrains from using it. Use these devices and avoid harmonizing with her."

Soft murmurs rippled through my guildmates. A few heads shook as she started distributing the contraptions. I was about to ask what the fuss was about when the scent of vanilla and peaches teased my senses. The projector was creeping up behind me. A shiver ran down my spine, but I shrugged it off with some effort.

There you are, I thought, fighting the urge to turn around.

The lieutenant approached, making me wait with my hand out like some common beggar. Her narrow, unsmiling grin pissed me off as she dropped the device into my palm.

"Now, if I could have your attention," she said, doing a one-eighty. "Attach the equipment under your left ear." She flipped her hair back to demonstrate first on herself. "You may feel slight discomfort. Proceed at your own pace." Not a single twitch betrayed that she might have felt a sliver of pain.

We got to work, our clothes rustling. I pressed the disk into the soft spot between my jaw and earlobe, hissing as hundreds of needles seemed to drill through my skull. The sensation felt like spiders crawling beneath my skin.

"Slight discomfort, my ass," I grumbled. The ache abated, but the pressure inside my head did not.

The pureblood resumed pacing, holding up a finger, her voice clipped and precise. "To contact each other, press the center of the disk and say their name. The nerve implant will register your command and connect the transmission wirelessly." She raised a second finger, scanning my guildmates with keen eyes. "For group chats, list names in order. Use your guild's name for the whole team." Her lips thinned, a hint of annoyance weaving into her tone. "And for the love of darkness, speak clearly. These things are still in beta."

The black jeans she had on whirred when she walked, rolling her hips slightly, shoulders pulled back a little to showcase her breasts. I couldn't help but notice how attractive she was, in that way that all immortals were—stunningly beautiful, with a heart of stone.

"So, we're your guinea pigs?" Hummingbird piped up.

The medic hissed, not even bothering to look at him. "As much as I hate it, iele, I'm here to save your ass if something goes wrong. Questions?"

Gale's hand shot up, the silver disk below her ear flashing blue. "Does the projector have one?"

"No. Your commanding officer will contact you through the Harmonization."

I caught Gale's eye. Her raised eyebrow said it all. *Yeah, the projector gets a free pass while we're stuck with these damn head leeches.*

Terraknight's hand shot up, a shit-eating grin plastered across his face. "Got a question for ya, shortie."

The lieutenant's eyebrow arched, but she nodded, inviting the inevitable disaster.

"You always got a stick up your ass, or did no one fuck you in a while?"

The yard erupted.

Laughter ricocheted off the old sandstone walls and rippled like moonlight on water. Phoenix folded in on herself, her auburn hair whipping as she cackled. Ember followed. Pearl's aquamarine eyes went wide, her palm shooting up to her mouth in a failed attempt to stifle her giggles. Hummingbird and Quakelord were shaking, tears streaming down their faces. Even Gale had trouble holding in her chuckle.

"Fuck's sake, Terraknight," I muttered, struggling to keep my own face straight. The colossal idiot was going to start a fight, but damned if it wasn't entertaining.

I glanced at the projector, half-expecting her Darklings to materialize and rip my vice-captain a new one. Her giggles carried despite her effort to hide them behind her hand. Her friend, though? If looks could kill, Terraknight'd be six feet under.

Alarm bells rang inside my mind, and I straightened up, prepared to intervene if she decided to blood magic his ass.

The pureblood's teeth flashed, white as bone and twice as sharp. "Offering your services, boy?"

I damn near swallowed my tongue. I'd seen guys twice Terraknight's size piss themselves at the sight of him. His bulk alone could intimidate a bear. If you had the misfortune of taking one of his punches, you'd be picking up pieces of yourself for a week. But this pureblood didn't even flinch.

"Damn, son!" Quakelord wheezed between laughs, slapping his knee. "She's handing you your ass!"

Terraknight, the cocky bastard, just grinned wider. I'd seen him charm the pants off anything with a pulse. We'd always joked about who'd lose their edge first and start showing signs of aging. Part of me had hoped something would knock him down a peg, mess up that human-perfect face of his. Make him more like the rest of us peasants.

Guess I was wrong.

All it took was one ice-cold immortal to have him ready to roll over and beg.

His eyes gleamed with challenge, but there was something else there, too. Something that said he'd met his match and was loving every second of it.

"My room's always open, shortie," he purred, full of promises. "I'll rock your world."

The pureblood's smile turned predatory. "Flattering, but I sincerely doubt you could handle me."

I exchanged a look with Gale, both of us thinking the same thing: This was gonna be one hell of an entertaining disaster.

AURORA

GALE'S LAUGHTER DANCED ON the night breeze as she twirled around the fountain, wings shimmering like living metal. "I like her." She giggled, balancing two steaming mugs in her hands.

I eyed the chipped ceramic cup she handed me, the inky liquid sloshing close to the rim. A rich, nutty scent tickled my nose and stirred a flicker of curiosity. Throwing caution to the wind, I took a generous swig.

Sweet Darkness, what a mistake.

My taste buds revolted, every nerve ending screaming in protest. It tasted like a horrifying brew of distilled essence of damp earth and bitter regret. I struggled to keep my face neutral, but my treacherous lips puckered as if I'd just kissed a dirt clod.

Gale's knowing smirk told me I wasn't fooling anyone. So much for my legendary poker face. At least I managed not to spit the vile concoction in her face. My mother's lessons in decorum were worth something, at least.

Her almond-shaped eyes sparkled with mirth. "Kafea," she explained. "It's... an acquired taste."

"I've had worse," I lied, mustering a weak smile. The truth was, it was so terrible even bacteria rebelled against it.

"Oh please," Gale snorted, downing her own drink without a wince. "If you think this is bad, wait till Terraknight breaks out his home-brewed mead."

We left our mugs perched on the fountain's edge—mine untouched save for that initial, regrettable sip—and ambled toward the captain. The bitter aftertaste still clung to my tongue, making me wrinkle my nose with every swallow.

Gale moved with an effortless grace, the kind of poise usually reserved for someone who'd grown up at court. Her wings, fitted neatly through artful slits in her shirt, rippled like crimson silk in the moonlight. A flash of ink peeked from beneath the fabric, sparking questions that I mentally filed away for another time—when I wasn't teetering on the edge of hysterical laughter.

Her boots, comically oversized and clearly 'borrowed', slapped the ground with each step. She looked like she'd raided some unfortunate giant's closet—Terraknight's, most likely. The contrast between her elegant bearing and those clownish shoes was my undoing, but I folded my lips and reined myself in. The last thing I wanted was to offend her.

Harbinger glanced up from his book and looked in our direction. His gaze landed on me. For a heartbeat, surprise flashed across his face, dark-blond brows arching high. Then curiosity took over, his scrutiny so intense it set my pulse racing. Those eyes shouldn't belong to someone looking shy of thirty—they held centuries, millennia even. Empires could have risen and fallen in the depths of that gaze.

I knew I was staring. Underworld's balls, I *knew* it. But I couldn't tear my eyes away from the sun-kissed planes of his face, the curve of his lips. The sharp edge of his jaw. His neck.

Unbidden, the memory of his blood flooded my senses. I ached to taste him again, to run my fingers along that golden skin and—

His features twisted into a sneer, dousing my wayward thoughts like ice water. I felt my face grow hot, equal parts embarrassment and irritation. I fought to regain composure. I was a professional, damn it, not some love-struck fledgling.

I held my shoulders upright, tamping down the inconvenient warmth in my belly. Time to focus on why I was really here.

His sneer deepened as I approached, but I refused to be intimidated.

"We need to discuss your mission logs," I said. "There are... discrepancies that need addressing."

Harbinger's jaw locked, fingers tightening on the book. "What exactly do you think you've found?" he snarled. "Those reports contain everything necessary. Nothing more, nothing less."

The Bloodthorn Nexus buzzed at my nape. I pressed the crystal, and Selena's acerbic voice flooded my mind. *"Having fun with your fake original? I'm heading back for our gear. Starving here."*

As her shadowy form melted into the forest, my body revolted. "Wait!" I cried, lurching forward. "I'll come with—"

"I've got this." Gale stopped me, her grip around my wrist firm, sure.

I hesitated, eyeing the lightening sky. Sel was strong, but alone out there... She'd need the extra help to haul the crate back in time. "Fine," I huffed. "But be careful. And hurry back."

Gale's wings snapped open like a thunderclap. One powerful beat sent her rocketing skyward into the pre-dawn gloom, the burst of air scattering leaves and pebbles and pelting the roof with a staccato of tiny impacts.

A plaintive mewl drifted down in response, sending a tremor up my back.

What in the eternal fires was lurking up there?

"Did you hear that?" I hissed at Harbinger, scanning the roofline, searching for danger.

Harbinger didn't even bother to lift his gaze from the book, his brows furrowing deeper as if my very existence was an affront to his concentration. "It's just the wind," he muttered through a rigid mouth. His fingers, long and calloused, flipped to the next page with intentional slowness, the message clear in the soft rustle: 'Already scared, princess?'

Just. The. Wind.

The sheer audacity of this man. As if I couldn't pick out each individual termite gnawing at the rafters, or the steady thrum of his own heartbeat. I fought the urge to snatch the damn book from his hands. Here I was, on high alert for potential Stalker threats, and this conceited, exasperating half-original was more concerned with whatever drivel he was reading. The same man whose sloppy reports were full of holes.

I unclenched my fists, giving him my best smile—the one that said I could speak presumption fluently—and bit back a scathing retort. I wouldn't let him bait me into losing focus. There was a job to do, and by the Moon, I'd see it through.

Forcing my attention away from him, I surveyed the looming mansion. The structure stood out like a forgotten Tenth Ward lord who'd stumbled into the slums—sandstone and red brick with Romanesque arches clinging weakly to their bygone glory. Its once-proud Victorian bones were now a centuries-spanning patchwork of architectural confusion, scarred by boarded windows and hasty repairs.

The building's haphazard array of ornate balconies looked one stiff breeze away from collapse. Kudzu had taken full advantage of the neglect, its dense tendrils scaling the walls, edges frosted by the encroaching cold.

Despite my enhanced senses—clearly superior to the oh-so-preoccupied captain's—I couldn't pinpoint the source of that earlier horrifying sound.

Let it go, Aurora. Focus.

I filled my chest with air, preparing myself for the confrontation ahead. "About the guild's battle logs," I said, keeping my voice level. "You sent the wrong ones. They all contained the same report—"

"What, you went through all of them?" Harbinger's head snapped up, glaring at me with narrowed eyes.

I held my position and lifted my chin.

Something swirled around his pupils, like amber feathers or brushstrokes of liquid gold. I found myself leaning in, breath catching in my chest. Red flecks danced in honey as if someone had placed them with tiny tweezers. The crimson circle pulsed once, twice, then vanished entirely. His irises transformed before me, melting into pure, bright citrine that seemed to glow from within.

It was beautiful. Terrifying. A reminder of his otherness, of the unknown power that lurked just beneath that tough exterior. I knew I should pull back, maintain some semblance of professional distance but—

"...the Hell? You're still doing that?" Terraknight's bellow shattered the moment.

I jerked and stepped back, spine ramrod straight.

He launched himself from the fountain, all rippling muscle and a sly smirk. For a man who looked capable of demolishing walls, he landed next to the captain with surprising grace, his gaze ping-ponging between us.

"Yes, I have," I told Harbinger, meeting his steely gaze. "I've examined all the reports since you took charge, including those of your predecessors."

He blinked. The golden wonder in his irises froze over. "What exactly do you expect to achieve with them? They seem pointless to me."

I couldn't believe my ears. Was he serious?

"Analyzing Stalkers' tactics isn't just a projector's responsibility, it's a crucial part of our survival," I retorted. "You've been battling them for decades. You, more than anyone, should understand the significance of being well-prepared."

After eighty years, Harbinger must have developed his own methods—his survival was proof enough. But I needed those details, the nuances of his countermeasures. Unlike my less-diligent colleagues, I'd made it my mission to dissect every facet of Stalker behavior. It ranked third on my priorities, right after mastering protective gear and keeping a ready supply of synthetic blood. Sweet Dark Father forbid I be caught unprepared or, worse, hungry during one of the Sparrows' missions.

If Harbinger had some secret method that he didn't want to reveal in his reports, I needed to know about it. And if he didn't... well, then we had a much bigger problem on our hands.

I softened my expression, offering a closed-lipped smile. "I realize you might have assumed no one bothered to read these reports," I said. "We've failed in that regard before, so I won't hold it against you. But moving forward, I need you to submit them regularly. I assure you, I *will* read every word."

My gaze never wavered from his. I was confident in my position, in my dedication. If he believed he could shirk his duties, he'd find out just how sharp my fangs could be—figuratively speaking, of course.

His lips—which I absolutely wasn't staring at—flattened into a hard line. The silence stretched taut before he turned back to his book. "I can't write or read well," he muttered. "I have more important things to do."

"The balls on you, I swear," Terraknight hissed, shaking his head.

I *almost* laughed in Harbinger's face. If I hadn't met him, read his eloquent letter, or seen Noica's name embossed on the leather-bound tome in his lap, I might have believed him. He wasn't illiterate any more than I was mortal.

Two could play at this game. I had a century of practice dealing with stubborn arrogance. My most recent difficult charge was Stoneheart, but he was only the latest in a long line.

I closed my eyes, silently begging for patience from any deity willing to listen. Father's voice echoed in my mind, a memory from the grand halls of Corvin Palace when he shared his wisdom.

'Restraint and understanding, my dear daughter, have been the cornerstones of Tepes' rule for millennia,' he'd said. *'Even Dracula, for all his bloodthirsty reputation, was a king who listened. He gave his subjects the benefit of the doubt, a chance to air their grievances.'*

His statement burrowed under my skin, stirring a pot of frustration that was already nearly overflowing. I despised being played for a fool, but how to respond? Match Harbinger's mockery or rise above it?

The decision was easy enough in the end.

I leaned in, close enough to see a tiny birthmark perched atop his upper lip. My mouth curled into a wolfish grin. "My mistake," I purred, running a finger along the corner of the book. "I assumed you'd penned that letter yourself." Our knees brushed, and I watched, transfixed, as those golden feathers completed another rotation around his dilated pupils. "But if that's not the case, well... these reports are the perfect chance to practice. I'm sure they'll be *tremendously* beneficial."

"Will they, now?" Harbinger grunted, his throat working as he gulped. Those otherworldly eyes spoke of violence... and a Blood Pact that could send you over the edge for a swift journey to the Underworld and back.

Heat pooled low in my belly, my rebellious flesh responding to his proximity with embarrassing eagerness. I filled my lungs with air, savoring his scent. My suit felt too tight, too confining. Especially when my mind wouldn't stop picturing him tangled in satin sheets, looking at me as he was right now.

My fangs dropped, aching to sink into his neck. Dear God. I had never *craved* someone like this.

After Lev, I never thought I'd tolerate a man's touch again. But something about Harbinger drew me like the sweetest drug, impossible to resist. For a few moments, he'd made me forget the scorching sensation of fangs piercing my unwilling skin.

I knew, as surely as I knew I was standing here on the battlefront with Selena and a guild of powerful mixed-breeds, that this fixation on him—on the man and the blood flowing in his veins—was going to come back and bite me in the ass. Hard. It was a certainty, like the rising of the sun or the phases of the moon.

That day was barreling toward me like a runaway train. And it was going to be bad. Catastrophically, earth-shatteringly bad.

I couldn't decide if this foreknowledge was a blessing or a curse.

"She's not wrong, you know," a lyrical voice drifted from the gravel path, pulling me back from the brink of utter mortification and drawing Harbinger's gaze away.

I sucked in a ragged breath, desperately clinging to the notion that it had simply been too long since the Sparrows' Initiation. Surely, the proximity to mortal blood was addling my senses. It had to be the bloodlust. Because if it wasn't... By Dracula's fangs, I couldn't even begin to fathom what this attraction to Harbinger meant, and that terrified me more than any Stalker.

Pearl glided to a stop beside me, her high ponytail swaying. The scent of saltwater and seaweed wafted from her like a breeze.

She winked one azure eye at me, blowing delicately across her steaming cup of kafea. "It could help you, Cap," she said, popping the 'P' with relish. "You're always nose-deep in some book. Is that Constantin Noica? 'Being and Logos' bored me senseless, but you seem riveted."

Harbinger's eyes narrowed slightly, a flicker of surprise crossing his face before he masked it.

Pearl's gaze slid to me, and I felt heat creep up my neck. There was something in her voice that beckoned you to follow her into the depths of the sea. A daughter of Kotys, the varva carried the very essence of the ocean in her tresses, shimmering in hues of turquoise, emerald, and sapphire under the moonlight.

Guessing Pearl's age was about as easy as nailing jelly to a wall. She exuded a timeless beauty that made centuries look like mere blinks of an eye. The way she carried herself—all regal patience, as if she and time were old friends—reminded me of Sonya in a way. It was that eerie calm you only get after you've seen all the world's wonders and horrors and filed them away like so many dusty books.

It took every bit of my resolve to tear my eyes away from her and remember I still had to sort things with the insufferable captain. "Harbinger?"

"Fine!" he snarled, slamming his book shut. "Will audio records suffice?"

I tilted my head, meeting his glare with one of my own. "No. I need handwritten reports. Summaries of all patrols for the past six months, combat included." With millions of purebloods at stake, I couldn't afford to let him off easily.

Harbinger's disapproving 'hmph' painted Pearl's cheeks a delicate shade of pink, but their silent exchange lacked the intensity of the stern looks he usually reserved for me. If I could've peeked into their minds, their wordless conversation might've gone something like:

"Sorry, I didn't expect her to push this hard," I imagined Pearl's downcast eyes saying as she scuffed her boot against the gravel.

He shook his head, exhaling a sigh that seemed to come from his very bones. *"Nah, this one's on me."*

The silence stretched, thick and uncomfortable. For all my skills at reading people, I could've been dead wrong. They might've been plotting my demise for all I knew, and I'd be powerless to stop it.

"To effectively counter the Stalkers, we need real-time intel," I said, forcing steel into my voice. "Your experience is invaluable. Work with me here, Harbinger. It's in everyone's best interest. Cooperation could save lives on all sides."

His eye twitched, but resignation banked the rage in his gaze. He gave a curt nod, so slight I almost missed it. The muscles in his jaw popped as if the very act of conceding caused him physical pain.

I held back a smirk, mostly because I understood. It wasn't easy to step over your pride and not get a little bit damaged. God knew I'd tripped over mine enough times.

This was progress. Painful, grudging progress, but progress nonetheless.

Footsteps faded onto dew-kissed grass as the rest of the Black Guild drifted toward the house. My gaze darted to the forest, and worry sank in my gut.

No sign of Selena or Gale.

The sliver of pre-dawn light peeking through the trees felt like a blade against my spine as my fists balled.

"One more thing," I said, maintaining a neutral tone despite the adrenaline thrumming in my blood. "These reports are twenty-five years old. Did you get them from another outlier, or have you been sending them all this time?"

A twig snapped, and I nearly jumped out of my skin.

"Yeah, Captain's been sending those fake reports for ages. Even before I met him," a husky male voice whispered in my ear.

I jolted, avoiding a near skull-to-skull collision.

Only by Derzelas' mercy did I stop myself from tapping into my magic and retaliating. "Dark Father Almighty! Don't do that!" I hissed, putting some much-needed distance between us. No man of his size should be that quiet, but he snuck around me like a ghost. It was... disconcerting.

Quakelord flashed a grin that would've made a shark proud. I showed my fangs in return, sizing him up. Six feet of pure muscle—not bulky, but far from lean. Thick, hard, and defined, the kind of strength that could send him scaling a roof or cracking a Limus skull with one well-timed slap. His straight black hair skimmed broad shoulders, and those hooded olive-tinted eyes... they radiated danger just like Katerina Wurdulak's.

An uneasy quiet fell between us, broken only by the whisper of grass in the gentle wind. Through the gaps in the boarded-up windows, flickering candlelight danced like trapped fireflies as the other outliers ventured deeper into the mansion.

I hugged my ribs, fighting the hollow ache in my chest. My eyes darted back to the woods for what felt like the hundredth time.

Where are they? What's taking so long?

Resisting the impulse to charge into the forest, I asked, "Did you know Harbinger before joining the Black Guild, Quakelord?"

Should I go after them?

The scent of moss and rain wafted over as Quakelord shifted his weight. I glanced at the trees and back at him, catching his easy shrug.

"Yeah, most of us go way back," he said. "Phoenix and Ember? Those two've been joined at the hip since day one of enlistment. I crashed their party seven years later." He jerked his thumb toward the others. "Hummingbird, Pearl, and Gale—they've been with Harbinger and Terra since forever." He squinted at the vice-captain, scratching his chin. "How long's it been, old man? Five, six decades? I lost track."

Terraknight's jaw stiffened as he gripped his ankle, crossing it over his knee. His eyes darted warily toward the treeline. "Longer," he muttered.

"How long since you were drafted?" I pressed, even as anxiety ate at me from the inside.

Quakelord seemed unnervingly calm. If he was worried about his guildmate being late, or worse, meeting any Stalkers, he hid it well.

"Me? Thirty-five years, give or take. Phoenix and Ember about four decades." He paused, shooting a sidelong glance at Harbinger. Something flickered in his eyes—Respect? Wariness?—before he took a hard swallow. "But Cap and the rest? Man, they've been out here longer than any of us can remember. Hell, sometimes I think they came with the forest."

I felt my eyebrows climb toward my hairline. Just how old was Harbinger anyway?

The long years of service explained Terraknight's position as vice-captain and their masterful control over elemental powers. Clearly, the Commander's intel had some gaping holes.

I caught myself staring at Harbinger and snapped out of it when he spoke. "With all the battles and patrols and everything else," he sighed, "it's exhausting to keep track." He grunted, making me painfully aware of my titles and privileges. His tone still grated on my nerves. "All I can say is that it's been a long time we've fought your war."

I bit my cheek, the sharp sting giving way to blood. Guilt settled on my chest. He was right, and I had no retort. I'd been out here for mere hours and was already stressed to my limits.

The sweet metallic scent permeated the air, catching Harbinger's attention. His eyes widened, those mesmerizing feathers looping in his gaze. The edges of his irises darkened, flickering red. His nostrils flared, and for a moment, I saw raw hunger shining in his eyes. It comforted me that I wasn't the only one.

He responded with a disdainful curl of his lip, but I could hear his pulse racing, matching mine beat for beat. A quick blink, and his eyes returned to normal, but the sneer on his face lingered.

"In that case," I blurted out, "you've all completed your service. You're free. You can return to the Republic—"

The words shriveled and died on my tongue. My stomach dropped with dread. I couldn't bear the thought of them going back, not with the Wurdulaks hunting outliers to sate their bloodlust. But I couldn't voice that fear. If I stripped away their last shred of hope for safety, what reason would they have to keep fighting?

"Who said we want to go back to living with those bloodsucking pigs?" Quakelord spat. "To be treated like scum again?" The ground shuddered, mirroring the drum of his raging heartbeat.

Underworld's fiery balls, I wished I could stuff those words back down my throat. You know that feeling when you vomit up sentences and instantly want to die? It was like savoring a rare vintage of synthetic AB negative, only to choke and spray it all over your favorite leather jacket. Disturbing, messy, and utterly mortifying.

Quakelord's fists clenched and unclenched, knuckles white as bone.

I backed away, every muscle wound tight. My vow not to use Blood Manipulation on them battled with raw survival instinct. I felt my power surge, ready to respond to his. My scent spiked, saturating the air—sweet with the sharp tang of copper.

"Quakelord!" Harbinger snapped.

The earth stilled, but Quakelord's face stayed flushed, his teeth grinding together. Quiet, seething fury smoldered in his gaze.

I kept my guard up, my magic humming just beneath my skin. "I didn't mean to offend." I spoke with forced calm.

Wings flapped overhead, nearly drowned out by the rush of blood in my ears.

"Our Creator will awake soon. You're free to choose your path," I added.

Quakelord grew silent, and I let my magic recede. Gale's arrival broke the tension as the supply crate hit the ground, dust erupting from between the planks. With a graceful twist of her fingers, she sent the particles swirling skyward before landing atop the crate, cat-like and silent.

I met Harbinger's blazing gaze. "If you don't want to go back, there must be places you want to see, to explore."

His eyebrow arched, the corner of his eyes crinkling with amusement. It was a look that said he thought the world was full of fools, and he found their antics entertaining.

And I, apparently, was the court jester.

A flush of heat spread up my neck. *Goddammit. What's wrong with me that I can't control my mouth tonight? As if sightseeing is a priority when their survival hangs by a thread.*

Harbinger's eyes remained locked on mine, even as Selena approached, weighted down by half a dozen leather bags. Her presence loosened the vice around my lungs, but Harbinger's bitter smile set me on edge.

"Perhaps," he said, voice as dry as ash. "One day, maybe we'll get to it."

AURORA

"How did a half-original end up on the battlefield? No, scratch that," Selena growled, raking her fingers through her hair. "How in the bloody Underworld does he even *exist*?"

I watched my best friend pace the room like a caged panther, her spiked heels gouging deep grooves in the golden pine floors. Dust billowed in her wake and caught in my throat. I longed to throw open a window, to let in even a whisper of fresh air, but the wooden boards nailed to the frame made that impossible. I wasn't even sure if there was glass beyond them anymore. Still, they did an excellent job of keeping the sun rays at bay while I slept.

Selena whirled on me, her eyes lit with fury. "He couldn't have been Changed," she snarled. "It's biologically impossible!"

I nodded, the weight of Harbinger's revelation settling on my chest like a granite slab. If anyone could figure it out, it was Selena. But out here, she didn't have her lab or her technology.

His mere existence had shattered everything I thought I knew. We were born, not made. Then again, I'd always believed we couldn't procreate with mortals. So much for certainties.

"Do you think the Commander knew about him?" she whispered.

"He couldn't have. The only thing that gave Harbinger away was his blood." I gulped, and it carried. I could still feel it rushing in my veins, warm and enticing, like an unrestrained river. "You heard him, Sel. He's been bitten before. I don't think his immortal side is strong enough to react to pure blood. But to original…"

A bitter laugh escaped her lips. "Oh, you raised something alright. At least one part of him stood at attention."

"Selena," I muttered, but my protest lacked conviction. My face flushed with heat, a ghost of that electric connection surging through me again.

When Elena pestered me about the blood banks, I gave in just to silence her. I could have ignored her like a bothersome fly, but then I risked facing worse consequences. So, I had complied, exploring the 'intricacies' of logistics she'd prattled on about. But when she had insisted I grasp the chemical and biological reactions between synthetic blood and our bodies, I drew the line. I knew my limits. Let the brainiacs handle the complex stuff. Just give me the results. Ruling was all about delegation, after all.

Now, I wished I had at least a modicum of understanding, and perhaps a microscope at hand, to witness the phenomenon coursing through me. I could never explain it in scientific terms, but I sensed him *everywhere*, in every cell. A feverish heat, an electric rush, an adrenaline spike—the rhythmic thump of my heart made me feel invincible. Within, tiny sparks ignited where HemaTech-9—my favorite blend—and the essence of the other outliers clashed with Harbinger's blood in its vicious rampage throughout my system.

I felt like I could uproot trees, deforest entire woodlands. Perhaps I could phase through solid walls and join Terraknight in laying waste to buildings just for the thrill of it. The power was intoxicating, terrifying, and utterly addictive. Half of me reveled in this newfound strength, while the other half recoiled at its intensity.

Was this what it felt like to feed from the vein? To be truly alive? Or was it his original blood changing me?

And yet, despite this rush, one question still burned in my mind, sobering me: What exactly was Harbinger, and what did his existence mean for our kind?

Abruptly stopping, Selena smacked a hand onto her hip, making a sharp sound. Her obsidian gaze narrowed into slits and scanned my face as if it held all the secrets of the universe.

Outside, skeletal trees scraped against the wooden boards, like oaken nails on a coffin lid. A breeze passing through and billowing the curtains carried the scent of decay and damp earth, adding substance to the moldy odor already persistent in the room. The sensation of the air gave a momentary reprieve from Selena's stare.

Inhaling a low, hissed breath, she blew a stray strand of hair from her face, her lip curling into a sneer. "Aren't originals usually paranoid about sharing their genes with just anyone?"

"So, you're pinning this on me? Unbelievable," I huffed as I sank onto the satin-covered window seat, my limbs suddenly too heavy to support me. My hand brushed the out-of-place fabric.

She dropped her gaze, scuffing the floor with the tip of her boot. "I'm sorry, I shouldn't have snapped at you, but this is... it's too much. It *terrifies* me."

"I know. It terrifies me, too. Harbinger, his existence... what if this changes everything?" I paused, gathering my thoughts. "I've never drunk from an original before, but I can tell you right now, his blood doesn't taste like any of the outliers I've sampled. It's not just intense, it's... transformative."

Selena's head snapped up, her eyes wide. "Transformative? What exactly do you mean by that?"

I couldn't tell her the truth: that it was the finest elixir to ever cross my lips, that it was the highlight of my life. But I had to say something.

"It's hard to explain," I began, choosing my words carefully. "Every sense is heightened, every emotion intensified. I feel stronger, faster, more alive than ever before. But there's also this... hunger. Now that I've had a taste, I crave more. It's terrifying how badly I want it." I snapped my mouth shut, realizing how that sounded. Like an addict frequenting the bloodletting bars, justifying their next fix.

I met Selena's concerned gaze, her brow furrowed deep enough to etch permanent lines.

"Am I losing it, Sel? Everything happened so fast, it's become a blur. The Sparrows' blood came in neat little vials. I'd never even seen a mortal up close before, let alone..." The mere thought of Harbinger's blood made my fangs ache.

Selena's face drained of color, her fingers curling into white-knuckled fists. The fear in her eyes echoed the anxiety swirling in my belly.

Who was I trying to fool?

I had fantasized about the taste of fresh blood since I was nothing but a foolish girl, lost in fanciful tales and romantic delusions. If I failed to come up with something close to what it really felt like to puncture a healthy, throbbing vein then, it was a hopeless cause now. Because deep down, a twisted piece of me wished to have joined the Wurdulaks in their massacre; understood why my forefathers brought humanity to the brink of annihilation. *I* wished Harbinger hadn't stopped me from taking more.

My stomach rolled, and although I hated myself for even thinking it, at least I now recognized what had triggered my anxiety since arriving. The thought of losing control, of hurting innocent people... It was almost too much to bear.

"I'll keep myself well-fed," I choked out. "But Sel, if you see me slipping... I need you to stop me. Promise me."

She gripped my shoulders, her floral scent grounding me. "I've got you, A. One hint of a black vein, and I'll do whatever it takes. Even if it means knocking you out cold." A humorless smile touched her lips. "But let's be real. You're the strongest person I know. If anyone can resist this, it's you." Her grip tightened. "Just... don't make me follow through, okay? I'd hate to break your neck."

She spun, her boots sending tremors through the floor. Porcelain figurines atop the maple vanity rattled like chattering teeth.

I sighed, grateful the Black Guild was out on patrol.

Selena snatched a ballerina mid-pirouette, clenching her fingers around its delicate form. "I've seen his eyes... but what are the chances he's a pureblood?" Her nose scrunched. "Please, for the love of holy darkness, tell me he's not one of us. We have enough assholes as it is."

Harbinger's blood had packed a meaner punch than any pureblood's I'd ever tasted. It was more direct, like a slap to the face rather than a tender stroke. Raw power with a side of danger, served straight up.

If he hadn't pulled away... My cheeks burned, imagining the spectacle I'd have made. The mother-of-all-orgasms, on full display for the Black Guild. I gulped, all too aware of how close I'd teetered on that precipice. How much I wanted to throw myself off it.

"He's not a pureblood," I admitted, my voice coming out a little husky. "But he's telling the truth about his bloodline. I sensed Derzelas' power in him."

"Then what is he?"

My heart pounded. "I have no idea."

The vanity groaned as Selena pushed off it. In a blur, she yanked me from my perch, wrapping me in her trembling arms.

"We better figure out his other half before it's too late," she murmured, combing her fingers through my hair as I bent to hug her. After decades of friendship, we had the height difference sorted out.

I forced down the knot in my throat and squeezed her tighter. While I didn't trust Harbinger any further than I could throw him, working with him was a necessity. And after witnessing Gale and Quakelord's power, I was convinced the Black Guild offered our best chance for survival.

The mountain of anxiety that had weighed on me shrank to a hill, a glimmer of hope peeking through the clouds of uncertainty. We had a plan, however tenuous. It would have to be enough.

"A?" Selena's hands stilled on my hips.

"Hm?"

She cocked her head, onyx eyes glinting with the light of candle flame. "Were you about to scream Harbinger's name when he pushed you away? Or just moan it really, *really* loudly?"

A snort bubbled up in my throat, followed by uncontrollable laughter. My life had gone from bad to worse to 'we're both going to die,' and here I was, still fantasizing about riding Harbinger like a bucking bronco. After everything that had happened, it surprised me how easily my thoughts flew to him. I had never thought a man would make me think like that.

"Oh, do tell," Selena teased, more in reproach than amusement. "Did you savor every drop? Did his hands leave scorch marks on your skin? Was his throbbing—"

"Selena!" I yelped, squirming out of her grip. A grin pulled at my lips as I bolted for the four-poster bed, a Victorian monstrosity that would make even the most reserved historian wince.

"A lady never kisses and tells!" I shrieked, diving onto the mattress.

She ducked under the velvet canopy, grinning like a lynx. "Since when are you a lady? Is that a blush I see? What are you, a swooning debutante?"

Armed with a tasseled pillow, I snorted, hurling it at her face. "I am not swooning!"

"Are too!" Her eyebrows disappeared into her hairline. "Was it that mind-blowing?"

"Let's just say it puts your Red Brownies to shame." I chuckled, unsure if it was Harbinger's blood or the man himself that had me so flustered.

The pillow smacked me square in the face. "Then keep your fangs to yourself, missy! I don't care how delicious he is, getting involved with a projector-killer is bad news."

Spitting out a mouthful of tassel, I protested, "I don't plan to—"

"To what? Jump his bones the second I turn my back?" Selena wagged her finger. "I've seen that look before. It usually ends with me bailing you out."

I gasped in mock offense. "Name one time!"

Her mouth opened, likely to remind me of the Belt Incident of '27, when tiny fireworks erupted under my skin. Tingles raced down to my fingertips, my heart pounding in anticipation.

Selena's words faded as I brushed the Nexus on my nape—the source of my distraction. It awakened with a burst of sparkling stars crowding my vision.

"Projector Tepes, Harbinger speaking," his urgent voice crackled over the Harmonization.

"I hear you, Harbinger. What's wrong?"

Selena dashed around the bed; her eyes latched onto mine.

"Prepare for battle. The Stalkers are coming."

"How do you—" My senses jolted with alarm. "Harbinger, don't get too close! You don't know how many—"

"I'm on my way. Wait for the briefing."

"Be careful—"

The thread linking us snapped.

My stomach flipped and squirted acid into my throat. I closed my eyes, fighting it. The image of Harbinger surrounded by Stalkers intensified the queasiness in my abdomen. Immortal or not, his original blood wouldn't save him from a brutal death.

Selena's hands on my shoulders jolted me back. Worry lines aged her face by centuries. "What did he say?" she asked, the cords in her neck taut like tree roots.

"The Stalkers are attacking. We need to—"

Electricity coursed through me again. I tapped the crystal. "Harbinger? Report, do you hear me?"

Silence, broken only by distant winds and a sinister howl. Selena's anxious gaze burned into me. I gave a slight head shake, about to speak when—

"Hunting party, do you read?"

Relief flooded me, until Harbinger's presence fragmented, brushing jagged against my consciousness. I winced.

"What is it?" Selena's voice sounded rough, but quiet.

"It's... different. Echoey. Like a weak radio signal." I strained to listen beyond the static. "Harbinger? Say something."

"Captain, what's the situation?" Terraknight's smooth, gruff voice cut in, clear and direct.

"I picked up on Harbinger's transmission," I told Selena, then quickly added, "Initiating Lieutenant Popescu."

Her consciousness collided with mine, a torrent clashing with a still river. Her Initiation had left me breathless before, but linking to her now felt like a fist to my gut.

"Aurora..." she groaned, but her words faded as the frequency shifted.

Harbinger's voice boomed in my head, *"Change of plans. We have visitors."*

My skull throbbed, splitting in two. His presence wavered, a glowing apparition devoured by shadows.

"When?" Terraknight replied, another wraith fighting for supremacy.

Head-jumping while harmonizing had always been effortless, like stepping from one room to the next, but now, I couldn't brace myself fast enough.

Darkness expanded within my consciousness, pulsating—once, twice—then stillness. The silence was liberating.

A ripple crossed the inky pool. A shapeless face lunged, jaws gaping as it spoke in Harbinger's voice. *"About two hours from now. A pack of Limuses regrouped with a mixed force trailing behind. They're probably tracking Mandrake's corpse. We should ambush them near point six-five-A."*

I ripped my eyes open. Two hours away meant the Stalkers were at least eighty miles out. He couldn't have seen them, yet he described their composition as if watching them with his own eyes.

Selena collapsed onto the mattress, ancient springs groaning from the strain. "How the hell does he know about the different Stalkers out there? Even our radars can't reach that distance."

I shrugged and shuffled to the window seat. Blackness consumed my thoughts, draining the fight out of me.

"Roger that. Meet you at the entrance to route twenty-five," Terraknight said.

Harbinger's reply landed like an avalanche. *"No Shepherd this time. They'll likely try to brute force us."*

Leaning against the rugged planks, I covered my eyes with my forearm, relieved to find the headache lessening as I relaxed into the conversation. Not that I knew how to silence the voices in my head, other than turning off the Harmonization.

I didn't want to do that. Not yet.

"Just a bunch of Sheep, huh? Like shooting fish in a barrel," Terraknight's apparition released a gruesome laughter, stirring the shadows.

"Even Sheep can be dangerous."

"Easier when they're not led by a Shepherd, though. We'll regroup with the girls at the lake on our way back..." The vice-captain's voice crackled. *"—Gale's turn on laundry duty."*

My hands clenched on my thighs. They were supposed to be on patrol. I scrunched up my face until it went numb, then released it, mentally yelling at them.

"I'll call Gale right away," Harbinger's specter said.

"Copy. See you soon."

The background noise faded into hungry darkness. Finally, my head quieted, the pounding subsided, and the nausea skedaddled with its ghostly friends.

I looked up, meeting Selena's stormy eyes. She stood with arms crossed, delicate eyebrows furrowed.

"You look like shit," she hissed, blunt as a kitchen knife. Stretching an arm into her back pocket, she pulled out a bottle of synthetic blood.

My mouth watered. "Gimme!" I blurted, curling my fingers in a grabbing motion.

She dangled it just out of reach. "How are you feeling? Does your head still ache?"

"Not anymore."

Selena tsked, unsatisfied.

"I was nauseated, and it throbbed at first, like a wrench pressed against my skull," I rushed out. "It got better once I stopped fighting it. I feel great now. Happy?"

"Good girl," she muttered, releasing the bottle into my keen hands.

The blood was cold, but I took a long swig, humming contentedly. "I don't know what I'd do without you," I said, flashing my most charming synthetic blood-stained smile.

She snorted, shaking her head. Her wit seemed to be on vacation. "What's with this Shepherd and Sheep crap?" she asked, tipping the bottle when I froze to digest her question. "Bottoms up."

I slurped the last drop with a gratifying sigh. I didn't want Selena to catch on to my frustration with Harbinger's lies.

"No idea. Don't worry," I muttered, eyeing the door as if he could pop up at any moment. "I won't force my blood magic on them, but I've picked up a few tricks from Elena. I'll uncover all their dirty little secrets when they come back."

Selena resumed pacing, cutting a circle into the floor. "Think about it," she said, tapping her finger against her lips. "The transmitters are clearly malfunctioning with your Nexus. Thank the Moon I was against it when you asked for a device for yourself—"

"What are you up to?" I interrupted.

She stopped, glanced up at the ceiling as if seeking divine inspiration, then fixed me with a stony gaze. "You could spy on them whenever they're out doing... whatever the fuck it is they're doing."

"Very mature," I scoffed. *But not wrong either.* "Your vocabulary gets more colorful each day."

"Don't give me that look! Yesterday, they treated you like a welcome mat, and you just took it. How much of their crap are you gonna take?"

"Fine, I'll do it," I conceded, springing up. "You want me to play dirty? I'll dive right in—elbows deep in muck. Get ready. They'll be here any moment." I needed the Black Guild to trust me, and to include me in their plans. If that meant getting cunning like my mother, so be it.

My bag lay against the pale pink wall, looking bleak surrounded by watercolor field flowers and magnificent sunsets. I snatched the leather belt, shuffling toward the bed with Selena trailing behind.

"You mean, 'get ready' for another boring night in your room." When I didn't correct her, she went full beast mode. "Are you out of your mind? Commander explicitly told us to avoid direct combat. It's too risky!"

"You didn't think I was going to sit back while they fought for us, did you?" I tried to sound calm, but I was too giddy. "This is what you signed up for. You said you were ready. And if I recall, you weren't a *total* loser at the Academy."

Selena's finger was sharper than a sword as she poked my ribs. "Screw you," she hissed. "I aced Combat class."

"Then show me what you've got," I puffed, folding at the middle. *That damn finger.* "If you don't want to engage, stay on the sidelines. But we're going. The Stalkers have mortal blood, and we know our magic works on them thanks to the Republic's armed forces."

Her stare bore holes into my forehead. "They are all dead, A."

Pain shot through my chest. For a moment, I saw their faces—family, friends, teachers, innocent immortals—all gone in an instant. I pushed the ache aside, their memory fueling the fire burning in my veins. *All the more reason to retaliate.*

I unzipped my bag, spilling its contents onto the bed. It wasn't much: protective leather suits, lightweight clothes for indoor wear, a worn photo of Father—his smile forever frozen in time—and my prized possession, the wristband that secured my combat needles.

I'd never been good with a sword, but these? These were an extension of me. Delicate, deadly, and deceptively innocuous. I plucked one from the band, its weight a reassuring presence in my palm.

With practiced ease, I gathered my hair, twisting it upward. The needle slid in smoothly, followed by a second, forming a secure knot at the nape of my neck. A ghost of a smile tugged at my lips. Ready for both battle and a night out—multitasking at its finest.

The remaining needles I gave to Selena, who accepted them with a raised eyebrow and a wicked smirk. She twirled one between her fingers, testing its balance.

I shrugged. "Just in case."

But the weapons weren't what I'd been searching for. The metallic box rolled out from the pile, landing on the bed with a satisfying thump. "The army didn't have this," I said, grinning as it opened at my touch and the soft blue glow lit up Selena's eyes. "With the Astral Visor, we'll identify the Stalkers before getting too close," I explained. "We'll know exactly what we're getting into."

Selena nibbled her lip, gaze darting between the Transpection device and me. She sighed heavily. "I can't believe I'm agreeing with this, but if we get hurt, I'm going to kill you!"

Aurora

The grandfather clock outside my room screeched like a bat, its 'pleasant' melody announcing thirty minutes past midnight. The Black Guild should arrive any minute.

I trailed after Selena in the dim hallway, ignoring the creepy eyes following us from the oil paintings lining the walls. Flickering candles danced in gilt-framed mirrors, the one in front of my door catching my reflection—pale skin, wide eyes, and surprisingly good-looking hair. Not bad.

Raking my fingers through the unrestrained locks framing my face, I rushed to catch up, but my boot caught on a frayed carpet edge and sent me stumbling. Thankfully, the antique side table was there to stop me from face-planting on the skirting. The priceless Stefan Luchian vase atop it teetered for a dramatic moment before crashing to the floor.

Because of course it did.

"Are you quite finished?" Selena asked, a grin stretching to her ears. At least someone was enjoying this.

Giving the shards of what was probably the finest piece of art in this decrepit ward one last pitiful look, I marched ahead. The landing greeted me with a chorus of creaking floorboards and a waft of musty air.

I'd been too flustered the night before to notice it, and we hadn't had time to explore. Seeing the foyer now was like unwrapping presents on Fateless Eve—if those presents were a vision plucked from the pages of history, all boxed up and ribboned in velvet. Nothing says 'ridiculous opulence' quite like enough gilt to blind a basilisk.

"Holy darkness," I muttered, gripping the banister.

Selena's eyebrow shot up, no doubt cataloging my every embarrassing reaction for future mockery.

Emerald and burgundy settees huddled against sturdy columns, intricately carved and dripping in gold. Crystal vases crowded gleaming marble-topped tables, surrounded by delicate porcelain figurines with vacant, judgy eyes. The cloying scent mingled with the musty, aged wood and burned wax, creating a heady perfume that made my head swim.

Selena's lips quirked, humor sparkling in her obsidian eyes. "Enjoying the view, princess?"

I shrugged, incapable of masking my fascination. Subtlety had clearly died along with good taste in this place. "It has a certain... charm."

"Don't get too attached," she warned, vaulting over the banister with feline grace.

Below the hanging chandeliers—untouched by electricity for the past century—and blocking a giant double door, stood the crate Gale had hauled in two mornings ago. It looked comically out of place, like a cardboard box in a jewelry store.

Selena circled it, her sharp gaze assessing every inch. "Still sealed," she muttered. "Good. I don't have to break any fingers for dipping into our supply."

I held back a sigh and lunged over the railing, landing on my toes. "We can always get more. If they need it—"

Somewhere in the house, a door banged.

"Shh," Selena hissed, tensing like a cat ready to pounce.

The air shifted, carrying a medley of scents: rain, moss, orange, marshmallows, rosemary, saltwater. My pulse quickened as familiar voices drifted from down the hall, a hubbub of bickering and laughter.

"Ready?" she asked.

I nodded and squared my shoulders. We moved in tandem, our footsteps whisper-soft on the lacquered floors. Dark wood paneling stretched endlessly to our right, punctuated by boarded-up windows that admitted slivers of moonlight. To our left, closed doors beckoned from a narrow corridor, the lingering scents heavy in the air.

My heart lurched as we rounded the corner. The ceiling dipped and rose, creating pockets of shadow that seemed to pulse with each thundering heartbeat echoing from the room ahead. Mortal hearts always sounded like they were in a rush. Probably because they had so little time to begin with.

Selena stopped so abruptly that I nearly plowed into her back. A choked laugh escaped her lips. Not the warm, infectious kind, but rather a cold, contemptuous bark that made my scalp prickle.

"Aurora, the children are home." Her voice bristled with sarcasm. "Aren't they adorable?"

Ever had one of those moments when time freezes, the world goes still, and it's so silent you could hear a pin drop? It's just you and the roaring drumming of your heart in your ears. You stand there, feeling like you've died a thousand deaths, only for reality to come crashing back, leaving you slack-jawed and brain-dead.

Trust me, it was not pleasant.

Especially when six outliers were staring at you like you were their next meal. Something with far too many legs crawled up my spine, and I suppressed a shudder as I imagined tiny, chitinous mouths nibbling at my skin.

Okay, maybe I was exaggerating.

But with enough firepower strapped to their bodies to level a small country and looks that promised slow, creative deaths, I felt like turning around and running for dear life. Their gazes pressed down from all sides, heavy as a steel grate.

I avoided their glares and darted my eyes around the room. 'Functional' was the immediate word that came to mind. The vast space, once host to grand banquets and probably a fair share of illegal bloodletting—if the smudged marks on the walls were any indication—now lay stripped bare. A lonely marble mantel stood out like a sore thumb in the emptiness, probably wondering where all its 'pompous friends' had gone.

Someone had shoved a long dining table against the windows, the organized chaos atop it threatening to spill onto the abused timber floors. A map of the Republic's Outer Wards sprawled across it like a tablecloth, at least ninety years out of date and sporting dark-brown cup stains along the edges. A rock lodged in my throat, cracked, and plummeted into my stomach. Floods, storms, earthquakes—they'd all left their mark, and even the slightest terrain change could prove deadly without the accuracy of our scanners.

The Black Guild was flying blind in a storm of stakes.

Heavy boots thundered outside, and the patio doors burst open, cracking against the wall. My heart did a front flip in my chest, and I had to lock my knees to keep from stumbling backward. So much for holding my bluff.

I hadn't wanted to meet with Harbinger after the bomb he dropped on us, but if I wanted in on the briefing—and I needed to be there if I hoped to join them in battle against the Stalkers—I had to put on my big girl fangs. Because he was a lying, mean bastard who seemed to get his jollies from making me squirm.

The room reeked of gunpowder, sweat, and Terraknight's tart signature scent, like ripe blackberries. A hint of coffee beans and roses trailed behind. Harbinger.

My gums itched in response, my tongue darting up in an attempt to soothe them, and I hated myself for it.

"You're late, Terraknight," Hummingbird roared, his volume inversely proportional to his size. "Thought you stepped on a landmine and went 'POOF'!" He mimed an explosion, slouching on a stool with his silver wings brushing the floor like cotton-white curtains.

Terraknight's glare could have extinguished the flames of hell. "Shut. The. Fuck. Up," he snarled. "Mandrake's stiff body is still out there."

The iele's face drained of blood. "Ah, shit... sorry," he stammered, clamping a hand over his mouth as if to catch the words and stuff them back in.

Gale rolled her eyes with the weariness of someone who'd heard it all before, claiming a seat by the window.

Quakelord glided away from the mantel, all smooth muscle and quiet menace. "The only constant in our world is death. Embrace it, birdboy," he intoned, squeezing Hummingbird's shoulder on his way to the other side of the table.

Selena hissed, "At least we found out who Mandrake is," nudging me in the ribs just as Harbinger crossed the threshold.

I cringed so hard that I nearly pulled a muscle. Of all the times to run her mouth, she had to pick now. My eyes darted to him, and suddenly breathing became an advanced skill.

The captain strode in, tall and broad-shouldered, moving with destructive focus. Black cargo pants hugged long, sturdy legs and tucked into combat boots. The black t-shirt he had on clung to him like a glove, outlining every ridge and plane to perfect detail. My eyes roamed, tracing a path up his body, lingering far too long on the way that shirt stretched across his chest.

He groaned huskily—and Derzelas, what a sound, thick enough to touch—and our eyes clashed.

Even with most of his face hidden beneath that ridiculous cowl, there was no mistaking the tightness around his eyes or the hard set of his jaw. Annoyance, irritation, disdain—the captain was practically radiating 'pissed off' energy. It was like watching a thundercloud roll in, promising one hell of a storm.

I wrenched my eyes away, finding the room's decor absolutely fascinating. Maybe there was another priceless antique I could probably break just by looking at it too hard.

Pull yourself together. He may have blood that tastes like liquid ecstasy, but he's still a conceited, arrogant half-original. No matter how well he fills out that t-shirt or how his eyes make you feel things you shouldn't, he's strictly off-limits. Harbinger is a complication you can't afford.

Remember who you are, what's at stake.

"We're all here. Good. Listen up," Harbinger announced, his voice a low rumble that sent an involuntary shudder along my spine.

He halted at Terraknight's side by the mantle. The silence that fell was as thick and oppressive as a burial shroud.

Adrenaline pumped in my veins, priming my body to jump into action. Beside me, Selena let out an exaggerated sigh that telegraphed 'bored to tears.' Nice try, but I knew better. It was her favorite mask against anxiety.

"Our mission: track down and neutralize the Stalkers," Harbinger continued, his words measured and precise. "All four types, about five hundred strong. Sibiu's main road is too narrow for a frontal assault, so they'll likely split up and come at us from multiple angles."

How in the Underworld does he know all this?

I stepped forward, ready to call his bluff, but Selena's grip on my wrist might as well have been forged with steel. Her onyx eyes flashed a warning clearer than any words. *Wait.*

I shot her a fanged snarl that promised payback and yanked my hand free. Ligaments tore, bones cracked, then knitted back together in an instant. The dull ache lingered, a reminder that immortality wasn't perfect.

Nothing spared us from the joys of physical pain. Sometimes, greater regeneration just meant greater suffering. But in the grand scheme of things, our wounds were as fleeting as a speck of dust in a sandstorm—here one second, gone the next.

"Shepperd?" Gale's voice was soft as velvet wrapped around a blade.

Harbinger shook his head. "Not this time, but don't get cocky. Limuses and Nebulas will bring the brute force up front. Glacies will hit and run. It's the Ignises we need to watch for—they'll be waiting to roast us when we least expect it."

He paused, his eyes narrowing. "I can predict their moves, but be ready for anything. Keep moving—it'll mess with the Glacies' aim. Pick off Limuses and Nebulas from a distance, and for fuck's sake, don't let an Ignis get you with a Magma Lance."

The room fell silent, Harbinger's words settling like lead in my stomach. This wasn't just another mission where my screens safely ensconced me. This was war, and we were about to dive headfirst into the fray.

The outliers rose as one, a united front brimming with suppressed elemental magic. Harbinger planted his feet wide, his voice a low, raspy command. "Hummingbird and Pearl, you're suppressing fire."

The pair nodded, already moving toward the patio doors with an eagerness that made my stomach drop. The remaining four stood waiting for orders, their eyes gleaming with anticipation like children pressed against a bloodcandy store window.

"Quakelord and Phoenix, controlling fire. Spread out along the main road." Harbinger's gaze shifted to the final duo. "Gale and Ember, you're vanguard. Take the ruins. Terraknight and I will play bait."

My heart thundered in my chest as I forced out the words, "What about us?"

All eyes turned our way, a mix of frowns and smirks that made me want to bare my fangs. Instead, I tilted my head back, meeting Harbinger's hard gaze.

"You're a liability," he snarled. "There's nothing you can help with. You're out of your league."

Heat bloomed across my cheeks, my fingertips itching to unleash the magic stirring beneath my skin. I bit my tongue, tasting copper. The urge to bite him, have one more taste, warred with the desire to knock him down a station or two.

This wasn't the time, and Harbinger sure as hell wasn't a man I wanted to fight. But I couldn't back down either.

I clenched my fists, nails digging into my palms. "No."

The word came out stronger than I felt, but I held my ground.

"No?" Harbinger's eyebrow arched.

"No."

He crossed his arms, muscles rippling beneath his shirt. "You know what I can't stand about you? Your complete lack of sense. You're in my house, jumping at shadows, and you have the gall to tell me 'no?' You'd provoke Death if you had a chance."

I stifled a laugh.

Was that what I was doing? Provoking Death? I let my gaze drift over him, from his boots to those maddeningly intense eyes. If Death looked like this, maybe a little provocation wasn't such a bad idea.

"Maybe Death needs a good provoking now and then," I said. "Keeps things interesting, don't you think?"

I darted my eyes to the others in the room. Gale watched with thinly veiled amusement, while Terraknight's hand twitched near his strapped weapon.

Harbinger's gaze flashed with a dangerous glint. "Interesting, huh?" His voice came like a scrape of claws on rusty metal. "Be careful what you wish for, princess. Death doesn't play nice, and neither do I." He raked dismissive eyes over me. "Do what you want, but don't come crying when you can't keep up. You don't have your precious shadows to back you up, do you?"

A growl built up inside me. How the hell did he know about my Darklings? The room temperature dropped with the flare of my magic, and I noticed Pearl take a step back, her beryl eyes wide.

"A, I know that look," Sel warned under her breath.

My blood boiled. This ended now. "I don't need them or any magic to take you down," I hissed, even as a voice in my subconscious screamed at me to stop.

The room stilled, the air thickening like syrup. Quakelord's teeth scraped against each other, his attention flicking between Harbinger and me. "Cap, you gonna let an immortal talk to you like that?" he lashed out.

Harbinger's lips curved into a smile that promised violence. He beckoned me, fingers curling. "Bring it on, then."

We circled each other, floorboards creaking beneath our weight. My Blood Manipulation stretched out, an invisible web skimming the edges of his mind. I wouldn't use it on him, but I'd be damned if I walked into this blind.

Hummingbird leaned forward, his wings rustling with an anticipation I didn't share.

Then, like a bucket of ice water, reality doused my anger. What in the Underworld's pits was I doing?

If we fought and I survived, I'd never uncover the truth about Projector Olaru's death. Worse, I'd be putting Selena in danger. If I got myself killed, my quest to challenge Lev and reclaim my crown would end here, in this dusty room, over wounded pride. Father's final request would go unfulfilled, all because I couldn't keep my temper in check.

The realization was a bitter pill to swallow, but it cleared my head. I had a duty to fulfill, a mission to complete. I couldn't afford to let Harbinger or my own ego derail that.

I halted, slowly lowering my fists. Choking down my pride felt like swallowing ground glass, but I forced the words out anyway. "I apologize. I'm not my own person right now," I said, pressing my teeth together. "We both have responsibilities that are bigger than this... disagreement. I propose a truce, at least until our mission is complete."

The admission cost me, but I kept my chin high. I'd embarrassed myself, but I wouldn't give him the satisfaction of seeing how much it stung.

His smile widened, turning smug. Behind him, I saw Ember's shoulders relax, the fire in her veins dimming. Her friend, Phoenix, wasn't of the same opinion, pale blue flame sparking at her fingertips.

"I'm here on official orders to investigate the murder of a fellow projector. If you think I'm a pain, trust me, you'd hate whoever they'd send to replace me." I met his gaze, unflinching. "I can't afford to fight you, and I won't use my magic. I just want to do my job and get out of here. Once I find the *killer*," I let the accusation hang in the air between us, heavy and unmistakable, "I'd be more than happy to indulge you."

The silence raised my blood pressure. Mortal heartbeats slowed down from their frantic pace now that this standoff would end—one way or another.

I extended my hand, the gesture feeling more like surrender than a peace offering. Despite trembling muscles, I centered myself and kept my fingers steady.

Harbinger studied me, his expression unreadable. For a moment, I thought he might reject my offer, might decide to put me in my place. Then he clasped my hand in his larger one. An electric shock raced up my arm, setting every nerve alight.

My breath stalled, my face battling to stay neutral, all too aware of the eyes watching me.

"Fair enough," he said, mirth gleaming in his eyes. They flared crimson, but the gold in them blazed like twin suns. "Right now, I'm not entirely my own person either."

We broke apart, and Harbinger nodded at the others. "Go. I'll meet you at point six-five-A."

The ieles mobilized, their movements a blur. Gale and Hummingbird burst through the patio doors, unfurling their wings in a dazzling display of silver and copper. My jaw dropped as I followed Quakelord's gaze skyward, and it hit the floor when Hummingbird folded his wings and plummeted like a stooping falcon.

My muscles tensed, ready to sprint outside. It would be a wild collision for both of us, but at least he wouldn't snap his neck and die. Before I could move, the air around Hummingbird began to churn.

Winds whipped into a frenzy, coalescing into a swirling vortex that cradled his fall. Rocks and dirt pelted the roof and windows, the wooden planks groaning under the assault. Hummingbird's face split into a wild grin as he brushed the gaping maw of the tornado with a wingtip. In a heartbeat, he vaulted through the clouds, leaving the tempest to howl with a longing cry before dissolving into nothingness.

"Birdbrain," Quakelord growled, but I caught a hint of admiration in his tone.

I'd encountered elemental powers before—some of the Sparrows had been formidable—but this... this was on another level entirely. "Derzelas," I breathed. "That control is magnificent."

Gale landed with the grace of a dove, a smirk playing at her lips. "You ain't seen nothing yet, Projector," she quipped before a gust of wind swept her off her feet and into the night sky.

My cheeks hurt from how wide I smiled. There was a comforting quality to Gale that reached deep inside me.

Leather creaked, drawing my attention back to Quakelord. The whole house began to tremble, the floor rippling beneath our feet like a waking giant. His muscles bulged, veins standing out on his neck as he raked long fingers through his tousled hair. The earth elementalist seemed to draw power from the very foundation. A dirt path arched straight from the threshold, three feet above the grass, like a serpent rearing its head.

Quakelord stepped onto his creation without a second glance, seemingly unconcerned that the far end hung unfinished over the lawn. As he strode forward, the earthen bridge slithered across the backyard, small holes appearing and sealing themselves in its wake.

On the other side of the room, Ember muttered something about 'unnecessary theatrics' in her rich, exotic lilt, while Terraknight grunted in agreement.

Pearl walked to the door, flashing an impish smile that made her look far younger than her years. She stepped onto the back porch, her purple dress splitting at the sides to reveal black pants and scuffed leather boots. Planting her feet shoulder-width apart, she raised her hands inch by inch, channeling water to the surface.

The air was saturated with the smell of the ocean—an in-your-face fragrance that made my nose twitch. The varva was powerful, and she wanted everyone to know it—wanted me to know it.

Pearl glanced over her shoulder, her white-blue glowing eyes zeroing in on me. "You might want to step back if you don't want to get wet."

I did.

The grass frothed, tiny rivers melding into a rolling wave. I half-expected to see fish hopping in and out of it and stifled a laugh. Pearl leaped onto the crest with a whoop and surfed ahead, following Quakelord's cheers echoing in the distance.

"See you, captain," Ember murmured, dazzling Harbinger with a toothed smile. She walked with a slight hip roll, shoulders back, and a confident stride that showcased her curves.

She had exchanged the first night's flowy dress for more practical attire: a dark green turtleneck, tight pants stuffed into yellow rubber boots, and her golden hair fashioned into a messy bun atop her head. Despite being only a few decades her senior, seeing her now made me feel... *old*.

Arms tucked into her sides, she spread her palms. Orange flames burst from her fingertips, crackling softly like tiny bonfires.

The heat hit me in the face. I licked my lips to wet them, tasting rosemary and honey in the air.

Phoenix stood at her side, her own fire burning a bright blue that turned her red hair and the freckles on her nose a dark shade of violet. She was all sharp angles: pointy elbows, prominent knees, a triangular face with a chin that could cut paper.

A patchwork of glowing veins slithered under their skin as they propelled into the night, creating a path of dwindling fire and smoke. The contrast between Ember's warm orange and Phoenix's cool blue was mesmerizing, like watching day and night battle for dominance.

I turned to Harbinger, a question forming on my lips, but the words died as I caught the expression on his face. There was pride there, yes, but also a haunted shadow that spoke of battles fought and comrades lost. Although he could be an asshole, he clearly cared about his guild.

"Time to move," Harbinger's voice resonated in the emptiness of the room.

His sudden decision to include us sent a burst of adrenaline through my limbs.

"You trust her not to run straight to the Republic?" Terraknight interjected.

My jaw went tight, molars pressing together as I fought to hold my tongue. Something felt off, a discordant note in the air that made my hair bristle. Beside me, Selena's eyes narrowed to slits, her body strung tight.

Harbinger moved forward at a deliberate, unhurried pace and grasped the edge of his hood, the gesture deceptively casual. "Might as well see what she's made of now," he said. "What's the Republic going to do? Banish me to fight their fucking war?"

Gold eyes flecked with crimson pinned mine. The intensity of them made the blood rush to my limbs. There was nothing especially threatening about his stare, but something behind those eyes made me want to raise my hands in the air and back away slowly until it was safe to run for my life.

"Besides," he continued, a smile curling up the corners of his mouth, "I'm curious to see how our esteemed Projector handles herself when the gloves come off."

He slipped the cowl from his head, and the sky came crashing down on me. My legs went weak, and I staggered, struggling to stay on my feet.

No. This can't... it's not...

A roar filled my ears, drowning out everything but the impossible sight before me.

My body rebelled, each nerve ending screaming in denial, but my eyes couldn't lie.

He stood there, undeniable. A living, breathing contradiction.

The foundations of my existence—the truths I'd *clung* to—the certainties that had shaped my world, all crumbled to dust in a heartbeat.

AURORA

A CASCADE OF WHITE hair, so pale it rivaled the moon, spilled down his forehead.

My heart gave a startled thump, then took off, stumbling over its own rhythm. The room lurched, faces melting into a whirl of color and shadow. My insides hollowed as if some unseen force had carved away my courage, along with my voice.

I opened my lips, but only a strangled whisper escaped.

Harbinger tilted his head, frost-white tresses framing his face. "Don't look so shocked, Projector," he drawled. A sinister pleasure laced his words. "Didn't you know, the enemy of your enemy is your friend?"

A slow, lazy, carnivorous smile touched his lips. Selena's hiss echoed as she leaped back, her floral scent thickening with magic. I stood petrified, my mind and body paralyzed with fear and disbelief.

That hair. There was only one race with such colorless manes.

The same race that had torn my world apart, stolen everything I held dear: my father, my people, our freedom. Every cell in my body begged to destroy him. I could almost smell the tart smoke, taste the bitter ash as

I imagined him burning—just as *they* had burned our homes, our hopes, our future.

And yet...

A whisper of conscience held me back. The memory of mercy I'd received as a child warred with the thirst for vengeance. An outlier, just like him, had appeared on our side of the battlefield and saved my life when all hope seemed lost. One of *them* had given *me* a second chance.

Where did that leave us?

Harbinger was the enemy—wasn't he? A nagging sense of debt held me back from striking. Should I end him now, quick and ruthless? Or hear him out, extend the same mercy I'd once received? What would my father have done?

A knot of panic wedged in my throat. I struggled with it for a few agonizing seconds and forced it down. "You're... a varcolac?"

"Half," he corrected, his amber eyes flickering with crimson. "And before you get any ideas, I take no sides in this clusterfuck you call a war."

Kill or spare. Vengeance or mercy. The fate of my people could hinge on this choice. I didn't believe he was a spy, but could I afford to take that risk? What did he gain from fighting the Stalkers, from defending *our* country for so long?

It made no sense.

I met Harbinger's gaze, my heart hammering like a blacksmith's forge in my chest. "Then why fight on our side?" I snapped, unable to hide the loathing in my tone.

His face darkened, a menacing growl rumbling in his chest. "That's not your fucking business."

I took a step forward, yanking my arm to pull free from Selena's unyielding clutch on my wrist. She didn't let go. "Make it my business. Prove that you're not a risk to my people, or I'll have no choice but to end you."

Harbinger's laughter was a silken threat. "Oh, princess," he sneered. "You're welcome to try. But if it makes you feel better, know that I don't give a rat's ass about your precious Republic. I've got my own reasons for being here."

He raised a hand, palm up. The air between his fingers shimmered and warped, like heat rising from a fire. The scent of fresh coffee and roses flooded the room, so thick it made my fangs drop.

I clenched my fists and forced my eyes to focus on the haze dancing above his hand, rather than on the need to bite his neck—or tear out his throat.

The air crackled and popped, a sound like the tearing of fabric. A dark knot materialized five feet from the floor, as if someone had ripped a hole in reality itself. It hovered, expanding until a good portion of the wall vanished, leaving a three-by-three, pitch-black circle in its place. Veins of pure gold zigzagged in and out of the void, hissing and spitting sparks, giving the 'abyss' a terrifying depth.

But it wasn't just a hole. It was a gateway. A magical portal. *Dear God, how many impossible things are you going to drop on me?*

The furniture around us began to vibrate, steel weapons rattling against the walls as the portal throbbed with untamed energy. Fear and shock gripped me so tightly I couldn't breathe.

Harbinger stepped one foot inside the void, his silver hair whipping about his face as if caught in an otherworldly wind. He looked at Terraknight, arching a brow. "Are you coming or not?"

The vice-captain paced like a cornered animal as a sickly pallor crept up his face. "Do I have another choice?" he barked, his voice collapsing slightly.

Harbinger shrugged and surrendered himself to the crackling darkness. "You can always walk."

Terraknight ran a hand through his short hair, cursing like a sailor. With a grunt that sounded more like a prayer, he leaped into the shrinking portal. His parting words spat out before the gateway dwindled to a narrow crevice, "You son of a bitch, if I puke on you, I don't want to hear it."

Selena's obsidian eyes darted between me and the spot where Harbinger and Terraknight vanished, her grip tightening almost to the point of breaking bone. Her breath came in short, sharp gasps.

"A fucking *varcolac*, Aurora?" she hissed, her voice trembling with fright. "That's it. We're out of here. Now."

I wrenched my arm free, panic clawing its talons up my throat. "And go where, Sel? Stroll through Stalker-infested territory back to the Republic? I can't shadow us!"

Full-body tremors hit me. Damn. The air crackled with Harbinger's magic, raising every hair on my body.

I'd never seen such raw terror etched into Selena's face. *I'd* never felt this kind of fear myself. A varcolac with original blood wasn't just impossible—it was an abomination, a cosmic middle finger to our sacred laws.

Her mouth twisted into a vicious snarl. "He opened a goddamn portal, A! That's not Derzelas' magic, and you damn well know it."

I choked down a swallow, tasting bile. "I know. But how? Varcolacs are mortal. Their bite shouldn't... Sel, I tasted his blood. Our Dark Father's mark runs in it."

She ran her fingers through her hair, leaving furrows like a farmer's field. "He's an anomaly. Varcolac toxin only works on mortals and daywalkers. They're compatible because they both produce blood until their clocks stop ticking."

I nodded in agreement. Immortality might be a treasure, but its price was steep. We needed blood to survive, forever chasing the moon, while varcolacs basked in sunlight. Like celestial bodies that could never share the same sky, we couldn't coexist.

Selena pinned me with a sharp glare. "There's only one theory left standing."

"They can't turn us…" My abdomen knotted. "But we can breed."

"Bingo."

I exhaled, low and long. Every belief, every lesson—down the drain. I hated being in my head right now. It was a warzone. "If we go back, we risk everything. The Commander's position, your job… and *Lev*." His name didn't just taste foul. It cut my mouth as I spat it out. "He'd use you to get to me. I can't let that happen."

Her face softened for a heartbeat before hardening again. "So, what, we play house with the varcolac?"

"For now, yes. We need answers, Sel. If we hadn't come here, we wouldn't know about Harbinger's existence. Who knows how many more lies we'll uncover out here? He's our best shot at understanding what we're up against."

"Or our fastest route to an early grave," she muttered.

"If there are more hybrids like him, the Republic won't stand a chance. Imagine an army of varcolacs with our strength and speed." My pulse thundered as I recalled the feral strength radiating from him. "We can't let that nightmare become reality. We keep it civil until we learn more. Two purebloods against one—the odds are in our favor."

Selena clicked her tongue. "He doesn't even acknowledge your authority."

"I'll make him listen. I'll use my magic if I must."

She held my gaze for a long moment, then nodded. "Fine. But if this goes sideways, I'm dragging you back to the Republic myself." She paused, rolled the word on her tongue, tasting it. "Varcolac." Her face twisted as if she'd bitten into something rancid. "There's a darkness lurking in his eyes, A. It's hungry, and I don't like how it's looking at you... like it wants to devour you."

It was clear I wasn't thinking straight when her words made frost slither across my skin, equal parts fear and... and something else I didn't dare name. The rational side of my brain recoiled at the thought, but another side, one I scarcely acknowledged, thrilled at the danger. I pushed the feeling down, burying it deep in the bowels of my mind.

I knew what had captured her attention. The crimson circle must have been too distracting for her to notice the monster peeking back. I'd seen that predatory glint before, in the eyes of the outlier who'd slain the enemy and saved my life. Harbinger wasn't him, but if you met his gaze at the right moment, something chilling stared back at you—a predator as ancient and deadly as our own kind.

"It's the varcolac in him," I explained, fighting a shudder.

Selena's brow furrowed. "What do you mean?"

"He's a wolf prowling in the dark woods. A shadow."

A snarl vibrated in her chest. "You may see a wolf, but I see cities in flames." She clenched her fists. "Innocents slaughtered. There's something profoundly unsettling about him."

I chose my next words carefully. "I trust my instincts, Sel. He's not a threat. Not yet, at least. His reasons for fighting our common enemy seem to outweigh any animosity toward us. We should use that to our advantage."

Harbinger was a wild card, but he was still the best shot we had to survive.

I could have told her about the varcolac, my savior. *It might cast Harbinger in a different light.*

But what did I truly know of him? He was a stranger, an enigma. We all harbored an inner beast that could break free at any moment. Selena had been there, witnessed the Wurdulaks' bloodlust firsthand. I'd rather meet Harbinger's wolf than go through all that again. Here, at least, I could serve my country.

Retrieving the Astral Visor from my pocket, I strode toward the porch doors. "He won't hurt us, not if I have any say in it. Come on, I know where they'll intercept the attack," I said and stepped outside.

Selena followed, but her footsteps faltered as we entered the garden.

I took a deep inhale, the rich scent of damp earth and night-blooming flowers filling my lungs. Jasmine, tuberose, and moonflowers danced on the breeze, their heady perfume a long way from the musty alleyways and unpleasant odors of the Republic.

"This place..." Selena breathed, eyes rounded with wonder.

I drank in the ethereal silver glow coating everything. "Like stepping into another realm."

A stream burbled as we hurried along, sand-colored tiles giving way to lush grass. Tall poplar trees stood sentinel at the garden's edge, flanked by manicured bushes and star-shaped blooms.

There was no going back now.

With a touch, I activated the Nexus. "Initiate Harmonization," I murmured. "Set Harmonization target, Outlier Harbinger. Open link, Lieutenant Selena Popescu." A tingle raced down my arms, and I sucked in a sharp breath, relishing the adrenaline rush.

Nature's light show came alive around us, outshining the Republic's artificial glow. Bioluminescent beetles rivaled the stars, dragonfly wings shimmered like liquid jewels, and fireflies wove gold patterns in the air. But I knew better than to be lulled by this enchanting facade. Monsters lurked in the shade—vicious, bloodthirsty, and relentless.

Adjusting the Astral Visor, I commanded, "Open Transpectre via Harbinger."

Selena's gloved hand yanked me to a halt. She leaped into the dry fountain, midnight hair whipping. "I don't like this, A," she hissed. "What if—"

"We need to know what we're walking into." The holo-screen descended with a soft whirr, cutting her off. "I'll get a headache. Nothing a little blood won't fix."

Through Harbinger's borrowed eyes, Sibiu's ruins trembled against the night sky. His steady heartbeat thrummed through me and countered my racing pulse.

I vaulted over a crater, my vision split between perspectives as I moved. "Calculate fastest route to Sibiu," I instructed the Visor, veering right into the woods.

A jagged yellow line flickered to life, slicing across the landscape, and merged with Harbinger's vision.

Branches lashed at my skin as I tore through the forest. Behind us, leaves crunched and twigs snapped—a feral cat giving chase, its snarls echoing as it struggled to keep up. The path seared itself into my memory.

"Show me Harbinger," I breathed.

The world spun, my stomach roiling as his sight became mine again. A desolate concrete road stretched out before him, flanked by crumbling buildings and skeletal trees. Beside him, Terraknight's steel-capped boot hammered an impatient rhythm into the ground.

At the far end of the street, down a gentle incline, a ghostly mist crept forward, tendrils snaking into alleys, devouring the city piece by piece.

Harbinger's gaze darted left and right, tracking the fog's advance.

"Take your positions," he commanded, his voice unnervingly calm as his guild fanned out around him in a crescent formation.

Harbinger's whispers formed words too quiet to catch. A last-minute strategy? A last prayer?

My left eye, still locked on the forest, caught the darkness giving way to a moonlit hill. I stretched out my Blood Manipulation down the slope, probed for hidden threats, and my senses screamed on high alert.

Harbinger's voice exploded inside my head, *"One hundred and fifty Limuses, one hundred and fifty Nebulas, one hundred Glacies, and eighty Ignises."* His arm shot forward like a spear. *"Prepare yourselves."*

Stars above, he hadn't been strategizing or praying. He'd been counting.

Frost spread through my veins, stealing the oxygen from my lungs. Something stirred in the mist. *How in the Holy Pits does he know their numbers, their formation, with such terrifying accuracy?* His half-original blood hadn't granted him our abilities. Our magic carried a metallic tang, but Harbinger's... smelled of rich coffee and honeyed blooms, like his very essence.

Fear coursed my body. But it wasn't the Stalkers lurking along the borders of my magic that filled me with paralyzing dread.

It was him.

"He's done it again, hasn't he?" Selena snarled. "How in Dracula's name does he know all of this?"

Before I could respond that it was exactly what I wanted to find out, a hair-rising howl pierced the night. More followed. Through Harbinger's eyes, I watched a silhouette emerge from the mist, and then another, and another.

"They're coming," his voice rumbled in my mind.

The Limuses burst from the fog, their grotesque forms coming into focus. Misshapen bodies swayed between backward-bent legs, maws showcasing rows of gleaming fangs.

Red neon letters blared across my Astral Visor. *Threat assessment: Potentially Deadly.*

"Oh, Sweet Derzelas." My knees felt like they would buckle.

Sand rose in swirling vortexes, clawing at the sky. Bloodshot eyes locked onto me—onto the captain—and bile scorched my throat.

"We have to go," Selena panted, dragging me forward.

Sibiu's church turret loomed ahead, a dark sentinel in the night.

I nodded, speechless. My focus split between Harbinger's sight and my Blood Manipulation mapping the battlefield. The Black Guild flanked the road while Harbinger and Terraknight stood their ground, living bait for the approaching horde.

"Hold," the captain ordered. *"At my command."*

Magic collided with a bone-grinding roar. Debris shot skyward as Nebulas unleashed their power, leveling buildings and splintering trees. Nine-foot-tall with oozing sores and four arms that could topple mountains.

Among them, the Glacies stood out—a hashish-inducing nightmare of human skulls and satyrs, with leathery wings scraping the ground. Dark ice surged from their cloven hooves, coating the concrete.

The holo-screen flashed the same chilling warning. My throat squeezed shut. *Maybe Selena's idea to stay in my room wasn't so bad.*

Her touch jolted me. I stifled a scream, meeting her terrified gaze.

"If we don't make it through this," she hissed, baring her fangs, "I swear I'll haunt you for eternity. And if we survive..." She let out a short, sharp laugh. "You'll wish we hadn't."

I drew in a breath to reply, but my voice failed me as the Limuses entered the kill zone, focused on Harbinger and Terraknight uphill. The Nebulas and Glacies followed, stepping into the Black Guild's trap.

"Open fire," Harbinger commanded.

The world held its breath. Time froze.

Then, chaos erupted.

Aurora

Ice and fire clashed in a thunderous roar.

Ember perched on the roof, her emerald eyes blazing with Gebeleizis' fire. Wind whipped her golden hair into a frenzy as she stepped onto the ledge, each strand pulsing with power.

"Time to light 'em up!" Ember's manic cry sent chills down my spine. "It's barbecue time, y'all!"

She thrust her fists over her head, veins igniting like Fateless Festival fireworks. Muscles and bones flickered beneath her clothes.

"Dance for me, you bastards!" she howled. "Burn, baby, burn!"

The night sky erupted. Celestial fireballs blazed to life among the stars, hurtling toward us with terrifying speed. As the ground shuddered, shooting cracks along the church wall, my body reacted.

"Selena!" I choked out, seizing her hand and yanking her toward the nearest alcove.

The church turret split apart, collapsing in a cloud of debris just as Ember's meteors slammed into the earth. Agonizing wails shattered the night before fading into eerie silence. I peered around the corner, choking on smoke and dust. Burning Stalkers filled my tear-drenched vision, and acid washed my tongue.

A rush of wind drew my gaze upward.

Gale had landed on the roof, her coppery wings unfurling like a metallic sunrise. She raised her hands, and the air responded with sudden fury. Smoke spiraled skyward, sucked into the growing maelstrom. Fires sputtered and died, snuffed out by the tempest.

The stench of charred flesh being whipped into the air nearly emptied my stomach.

The Astral Visor shifted with Harbinger's gaze, revealing Phoenix, Quakelord, Hummingbird, and Pearl taking their positions. My Blood Manipulation tugged at my mind.

We were still vastly outnumbered, and the Ignises had yet to reveal themselves, and—

Magic fizzed through the air, raising goosebumps along my skin.

"Holy fangs," Selena gasped beside me, "do you sense that?"

I nodded, words failing as their magic surged in perfect sync.

Phoenix's skin flashed, blue fire erupting from her clawed fingers. Two dozen Stalkers incinerated instantly, their howls silenced mid-screech. A hundred paces away, Quakelord grinned at the carnage. The ground roared, clay spears impaling Stalkers in droves.

My magic fluttered in response. I rubbed my hand over my face, forcing it down. Not yet. I had to be smart and find the right moment to strike. *Can I tap into the Stalkers' minds, take control over their blood?* I'd never tried outside of Academy drills, but now seemed as good a time as any.

Pearl's arms shimmered with iridescent scales as massive water bubbles rose around her. Stalkers thrashed in her liquid coffins, clawing futilely at their throats. Beyond her reach, more Stalkers wailed and choked on air.

"Hummingbird," I gasped, my pulse rising.

Selena clicked her tongue. "Hey, that's my move, asshole!"

Hummingbird leaned against a wall, hands in pockets, stealing breaths with casual ease. When we first met, I thought him pretty. Now, with honey-brown curls falling on his forehead and eyes, which were slightly darker than the captain's, sparkling with dark delight, he looked positively handsome.

My magic yanked at me, invisible threads thrumming with dark, viscous power. Everything stopped. My heartbeat roared like a battle drum. Ignises marched through the mist, crushing my mind like a vice.

Pressure built in my skull, ready to burst.

I snapped my eyes open, stars swimming in my vision. "Clear the way!" I screamed, but the earth answered first, rupturing with a deafening blast and swallowing my warning.

A colossal tide of liquid fire surged up the road. The world dissolved into blistering heat and harsh smoke. I staggered from the alcove, a burning stench filling my nostrils as the suit melted with a sizzling hiss. Dread held me in place, the advancing inferno searing my eyes.

"Aurora!"

Selena slammed into me, sending us tumbling away from certain death. Stones and mortar pelted us as we crashed into the building.

The Astral Visor went dark. My head throbbed like a hammer blow.

Choking on ashfall, I forced myself up. "Sel?" I croaked, squinting through the haze. "You okay?"

Her groan was my only answer while I fumbled with the unresponsive Visor. Fear chilled my blood. We needed eyes on the battlefield before the Ignises struck again. But first—

"Set Harmonization target, Black Guild," I rasped, dread tightening.

Connections blazed to life in my mind. I leaped from consciousness to consciousness, heart pounding in my throat.

Phoenix, Ember alive. Quakelord, breathing. Gale, Pearl, Humming-bird, good. Terraknight, Harbinger—all safe. Relief surged through me, so intense it brought tears to my eyes.

The lava receded, leaving a gaping chasm along the road. I helped Selena up, ignoring her death glare. Then I gave one back that said, *we don't have time to argue.*

"Dear Lord," she gasped, her hand flying to her mouth.

I glanced uphill, my heart sinking at the sight of the church reduced to rubble. "Come on. We should move," I muttered, tugging her along.

We inched forward, the ledge shrinking with each step. Across the chasm, sheer smoldering walls belched thick smoke. A disturbing realization hit me.

"The Ignises," I breathed, "they aimed for Harbinger and Terraknight."

Selena squeezed my hand, a small comfort as the Astral Visor flickered back to life. What I saw made my blood run cold—a creature I'd only heard whispered about in terrified tones.

No outlier had ever seen an Ignis and lived to tell the tale.

Harbinger crouched among ruins, a smoldering tree trunk at his side. His breath came in ragged gasps, but his heartbeat remained steady. Beyond his silver locks, I glimpsed Terraknight's tanned arm, moving in slow, perfect circles.

The fog parted.

The Ignis rose in ribbons of heat, flames dancing around its ten-foot frame. Its skin gleamed like freshly forged iron. Curved bones sprouted from its elbows, ending in sharp, clawed fingers, rivaling the fiery horns crowning its head. It fixed blazing orange orbs on Harbinger, and my bones liquefied.

My Astral Visor screamed: *Threat assessment: Lethal.*

The Ignis' cry agitated the earth.

I pressed against the wall, shielding my face as a wave of heat tore through the street. Trees snapped like twigs, the stench of sulfur reaching us moments later.

"We're close," I yelled to Selena, trying not to gag on the taste of rotten eggs.

I released her hand, trusting her to follow as I inched along the buildings. One eye on the battle, the other watching my steps, we moved painfully slow. The smoking chasm yawned to our left, promising eternal death with one wrong step.

"I should have listened to you and stayed in my room," I muttered under my breath.

Selena's bitter retort raked like thorns down my back. "Don't make me smack you! I told you—I fucking told you not to come."

The gurgle of lava mixed with the sounds of battle. Shivers ran through my body, both from heat and fear. I wondered which was worse—one misstep straight to our deaths, or walking into the bloodbath unfolding on my Visor.

BOOM!

A massive explosion rocked the ground, nearly knocking us off our feet. An entire row of houses collapsed between us and the battle, raising a billowing cloud of dust that stung my eyes and choked my lungs. On the holo-screen, Gale's scarlet wings swept the debris away, revealing the outliers' strategic positions.

They had the Stalkers cornered.

"*Unde esti? Hai si prinde-ma, lasule!*" The captain's faint words carried a chilling familiarity.

"*Hey, you alright?*" Terraknight's deep baritone rumbled through the Harmonization.

Stairs of sandstone materialized before them, propelling them over a broken fence. Harbinger remained ominously silent.

"Did he lose it again?" Hummingbird cried out. *"Not the time to retreat into your enormous head, Captain."*

"What did he say?" Phoenix unleashed a fiery blue arrow. It hit its target, igniting a Nebula on the spot.

"Asked the Shepherd to come get him, I think," Hummingbird replied. *"My Russkayan's rusty."*

Quakelord crashed a building down upon a dozen Stalkers. *"Creepy, Cap. Don't do it again,"* he warned.

Selena's fist slammed into the wall, pulverizing it. Her eyes, decidedly murderous, locked onto me. I flinched, remembering the last time I'd seen her this furious—when her parents had disowned her after the Academy.

"He speaks their language!" she spat, ripping off her torn glove. "He's a traitor! Varcolacs have no honor, Aurora. He'll slit our throats first chance he gets!"

Doubt crushed my chest. Was Harbinger here on Russkaya's orders? My Russkayan was less than rudimentary—I'd have to brush up the first chance I got.

My doubt plummeted, then soared. The Commander had sent me to investigate him. That's what I'd do, even if it meant confronting him directly.

The road bent, and I could see Harbinger and Terraknight without the Visor. Ice shards rained down on them, clashing against the vice-captain's earthen blocks. The Glacies met their end, impaled on a forest of spikes.

Harbinger moved in a blur—and even I had trouble keeping up with him—changing directions and plunging into the fray.

Alone.

"Harbinger, what are you doing?" I blurted.

If my voice surprised him, he didn't show it. He leaped between the storming Stalkers, his heart thudding with a terrifying excitement that echoed in my chest.

Froth-mouthed Limuses led the charge, followed by a horde of Nebulas and Glacies. In one fluid motion, Harbinger unsheathed a short sword, so dark it melded with the night. It hissed along the scabbard like a whisper of scales on rough stone.

A Limus leaped, jaws snapping for his throat. Harbinger's blade flashed, and the creature split apart in mid-air.

I'd missed the strike.

Sand twirled around his weapon as he pivoted, ducking under another Limus. The hellhound's head hit the ground before its body finished falling.

Harbinger pressed forward, his actions merging into a haze. A Glacie's eye exploded in a spray of gore, the deadly ice shard shattering to the ground. Before its scream faded, Harbinger had already vaulted onto a Nebula, slicing its throat with surgical precision.

"How is he so fast?" Selena snarled, her teeth gnashing together.

I couldn't answer her, my throat tight with dread. A knot fisted my stomach as I watched him flicker across the battlefield, each swing of his sword dealing a fatal blow.

Then, a murmur through the Harmonization. Harbinger's voice, cold and distant, spoke in the Republic's language, *"Ah, you won't come out this time, either, will you?"*

My heart shriveled, dropping into my guts with a painful thud. This wasn't the calculating captain from the war room. This was... He was a different man.

Harbinger moved like a whirlwind of steel, cleaving through bodies without pause. When his blade met flesh, it tore. It was a lethal dance, and only he could hear the music. He wasn't just fighting. He was reveling in it. The thrill of killing enraptured him, and a piece of me recognized that dark euphoria all too well.

I felt like I was witnessing my father's chronicles come to life. They called him Vlad the Impaler because destruction trailed behind him on the battlefield, like the ravens in ancient folklore.

If my father was the messenger of Death, then Harbinger was its scythe.

My magic prickled a warning. A horde of Stalkers poured from between the buildings, heading straight for Harbinger. The captain, lost in his battle frenzy, seemed oblivious to the approaching threat.

"Harbinger!" I shouted, quickening my pace as the chaos swallowed my voice.

Gritting my teeth, I extended my Blood Manipulation in a desperate attempt to halt the oncoming Stalkers, but their minds slipped away from my control like vapor.

"Stupid, bull-headed—"

A snarl was my only warning before a Limus slammed into me. We skidded across the ground, its jaws snapping inches from my face. Pain seared through my abdomen.

I unleashed my magic, feeling it surge through me like scalding lava. The fragile barriers of his hollowed mind shattered, and I invaded, bending its will to mine.

It froze, yellowed killing teeth inches away, drool splattering my face. *Yuck.*

"Aurora!" Sel's cry broke my concentration.

The Limus' eyes flared red, and it shook its head as it regained control.

I yanked a needle from my hair and jammed it into its bloodshot eye. It yelped, giving me the opening to kick it off.

Another lunged. I sidestepped, scoring its neck with my nails.

Then it spun and burrowed its claws in my thigh. Ignoring the pain, I rammed my fist into its throat, tearing through arteries and bones.

The Limus collapsed, spewing rotten blood.

I twirled, searching for Selena as the foul scent penetrated my nostrils. She was extracting a spine shard from a third Limus with her bare hand, looking as gore-splattered as a Goya painting.

"Stay on the sideline," she spat, throwing my earlier words back at me.

I rolled my eyes. "Oh please, you handled yourself just fine. Now, are you going to help me save the idiot captain, or cry into your fist?"

Selena's mouth opened, then snapped shut with a groan.

"Keep up, slowpoke" I called over my shoulder, already racing toward him. "Harbinger!" I shouted. "Enemy at your ten!"

He ignored me, lost in his rampage. Glacies and Nebulas fell before him, bodies piling up like gruesome trophies. The Stalkers were circling, hunting him. Anger boiled in my veins to the point I could *hear* it.

Enough.

I wouldn't stand by and watch him get himself killed. Not when I needed answers to so many questions. *It was enough.*

"Sel, slow the Stalkers rushing Harbinger. I'll help, then try to stop him, but I need backup if I fail."

She nodded grimly. "On it."

I reached out with my Blood Manipulation, digging my nails into the slippery, tar-soaked threads of the Stalkers' minds. Their vacant consciousness yielded easily, bodies freezing mid-charge. I felt Selena's magic brush mine, reinforcing the hold.

Harbinger's mental barriers were another story. His blood, still fresh in my system, made finding his link simple. But penetrating his mind? Like breaching a fortress.

His consciousness was intricate and vast, a labyrinth. I slipped through his initial defenses, meeting resistance like pushing against rubber. Then the walls came up, shoving me back.

My head throbbed as he fought to keep me out, but I held on. If I could just make him see reason, make him understand the danger—

I yanked at his thread. *"Harbinger, stand down!"* I roared into his mind.

His body halted mid-swing, the blade hovering. For a heartbeat, silence fell over the battlefield.

Then came his feral roar—defiance and anguish combined into a horrifying sound. It didn't matter if I was right; like a petulant child, he rejected reason.

The pressure in my skull mounted to unbearable limits. This was what a walnut must feel like in a nutcracker. And still, I sensed he was holding back.

"Get out of my head, Projector!" he snarled.

His presence became a tempest, raging against my grasp. I felt my control slipping, cracking under the assault. A tidal wave of power slammed into me, infiltrating my mind, squeezing, bombarding, trying to wrest control.

With a terrifying growl, Harbinger shattered our link. It snapped, crumpled. And a void slammed into me like a hammer to the chest.

I took a step toward him—or attempted to.

A streak of heat ran up my spine and exploded into jagged pain at the base of my neck. It ripped at my bones, twisted my tendons, and dragged me to my knees. The world tilted and blurred, voices shouting indistinctly over the thrashing in my head.

Blood filled my mouth, metallic and warm.

As darkness swallowed me, one last thought haunted my thoughts: I'd failed. I'd failed us all.

AURORA

I WOKE UP TO the awareness of someone watching me.

"Get up, damn you!" Selena's voice sliced through the fog, yanking me to consciousness like a hook in deep water. I held myself still, refusing to flinch, waiting for reality to settle before taking the irrevocable step of opening my eyes.

Once you admit you're alive, playing dead becomes a luxury you can't reclaim.

I cracked my eyelids to find her face an inch from mine, her features twisted with worry and rage. We locked eyes, a silent exchange passing between us as the stench of rotten guts and viscera polluted the air around us.

"You're not going to die?" she asked softly. *Too softly.*

My blood pressure started to rise. "Not right this minute." I grimaced, half-expecting a chunk of space debris to come hurtling through the atmosphere and smash my skull into oblivion.

"That's good," she snarled, her tone suggesting anything but happiness. "I was afraid of being robbed of the pleasure." Her slap stung and snapped my scattered thoughts into focus.

Memories flooded back—the battlefield, Harbinger cutting through the horde like a possessed demon. And myself, foolishly attempting to control him, breaking my promise to Sel.

So much for not letting the Nexus hurt me.

I could still feel the repercussion of the severed link. It throbbed with each heartbeat, as if someone had taken a sledgehammer to my head, then poured acid into the cracks. But even that agony paled in comparison to the crushing guilt. I'd endangered not just myself, but Sel too.

"I'm sorry," I croaked and tried to rise on my elbows.

A splintering current zinged through my body. My dry throat rattled like gravel, and I bit down hard, each movement sending fresh waves of pain through my skull. The world tipped and swayed, the ground seeming to ripple beneath me like choppy water.

"Don't 'sorry' me," she spat. "Do you have any idea what it was like? Watching you drop like—like a stone, convulsing on the ground, completely unresponsive? You promised me you'd be careful, you reckless idiot!"

I gulped, and it went down like nails. "I know... I'm so sorry for putting you through that. I just... thought I could control him. His immortal blood, it's like a fortress around his mind."

Sel's lips curled, disgust giving way to anger. "Should've let the bastard die. I certainly wouldn't shed a tear." She grabbed my arm, her grip bruising as she yanked me up onto my feet. "Now get up before I fucking kill you myself—or the Ignises beat me to it and turn us both to ash."

I complied, swallowing a groan. The temptation to play possum a little longer was strong, but Sel's fury was stronger. The mother of all migraines hammered at me, and my Blood Magic clung weakly to the Black Guild's outliers.

Locking my knees, I was determined not to fall again. My legs trembled, muscles protesting every movement.

"Was this how he harmed his projectors? By pushing them out of his head?" I muttered, more to myself than to her.

"Must be." She lowered her voice, a tremor breaking through her rage. "You died, A... for five minutes, you were dead cold."

A twist of fear wound deep inside my belly. My breath struggled past the boulder in my throat. I held her tightly, pulling her close.

"I'm fine. I swear to you I'm okay now." I paused, managing a weak smile. "I'm a little hungry, though. You wouldn't happen to have some blood hidden under your coat, would you?"

She squeezed me tight before pulling away. "Here," she growled, shoving a half-bottle of Hematech-9 into my hands. *Where does she even keep them?*

I gulped it down like air, feeling strength seep back into my limbs. The synthetic blood coursed through me, dulling the edge of pain and clearing some of the fog from my mind. "Thanks," I said, licking my lips. "Are we good?"

Selena's eyes flashed like a glint of a blade. "Not even close."

I nodded, guilt twisting in my gut. "I'll make it up to you. I promise."

The distant roar of battle still echoed around us. I straightened my shoulders, wincing as my spine popped and cracked. We had a mission to complete, and I had a lot to prove—to Selena, to the Black Guild, and to my own battered ego. Plus, I owed Harbinger a piece of my mind... and maybe a swift kick to his thick skull.

Terraknight's voice roared through our mental link, making Selena stiffen beside me. *"Hummingbird, Ember, northeast. Distract and retreat. Second unit, hold position. Rogue Limuses and Glacies incoming."*

A flurry of responses followed. Each determined voice solidified my resolve. But one look at Sel's vicious glare doused my enthusiasm like a bucket of arctic water.

"Don't even think about it," she hissed, threatening me with her lethal forefinger. "He almost—no, he killed you, Aurora. And you want to help them? They are not our allies. I refuse to put my life and yours in danger for these traitors."

I gnawed at the edge of my lip, searching for words that wouldn't sound like weak excuses. "I don't think he meant to hurt me like that. When I slipped into his mind, he reacted like... like it spooked him, turned defensive. Sel, I'm not sure if he understands what being an original means." Like he didn't know what happened during the Blood Pact. Harbinger had stopped it just as I'd brushed his mental walls.

Her onyx eyes drilled into me as if trying to peel back my scalp and read my thoughts directly. She let out a long, strained breath. "Fine. One more chance. But if he so much as twitches wrong, I'm taking him down myself."

"And I won't lift a finger to stop you. Let's split up—you take Hummingbird and Ember, I'll check on the *others*." I avoided giving specifics, but Sel's parting look told me she wasn't fooled.

She melted into the shadows, her floral scent trailing behind her.

I started north and hugged the buildings. My hand kept twitching toward the Astral Visor nestled in my hair, but fear stilled me. The thought of Harmonizing with Harbinger again made me sick, but I needed eyes on what lay ahead.

Oh, to hell with it. He's not the only outlier in Black Guild.

"Initiate Transpection via Terraknight," I muttered.

The holo-screen whooshed over my eye, and I found myself staring at Harbinger's back—his very naked, muscled back, glistening with sweat. *Great. As if this night wasn't complicated enough.*

He turned to face Terraknight, and my pulse did a rebellious little dance. Every line of his body broadcasted danger and power. Not the mindless brute force of the varcolacs or the refined might of purebloods, but an intelligent, stubborn strength. It manifested in the set of his broad shoulders, the turn of his head on his solid neck, and the angle of his square jaw.

His body tensed, muscles flexed, hands poised to grip and crush. His eyes, alert and radiant with the electric amber glow of his wolf, missed nothing. I could easily picture him centuries back, sword stained with blood, striding alone onto a drawbridge to defend his castle against a horde of invaders with that exact look on his face.

Ice-cold dread gripped my body. Somehow, I knew that before sunrise, I'd end up face-to-face with him. And if we fought—*really* fought—I wasn't sure I could win.

No, scratch that. After seeing his magic and the way he used it in battle, I was sure I couldn't win. He'd kill without blinking.

His voice, calm and commanding, reached me through Terraknight's linked hearing-sense. *"Black Guild, cease fire and spread out."*

The outliers obeyed, scattering into the shadows. Only Terraknight held his ground. As they moved, I felt an alarming tug on my magic.

The Ignises... They were gearing up for another assault.

A piercing screech split the air from the northeast. Before I could blink, a colossal tide of lava erupted, bisecting the road. Sixty feet high and twice as wide as the street, it annihilated everything in its path.

The attack missed Harbinger and Terraknight, but the collateral damage was catastrophic. Buildings crumbled, cobblestones exploded, and thick, black smoke choked the air.

My Blood Manipulation flared in warning—another pull, this time much closer, stronger. I skidded to a halt, squeezing my eyes shut to focus on the threads of life around me.

Almost a dozen Ignises stood motionless, gathering power for another strike. I delved into the outliers' minds, mapping their positions and combat status. Two were available.

It was now or never.

"Projector Tepes to Pearl and Gale," I called out. "I'll stop the Ignises. Seek cover across the road and eliminate the group to your southwest."

Their responses came quickly. Gale's confident reply, "Roger. On it," followed by Pearl's melodious, "Ready when you are."

"Wait for my signal."

I pushed my magic outwards across the ruins of Sibiu, my scent—vanilla orchids and pennies—thickening the surrounding air. The world faded into pulsating threads of energy, outliers glowing faintly blue amidst the viscous darkness of the Stalkers.

Fixing on the motionless Ignises, I slammed my consciousness at them like a juggernaut. I invaded their minds, seizing control of their blood, and halted all functions.

If storms could bury villages under snow, I was an avalanche, unstoppable and all-consuming. Their empty minds collapsed under my assault, offering no more resistance than tissue paper.

But even as I breached their defenses, I realized with horror that I was too late.

Two had already launched their assault.

Their magic fizzled out under my iron grip, but the lava was already hurtling toward me.

Heat seared my eyelids, muscles locking in primal fear. Panic set in, bitter and choking. A dribble of warm liquid trickled over my lips, the fruity coppery tang of HemaTech-9 too familiar.

Every instinct urged me to run, to save myself. But I couldn't. I wouldn't.

If I let go now, the Ignises would attack again. And next time, it might not be me in the crosshairs. It could be Selena, or Pearl, or any of the Black Guild members who, despite everything, I'd sworn to protect.

Selena is going to kill me if I don't die first, I thought hysterically.

"Now!" I screamed, raw desperation tearing at my throat. Agony pierced through my head like a blazing bolt of lightning, but I dug my heels in.

I'd failed before. I wouldn't fail again.

The oily threads vanished from my mind as Pearl and Gale struck down the Ignises. The air sizzled, scorching hot, as if I'd stepped into an oven.

Lava only feet away from consuming me whole.

Tears trailed down my skin, evaporating almost instantly in the blistering heat. Too hot, then—

Cold water lapped at my ankles, rising quickly past my chin. I'd never admit it, but in those last moments, I'd surrendered. With pride, knowing I was giving my life to defend my country.

Holding my breath, I slowly opened my eyes... and choked on brine, the salt burning my throat. A thick sheet of ice-cold water stood between me and certain death.

"Pearl, you saved me!" I sent her a mental squeak.

Her smile was warm even through the Harmonization. *"You'd do the same."*

The world beyond Pearl's bubble glowed like a sunrise. I tilted my head, seeking the moon for orientation, and willed my heart to settle. We still had hours until dawn. Inside, it was hot but bearable. For the first time, I felt... mortal. I felt the sacrifice of all the mortals who'd died for the Republic.

The lava receded with a hiss, and the bubble burst. I gasped, coughing and sputtering.

Gale's giggle rang out from above, *"Here you go, Projector,"* as a warm breeze caressed my skin, drying me off.

"Thanks," I managed, running my fingers through my tangled hair.

A guttural sound rumbled from the bottom of the chasm and vibrated through the ground. The stench of sulfur and decay hit me like a fist to the ribs. I stumbled back, hand pressed against my mouth. Never again would I take immortality for granted.

Refocusing on the holo-screen, I spotted Terraknight balancing atop a wall, moving with a grace impossible for his massive frame. I sprinted toward him, trying in vain to avert my gaze from the bodies littering the pavement.

Nebulas lay among the fallen Ignises, their gray skin covered in oozing boils. Mounds of Glacies bled dark crimson rivers, painting the cobblestones. My stomach lurched and tried to crawl sideways.

"Terraknight," I projected, *"three dozen Ignises incoming from the next block."*

He acknowledged with a grunt, then dipped and spun, narrowly avoiding a barrage of ice shards.

I didn't breathe until he disappeared into the ruins, then I raced after him. Dracula's statue loomed in a courtyard, its white marble incongruously pristine amidst the destruction.

My blood magic placed Terraknight fifty yards away, but I heard two heartbeats.

A figure emerged from the shadows. Someone else had beaten me to him.

AURORA

"Like shooting fish in a barrel, huh?" Harbinger quipped, mimicking Terraknight's voice.

Moonlit hair fell onto his forehead as he wiped his blade against his thigh. His unexpected grin made my breath hitch. Moonbeams glinted off his sweat-slicked skin, highlighting every ripple of muscle. If only he weren't so infuriating, I'd freeze this image for later study. But, Derzelas, he was driving me insane.

Terraknight barked a laugh, his vision shaking with mirth. In his periphery, Harbinger's citron irises blazed with unquenchable fire, staring straight at me. A muscle twitched in his jaw, making my pulse skitter.

He narrowed his eyes, then fixated on a shadow in the street. *"Harbinger to Black Guild. Let's wrap things up."*

Hummingbird's response made me jump. *"Roger that. Captain... make them suffer."*

"Kill them all," Quakelord interjected, followed by Gale's softer, *"Be careful."*

Similar replies flooded in, but none clued me in on Harbinger's plan. My teeth hurt as I grunted, "Set Harmonization target, Outlier Harbinger."

The familiar pressure in my skull returned as I restored our link. "Harbinger, wait for—"

"Projector Tepes!" he growled, whirling to face Terraknight. Adrenaline surged through him, that same rush from his earlier rampage. *"From this point forward, I need you to stay silent. You've done enough."*

Asshole.

Oh, he and I were definitely going to have words. Loud, violent words.

The ground shook, walls groaning as another lava wall rose, dimming the stars. Fear coiled in my intestines like a thorny vine.

Harbinger looked up, the blazing glow illuminating his features. Good God... was he smiling?

"If you won't punch him, I will," Selena muttered in my head.

I shifted Transpection to check on her and met half a dozen Stalkers staring blankly at me. Dark blood sprayed everywhere while Hummingbird and Gale sliced the immobilized creatures with invisible air blades.

Wrinkling my nose, I shifted focus back to Terraknight just as a blue fireball streaked past and intercepted a barrage of ice shards meant for him and Harbinger. The fire sizzled, then died out.

Harbinger leaped into the open, zigzagging between lines of fire. Alone. Again.

Worry and frustration battled for dominance.

Five Nebulas closed in, trapping him. Harbinger blurred, ducking and spinning to evade their leprous arms. Instead of killing them or fleeing like any rational outlier, he circled back, toying with them.

"Anytime now, Terraknight," he bellowed, skirting a blow aimed at his face.

My boots pounded against the broken pavement, but I heard nothing over the high-pitched shrill ringing in my ears. A legion of Glacies soared at the captain, their matted gray hair gleaming like tarnished silver. Breathing raggedly, I halted and hurled my magic at them. Blank minds fell apart, winged bodies falling limp like broken dolls.

Terraknight groaned, thrusting his fists downward. The earth responded, erupting in jagged spikes and massive boulders, obliterating every Stalker in range. But more were coming, their savage, bloodthirsty shrieks tearing through the darkness. More always came.

"Black Guild, take cover!" Terraknight commanded, joining his palms. The earth quaked and rolled, sending shockwaves that reduced his creations to fragments.

The outliers obeyed, but I was too late. An explosion of miniature shards hovered for a second, then slashed through the incoming hordes like a flock of razor-sharp birds. A searing cut sliced my cheek, healing on the spot. Dozens more stung my right side, ripping through my suit. I shielded my face, my arm absorbing most of the impact as the remaining fabric of my suit soaked up blood from already-healed cuts.

My pulse throbbed, syncing with Terraknight's heavy breaths. He looped the debris in a wide circle and settled it on the ground, the scrape of stone against stone hurting my eardrums.

Across Harmony Street—the irony!—a ten-foot Ignis extended its limb, tracking Harbinger. A hiss forewarned the eruption of lava beneath the captain's feet.

No!

I braced for his death, the pungent smell of struck matches burning my nostrils. But just before the inferno could touch him, Harbinger... vanished.

He reappeared like a glitch, hurling a portal like a frisbee, cleaving the Ignis in half. The steaming torso flickered and disappeared. A fountain of black, rotten blood showered over Harbinger, darkening his moon-white hair. The stench of putrefaction stung my eyes.

The bottom half swayed and slammed down. Guts spilled from the stump. My stomach spasmed, and I retched, almost soiling my boots.

Harbinger wasn't just portalling at speeds I could never hope to penetrate his mind—he was butchering Stalkers and sending their parts Derzelas-knew-where. Another heave wrung my insides. *How am I going to survive him?*

The earth buckled, nearly sending me sprawling. A seven-foot stone wall ground upward and forced me to stagger back. Only then did I register the savage claws raking the other side and the bone-chilling howls.

I'd been so lost in my thoughts, I'd missed the Limuses charging at me. *Dark Father, help me.* Lead filled my bones, rooting me to the spot. A spike of adrenaline made my insides curl, wither, and die.

Terraknight materialized inches from my face, his narrowed gaze assessing me like he was sizing me up for a coffin. His grip on my arm was iron clad.

"What the fuck is wrong with you?" he snarled, giving me a brutal shake. "You either help or get the hell out of here. I can't keep you alive and do my damn job!"

"But Harbinger..." I protested weakly, my voice sounding pathetic even to my own ears, "he's—"

"He knows what he's doing," Terraknight cut me off with a shove. "You clearly don't!"

He vanished between the buildings, leaving me alone in my shame. It seared within me, consumed me. I'd been so desperate to prove myself, I'd lost sight of the mission: defeat the Stalkers, save the Tenth Ward. Harbinger was more than capable without my interference.

I... I was a liability.

Jasmine bloomed among the choking smoke and spilled guts. Selena blurred at my side, a mean scowl twisting her brows. Her wide eyes locked onto Harbinger.

"What'd I miss?"

I followed her gaze to where Harbinger was warping in and out of existence, leaving a trail of smoldering, incomplete bodies in his wake. I counted the Ignises surrounding him. One lingered close, while six others circled at a distance, likely pooling their power for a Magma Lance. His presence had distracted me from the goal. His well-being had clouded all judgment. Why did I care? Why did his mortality plague me, above even my own safety?

"My pride getting kicked in the gut," I muttered, though I doubted she heard me.

Harbinger raised his hands, grasping the air with curled fingers. Veins bulged in his arms as the space before him shimmered, then tore open with a crackling hiss. He molded the smoky rip into a crescent shape, sharp on both ends, spun, and jammed it into the Ignis sneaking up behind him. The Stalker vanished as the 'weapon' expanded into a vertical portal.

Selena's jaw went slack. "Holy fuck, is he—"

"Yep."

"How... how did he manage to trick the system?" Her voice trembled, thick with fear I'd never heard from her before.

"I don't know. Maybe he concealed his magic in the camps, or he came into it after deployment. But this..." I gestured helplessly at the carnage before us, "taking down multiple Ignises on his own? It's unheard of."

"A," she gripped my hand, "what does this mean for us?"

It physically hurt to admit. "It means he's right. We're in way over our heads."

The Sparrow's battles had never reached this level of complexity. If only he'd briefed us properly—

"Pearl, create a thirty-foot tide to push the Stalkers south," Harbinger's voice resounded in my head. *"Make it dense enough to withstand their heat."*

"Roger that," Pearl replied swiftly.

He tore through another Ignis, kicking its remains aside. *"Quakelord, raise a mud wall to the north. Nebulas can't penetrate it. The rest of you, herd the Stalkers toward me and secure the flanks. Box them in."*

Pearl and Quakelord emerged from the wreckage, eyes aglow with power. Her opalescent scales shimmered as she drew water from every source, even from the air itself, feeding the colossal liquid barrier. Opposite her, Quakelord's hands sank into the earth, conjuring a thick mud rampart to meet her tsunami.

A high-pitched wail froze the blood in my veins.

Selena yelped, and we both spun around as dozens of Stalkers poured out from the shadows between buildings. Some took flight, leathery wings stretching out before Ember's fiery anvil reduced them to ash. Others snarled and snapped at each other.

On the flanks, Gale and Hummingbird corralled them with invisible walls, herding them like sheep to the slaughterhouse.

Terraknight joined Quakelord and Pearl, his stone barrier rising as Phoenix's wall of fire completed the cage, trapping the Stalkers inside. He crouched atop the wall, gaze fixed on the writhing mass of bodies below.

Through our link, I felt his focus, sharp as a knife. Above, the ieles hovered like vengeful angels, while Ember perched on a nearby roof, scanning for threats.

Harbinger portalled atop Quakelord's mud bulwark, his feet planted wide, hands drawing circles in measured, large loops. His movements held a magnetic grace that belied the untamed power coming off him. He was a deity of pure violence. His citrine eyes were luminous as a rising sun, no longer appearing mortal.

The air flooded with his scent.

My stomach revolted, not in repulsion, but with a primal craving for blood—his blood. The weight of his growing magic consumed my reserves, his presence dominating my mind. I slid to the ground, leaning against a crushed boulder, each breath a struggle.

Between Harbinger's hands, a dark cloud writhed like a miniature storm, flashing with golden lightning.

Terraknight looked down, and I gasped.

"Do I even want to know what you see?" Sel asked.

"No."

Midway down the cage, a colossal pitch-black portal descended at a slow pace, grinding against the elemental walls with a sound like tearing metal. I held my breath, my head throbbing as if my brain was a balloon about to burst.

Howls screeched, bones cracked, and the earth absorbed every single cry. I felt them reverberating in my bones to my core.

The portal imploded with a thunderous crack, and I remembered to exhale. Moonlight glistened on the carnage like onyx gemstones. Viscous blood flowed freely from butchered carcasses. Every single one of them destroyed. Put down in the blink of an eye by his immense power.

I gagged, tasting rot, and switched to mouth-breathing as I shut off the Visor.

Today had been a nightmare. I'd discovered my guild captain was a varcolac—the Republic's worst enemy. I'd died for five minutes, survived Selena's rage, failed at blood magic, and witnessed Harbinger's city-leveling rampage. The pain of our severed mental link still burned. If I could, I'd punch today right in its smug face.

Phoenix's fire wall dissolved into a disk of wildfire and plunged us into darkness. Pearl's water tide burst into rainfall, washing away the gore. The other two barriers sank back into the earth with a rumble.

And then silence.

I struggled to my feet, recalling my blood magic. The remaining Stalkers retreated north, back to their territory, their losses too great to continue fighting.

Harbinger portalled a hundred feet away, eyes still blazing gold. His gaze locked onto me, hot and pointed as an arrow, making my spine tingle. He stalked toward me, all lethal grace and simmering power. Every step promised instant violence if provoked, and I had not an inch of a doubt he'd deliver.

I knew I deserved it, but I wouldn't take it quietly.

"You," he snarled, and the sheer amount of pure contempt nearly knocked me over.

AURORA

Fᴇᴀʀ ʀᴏᴏᴛᴇᴅ ᴍᴇ ᴛᴏ the spot, a primordial instinct screaming to stay perfectly still. But terror had always had a funny way of unlocking my tongue.

"Me," I replied, sharp and defiant.

His right hand twitched, cords of muscles boiling under golden skin. He flickered and lunged to grab my throat.

I ducked, muscle memory kicking in, and spun away. His fingers grazed my cheek as I shoved Selena clear. This was between me and him.

We circled each other, predator and prey, though I wasn't sure who was which.

"What the hell were you thinking?" Harbinger growled. "You could have gotten us all killed!"

I lifted my chin, keeping the tremor out of my voice. "I was saving your ass, you arrogant prick. Or did you miss the Stalkers sneaking up while you played god?"

His nostrils flared, a quiet grumble building in his chest. "I had it under control."

"Clearly," I scoffed, gesturing to the carnage around us. "Is leveling half the city your idea of 'control?'"

He lunged again with a growl. This time, I wasn't fast enough. His fingers wrapped around my neck, the world went dark, unfamiliar, and icy-cold, then he was slamming me against a wall. Debris rained down on us.

Like a brand, his touch seared my skin, the heat of his body seeping into me, leaving a fiery trail in its wake. All this I figured out later, but this was his varcolac surfacing—his erratic heartbeat, the molten gold in his eyes, the fever-hot skin. Harbinger always ran warm, but when he let the beast loose, he became an inferno.

"Listen carefully, princess," he snarled, face inches from mine. My feet felt no ground. "Pull that stunt again, and I'll—"

"You'll what? Kill me? Like to see you try."

The realization that I was once again at a man's mercy ignited something primitive inside me. Rage and terror collided, my vision blurring crimson at the edges.

No. Not again.

Never again.

My body moved on pure instinct. I gripped Harbinger's wrist, reached for the silver needle in my hair, and drove it deep into the nerve between his thumb and forefinger.

A shudder ran through Harbinger's arm. His fingers spasmed, his grip loosening just enough.

I dropped, sweeping his legs. The mighty Harbinger toppled, a look of utter shock flashing across his face. I rolled, putting precious distance between us before springing to my feet. Harbinger was already rising, muscles coiled tight, eyes savage. Ravenous.

The entire exchange lasted mere heartbeats. Our audience stood frozen, mouths agape. Selena's face was a mask of horror, while Terraknight's hand held onto her, twitching as if unsure whether to intervene.

Harbinger pulled out the needle and dropped it to the ground, never taking his eyes off me. "You've got a death wish."

Nervous laughter bubbled up. "And you've got an ego the size of Transylvania. Quite the pair we make."

Harbinger charged.

I darted forward, aiming to slip under him and ram my fist into his ribs. Instead, we both slammed into Terraknight's brick wall of a chest.

"Enough!" the vice-captain barked, restraining us both. His eyes ping-ponged between us, like he was dealing with troublesome children. "Stand down. *Now!*"

I bared my fangs. "If I hadn't been guarding your flank, you'd be nothing but Stalker fodder—"

"A, let it go," Selena pleaded, pulling at my wrist.

Harbinger's eyes flickered, gold bleeding to crimson. "Why risk your neck for halfbloods? What's your game, Projector?"

"Because I don't want to see you hurt. Any of you."

Then I saw it—my silk scarf dangling from his fingers like a trophy, and my stomach dropped to my toes.

Cold air lapped at my neck. My hand flew to my throat. Bare. Exposed.

No. No. No!

Harbinger's gaze followed, his perpetual scowl softening a fraction as he took in the scars. Understanding dawned in his eyes, but it was too late. Shame burned through me like poison.

My pulse slowed. My face grew hot, my fingertips cold.

No. Please, no. His anger I could tolerate, but his pity... I wasn't sure I could bear it.

"Shit," Selena hissed, yanking harder.

I gently removed her hand, squaring my shoulders. "Give. That. Back." Breath rolled around my lungs like a block of ice. The derelict side buildings closed in around me, choking me.

Harbinger dangled the scarf like a matador's cape. Silver light glinted off his fangs as he grinned. "Tell me why you care, and maybe I will. Or come take it yourself, princess."

That bastard.

I could use my magic, force him to hand it over. But my reserves were as drained as his. Engaging him on the mental plane might plunge me into bloodlust. The risk was too great.

Harbinger smirked, stuffing the scarf in his pocket. "What's wrong? Scared?"

Terrified. Humiliated. Absolutely livid. "Of you? Please. If you open a portal, I might scramble your brain." Total bluff, but I refused to let him see me crack. I forced a shrug. "I've seen what's rattling around in your head. Not exactly impressed."

Terraknight shook his head, his massive hand curling around Selena's arm. "Come on, shortie. Let them sort out their problems."

"Aurora, don't—"

Terraknight threw her over his shoulder and whisked her away, a torrent of obscenities trailing behind them. Perhaps I should've listened to her. But I couldn't show weakness—they'd never let us stay if I did. I turned back to Harbinger, his blazing eyes still fixed on me, promising a reckoning.

Harbinger closed the gap in a single leap.

I stumbled back before steel fingers clamped around my wrist, his other arm snaking around my waist.

He pulled me close, as if to dance, his minty breath hot on my face.

I thrashed, but it felt like battling a mountain.

"You expect me to believe you'll play fair? That you're not a cold-blooded viper like the rest of your kind?"

I recognized the shift in his hips a second too late. "Harbinger! Don't you dare—"

The world spun. I sailed through the air and landed flat on my back. Air whooshed from my lungs.

Ow. Bits of gravel dug into my palms.

"Impressed yet?" His shark-like grin stretched like a white stain over his face.

He was *playing*. The bastard could have snapped my spine, but no—he'd cushioned my fall, made sure I landed right.

"Big bad original, laid out by a *mutt*." He laughed. "I'd be blushing if I were you. At least try some magic, princess."

Oh, he asked for it.

I gathered every scrap of power I had left, focusing it into a battering ram against his mind. The effort made my vision swim, a dull ache building behind my eyes.

"Kneel."

He grunted, face contorting like Atlas shouldering the heavens.

I stood on shaky legs, adrenaline covering up the bone-deep exhaustion. Harbinger remained locked in place, every muscle straining against my command. He didn't kneel. He *wouldn't* kneel.

Even with his defenses down, my all-out attack still wasn't enough to defeat him. When he broke free, there'd be hell to pay.

Warning sirens blared in my head. My last shred of self-preservation screamed, *Release him and grovel, you idiot!* But the damage was done. He was under my control, though only just, and I needed answers before he'd *probably* kill me.

"Did you know severing the Harmonization would hurt your projector?" The words came out ragged, each syllable an effort.

He fought the dual commands, but a troubled expression disturbed the sneer on his face. "No," he grunted.

Truth. Which meant he was innocent of harming me, and maybe others. But Olaru's death... No sane pureblood would give up their life over a trivial amount of pain.

I felt him slipping away. "What's your mother's name?" I pushed harder, ignoring the hunger clawing in my gut.

A deep, throaty sound bellowed in him. It was a sound of rage and pain rolled into one.

Oh no.

"What happened to her?"

Sweat beaded his brow. "Your precious Republic happened," he snarled. "What do you think those fuckers did to a Russkayan diplomat's wife?"

Remorse dug at me, but I pushed it away, concentrating on the implications. Only an original raised at court would marry into an alliance. A high-ranking pureblood, sacrificed for politics. They should have spared her. Killing or hurting our own was against our law, an offense punishable by sunrise.

I studied him, trying to place his bloodline. Not Tepes—I would have heard of his mother's execution, no matter how hard the Republic tried to hide it. Wurdulak or Hansen, then? Hard to tell with the mixed blood. And political machinations meant that no one would freely speak about their traitorous relative.

His skin was too warm, too golden for a pureblood. Silver-white hair framed a face that lacked the sharp angles of Derzelas' children. Only the crimson ring in his eyes and the potency of his blood betrayed his heritage. Everything else about him was too rugged, radiating a raw masculinity that could only have come from his father.

His *varcolac* father.

Visions of my wrists shackled beneath the Tribunal's oculus flashed before my eyes. My blood turned to slush in my veins. Elena would fight for me, but if the Council discovered Harbinger's true nature—and that I'd kept it secret—not even my brother's rank would save me from execution.

I leaned close, my breath forming a small cloud in the crisp morning air. "I'm so sorry. The Republic should have protected her... and you."

With a low growl that raised the hairs at my nape, he finally straightened. "Save your pity for someone who gives a damn, princess." His eyes flashed red, then pure gold. "Shall we dance?"

"It will be my pleasure." I tried to sound confident, but my use of magic on an empty stomach was taking its toll.

I stayed light on my feet, ready to dodge. The rubble and uneven cobblestones made footing treacherous. If he grappled with me, it was over.

He lunged once more.

I twisted past, the rush of air from his movement ruffling my hair. My kick connected with the side of his leg, the impact reverberating up my leg. It should have shattered concrete.

"Tickles." He chuckled darkly.

His hand clamped around my arm like an iron vise and tossed me across the street.

The impact was barely noticeable, and I rolled, scrambling to my feet.

Harbinger's smug grin greeted me. "You're fun to play with. Good training dummy."

Dummy?

His smile turned feral as he prowled closer. "Terraknight fills them with wheat bran. Nice not having to sweep up after smashing their heads."

"I'm not your damn punching bag," I snapped.

"Prove it."

Blood drained from my face. My mouth turned into a desert. "I out-rank you, you insubordinate ass!"

He pulled me into a crushing bear hug, his heat enveloping me, his scent overwhelming. "Rank means shit out here, princess. You've done nothing but piss me off." He tilted my chin with a knuckle, all humor fading from his eyes. "My turn for questions. Who did this to you?"

Though his touch seared my skin, I didn't pull away. His fingers ghosted over my scars, and I clutched his wrist, fighting back the flood of nightmares threatening to drown me.

"Don't," I whispered so quietly that even I couldn't hear my voice. Every proud fiber of my being strung tight, and my eyes snapped to his.

He released me and took a step back as if the air between us had grown red-hot. The cold night air rushed in where his warmth had been. "Have it your way," he said. "But here's the deal. You want to play, Projector? Fine. But you and your little friend follow my lead. No exceptions."

AURORA

Selena yanked at her leather sleeves, the zipper's teeth gnashing as she rolled them up to her elbows. "What's next? Cooking their meals and tucking them in at night?"

She plunged into the knee-deep icy water, attacking the soiled pants as if they'd insulted her work. The spray and flood of muttered curses silenced the chorus of crickets and frogs hiding in the bank.

I bit my lip, stifling a snort. "I think cooking's the last thing they'd expect. Besides, you couldn't handle mortal food if it came with step-by-step instructions and a personal chef."

Three weeks had slipped by since we'd fled the Republic. Six more sorties with the Black Guild had left me bone-weary but alive—and so was everyone else. Praise Derzelas for small favors. The missions had been a crucible, forging my control over the Stalkers in ways I could've never hoped to achieve. I felt my magic hum through me in waves of strength I'd never experienced.

Harbinger, though... He remained an enigma, his knack for predicting Stalker attacks both infuriating and fascinating. We'd found common

233

ground, if you could call shifting sands stable. He'd started to harmonize with me, actually listening to my ideas during strategy meetings. Sometimes, I'd catch a glimmer of *something* in those scarlet-gold eyes. Not quite contempt, definitely not approval. Perhaps curiosity? I couldn't be certain—it vanished too quickly to name.

Even when he ignored my suggestions—which was often—I counted it as progress. Baby steps. I dipped my hands in the water, scrubbing at a stubborn stain. *Humans,* I reminded myself, *hadn't built their empires in a day.* And neither could we.

Selena tossed the still-dirty slacks into the basket by our boots. "Hey!" she snapped, stretching to retrieve another piece of laundry from the pile beneath the willow tree. "You didn't complain when you stuffed your face with my Red Brownies!"

"I have no idea what you're talking about," I quipped, then noticed what she held in her hands. I pressed my lips together, trapping the laughter bubbling in my throat.

Selena's face was a study in dawning horror as she looked down.

Her eyes widened, mouth slackening as if trying to form words her brain couldn't quite process. No sounds came out. She examined the black *male* boxers in the soft lantern light, her left eye twitching spasmodically. Then her nose wrinkled, lip curling over her fangs in a look of such utter revulsion that it nearly sent me doubling over.

Her screech echoed off distant, snow-capped peaks. "Ugh! I *touched* that!" The offending garment flew, landing on the rocks with a wet slap.

"That's it!" she yelled, throwing her hands up. "I quit! I'd rather sunbathe than wash another stitch of their underwear!"

"Careful, pureblood," Phoenix called out, her grin stretching to her ears. "Wouldn't want you catching cooties or anything."

Selena's response was swift and decidedly non-verbal, involving a certain finger and *a lot* of feeling.

I lost it then. Tears streamed down my face as I burst into laughter.

"Et tu, Brutus?" Selena rounded on me, jabbing an accusing finger in my direction.

I raised an eyebrow, still chuckling. "What? It was funny. A little laundry won't kill you. You've survived worse."

Ember dove into the lake, veins igniting like bioluminescent deep-sea creatures. Her fire magic pulsed through the water, bubbled, and sent up spirals of steam that condensed into a ghostly fog around us. The high-waisted drawers she had on puffed up, bobbing behind her like a Victorian cotton buoy as she glided beneath the floating laundry.

Phoenix arched her back, stretching her arms skyward. Electric-blue sparks crackled between her fingertips before she plunged her hands into the lake. A fresh wave of steam billowed up, carrying her scent of roasted marshmallows. Unlike the other balaur, Phoenix wore garments from this century: a black sports bra paired with low-slung maroon cargo pants, both now plastered to her body and dripping water.

Selena's hand shot out, sending a spray of icy water into my distracted face. The shock of cold made me gasp, droplets clinging to my eyelashes.

"I'm putting my foot down, A!" she growled. "I didn't claw my way through decades of military bureaucracy and Healing Corps bullshit to end up as some halfblood's laundry wench!"

I wiped my cheeks, the spark of stubborn challenge in Selena's eyes almost worth the impromptu face wash. "No one's forcing you, but if we want to stay, we pull our weight. Come on," I nodded toward the discarded boxers. "Show me that famous pureblood pride. Pick those up."

Her glare could've frozen the entire Black Sea. "I. Loathe. You," she hissed, reaching for the willow. Branches snapped under her grip, startling a nightjar into a hasty flight. Frogs leaped for safety, creating tiny splashes in the pond.

Twisting the twigs into a makeshift rod, Selena stomped to shore. Her leather suit creaked as she bent, gingerly hooking the briefs. Tears of mirth blurred my vision.

Pearl hid her amusement behind her hand, but the balaurs, less tactful, giggled shamelessly.

"Over here, Lieutenant!" Gale called. Her infectious smile matched the excited flutter of her coppery wings. "I'll lend a hand, just this once."

Selena's arm blurred, swinging her improvised bat. The underwear sailed through the air, a dark kite against the moonlit sky. Gale snatched it mid-flight, balled it up, and tossed it to Pearl.

The varva's hands became a whirlwind of motion, conjuring a soapy bubble that smelled of homemade lavender bars. It intercepted the 'ball,' tumbling it for one, two, three seconds before flinging the now-clean boxers into a small vortex swirling on the bank.

Two minutes, start to finish.

"Show-offs," Selena muttered, a reluctant smirk hovering on her lips.

Pearl's shoulders stiffened. Her hand flew to the transmitter, her enchanting giggle cutting off. "Understood, Captain." She glanced first at Selena, then at me, letting a vixen smile curl her lips. "Almost finished. Our guests could use a little more time." She winked, then murmured in the softest voice, "Stay on the line for a bit."

Raising her voice, Pearl hollered, "Our stern-faced captain just called, ladies. Dinner's ready."

I froze.

Water lapped at my calves. A faint alarm bell rang in the back of my mind. Why would Pearl lie about Harbinger still being on the line? Curiosity got the best of me. Meeting Selena's gaze, I gave a subtle nod and brushed the crystal at my nape. *Initiate Harmonization. Set target, Outlier Pearl. Open link, Lieutenant Selena Popescu.*

The connections blossomed in my mind like moonflowers blooming at twilight, eclipsing Harbinger's spectral presence. Warmth spread through my chest, accompanied by an electric tingle of anticipation.

My gamble paid off—the Transmitters were malfunctioning again, just in time to catch Harbinger's grumble. His voice, deep and irritated, sent a conflicting wave of excitement and apprehension through me in a shiver.

"Pearl, I don't have time for this."

Pearl ignored him.

Ember erupted from the lake as if chased by a river monster, an empty laundry basket clutched to her chest like a shield.

"Whoa, Ember." Pearl chuckled, waggling her eyebrows. "Careful not to break your neck. We might need to orchestrate some alone time for you two next laundry day."

The balaur's face flushed crimson. She fumbled with the basket, nearly dropping it on her folded dress.

"W-what? No! It's not... I mean, we're not..." Ember sputtered, catching my amused gaze and narrowing her eyes.

Oh yes, it was *exactly* like that.

Pearl tossed her thick braid over her shoulder with dramatic flair. "I just don't see the appeal. The man's a walking statue. You can never tell what's going through his head."

Ember stomped her bare foot, chittering like an indignant squirrel. "For the last time, I don't see him like that!"

Harbinger's spectral presence stirred. Impatience radiated from him, yet he lingered, eavesdropping. *Curious.*

I focused on scrubbing one of his shirts, sneaking a glance at Selena. She lounged on a flat boulder, inspecting her manicure with an expression of long-suffering boredom. Her drama allergy was acting up again, no doubt.

"So, Projector," Pearl spoke with a layer of faux innocence, "what's your take on our illustrious captain?"

My heart did a spectacular belly flop. *Nice try, vixen.* Harbinger's presence went eerily still.

"That's hardly appropriate," I managed, proud of my collected tone.

"Boo! What's the point of immortality if you don't live a little?" Pearl pouted, sweeping her arm to assist Gale with the remaining laundry.

I parted my lips, ready to tell her I had better ways to spend my eternal time than thinking about her captain, when the lake decided to upstage us all.

A colossal wave rose, its crest morphing into... was that a *Carpathian bison*?

My witty comeback evaporated as the watery beast huffed and bellowed, snatching the clothes in its jaws before melting back into the lake.

Gale sauntered to shore, her newly cleaned clothes floating above her head like Aladdin's flying rug, trailing the scent of lavender and citrus. "Silent and stoic?" She grinned. "Sign me up."

Her plain jeans and dark, long-sleeved shirt were completely dry. There was something in the way she walked—a subtle sway, shoulders squared beneath the weight of her wings—that inspired me to picture her in blood-red silks, a priestess in Derzelas' temple.

"Gale!" Ember shrieked, her jade eyes as wide as saucers. She scrambled into a knee-length corduroy dress, somehow managing to look adorable despite the garment's stiff A-shape and kitsch embroidery. The balaur could make a burlap sack look chic.

Pearl's hearty chuckle filled the air like warm honey, but Gale wasn't finished. Her tone shifted, turning serious. "If none of you have dibs," she said, gliding the folded clothes into her crate, "maybe I'll make my move today. A little midday visit to the captain's quarters—"

"You may want to hold on to your plan," I interjected, aiming for nonchalance as I tossed Harbinger's top toward the basket. "He and I have a thrilling date with reports and shipment logistics. Could take hours."

My casual toss turned into a laundry catapult. The hamper skidded along the rocks like a shipwreck washed ashore, leaving a thirty-foot trail behind it. I stopped breathing, counting to five.

Maybe no one—

"What the actual fuck was that?" Selena's voice slapped me from two directions—both mentally and out loud. *Perfect.*

I plastered on my best 'nothing to see here' smile, mentally kicking myself for the blatant lie with the captain eavesdropping on the other end. Since when did I care which one of them warmed his bed?

Harbinger's echo in my mind got several hundred pounds heavier, pressing against my thoughts like a lead blanket. It was all I could focus on. He was all I ever seemed to focus on.

"Tomorrow's another day?" I suggested weakly.

Gale's grin could've lit up a small city. "It's on. Thanks for letting me know, Projector." She turned to Ember, giving her a shrug. "Tomorrow it is."

My smile felt as genuine as a plastic plant. This shouldn't bother me. *Chokehold,* I told to the spike of unwelcome jealousy, and it dissipated like smoke in a windstorm.

"Gale!" Ember wailed; her fair brows knitted in distress. "It's not proper! He's... he's our captain!"

Phoenix, emerging from the water with an armload of dripping clothes, let out an ungraceful snort. Gale shook with silent laughter, tears rimming her eyes.

"Oh, you prude!" Pearl cackled, just as Selena muttered, *"Fucking children,"* her exasperation as thick as a slab of clay.

I clenched my teeth to keep from laughing, too.

"You're all awful! I hate you!" Ember stomped her rubber-booted feet again, looking about as threatening as an angry kitten.

A rustle at the forest's edge sent everyone on high alert.

"Wait—" I started, but Gale'd already leaped into action. Eyes aglow, wings spread wide, she unleashed a whirlwind that would make any twister run for its money.

The night cracked open as half an acre of innocent trees toppled with a mere flick of her wrist.

Quakelord let out a surprised yelp, announcing his presence to the world. His magic, previously a whisper, now saturated the air with a cocktail of moss and rain.

Several things happened at once. Branches snapped like brittle bones, terrified rodents fled their homes in a furry exodus, and the lake shrank as if someone had pulled the plug.

Quakelord, quick on his feet, rolled and dodged, whooping in excitement while the earth roared to his defense. His mud walls crumbled under the elemental onslaught—water, air, and fire combining into a force that would give even a legion of Stalkers pause.

Phoenix, ever the silent one, reached into her thigh pocket, drew out a short blade, and swept her arm in a broad arc.

"What the hell?" Quakelord squeaked, plastering himself against a barricade. "Who threw that? You trying to turn me into a pincushion?"

"You pervert!" Ember bellowed, hands on her hips.

Twin fireballs, one golden, the other green-blue, arced around his shield and exploded in a cascade of sparks.

Panic seized my chest, squeezing the breath out of me. "Quakelord!" I shouted, but the crackling flames and shattering earth muted my voice.

He let out a war cry and dashed along the shore, his dark hair glistening in the firelight. My bloodstream buzzed, sending my heart into overdrive.

I called my magic, ready to stop them before someone got hurt. This was spiraling out of control.

"Doesn't anyone care if I'm bleeding? I could be dying here!" he wailed from his latest mud fortress, a trace of humor breaking through.

Tension drained away from my shoulders. *They are... playing?*

Gale landed atop his mud igloo, her wingtips brushing the clay with soft whispers. "Don't be such a baby," she teased, rapping her knuckles on the dome. "Come out and face your punishment like a man."

Pearl's steel-toed boot connected with the base of his shelter. "Fess up, creeper. How long were you watching us?"

"Long enough to hear you lot saying that you *luv* Cap!" Quakelord's muffled voice rang out, shaking with laughter.

Ember's wail of despair could've shattered diamond.

I snorted, shaking my head as I returned to my laundry duty. How they could switch from hardened warriors to squabbling children in the blink of an eye was beyond me. Playing such games at court was unheard of—and would likely end in death.

Quakelord's mud cage finally surrendered with a dramatic groan. He erupted like a raging volcano, finger pointing skyward. "I've got it!" he crowed. "Let's trick Ember into confessing her love while Cap's tuned in!"

If only he knew what a show they were putting on for him.

Gale touched down with nimble agility. "Captain wouldn't even twitch an eyebrow."

Ember's face reached a new shade of crimson. "I never said that!" she screeched, swatting at Quakelord as if he were an annoying gnat.

In the recess of my mind, Harbinger's specter grew restless. His presence expanded, darkness weaving through Pearl and Selena's connections, nearly engulfing my consciousness.

"Listen up, Black Guild. Your 'silent and stoic' captain speaking. Return to base thirty minutes before moonset."

Ember's face paled to match the moonlight. Quakelord shrugged in the way boys often did when caught red-handed, while Pearl's grin stretched wide, almost splitting her face in two.

"You are no fun, Harbi—"

Click.

His presence vanished before Pearl could finish, leaving an emptiness that shouldn't have bothered me as much as it did.

The Nexus buzzed, and I reached to tap the crystal. A familiar warmth bloomed in my chest, tingles racing along my skin as Harbinger's voice rumbled through our direct link. *"Projector, we both know there aren't any reports for you to review."*

My pulse quickened, fingers tightening on the fabric in my hands as I raced to excuse my lie. "I need to send a letter to the Republic," I countered, the half-truth sour on my tongue. Our dwindling blood supply was my burden to bear, not his.

"Then you'll want Terraknight. He's in charge of the carrier birds."

The connection ended with a whisper-soft pop, just a breath against my senses.

Then the Bloodthorn Nexus cooled at my nape, leaving me oddly bereft. It wasn't the skull-splitting agony of before, but a gentler dismissal that somehow stung worse. How considerate of him to spare me the headache while still wounding my pride.

It took physical effort not to reach back and yell at him, focusing instead on the cool night air against my flushed skin. The moonlight felt too bright, the sounds of the forest too sharp. Everything grated on my nerves.

I clenched my jaw, feeling the tension spread down my neck and shoulders. Why did his dismissal affect me so much? He was just a rude, egotistical man, nothing more.

Selena waited for me on the shore, the daring smirk on her face making me want to dunk her in the lake. Around us, the others were gathering their things, following their captain's orders with quiet efficiency.

"Not now," I hissed.

"Jealous, Aurora?" She smirked.

"You're delusional," I scoffed and bent to pick up our laundry crate. Maybe if I ignored her, she'd stop talking.

Selena nudged me with her elbow, her eyes drilling into me. "You know, denial isn't just a river in Solanthia."

"Go away."

She let out a cackle.

I squared my shoulders and crushed my irrational anger beneath my iron will. Bigger problems demanded my attention—our blood supply diminished by the night, and the Commander's explanation about the delayed shipment had failed to arrive.

The forest's shadows deepened around us as we trudged back to base, and I made a silent vow. These confusing feelings, this pull toward Harbinger, I'd bury them deep. I had to figure out if Sel and I had enough to feed on before it became a real problem—and I'd be damned if I let my irrational emotions stand in the way.

Aurora

THE JOURNEY BACK PROVED brief and uneventful, save for Quakelord's attempts to mend ties with his guildmates. His voice carried on the breeze, his earlier transgression apparently forgotten.

We marched up the overgrown path, following the smell of seared meat and spices to the back of the house.

"I'm telling you, that knife was sharp! Did you see how I—"

"We were there." Gale rolled her eyes. "We saw."

Ember skipped ahead, her exotic voice floating back to us. "We're ho-ome!"

I hung back as the others filed onto the back patio, smoothing my silk blouse while I drank in the scene. Candlelight danced across the weathered oak table and faded velvet seats. Hummingbird sat on a stool, his wings spread around him like a silver cape. One twitched, sending shadows skittering.

"What's for dinner?" Quakelord smacked his lips and rushed after the balaur. He'd lost his hair tie at the lake, and his dark, glossy locks now flowed about his shoulders.

Terraknight emerged from the outdoor kitchen—one of the many additions this house suffered over the decades—balancing a laden tray. His eyes met mine, then Selena's, one side of his lips quirking up. "Venison stew, forest mushroom medley, garden salad, homemade seed bread, and..." he paused for effect, "berry tart."

"Don't forget the fancy wine we scavenged!" Hummingbird chimed in.

"Hell yeah!" Quakelord's fist connected with the table and nearly toppled off the candelabra at the center.

My stomach clenched, phantom pain ghosting through me upon seeing the steaming dishes. The memory of my first—and last—mortal meal flooded back, along with the week of searing agony that followed. I gulped, choking back a wave of nausea. I'd been just a curious child then, eager to try what the mixed-breeds enjoyed. Their ability to savor both blood and hard foods had always fascinated me. How could I have known our bodies would reject it so *violently*?

Terraknight neared the table, his leather apron creaking against his flexing muscles. The air thickened with the scent of ripe blackberries and fresh soil—his magic's signature. Flagstones quivered beneath our feet, then rippled like water, and nudged chairs aside.

He set the tray down on the cotton runner, flashing a grin at the overenthusiastic balaurs.

My gaze swept the table.

Quakelord's tongue darted out, wetting his lips. Pearl perched daintily across from Ember, who was already reaching for a glass. Terraknight settled into the corner seat with a satisfied sigh. But one chair remained conspicuously empty—

Gale's feathers tickled my arm as she leaned in close. "He's in his room," she whispered, her breath warm against my ear.

A frisson raced down my back, which I blamed on the crisp night air.

I cleared my throat. "Sel, I need to go over the next shipment with Harbinger. Save me a spot?"

Her eyes narrowed, but she nodded, dragging her feet to the other end of the table.

I turned to leave when Hummingbird called out, "Projector! Join us!"

A sharp smack echoed, followed by Pearl's voice, dripping with innuendo, "Leave her be, wonder-boy. She and Captain are *bee-zee* tonight!"

Everyone was a comedian. I sighed and walked inside, willing myself to ignore the chorus of laughter and exaggerated kissing noises that followed me into the war room. My neck burned, heat spreading to my ears.

I'm just being responsible. The synthetic blood supply is getting low. But even as I thought it, a defiant voice whispered that Terraknight was perfectly capable of handling the guild's cargo demands. I didn't *need* to see the captain for this.

You're being ridiculous. This is strictly business.

The foyer greeted me with shadows, a solitary candle flickering on the coffee table. Peeling gold wallpaper curled at the edges because of water seeping through the walls. I snatched a bottle of blood from the crate, quickly recounting the last three dozen. The commander's delivery was a week overdue. We shouldn't have waited this long.

I gulped it down with a tight stomach, an anxious knot gnawing at me.

Halfway up the creaking stairs, my courage melted away. My heart pounded against my ribs, mocking my feeble excuses for seeing Harbinger.

Liar, it seemed to say. *Liar, liar, liar.*

I paused outside his door, drawing a deep breath.

Who was I fooling? Certainly not myself.

My hand hovered inches from the door when it swung open. Harbinger filled the frame, his broad shoulders blocking the dim light from within.

Liar, liar, liar.

"Projector," he rumbled, his gravelly voice triggering a sudden rush of adrenaline.

I jumped two inches into the air and stumbled back, my heel catching on the loose carpet.

His topaz eyes locked onto mine, unblinking. "Jumpy tonight, aren't we? Or is it just my presence that sets you on edge?"

If I smacked his chest, it would only drive the point home. Instead, I lifted my chin, keeping a firm grip on my voice. "Maybe it's your charm that repulses me. It tends to have that effect."

"Interesting," he mused, leaning against the doorframe. "And yet you stand in the way of Magma Lances without flinching. Curious priorities you have, Projector."

"Some things are worth the risk. My guild's safety, for instance."

"Hmm." His lips quirked into a humorless smile. "I can't figure out if you're really this naïve or you mean it."

"Stick around, and you might figure it out." It was always like this with him. The more he got under my skin, the more my mouth ran.

We stood there, neither willing to break eye contact. I studied his face. Angular, devoid of softness: a firm chin, square jaw, smart amber-yellow eyes under blond eyebrows. My father had taught me to acknowledge my opponents by looking straight into their eyes; they told you the true nature of a person. When I met Harbinger's gaze, I saw a predator—calm on the surface, yet promising violence beneath.

I sensed it the way one killer sensed another. Like calling to like.

He stepped aside, gesturing for me to enter, but I faltered, suddenly questioning the wisdom of putting myself in such close quarters with him. The hallway felt infinitely safer than the confines of his room.

"Well?" he prodded, his tone growing bored. "Are you coming in or not?"

"That depends. Are you planning to behave yourself?

A daring smile spread across his lips. "Do you *want* me to behave myself?"

Oh, sweet darkness. Embers ignited beneath my skin, stirring in my lower abdomen. Fourteen months. That's how long it had been since I'd last shared my bed, my blood, my trust with someone. And now my eager body thrummed with need, responding to this aggravating man as if he were water in a desert. I could hear his blood whispering just beneath his skin. My fangs ached, desperate to break through.

I ground my teeth, forcing myself to remember why this was a terrible idea. For me, casual sex wasn't just an oxymoron—it was a risk. A Blood Pact placed me in a position of vulnerability, and there was nothing casual about that. I'd always sought a level of trust, admiration, a connection deeper than mere physical with the men I slept with.

I knew enough about Harbinger to know I couldn't trust him. Admire him? Perhaps a little. Surviving the Stalkers for this long was no small feat. But that wasn't nearly enough. Especially when his white hair reminded me every second of his ancestry.

Yet here I was, one taste of his blood and one lingering look at his perfect lips, and I was ready to throw caution to the wind. I'd nearly forced us into a Blood Pact, for Derzelas' sake. What was wrong with me?

Swallowing the ball of lust back into the pit of my stomach, I brushed past him into the room, catching the slight hitch in his breath, the momentary tensing of his muscles. I wasn't sure if his reaction came as a response to his hatred, or if our proximity affected him, too.

His room was sparse and utilitarian, smelling of gun oil and him. A wall-to-ceiling bookshelf hugged the wall by the door, filled to the brim with books in different states of deterioration. Faded olive paint bore patches of original floral wallpaper, a shade darker than the tattered curtains framing the barricaded window.

To my right, a double metal bunk bed took almost all the space, strategically positioned under a Rorschach test of water stains. I wondered if Harbinger saw omens in those brown splotches each morning when he went to bed.

A well-worn notebook lay open on the nightstand, dotted with red marks over a basic map drawing. Next to it sat a metal box, glinting in the candlelight. I glimpsed jewelry inside before Harbinger shifted, blocking my view. The thought of him collecting trinkets was jarringly at odds with the ruthless fighter I knew.

"I want to discuss the supply shipment," I said. "Are there any specific details the Commander should know about your needs?"

Harbinger scoffed, moving to his desk with unhurried finesse. He dropped into the chair like it was a throne, regarding me with thinly veiled disdain. "The Republic has nothing we need," he drawled.

I became hyper-aware of every inch between us, of the way the room seemed to shrink around his presence. I could gag at how awkward I felt. "Are you certain? What about reinforcements? You're operating at less than a third of a guild's capacity."

He leaned back in his chair, the old wood protesting beneath him.

My gaze wandered, the traitorous thing that it was, over his form. Harbinger had swapped his 'ready-to-murder-Stalkers' ensemble for something more relaxed: scuffed boots, leather pants that had seen better centuries, and a black shirt with its sleeves torn off. His arms were sculpted, neither overly bulky nor too lean. Just... perfect.

Desiring him probably qualified as a catastrophic lapse in sanity, but at least nobody could fault my taste.

He was all hard edges and rough surfaces. The tableau only lacked a hefty bat or an ax propped against those sturdy thighs as he glowered.

Thick. He was just thick all over.

It got me thinking about what else might be thick, and—oh, blood and ashes! *Aurora Tepes, get your mind out of the gutter.*

"You were saying something?" I quirked an eyebrow at him, aiming for cool detachment. After all, feigned indifference was the best disguise for drooling.

His voice rumbled low and a little rough, as if caught on the edge of a growl. "I said, 'Thank you, Projector, but my answer stands. We are enough as we are.'"

I pinched my lips together, hands clenching at my sides. "Why are you like this?" He knew they needed more people. I knew it. They had a death tally dangling on the front of the house, for pits' sake.

His jaw muscles ticked. "Like what?"

"Are you trying to prove something to me? Because refusing help doesn't strengthen your position."

"Don't flatter yourself, Projector." He leaned forward, resting his elbows on his knees, golden eyes boring into mine. "We don't need reinforcements because we collectively agreed not to bring any more people to this shithole. Does that answer satisfy you?"

His words knocked the wind out of my lungs. Shame seeped through me. I couldn't meet his gaze, couldn't bear to see the aversion I was sure lurked there. How had I misread this so completely?

Without another word, I spun on my heel and fled, not even registering the sound of the door closing behind me as I escaped into the hallway.

Aurora

Selena inched closer, her voice thick with smug delight. "I take it things didn't go as planned with our *dear* Captain?"

I swallowed a sigh. For all her virtues, my best friend had the emotional intelligence of a brick wall. Ever since Harbinger broke the Harmonization in Sibiu, she'd been seething, despite my assurances—and his confession—that he hadn't known the pain it would cause.

Forcing my attention away from her, I focused on Ember's animated storytelling. Her fingers scuttled across the table, mimicking rodents. "And then," she gasped, bottle-green eyes wide, "I saw one *this* big munching on the plaster!"

Groans and bubbly laughter rippled around us. I raised my cup, the metal rim glinting in the flickering light. Above, a crystal chandelier swayed on a rusted hook, painting our faces with kaleidoscopic patterns.

Gale's feathers ruffled as she traced the colorful beams on the tabletop. "Terra outdid himself with this one." She pointed to the porch ceiling. "Who knew he could appreciate anything finer than a well-toned bicep?

Though I suppose his right hook is quite the work of art," she quipped, flexing her arm with an exaggerated grimace.

"Keep this up, Terra," Hummingbird cut in, his tone equally mocking, "and we might start thinking you're more than just muscle and scowls."

"Softie." Quakelord snickered, then wheezed as Terraknight's open palm connected with his sternum.

The vice-captain peered around Pearl, his wink the stuff of any woman's dreams. "Can't have my ladies feeling neglected, now, can I?"

"Oh, how *noble*," Selena drawled with a venomous sweetness. "Such a hero."

His grin sharpened, all teeth and lethal charm. "Always at your service, shortie."

"Y'know," Hummingbird said, leaning forward as if he was about to share a secret, "a couple years back, I saw this meteor shower. Sky lit up like... like someone spilled a whole bucket of stars." His eyes sparkled with innocent glee. "Never seen anythin' like it. Beautiful don't even come close."

"Really?" I gazed at the bottomless night and imagined an upside-down ocean studded with falling jewels. "That many shooting stars?"

Hummingbird nodded, then prodded Phoenix with his chin as he reached for the card deck. She tilted her head, copper curls bouncing, while she deliberated her options.

"I remember that night," Terraknight grunted. "Harbinger and I were buried under Stalker corpses, searching for our friends' bodies while the sky celebrated." His eyes met mine, hard as flint. "Wasn't exactly the romantic evening some might imagine."

Funeral silence blanketed the table.

I studied Terraknight's expression—the tightness around his mouth, the muscle feathering in his jaw—and wondered how many guildmates he'd buried since his conscription. Dozens? Hundreds?

A low hum, like a murmured hiss, whispered through the night air.

Behind Hummingbird, the veil to our reality shimmered and twisted, birthing a fist-sized knot of darkness that crackled with a miniature thunderstorm. It grew wide, wider, until it devoured the crackling campfire and a good portion of the old oak. The aroma of roasted coffee and delicate roses—Harbinger's essence—intensified, flooding my senses.

I gulped down my HemaTech-9, desperate to relieve the itch in my gums.

His original heritage explained the magnetic pull I felt toward him. Among common purebloods, fresh blood addiction often bred possessiveness and danger—hence the Republic's draconian feeding laws. Bloodletting bars catered to those who acknowledged their cravings, a stopgap against the torment of perpetual hunger.

But I was neither common nor weak.

Yet... Harbinger's undiluted blood lured me in with a seductive melody of power and long-lasting satiation. Rich with his mother's legacy and spiced with varcolac genetic makeup, it promised a flavor so intoxicating, so potent, it made me ache with longing. A life without another drop led my thoughts into dark places.

Harbinger emerged from the portal, his snow-kissed hair windswept as if he'd battled a tempest. He settled onto the log by the fire, a leather-bound tome sprawling across his thighs. The firelight softened his features, melting away the ever-present tension in his jaw.

It was like glimpsing an alternate version of him—unburdened by the constant threat of death, with no one to impress or command. Just him and his book, tired yet at peace, stealing a few precious moments of respite.

And incredibly erotic.

Wait, what? That last thought came out of nowhere. Must be Hummingbird's breathtakingly romantic meteor shower getting to me. Had to be.

"On the bright side," Terraknight drawled, draping his arms over Quakelord and Pearl's backrests, "I figured if those stars were the last thing I saw before a Stalker ripped out my throat, at least I'd die with a view. Meteor showers, what are they—once a century? Doubt I'll live to see another."

Ember rose on silent feet, her blonde brows furrowed in concentration as she loaded a plate. Moonlight caught her blush as she approached Harbinger, hips swaying beneath her oversized dress.

A sudden, sharp pang of jealousy caught me off guard, its intensity almost dizzying.

Harbinger accepted the plate with a distracted nod, his attention never leaving his book. Ember settled beside him, drinking in his profile as if it were the most fascinating sight in the world.

I wrenched my attention back to Terraknight and ignored the discomfort in my chest. He wasn't mine.

"That's…" I fumbled for words, suddenly aware of how trivial my annoyance with Elena's dinner summonses seemed in comparison. "I'm sorry. I can't even begin to imagine—"

"Can't see the stars over there?" Hummingbird asked, gesturing south.

I shook my head, but Selena answered before me. "City lights. They never dim."

"Huh." He nodded. "It's pitch-black here. Few people, mostly candles. It's nice, I s'pose. Great for stargazing—one of the few perks of this place."

I choked on my breath. An outlier had just called the battlefront 'nice.'

"The sky here," Harbinger broke the quiet. "Reminds me of the Republic's fireworks. Are they still doing that?"

"Yes! They are. On the Fateless Festival. Do you remember it?"

He turned a page, the whisper of paper loud in the hush. "I remember the lights in the sky. The fountain at the base of some towering building. It was loud. Crowded."

My eyes widened. "That's Corvin Palace! Did you live in the First Ward, Harbinger?"

The First Ward had a rich history as an affluent neighborhood with venerable noble houses. It made sense for Harbinger to have lived there, given his mother's bloodline and Russkayan ties. I could almost see a young, silver-haired boy there, shielded from the struggles of the lower wards where mixed-breeds often lived. The Republic wouldn't have allowed his father to glimpse our nation's less polished facets.

After all, ignorance in our enemies was a weapon in our arsenal.

"It's been a long time," Harbinger said, staring into the popping logs. "But yeah, probably. With my family. I remember Ma taking me to watch the fireworks on a wide balcony."

I winced, realizing the minefield I'd stumbled into. "I'm sorry."

His eyes darted to me, amber flashing crimson. "What for?"

"I didn't mean to pry."

He shrugged. "It's fine. I can hardly remember it anyway." But the tension in his shoulders told a different story.

Dread swept over me like a lawn roller. I met their gazes one by one, each hard stare adding weight to the question swirling in my thoughts.

Pushing words out was like trying to carry a boulder the size of a house up a mountain. "Do you... resent us?"

"A, don't go there," Selena hissed a warning.

Phoenix and Hummingbird traded loaded glances over their cards. Gale's wings twitched, her eyes suddenly fascinated by the used napkin on her plate. The rook in Pearl's hand trembled, suspended over her chess game with Terraknight.

Their silence was answer enough for me.

It was Quakelord who spoke first, his voice surprisingly measured. "Being treated like dirt? It sucks. Those camps were hell, and every battle here..." He shook his head. "Yeah, I hate the purebloods with all my being. Who made them gods to decide we are disposable just 'cause we're not immortal?"

I moved to speak, ready to tell him that not everyone shared this view, but snapped my mouth closed. Platitudes wouldn't change their reality. Only power would.

"But," he continued, assessing me with sharp, hard eyes, "not all purebloods are monsters. Just like not all halfbloods are saints. Hell, my own people gave me grief for my slanted eyes in the camps."

Gale's low growl startled me. "Being an iele was no picnic either. Wings made us easy targets." Her gaze flicked to Hummingbird. "World's cruel to anyone different, pureblood or not."

"Point is," Quakelord added, "we know there are good purebloods. So no, we don't resent you for who you are."

The anxiety in my chest loosened. "Your experiences are valid, and your anger is justified." I straightened, channeling Miss Harambea's etiquette lessons. "I can't undo the past, but I can change the future. I will fight to create a world where no one faces such discrimination, pureblood or mixed-breed alike."

The quiet that followed was different—less hostile, tinged with a hint of respect. I'd meant every word. I hoped I could prove it to them.

"I've got a question for you, too." Terraknight lounged back, his eyes fixed on me. "How come *you* aren't resenting us? I haven't met a projector yet who doesn't loathe our bones."

"Resenting you would be... hypocritical," I said, weighing each word on my tongue. "And short-sighted. My views on mixed-breeds shifted long ago..." I took a deep breath, letting it out slowly. "Ever since an outlier saved my life."

I deliberately omitted any mention of his nature, wary of giving Harbinger any more information if he proved to be a Russkayan spy.

Bodies tensed and leaned in. Even Harbinger gave up on his book, his attention snapping to me with sudden interest. I could feel Selena's worried gaze drilling a hole into the side of my head. I'd never spoken it out loud before.

"I don't know what became of him," I continued. "But when I asked why he didn't let me die, he said something that has stayed with me ever since."

Selena clicked her tongue in disappointment. We didn't keep secrets, she and I, but this... Some truths were too personal to share, even with her. Knowledge of a varcolac could have put her in danger, and I convinced myself that withholding the information was the lesser evil. It was better for her to remain ignorant of his existence. At least, that's what I told myself to ease the guilt that had been eating at my conscience. Now, I only hoped she'd forgive me.

Hummingbird propped his chin on his fist, rattling the cutlery. "What did he say?"

I closed my eyes, battling the tide of memories. "He told me, *'We're Republic citizens, born and raised. But people have forgotten that, so we must prove ourselves. We fight and protect to show our commitment, so they can never again—"*

Harbinger shot to his feet, his book hitting the ground with a thunderous thump. The scowl on his face promised murder, his eyes beginning to glow with the beast inside of him. Fear punched straight into my chest, but I held my chin high and refused to cower.

"—claim we're undeserving of citizenship," I finished, a little louder than a breath.

I could see the effects of my words on him—surprise, skepticism, and perhaps, just perhaps, a flicker of hope.

Shock rippled through the outliers, a wave of gasps and widened eyes. But it was Harbinger's reaction, not my savior's declaration, that had stunned them. Only Terraknight maintained a facade of calm, betrayed by the wine trembling in his unsteady hand.

My mind raced.

Harbinger had known the varcolac. Closely, if his rage was any indication. Was it the words themselves, or the underlying sense of justice that had struck such a nerve?

"Instead of letting me perish, he gave me a second chance." I stood up, just in case I needed to defend myself. Or run away. "Those words became my guiding light, my purpose. Our differences once made the Republic great. It's everyone's responsibility to protect their homeland. And I intend to honor that duty, whatever the cost."

The glow in Harbinger's eyes dimmed, crimson bleeding into amber. When he finally spoke, his voice was rusty, as though he hadn't used it in years. "Pretty words, Projector. We'll see if you back them up."

"I intend to," I said, hoping no one noticed the rapid drumming of my heart.

Hummingbird piped up, his voice light but probing. "Say, Projector Tepes, you're a bit of an idealist, aren't you?"

Selena snorted, nearly choking on her drink. "Oh, she's definitely one of those."

"An idealist in the Black Guild? Now I've seen everything!" Quakelord put his head down on the table, his shoulders jerking.

I felt a hot flush traveling up my neck. Harbinger's solid frown cracked, a wisp of a smirk tugging at his mouth. Pearl caught my eye, mouthing a sympathetic 'sorry' as she tried to stifle her giggles.

My forehead wrinkled. "Is he choking?" I asked, nodding at Quakelord.

"No, he just needs a moment," Terraknight said. "He's young. Easily excitable."

I straightened my posture. "And what if I am... an idealist?"

Hummingbird held up his hands. "No offense meant. It's... well, the Tenth Ward has a way of shattering illusions."

Quakelord rose in his chair, his tone turning serious. "Look, you're not a bad person, Projector. But this job? It's not what you think it is. We're not fighting for some noble cause."

"Quakelord..." Harbinger's low growl held a note of warning.

The earth-mover shrugged, unfazed. "I'm just saying, maybe you should reconsider before you get in too deep. Switch with someone else before you end up regretting it."

"I appreciate your concern," I deadpanned. "But I'm not here by accident or mistake. I know exactly what I'm doing, and I'd prefer not to discuss my motivations further."

Harbinger's eyes narrowed, studying me with renewed interest. "Do you now, Projector? We'll see about that, too."

Aurora

I GRIPPED THE WINDOWSILL, the worn stone rough beneath my gloves. My fingers trembled, and I squeezed harder, willing the shaking to stop.

Seventy-six hours without synthetic blood.

Eyes closed, I inhaled from my stomach up to my chest and held the night air in. *I can manage this. I've gone days without blood before.*

But never this many. Never when it mattered so much. Never when every day pushed my body to new limits.

And Selena...

A pang of worry tightened my insides as I pictured her alone at home, curled up on the floor, fighting her own battle against the hunger. Or was this twisting sensation just my own craving? The two were becoming harder to distinguish.

I flexed my hands, and the leather creaked unnaturally loud in the quiet tower. My arms ached from the strain of holding on so tightly, but I couldn't bring myself to let go. That windowsill was my anchor to reality, to control.

"Projector Tepes to Black Guild," I called, extending my Blood Manipulation to its limits. "Enemies approach from the northeast."

A searing cramp ripped through my stomach.

I bit back a groan, breathing through set jaws. *Waves. Just waves. They'll pass.* But the vexing voice of reason whispered, *Until they don't.*

The madness would come, and the hit would be catastrophic.

Moonlight spilled across the stone floor, drawing long, writhing shadows on the walls. On any other night, I might have appreciated the view—the star-speckled sky, the crescent moon. It was a perfect moon, the kind that inspired terrible love songs. Now, it only made me more aware of the passing time—and the outliers that moved below.

My eyes clawed at the inky sky, but each shadow mocked me, withering my hope. The vast darkness swallowed my silent screams. *Where is that damn shipment?* Dread pooled in my gut, cold and heavy.

Terraknight had sent my letter to Commander Enescu two weeks ago. Surely, my godfather knew we'd be out of HemaTech-9 by now.

My heart raced, pumping the last dregs of synthetic blood through my system. *What if it never comes? What if Selena and I lose control?*

What the hell would I tell Harbinger when the bloodlust kicked in?

It was too late to send us away now. I might last another day, two if I isolate myself, but Selena... She'd hunt them down, and I'd be too weak to stop her.

They'll have to kill us.

The thought turned my legs to jelly, but part of me welcomed it. Better that than becoming the monster Lev and Elena tried to make me.

I forced myself to take another deep breath, tasting the breeze on my tongue. *Focus on the mission. Just get through tonight.*

"The enemy's primary force is a mix of Ignises and Nebulas," I continued, relieved as my voice held steady. "With a Limus and Glacies company on their—"

"I've confirmed their location, Projector," Harbinger cut in, his voice sharp through the Harmonization. *"We're ready to intercept them at point ninety-seven. Focus on monitoring the perimeter."*

My anxiety vanished, replaced by a hot flash of irritation. My fangs ached, desperate to extend. I breathed slowly through my nose, willing my hammering heart to slow. *Don't snap. Don't let him see how much the hunger is affecting you.*

But all I could think about was how quickly I could sink my fangs into his neck. The image was so vivid—the warmth of his skin, the rush of his blood—that I had to physically shake it away.

"Cap, Ember's in position," Terraknight's voice thundered through our link. My head throbbed as if goldminers were digging inside my skull with pickaxes.

"Pearl to Harbinger, I'm ready."

I leaned against the window, waiting for the others to take their positions. Fourteen hundred yards stretched between me and the Black Guild. A safe distance. Enough time for them to run if... if the worst happened.

My gaze darted from the decaying staircase at my side to the gap in the wall. A tight squeeze, but a potential escape route if the Glacies snuffed me out and flew up the shaft.

Another spasm hit, bending me over in pain. I pressed my forehead against the cool stone jamb, waiting for it to pass.

Outside, Bethlen Fortress sprawled beneath a cobalt sky. Its red roofline zigzagged like a drunken serpent, drawing my attention to the haphazard stack of three towering stories. Ornate cornices, wrought iron balustrades, porticos, and battlements swam before my vision in a dizzying blend of Victorian and Wallachian Renaissance. I blinked hard, trying to focus, but it all blurred into a nightmare of brick and stone.

A flicker of movement caught my eye.

Dark shadows swarmed the Transylvanian hills, flooding the narrow cobblestone streets like a plague of locusts.

My knees buckled, and I clung to the windowsill to stay upright. "Harbinger," I called, pulling up Sighisoara's old map on my Visor. "Have Ember change her location. Post her at three o'clock, two hundred yards from her current position."

The Harmonization crackled with dead air. Harbinger's silence pressed heavily on my already frayed nerves. Just as I was sure he was ignoring me, his hoarse voice broke through.

"We'll confirm the location... Ember, can you see that point?"

"I'll check—give me ten seconds." Ember's voice was tense. *"Yeah, I can see it. Moving over there now."*

"The new position has higher ground and is opposite Pearl," I explained. "They'll both serve as vanguard. Ember will deceive the Stalkers in the early phases before you split up into individual confrontations."

Terraknight chuckled. *"So she'll be the bait. Princess, you've got guts for such a pretty voice."*

"Nebulas and Ignises can't attack on elevated terrain." Another cramp twisted my insides. I breathed in and out, exhaling anguish. "Once she's up there, they shouldn't be able to reach her. If they change positions, the bank will provide cover—"

"Don't get me wrong. It's a good plan. Ain't that right, Ember?"

To Terraknight, she answered eagerly, *"I'll do anything to help."* But when she addressed me, her tone turned sharp. *"Did you find a new map or something? Must be convenient."*

I fought to keep my voice neutral. "It's the map the Republic's ground forces detailed at the war's outset. Want me to share it with you *later*?"

If we both survive this night. If the hunger doesn't consume me first.

I glanced down the stairwell again, gouging the distance to the ground. Fourteen hundred yards had seemed like such a safe buffer when I chose this position. Now, with their glowing blue threads stretching in my mind, each one screaming *prey*, I wasn't so sure.

Terraknight tsked. *"Sure you wanna do that? You'd be divulging military secrets to traitors."*

This time, I didn't hide my frustration. "What's the point of having this information if we don't use it?"

I'd unearthed the map from a dusty cardboard box in the Archives. How confidential could it be if no one had bothered to file it?

"Also, you are not traitors," I rebuked. "If nothing else, I've never seen you that way."

"Yeah, yeah—" Terraknight's reply was cut short. *"Shit. They're coming."*

A feral roar split the night, shaking the tower to its foundations.

I staggered, my boots catching on the uneven stone. My fight-or-flight response kicked in, pumping adrenaline through my veins. Every nerve howled at me to run, to abandon this rundown deathtrap while my legs could still carry me.

I closed my eyes and reached out with my magic. The ties to Terraknight and Harbinger stretched taut, a tangled web of blue lightning. Their movements came in flashes—dodge, strike, retreat—a frenzied dance against the encroaching Stalkers.

"Open Transpectre via Harbinger," I hissed through gritted teeth.

Pain exploded behind my eyes. Harbinger moved in a blur, too fast for me to follow. Cursing, I shifted Transpection to the others.

A mile to the east, a blinding flash lit up the sky, and heat seared the air as an Ignis hurled a Magma Lance across the city. The tower swayed. Chunks of masonry crashed around me.

I lurched. The window provided cover.

To the north, the Black Guild's elemental fury tore through the streets. Buildings crumbled like sandcastles. Twin tornadoes ground against each other, clearing the mushroom of dust and smoke.

The battle moved into Citadel Park—a place once a modest grove now sprawling over fifteen hundred acres. Water jets arced over rooftops, flooding the roads, and fractured the Stalkers into smaller groups. Fire lanced between trees, igniting canopies like candle flames.

Another bestial roar, closer this time.

Ice shot through my veins. I didn't consider myself a coward. Out of millions of purebloods, I was the second-longest survivor in the conscription zone—or third, counting Selena first. But this...

Desperate for a clearer view, I latched onto Phoenix's perspective. Moonlight filtered through freshly budded leaves, illuminating her hand as she pricked her finger with the point of her sharp blade. A single drop of blood welled up.

My world went red.

Saliva pooled in my mouth. My fangs dropped, razor-sharp and aching.

No, no, no, no.

I doubled over, my left hand tightly pressed against my mouth, the right one scrabbling at the stone wall for support. The hunger roared louder than any beast outside, threatening to take over my senses, my duty, my very self.

I screamed internally. *They need you. You can't give in. Not now.*

Phantom scents of cedarwood and toasted marshmallows—Phoenix's smell—tricked my nose.

My stomach gnawed. I jerked my head, trying to clear the hallucination, but my grip on reality slipped by the second.

Through Phoenix's eyes, I saw the forest transform into a deadly maze. The Limus' sand magic infested every shadow, turning the terrain treacherous. A deafening crack split the air, and my heart soared into my throat. A massive blue spruce hurtled through the mist, straight at Phoenix.

Her pulse spiked, and mine raced to match it. *Move.*

Phoenix twisted, the massive trunk missing her by inches. She rolled to her feet in one fluid motion, fire igniting in her veins. Her hand slashed through the air and sketched a foot-wide archway. A perfect, pulsing sphere of blue energy bloomed from the sparks dancing on her fingertips.

One heartbeat. Two. Three.

The sphere erupted, unfurling into a spiral of green-blue flames.

Wow. *So that's Blazeorb.*

An anguished cry pierced the mist—she hit the Nebula that had attacked her.

Phoenix bolted, weaving between gnarled trees, thorns tearing at her clothes. Each stray thorn that almost pierced her skin made me flinch.

Ahead, moonlight painted a small clearing silver. It beckoned like a beacon of hope, but in this situation, open spaces meant vulnerability.

I studied the map on my Visor, searching for another route for her to join the others, when the holo-screen blared in alarm. Two Ignises were closing in, but she couldn't see them through the fog.

"Get away from there, Phoenix!" I shouted, already vaulting over the rotten banister and plunging into the dark maw of the stairwell.

Wind whipped my face, the ground rushing up to meet me. Floors blurred past. My stomach rolled from hunger and vertigo. I tried to angle my body, but my limbs felt leaden, unresponsive. Normally, I'd land this with flying colors.

But not today. Not with my blood level running so low.

I hit hard, my right leg twisting with a vomit-inducing crack. White-hot agony exploded through my knee and robbed my lungs of their air. The world darkened, dissolving into a sea of bright, tiny stars.

I clamped my jaw shut, swallowing a scream. Through the haze of tears, I forced my attention back to Phoenix through our link. The scene on the holo-screen sharpened with horrifying clarity.

Where the map had shown solid ground, Phoenix now thrashed in a boggy mire. Murky water lapped at her thighs, rising with each desperate movement. Her hands scrabbled at the sodden earth, grasping for roots or stones—anything to halt her slow descent.

Mashing my teeth together, I popped my knee back and staggered to my feet. I burst from the tower, stumbling on weak legs. Every step was torture. My muscles screamed for blood I couldn't provide.

I moved on momentum and terror, catching myself against a tree, bark cutting into my shoulder. "Dammit!" I snarled and pushed off.

I'd always healed fast, so this... this bone-deep weakness was new. Terrifying. For the first time, I truly feared I might not make it before sunrise.

But Phoenix needed me. So, I ran, cursing my frailty with every faltering step.

In front of her, a mound of reeds erupted in billowing steam. Dirt and vegetation sloughed off like melting wax, revealing nightmare made flesh. Twin behemoths rose, their steel-gray skin pulsing with inner fire. Twisted horns, glowing orange at the tips, curved from massive skulls.

Four eyes, bright as molten metal, locked onto Phoenix—onto me.

Phoenix's terror slammed through our connection, so raw it nearly brought me down. I watched, helpless, as she lashed out with her magic. Unearthly shrieks filled the air as the Ignises recoiled. But the balaur's power faltered. Steam dissipated. And she fell back with a splash, sinking faster.

A horrible growl shook the forest. *Harbinger.* "Phoenix!"

The hair on my nape stood up. A dry-stone wall materialized out of nowhere. I dove through, sharp edges slicing my arms. The blood loss slowed me, but desperation drove me on. Downhill, my legs found new speed.

I leaped the Small Tarnava Creek, my lungs burning as I charged uphill toward the forest. Dread squeezed my stomach. My pulse echoed in my ears. As erratic and fast as any mortal's.

Phoenix yelled, defeated, *"I can't get out! I'm scared!"*

I'm coming. Just hold on.

The Ignis's twisted face contorted, its black tongue flicking out. Beside it, its twin's eyes flared as lava bubbled up in its maw, blazing like a captured sun.

"No…" her cry reached me now. "I don't want to die."

Something snapped inside me. I crashed to my knees at the glade's edge, unleashing my magic with a savage roar. Every inch of me screamed as I poured what little energy I had left into the assault. Darkness edged my vision, my skin on fire as if someone flayed me open, vein by vein, layer by layer.

I hissed through the agony and slammed my consciousness into the Ignises' hollow minds. I seized their putrid blood, commanding it to burst.

Rotten gore erupted from their eyes, their howls fracturing the night. Magma balls dissolved in their throats.

I screamed louder, clenching my splitting head between my hands. Every drop of their blood I spilled tore another piece of me apart.

Phoenix dragged herself from the marsh inch by inch, mud masking her freckles. Her clear, drift-glass green eyes widened in terror, fixed on something behind me.

A twig snapped—too close. Every instinct begged me to turn, but I couldn't risk losing my grip on the Ignises. One moment's lapse and Phoenix would die.

I should have looked. Should have prepared.

Tree-trunk arms crushed my middle. Ribs snapped like sticks.

The Nebula yanked me back, its roar deafening in my ear. My hold on the Ignises vanished as I clawed at the oozing limbs, desperate to break free. It squeezed harder, trying to pull me into its putrid body. Acidic drool stretched from its maw, sizzling on the ground and coating me. Burned grass and rotting flesh assaulted my nose.

I clung to awareness even as the world began to dim. My muscles quivered, fighting its grip. More bones crunched. Agony, with a capital A, coiled around my spine. I couldn't breathe, couldn't think, couldn't fight.

The Ignises summoned their magic. Two massive magma balls hurtled toward Phoenix.

I called her name, but nothing came out.

She neutralized the first one with a Blazeorb. The second struck her square in the chest. She flew back, spine cracking against a tree before she slumped to the ground.

Our connection went silent.

Harbinger roared, and the sound shook the forest. Grief and thunder rolled and combined, nearly bursting my eardrums as my hearing threatened to fail me next.

"Phoenix…? Damn it!"

"Harbinger, I'm going to retrieve her. Buy me a minute—"

"Don't, Pearl… They're using her body as a decoy. It's an ambush."

The voices hammered in my skull. Tears or Nebula saliva streaked my face—I couldn't tell which. Waves of crushing pressure pulsed through my body.

I screamed until my throat was raw, my awareness fracturing like glass under a hammer blow.

I'd never truly hated my immortal lineage until now. We might be hard to kill, but we weren't immune to pain. And this... this was beyond endurance.

A pool of crimson spread beneath me. Even with blood, recovery would take a whole day. A day I didn't have, with sunrise mere hours away.

The Nebula's grip tightened, grinding my shattered bones. I had no strength left to scream. Darkness beckoned, promising sweet oblivion.

I tried to swallow, but it hurt too much, and I gave up. Just let me pass out already. My head felt impossibly heavy, as if someone had filled it with rocks.

"Aurora!" a voice called. Familiar, but I couldn't place it. Couldn't think. Couldn't...

The Nebula twisted, and something in my spine shattered with a sound like splintering ice. The pain vanished. My body numbed, weightless.

Darkness rushed in, thick—suffocating.

Phoenix... I'm sorry. I-I tried...

Then, nothing.

AURORA

SOFT FOOTSTEPS PADDED ACROSS the floor. A wooden slat creaked—a sound so faint it could have been my imagination. Someone was in my room.

I willed my pulse to slow down and feigned sleep.

Close. Closer. Fabric rustled—he was reaching for me. My muscles flexed beneath the comforter, ready to react.

Now!

I catapulted, sheets flying as I lashed my leg out in a vicious strike. It connected with a solid mass, and a distinctly male grunt rewarded my efforts.

He went down.

I vaulted off the bed, fingers already grasping for my needles on the nightstand.

Empty. Damn it.

Panic flared, sharp and acrid in my throat as I dropped to my knees and scanned the shadowy floor. A glint caught my eye—there, on the far side of the bed. The bastard must have tossed them on his way down.

I crawled, but warm fingers clamped around my ankle. He yanked me backward, and I twisted, kicking out with every ounce of strength I could muster. I felt fuzzy, weak. My heel hammered his shoulder, and in the flickering candlelight, I caught a glimpse of familiar citron eyes.

"Harbinger!" I gasped.

What...? My head spun. I'd thought Lev Wurdulak was sneaking up into my room, finishing off what he'd started.

That split-second cost me. Harbinger dove at me. A wall of heat and muscle. The rush of blood in his veins became my whole world as he slapped my fists aside and pinned me to the floor. We wrestled for a hot second, the rough wooden boards scraping against my back. Then his legs trapped mine, and he leaned over, securing my right wrist above my head while my left arm pressed between us, against my sternum. He wrapped me up like a pretzel.

"Good morning, princess," he rumbled, his hot breath brushing my cheek.

A shudder zipped through me—two parts hunger, one part lust, and the rest frustration with myself. I hated how my body betrayed me, craving him even as my mind screamed danger. The impact of all that masculinity should have waned by now. I should have developed immunity. Yet, here I was, once again, taken aback by the little golden feathers swirling around his pupils.

Harbinger tightened his grip, making the carved biceps in his arm bulge. I clearly recalled those iron-hard muscles flexing as he lifted me by my throat.

I squirmed beneath him, but it was like fighting a steel trap. "Funny," I growled, "I don't recall ordering a wake-up call."

His lips quirked, revealing a hint of fang; he seemed pleased with himself. "Consider it a complimentary service."

"Well, consider me serviced. You can let go now."

"Hmm," he mused, not budging an inch. "And miss out on all this quality time?"

"Let me go and I promised not to stab you."

He chuckled, a low vibration I felt coursing through my bones. "Such a tempting offer. But I think I'll stay right here. The view's quite nice."

Exhaustion weighed on me, the crushing hunger in my gut making it worse. I couldn't out-muscle him, but a reckless part of me relished this proximity.

"What are you really doing here, Harbinger?"

His expression hardened, the cocky grin fading. "Checking up on you. Can't have you making any... unfortunate decisions while your hunger's still fresh."

"How gallant," I muttered. "And here I thought you'd just come for the sparkling conversation and—"

My stomach chose that moment to unleash an embarrassingly loud growl. Reality came crashing down; memories of the night before flooded back with nauseating clarity. The bloodlust ravaging my body, the putrid smell of the Nebula shattering my bones, Phoenix's limp body crumpling to the ground. A heaviness seeped into my chest, and my spine turned to wet cotton.

The guilt I'd buried deep within me erupted like a volcano. Every regret—fleeing the Republic, abandoning my coven—every worry and pain I'd meticulously locked away so I could function... It all swelled into a crushing pressure.

Phoenix's final plea echoed in my mind, shattering what little composure I had left. *'I don't want to die.'*

My vision blurred, crimson haze bleeding into tears. Grief and hunger twisted together, awakening the monster lurking beneath my skin. I fought to contain it, muscles trembling with the effort, but it was like trying to hold back the ocean with my bare hands.

Then Harbinger's scent hit me—roasted coffee beans and roses and something uniquely him. A flash of memory: his arms around me, keeping me safe as the world fell apart. It was the final crack in my defenses.

The floodgates burst open and drowned me.

My fangs descended with a painful snap. Every muscle in my body went rigid, my scalp prickling as if each individual hair stood on end. I could *feel* the change overtaking me, black veins creeping out from my hairline, spider-webbing across my face.

The monster was winning, and I was powerless to stop it.

"Fuck. This is what I was afraid of." Harbinger's hushed growl vibrated through me. His amber eyes darkened, a flicker of something—concern?—passing over his face. "Let it out, princess. I'm here. I won't let you hurt anyone."

But the remorse was stronger than the bloodlust, ripping me apart from the inside. A sob ripped from my throat, raw and fractured. "I had them... The Ignises were under my control. I thought... I thought..."

My heart thudded against my ribs, battering me with pain. I couldn't tell where the hurt originated anymore—my chest, my gut. Everywhere ached. I craved release, but my eyes remained stubbornly dry, the pressure building and building with nowhere to go.

Shivering despite the heat radiating from Harbinger's body, I clamped my jaw to keep my teeth from chattering. The dagger point of a fang caught my bottom lip, and the metallic tang of blood flooded my mouth.

Harbinger shifted, and his face came into sharp focus.

Our stares collided. I saw my own hunger reflected in his scarlet-rimmed irises. It would take a dead woman not to respond to that, and I wasn't dead. He'd saved me. Sliced through the Nebula, cradled me in his arms as my consciousness had slipped away.

His body pressed against mine, impossibly hard, hard thighs pinning me in place. The slightest movement would bring us even closer, dangerously so.

My senses heightened to a painful degree, aware of every point where we touched. "You shouldn't be here," I whispered, blinking away the red haze in my vision. He was too close, too warm, smelling delicious. "Why risk yourself when you know I'm on the edge?"

"Mmm." His gaze roamed my face, lingering on my eyes before drifting to my lips. It made my skin tingle. "Are you hungry? The blood I shared... it should have healed the worst of it."

His hold loosened.

I lay limp, caught between the urge to flee and the growing desire to draw him closer, to lose myself in him and escape the weight of my conscience, if only for a moment.

Hunger wore me down, but Harbinger's face was a map of exhaustion and sorrow. I swallowed hard. "I'm fine. Thank you."

His eyes narrowed. "Lying to me is a problem, princess. Bottling things up makes you easy prey."

"Oh? You've got me all figured out, then?"

"I understand your motivations. It's your methods that piss me off." His jaw clenched. "Throwing yourself into danger won't help anyone."

A band tightened around my chest. If I'd found that marsh sooner, I could have warned Phoenix. She wouldn't have gone to that glade alone. I could've saved her.

"I assure you, your feelings keep me up during the day," I retorted.

A sound between a laugh and a growl rumbled in his throat. "Provoking me won't work. Why were you there alone, without backup?"

If he knew how close I'd been to bloodlust... How it'd weakened me. I needed to change the subject. Fast.

"I work better alone. Like you. Or is stalking me a team sport now?"

"I'm not stalking—"

"What do you call this, then?" I glanced pointedly at our compromising position.

"Restraining a potentially dangerous opponent."

"Right. Did you take a good peek while changing me?"

Disbelief flashed across his face, followed by indignation. "For your information, Miss Popescu changed you. She insisted on making you more... comfortable." His gaze flickered downward for a fleeting second before snapping back to my face, a muscle twitching in his jaw.

Selena. Worry crystallized into a hard, cold knot in my stomach.

The need to know she was alright blinded me. I wrenched my arm free and slammed my elbow into his solar plexus.

He gasped, eyes widening in surprise.

I threw my weight to the side, twisting my hips, and landed on top. My knees pinned his arms, my forearm pressed firmly against his throat.

"*Where* is she?" I demanded. "Where's Selena?"

"Safe. Terraknight's been with her since we returned."

"The *vice-captain*, Terraknight?" Eloquence, thy name is Aurora.

A grin spread across his face, revealing those infuriatingly perfect dimples. "Seems she doesn't mind the *boy* after all."

Oh.

He adjusted to the new position, gold flashing in his eyes. "She suggested I give you small amounts of my blood, then let you feed until you're satisfied."

Harsh fabric scrapped against my thighs, and I glanced down. No. I was straddling Harbinger in nothing but a flimsy nightgown, the gossamer-thin material covering absolutely nothing. Completely bare underneath. *I'm going to kill Selena.*

His smirk was pure sin. "We haven't gotten to the last part yet, have we, princess?"

Without warning, he jerked his arms out from under my knees, pulled me to him, uncaring of my elbow crashing into his windpipe, and pressed his blood-coated lips against mine.

Harbinger's blood hit my tongue—intoxicating, undeniably original, spiced with varcolac.

The universe imploded. Stars rained down on my skin and obscured my vision.

A cramp wrenched my insides like a gasoline-drenched towel wrung out and set ablaze. I flicked my tongue, brushing his lips. My head swam.

Drunk on his taste and scent, I sank against him, seduced by the hard planes of his body. Every point of contact sent sparks skittering across my skin.

More.

"No!" Panic cut through the craving. I shoved against his chest, my palms burning with the touch. He held on a moment too long, his fingers digging into my hips before releasing me with a low, hungry growl.

I scrambled away, unsteady on my feet. "Are you insane? Flashing your blood at me like that?"

"You need to feed," he said, matter of fact.

"Get out."

He gave a dramatic sigh and leaped to his feet without the help of his hands. The candlelight caught the hard contours of his face, throwing shadows that accentuated his sharp cheekbones and the curve of his mouth. *His sweet, sweet mouth...*

I stumbled backward until my thighs hit the vanity. Pain throbbed through every inch of me—my throat, head, even my teeth. The room tilted and swayed, as if I were on the deck of a storm-tossed ship. It felt like someone had replaced my brain with molten lead, and now it sloshed and clanged in my skull.

Harbinger cornered the bed, looking sinfully tempting with his lips stained a deep red. The amber in his eyes blazed.

I pressed the heels of my hands against my eyes, trying to push away the bone-deep fatigue and the overwhelming urge to give in.

Despite it all, I craved him—to bite into his flesh, to run my hands over his body, to feel his mouth on mine.

No.

No biting. No touching. No. Just *no*.

I pointed to the door, my arm trembling. "Leave." *Before I lose control.*

Harbinger ignored me. "After your injuries, and not feeding for days? You must be dying to sink your fangs into a throat." He tilted his head, exposing the strong column of his neck. "Take what you need, princess. I don't mind."

The way he looked at me as if I were the most important person in the world, would have weakened even the staunchest priestess in the knees. My rational side wavered, but primal instinct won. I lunged, slamming the vanity into the wall. The mirror cracked. Dozens of ceramic figurines took flight and shattered on the floor.

Harbinger caught me in his arms. His strong hands gripped my thighs and hoisted me up.

My fangs pierced golden skin, and he groaned—a deep, vibrating note that resonated straight to my core. I wrapped my legs around his waist, molding myself against his solid frame.

The world narrowed to a singular focus—nothing existed beyond the irresistible flow of his blood.

He carried us to the bed, the ancient springs protesting as he sat, me straddling his lap. His life-essence coursed through my veins, staunching the ravenous hunger and warming me in all the right places. Even if I wanted to stop—and by the stars, I didn't—I couldn't now.

I circled my arms around his neck, pushing my pebbled nipples against his chest. The hard muscles of his back bunched under my fingers.

More. I needed more.

I kissed his throat, his jaw, nipping his earlobe and licking at the sensitive spot just underneath. I savored the saltiness of his sweat and the sharp touch of stubble on my lips.

I bit him again, this time in the nook of his shoulder.

He made a quiet, masculine noise—half-growl, half-purr.

Oh, my God. His hands roamed my back, leaving trails of fire in their wake, drawing me closer until I felt the hard length of him pressed against me.

Oh yes.

"Aurora." The husky timbre of his voice sent shivers cascading down my spine. He nuzzled my neck, his fangs scrapping the skin before he stilled. "If you don't stop, I won't be able to control myself any longer. I don't want to hurt you."

That did it.

My mind snapped into focus and pushed me through the fog of hunger and desire with an ice-cold hand. It shoved me past the brink of mindless want and back into the land of good judgment.

I froze, conscious of my nightgown bunched around my hips, my breasts pressed to his chest. A wave of pure lava rushed through me as I eased back, slowly uncurling my arms from his neck.

"You wouldn't... hurt me," I croaked, and meant it.

It wasn't lost on me how naturally I trusted him with this. I didn't think I would long for a man's bite, but he made me feel safe against everything that went between us. He'd hurt me, and I was pretty sure he hated me. Despite that, Harbinger had saved my life when he could've just let me die. It would've been so easy for him to let me die.

"I'm sorry," I sputtered. "I got carried away."

Golden eyes... I looked into those eyes and saw little ruby fragments twirling in their depths. The ring around his irises glowed a bright crimson. And my heart made a little jump.

I'm in so much trouble.

I shifted, trying to cover myself, but the movement only caused more friction.

A deep grunt stirred in his chest. His eyes hooded, and for a heartbeat, I thought he might bite me back. Instead, he gripped my waist, lifting me effortlessly, and bolted to his feet.

"I wish the lieutenant had dressed you in something"—he leaned over to snatch the duvet, paused, then offered it to me—"more."

I ignited. If the ground didn't open up to swallow me, I'd dig a hole in the back garden and bury my head like an ostrich.

Our fingers brushed. He felt like fire. I was ice.

When I tugged, he didn't let go.

The heat in his eyes cooled, and I sensed him raising his walls. "You were calling your father in your sleep."

My heartbeat slowed. An icy claw gripped my chest, freezing the breath he had warmed in my lungs. "Sometimes when a mission goes wrong, his death haunts me," I whispered.

He released the quilt, and I wrapped it around myself like armor.

"You were there when he died. Is that how you got your scars?"

Of course he had to bring that up.

I shook my head, not trusting my voice.

"You mentioned someone else—an outlier." Any trace of softness in Harbinger's demeanor vanished, replaced by something harder. Dangerous. Lethal. "Is he the one who saved you that night?"

The change in him extinguished whatever spark had kindled between us, and it struck me. Was this why he'd *saved* me? Watched me sleep, pinned me down, shared his blood—all an elaborate ploy to interrogate me about the varcolac?

I should have broken his nose. Instead, I'd fallen right into his trap, seduced by those cursed lips and my desperate hunger. And worse—I still wanted more.

"Yes." My voice came out flat, a one-note gathering of words stripped of any feeling.

"What's his name?"

"I'll tell you, if you tell me about your magic."

"Fine. You go first. Start with what happened that night."

I arched an eyebrow. "What are you, a child?"

He crossed his arms, giving me a condescending look. This was my chance to learn more about him, too. Better that the gloves came off.

I inhaled deeply and let the air out slowly, exhaling anxiety with it. The only thing I loathed more than recounting my last birthday was revisiting the night my father died.

Pulling the comforter tighter, I settled cross-legged on the bed. "I was thirteen when Father took me on that surveillance flight," I said in a quiet rasp. "He was the General of the Republic's Great Army. Finding a pilot willing to fly us into the congested zone was child's play."

Harbinger's eyes took on a steely glint. "And why would the great Vlad Tepes risk his daughter's life?"

"To teach me a lesson. To show me the true face of war." My heart clenched as I remembered his forlorn expression, the firm grip on my shoulders as he spoke what would be his final words.

'Aurora, one day you'll take my seat,' his rich voice resounded in my mind. *'As Dracula's successors, it's our duty to protect the motherland and all citizens of the Republic. I failed, and I'll carry this burden to my grave.'*

The tightness in my windpipe swelled, choking my words. I swallowed, once, twice, before I could continue. "He believed it wasn't too late to stop the injustice. He said we needed allies, people to support us, to prevent another incident like the Seventh Ward.

"It wasn't until years later that I realized he was talking about the Total Rendition." It came out as a strangled whisper, but I forced myself to meet Harbinger's hard gaze. "The council had outvoted him. While he led the army against Russkaya's abominations, the government betrayed him, betrayed its own people."

"Betrayed?" Harbinger snarled, his irises starting to glow. "You're either lying through your teeth or you're pitifully ignorant, princess. What *your* government did wasn't just betrayal. It was a slaughter. Brutality on a scale you can't even imagine."

An aura of menace radiated off him that raised the hair at my nape. I'd seen him cut through Stalkers with the same force as a tempest and witnessed his cold, calculated rage. Both were equally terrifying. But this...

The gold fire in his eyes triggered something primal within me, a fear as old as the first spark of darkness. It bypassed all reason and logic, addressing to the most ancient part of my being. That fear didn't just paralyze me—it threatened to devour me whole. I couldn't rationalize it away, couldn't fight it with mere willpower. If he unleashed the glare to its full intensity, I knew I'd break apart.

"Were you there?" I tried to hide the tremor in my voice, but it slipped through.

He drew in a harsh breath, a storm darkening his features. "I was too late. The evacuation had already begun. My parents... the Republic murdered them before even announcing the War Act. They herded everyone with mixed blood into the Seventh Ward for 'relocation' and left lower-class purebloods in charge. Not guards—just violent, bloodthirsty scum who'd played gods with their magic. Things went to hell quickly."

"Did they... hurt you?"

He shook his head. "I was among the first loaded onto the trucks. Most surrendered, but those bastards killed at random anyway. Two young varvas watched their parents beaten to death." His voice tightened with his rage. "Those pureblood bastards found it amusing. The older sister's defiance, her refusal to cry... haunted me for years. Like many others, those girls will never forgive the Republic."

My heart shattered into a thousand razor-sharp pieces, each one cutting deeper than the last. Derzelas, I knew it had been bad, but this... How sheltered had I been in Father's fortress? Why wasn't this common knowledge?

My plans to unite the Republic, to bridge the divide between purebloods and mixed-bloods, suddenly seemed laughably naïve. Not even an eternity would be enough to heal these wounds, to bring these fractured people together.

The future I'd envisioned—a strong, united Republic—went to dust before my eyes. How could I possibly make amends for the atrocities of the past?

Harbinger crossed his arms, his muscles bulging. "Your father's zeppelin—did it fly over the battlefield?"

I nodded, recalling how the First Ward's grand gates had shrunk beneath us, giving way to barbed wire and minefields. "Father insisted on showing me the frontline. The Stalkers shouldn't have attacked so close to sunrise..."

"Projector, did the Glacies attack that night?"

"No, it was too overcast. A Magma Lance struck the back propeller—"

"It was the Gloom," he muttered.

"What was?"

"It wasn't clouds you saw. It was sand."

"The Limus-sand mist? But we were airborne!"

Harbinger vanished, then materialized in a crouch before me, and I gasped, clutching my chest.

"Ever wondered why you're cut off from other countries?" His eyes twitched, searching my face.

"We're not 'cut off,'" I protested. "They shoot our carrier birds down from the sky."

He scoffed, raking his fingers through his frosted locks. "That's the biggest load of bullshit I've heard in a while, princess. And that's saying something, considering I'm living with Quakelord. The Gloom is sentient. It communicates with other Stalkers. That magma attack? Wasn't random." Harbinger shook his head. "They *knew*. They knew exactly where you were."

He rose, lifted the oak chest by the end of the bed, and dropped it in front of me. Plopping down on the lid, he propped one leg over his knee. "The Limuses blanket everything north of Brasov. Nothing gets in or out without their knowledge." He lowered his voice to a hush as if sharing a secret. "Still believe someone's shooting your birds from the sky?"

HARBINGER

I USUALLY TRIED NOT to be an asshole, but sometimes the bastard in me just couldn't help itself. Old habits die hard, and all that. But hell, if an original could defy her nature and risk her immortal ass to save a mixed-breed, maybe I could try not being a complete dick. Be the bigger person.

You just don't mess with a Nebula if you're not ready to meet your maker.

She hunched over, looking like her world had just imploded, and guilt sucker-punched me in the side. Maybe I should've softened the blow, eased her into our fucked-up reality. She appeared as green as they come, naïve enough to think coming here beat whatever shitstorm she'd left behind.

What lies did the Republic feed people about the Outer Wards? Some fantasy land where we braided each other's hair and shat rainbows?

Rage burned through me, hotter than an Ignis. Ever since Princess Tepes crash-landed into my life, my varcolac had been howling for blood, clawing at its cage. It made me reactive, irritable. The constant hard-on sure as shit didn't help.

Maybe I'd drag Terra's naked ass from the lieutenants' bed out for some sparring. Nothing took the edge off like breaking a few ribs—mine or his, it didn't matter to me.

A tremor tickled my thighs. I glanced down to where our knees touched.

It wasn't me shaking. It was her.

Crimson eyes brimmed with tears, and my heart sank. Fuck. I'd done it now. I'd officially terrified the original.

"How..." her voice cracked, hoarse as if she'd screamed her cords raw, "how could the reconnaissance teams be so wrong? We could have saved so many. My father..."

The duvet slipped, and she once again lay bare before me, all curves and vulnerability in that flimsy excuse for a dress.

My mouth went dry. Thoughts spiraled into dangerous territory. She had a big mouth and fought when she should flee. None of it should've endeared her to me. And yet...

I wiped my face and tried to banish the image of those tight, pink nipples from my mind. From the moment her fangs sank into me, it was like a switch had flipped. I couldn't focus on anything else but her squirming under me, moaning my name.

Fuck me. It took every ounce of willpower not to adjust myself, to free my poor cock from the chokehold of my waistband.

"Hey," I said, voice rough as gravel. My hand squeezed her knee through the quilt, as gently as I could manage. "You alright?"

She looked at me with dewy eyes, doing a terrible job of hiding her sniffle. "I'm fine," she murmured.

Bullshit. But I knew a wall when I saw one.

"If you say so." I started to rise, giving her space. "We can pick this up—"

"Wait!" She made this gasping sort of squeal, and it was the most astonishing sound I'd heard. Her hand shot out, gripping my shirt. "Please."

I froze. Damn, she looked young. That perfect, ageless beauty all those Republic bastards had, like the marble statues Ma used to collect for her summer garden. If the projector hadn't mentioned her age earlier, I might've pegged her close to Ember.

But, then again, those eyes. Those scarlet pools that had seen too much. That gaze added a good five decades she had on her.

You rarely got that look before hitting a century.

"Anything to learn what I can do, right?"

A trace of a smile teased at her lips, fragile as spun glass. Her shoulders hunched, a subtle flinch rippling through her body. She looked... breakable, like something daintier than flesh and bones shaped her underneath. Prolonged hunger did that to purebloods, wore them down to something *almost* mortal. It unsettled my stomach to see it.

Guilt, anger, and—fuck it—concern for the original tossed and roiled inside me like a toxic cocktail. Pearl had told me their blood supply ran dry days ago. I'd let my hatred blindside me, missed her running on empty. Great leader I was.

If I'd made sure she was at full strength, maybe... No. That road led nowhere good. Phoenix was gone, and no amount of self-loathing would bring her back.

I sank back down, holding myself back from reaching out. "Alright, princess. I'm all ears."

She released my shirt, chin trembling, and something squirmed in my chest. Like a swarm of worms wriggling in the muck. Damn it. I shouldn't care. Shouldn't want to...

"I can't be certain how long I was unconscious," her voice strained, "but when I came to, everything was engulfed in flames. The heat was overwhelming."

Her throat worked as she swallowed, and a mind-numbing craving to taste her blood slammed into me. *Get it together, asshole.*

"Father," she rasped, and for a second, I believed she might break. But she straightened her shoulders, pressing on. "His upper body was... there was nothing left but charred remains."

Oh, you absolute dipshit. I'd pushed her too far.

I combed my fingers through my hair, gripping my nape. Part of me wanted to shut this down, but I needed the whole story. Had to know if this was the outlier I'd been chasing.

A shiver wracked her frame, and I helped her pull the quilt over her shoulders. "Go on."

She gave a wan smile, clasping the fabric with trembling hands. "There was a terrible wailing from outside," she said, her eyes growing unfocused, lost in the memory. "I managed to crawl out of the hatch and saw... a monster. It was massive, its skin gleaming like jewels—emerald, sapphire, ruby. I thought it beautiful, until I saw its face. Those eyes, bright orange, piercing... they stared right at me."

Her breath hitched, and I leaned in.

"The pilot... he shouted for me to run. Opened fire. But it just kept coming. The bullets sparked off its steely hide in bright flashes. Then it..." She jabbed her arm forward, fingers splayed like a claw. "Thrust it right through his stomach and ripped his heart out."

She shuddered, and without thinking, I reached out, my hand hovering near hers. She didn't seem to notice.

"I screamed myself hoarse. Thought I was alone, but then..." Her eyes locked onto mine, glistening. "Someone came. He burst through the smoke and fire, wielding a beveled sword, just like yours—"

The whole damn sky crashed down on me. Her lips kept moving, but I couldn't hear a thing. My lungs seized, each breath slicing through my chest. It felt like invisible hands were strangling me.

"Did he... did he kill it?" I managed to choke out.

She nodded, a troubled expression crossing her face. "He moved like lightning, his blade cutting through the beast like a knife through butter. I was young, in shock. I couldn't comprehend such speed. Now I understand better.

"He saved me, but... I was terrified of him," she continued, her gaze dropping. "Even then, I knew what silver hair meant. What he was..." She hesitated, then looked up at me. "Um... Harbinger?"

"Hm?"

"What is your family name?"

"Lowe." My voice sounded distant, miles away.

Her eyes widened in recognition, and something inside me cracked. "Lowe..." She rolled it off her tongue, her accent giving it a subtle lilt. "My savior said his surname was unique to his father's clan. He mentioned an older brother, too serious for his own good, but I remember his eyes." She leaned closer, her fingers ghosting over my forearm. "A shade darker than yours, but they would light up like a flame when he talked about him. His name was Conin, and—"

"My little brother." I felt like I'd been gutted.

"I thought as much." She slipped her feet to the floor, gripping my hand. "He took me to his base, kept me safe until Father's men came. The way he spoke about you... it was clear you meant everything to him. He was eager to get back to you, said he'd nearly completed his service. Did he... did he not make it?"

Ice seeped into my veins, the kind of cold that settled in your bones and never left, no matter how much wood you fed to the fire. I'd gotten used to it. So why the hell was I letting her touch me? Seducing me with a warmth that would never be enough to thaw my heart.

"He died in the line of duty. Eastern front, thirty-five years ago."

"I'm so sorry."

Her constant apologizing made me seriously consider putting my fist through a wall. I yanked my hand away, my softness becoming a hardened shell again. "What for? You didn't kill him."

She bit her lip, and I cursed myself for noticing.

"My magic manifested after Dad died. That's when I learned about his sentence," I said, honoring our deal.

Her eyes went wide. "Is it hereditary? Can all varcolacs do what you do?"

I barked out a laugh. "Wouldn't that be something? It runs in my clan. Conin should've had it too, explains why you couldn't keep up with him." Pride swelled in my chest, and I thumped it away. "Chronoportal's a type of time travel. Opens little pockets in other dimensions."

"You can see the future?" she breathed.

"Not far. Risk getting stuck otherwise."

"Has that happened? Getting trapped?"

"Yeah, at the start. Before I knew how to control it. Thought I could end this war." My teeth were clenched. "Chronoportal doesn't work like that. Can't change the future. I got stuck in between worlds. Took me three years to find my way back, though only minutes passed here. Learned my lesson about pushing it too far."

She sighed, relief painting her face. "Thank the Moon you returned."

I studied her, trying to figure out if she really meant all that talk about halfbloods not being the enemy, about her government's injustice. *What makes her different from the rest of her kind who think we are scum?*

"Remember when you asked what I wanted to do when the war ends?"

"Y-yes, of course."

"Hard to plan when you might not see tomorrow." I stood, and she craned her neck to meet my eyes. "But there's one thing I need to do. Been doing it for thirty-five years—searching for my brother."

"You mean... his remains? But you said—"

"We should get going."

Why bother telling her? She'd be gone before she learned the truth anyway.

I grabbed the chest, tossing it at the foot of her bed just as Terraknight's voice boomed through the door. "Cap, breakfast's ready."

I scrubbed my skin raw, but her scent clung like a parasite. Vanilla and peaches. Fuck. The storm outside matched my mood, rain hammering the boards nailed over my window.

I cranked the hot water till it burned, steam choking the cramped shower, but it did jack shit to wash away the memory of her touch. Of her bite. Of her.

Slamming the faucet off, I stood there, dripping and seething. I growled, snatched the towel, and stormed into my room, dripping water behind me.

The baby zmeu launched itself from its favorite perch atop the bookshelf, scuttling under the bed with a frantic scrape of claws. Its fat little ass wiggled as it squeezed into the tight space. Any other day, I might've found it funny. Not now.

I yanked on my leather pants and grabbed the navy T-shirt off the bed. Before I'd even pulled it down, I was out the door, fabric still bunched around my shoulders.

Halfway down the stairs, I realized I'd forgotten my boots. "Shit." I glanced back, weighing my options. Fuck it. Who needs shoes when the world's going to hell?

That's when I heard her voice, soft and hesitant, drifting down the foyer. "About Phoenix... I'm truly sorry. If only I had reached her sooner..."

A snarl built in my chest. Was she trying to get herself killed? Empty apologies were the last thing my guild needed right now. I picked up the pace, my jaw clenched tight enough to crack a molar. *Princess and her fucking sorrys.*

The war room was so quiet you could hear the bugs crawl in the corners. I slid into my seat, eyeing Terraknight's spread for Phoenix's wake—fresh bread steamed next to a tub of golden butter, mashed potatoes towered in a pot, and a rib-eye roast lorded over a bowl of cabbage soup. My stomach growled, reminding me it had been way too long since I'd eaten.

But nobody dared make a move.

Terraknight broke first, ripping into the bread. I watched, mouth watering, as he slathered on butter, the fat melting under his blade like a snowflake above fire.

"You're sorry?" Hummingbird exploded, leaping to his feet. The tablecloth came with him, sending my fork and knife clattering to the floor. "What the fuck are you apologizing for? You don't give a shit if a halfblood or two die, as long as you get home safe, right? Cut the crap with that meek act."

I shot Terraknight a look, eyebrows raised. He shrugged and tore into his bread. *The bastard.*

The projector's face flushed red. Her mouth opened and closed, but no words came out. It only fueled Hummingbird's rage.

"Listen," he snarled, knuckles white at his sides. "We can play pretend when we've got nothing better to do. You say you never discriminate, you're so pure and noble, you're a bloody saint. But read the fucking room!" His voice broke. "We just lost one of our own. We can't stroke your ego right now, so get a goddamn clue, you hypocrite."

"Hyp—" she gasped, color draining from her face. Beside her, the lieutenant tensed like a coiled spring.

I reached for a piece of bread, needing something to occupy my hands. My appetite waged a losing battle with the growing tension in my stomach.

"Or what?" Hummingbird went on, spewing venom with every word. "You think we don't care that our friend's dead? Oh right, to you, halfbloods are expendable. Just stupid animals, not worthy of your precious pureblood attention, *right*?"

Tears welled in her eyes. "That's not true! I never—"

"Not true?" Hummingbird slammed his hands on the table, making her flinch and my bread fall from my fingers. "You're safe inside your walls while we fight in this hellhole your people created. Living in comfort while we suffer. If that's not treating us like livestock, what is it? Why the fuck are you even here?"

She dropped her gaze, hands twisting in her lap. I wanted to defend her—she didn't deserve Hummingbird's full-on rage—but she needed to hear this. Better to face reality than to live in a fairytale. Maybe then she'd leave. We could get back to our fucked-up normal, and she'd go back to what? Parties in castles and plush pillows. But even in my mind, the lie rang hollow.

My guildmates nodded along, some indifferent, others seething. That dull, resigned look crept back into their eyes. It made my blood boil, killing what little appetite I had left.

"You never called us halfbloods? Bull-fucking-shit!" Hummingbird's voice rose to a roar. "You think we're out here for fun? You've trapped us like animals, forced us to fight! Millions dead, and you think showing up here with your holier-than-thou attitude makes it right?" He jabbed a finger at her. "You've never even bothered to learn our real names!"

That sent her tears rolling down her cheeks. Miss Popescu, stiff as a ramrod, wrapped her arms around the projector's slumped shoulders. I wanted to comfort her too, and the thought hit worse than Terraknight's punches. *What the fuck is wrong with me?*

"Hummingbird." Terraknight's voice was low, a warning.

"What? You gonna defend this blood-eyed—"

"Enough!" I roared, driving my fist into the table. Everyone snapped their eyes to me like I'd grown a second head.

"Fine, I get it," Hummingbird drawled, slumping into his chair. But the fight still burned in his gaze.

Terraknight sighed and pinned the projector with a hard stare. "You should leave."

She looked up, eyes red-rimmed and pleading. "Terraknight, I—"

"We're not on the battlefield," he cut her off, his voice like ice. "There's no need for you to give orders. Hummingbird went too far, but that doesn't mean we're in the mood to play nice right now."

I knew he wasn't blaming her. None of us were. Losing Phoenix had ripped us open, and we were desperate for any target to unleash our rage on. The projector had happened to be in the blast radius.

Her chair screeched against the floor as she bolted up. She stumbled toward the porch doors, looking like a wounded deer. I wished I could call her back, say... something. But instead, I bit my tongue and let her go. It was better this way—for all of us.

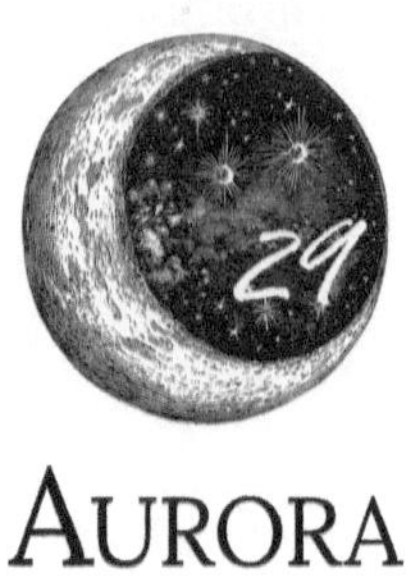

AURORA

"Aurora!" Selena's voice thundered like a cannon, rooting me in place. Her iron grip clamped my wrist, yanking me back from the porch doors. "You stay right there."

I whirled to face her, breath catching in the back of my mouth. Hummingbird's words rang in my mind, each syllable stoking the fire that clawed its way up my chest. Shame and self-disgust roiled, searing away my assurance. I clamped my free hand over my mouth, fighting the urge to retch, to run, to hide from my arrogance.

What terrified me most was how easily I'd slipped into looking down on these people—people who'd offered shelter and protection. I treated them with the same cold indifference my mother would have shown. Her icy voice slithered through my thoughts, *'When will you learn, child? You treat animals like animals,'* and the realization shook me to my core. I'd become everything I'd sworn to fight against.

"Let go," I hissed and tugged against her grip. "I need to—"

"No." Selena's fingers tightened, her face hardening into that 'don't even try me' expression I knew all too well. "We clean this up now."

Terraknight rose, his massive body tensing like an angry bear. "What the hell? I told her to leave."

"Oh, you told her..." Selena's laugh was brittle, bordering on hysterical. "How stupid of me."

The air hummed, thick with the scent of jasmine and cuscus grass—Selena's magic awakening. She sank her nails into my skin, nostrils flaring like a dragon about to breathe fire.

With a twist of her hand, she slammed Terraknight back into his chair. The whole room shook, dishes clattering, spoons clanging against plates.

"Selena!" I gasped, wrenching free. "We had an agreement. No magic!"

Her eyes burned with a fury that stole my breath. "The hell with agreements. *Civility?*" She spat the word like a curse. "Look where that's gotten us! I'm done watching you get hurt while playing nice. If they need a reminder of who we are, I'll fucking show them."

"Miss Popescu," Harbinger said, voice cold as midwinter frost. "Release my vice-captain. Now. We can discuss this like—"

"Like what? Rational adults?" Selena snarled. "Tell that to bird-boy."

Hummingbird leaped up, soup sloshing over his overalls. "You crazy bitch!"

Oh no. He didn't just call her *that*.

It happened in a heartbeat.

Selena's hand clawed the air, her Blood Manipulation surging. Hummingbird went rigid, then tumbled like a marionette with slackened strings. His chair wobbled on its back legs, then crashed to the floor with him.

Pandemonium erupted. Everyone lunged, some toward Hummingbird, others in our direction, but Selena's magic caught them mid-motion and forced them back into their seats.

They froze, faces contorted in shock and rage, muscles straining against invisible bonds.

Even Harbinger stilled, surprise flashing across his face before his eyes narrowed in concentration. I sensed him gathering power, preparing to shatter Selena's hold.

My heart hammered. "Selena," I whispered, fear tightening my throat. "Stop this. Please."

"No, Aurora. Enough." She shook her head. "It's time they learned. It's time *you* learned. We're not anyone's prey."

I met Harbinger's gaze over Selena's shoulder and saw his muscles bulging with the strain. He was seconds from breaking free, and when he did...

My mouth dried. Whatever happened next, there would be no going back. I wouldn't let him hurt her. I'd kill him if I had to. Even though it was my fault, my pride, that had brought us here.

"Listen, all of you," Selena seethed, stalking the length of the table. Her finger jabbed the air like a loaded gun. "You despise us, we loathe you. It's no secret. Aurora and I could end you all right now, and no one would bat an eye. The only reason we don't is out of *her* respect for you—the one pureblood in the entire Republic who doesn't hate your guts. And you've treated her like dirt!"

Their smoldering gazes turned my knees to rubber. I forced my spine straight, digging my heels into the timber floor. I'd stood up to my mother. I could face this too.

"Your friend's death is tragic. I get that," Selena continued, raising her voice. "But how can you blame us? We were kids when the War Act passed. We had no say! The Republic feeds us lies daily, denying you even exist. Parents use you as the boogeyman, scaring children into behaving. You know who saw through that bullshit and fought for your side?" She pointed at me, and my face tingled with warmth. "Aurora did."

"We won't apologize, if that's what you're after," Ember muttered, her teeth set in a hard line. Her fingers twitched, sparks dancing between them. Either she was resisting Selena's blood magic, or my best friend's control was slipping. My money was on the latter.

Selena's head snapped toward her, onyx hair whipping like a razor's edge. Her eyes, sharp as blades, narrowed to slits. Pure predator. "To hell with your apology, and to hell with you. You think we want to be here? After what Aurora endured—"

"That's enough, Selena!" I barked. I'd never pulled rank before, but her pledge to the Tepes Coven bound her to my orders. These were *my* secrets, *my* shame. I wouldn't let her speak of them without my permission ever again.

She bowed her head. "They *need* to know."

"Know what?" Harbinger rose to his full height, slow and methodical, as if encased in barbed wire—stiff, shoulders rigid, unnaturally straight.

His honey-colored eyes betrayed what his blank expression tried to hide: hard and backlit with contained fury. Those eyes now pierced through me, burning with questions I wasn't ready to answer.

"Nothing that concerns you," I snapped, my fingers instinctively tracing the scars hidden beneath my silk scarf. "You have your secrets, I have mine."

Harbinger flickered, reappearing before Selena, and slammed her against the wall. Plaster cracked, weapons and stone fragments raining down.

The air rushed from her lungs, her magic slipping away like sand with the tide. That black crescent-shaped weapon—the one I'd seen slice through Stalkers and tear holes in reality—hovered at her throat.

My pulse roared in my ears.

Chairs scraped.

The outliers rose, flexing stiff fingers. Gale's wings unfurled, casting long shadows across the room. Pearl and the vice-captain lingered behind as the others closed in on me, a pack of wolves circling wounded prey.

Harbinger leaned in, his face inches from Selena's. "You attacked my guild—*again*," he hissed. "Tell me, Lieutenant, if I retaliate now, am I the boogeyman, or is it just self-defense?"

Selena bared her fangs, fear and defiance etched into her face. "Kill me, prove my point."

Time stretched like taffy, and my heart plummeted. I had to act before Harbinger hurt her.

Magic surged through me, natural as breathing. I let it rise but kept it to a low simmer, wary of detection. While all eyes fixed on him, I reached for the blood samples I'd collected during the Initiation. Tendrils of his essence responded to my call, eager and familiar.

I'd been inside his mind before. Brute force wouldn't crack his mental shields. So, I began 'knitting'—a delicate task made harder by the need for subtlety. My temples throbbed in protest, every nerve screaming for caution.

Silence. Focus.

The first blood thread slipped through his defenses undetected. Emboldened, I wove two dozen more, creating a blood mesh over his motor cortex. One wrong move, and I'd paralyze him completely. Not even his precious Wolf God could save him then.

I tugged the reins, just a whisper, letting Harbinger know I was there. His right eye twitched. He backed away from Selena, a crazed laugh merging with his growl. "You insufferable woman!" he snarled at her, lowering the yatagan-like blade at his side. His glowing eyes locked onto me. "Start talking, projector."

I bared my fangs, the temptation to tell him to go fuck himself burning on the tip of my tongue. But his proximity to Selena made my stomach clench. I hated it, but I couldn't risk Selena's safety for the fleeting satisfaction of standing up to him and hiding the truth.

"We can't go back," I hissed. "Not until our Creator awakens."

Quakelord scoffed. "So, you've been exiled. What did you do?"

"We haven't been exiled," I rasped, fighting to stay upright against Harbinger's mental assault to expel me from his head. Not a chance. As long as he threatened Selena, I'd remain lodged in his psyche like a thorn.

"Then why can't you return home?" Gale asked over Quakelord's shoulder.

I leveled my hardest glare at them both. Lev's... actions were a wound I'd cauterized, buried deep, and refused to let fester. Speaking of it would only tear open the scar. Relief unknotted my stomach when Gale finally looked away, pulling Quakelord back.

Harbinger's voice rolled like a far-off storm. "Tell us about the Red Moon."

Selena seized her chance, slipping past him.

His jaw popped, but he only shook his head, so I exhaled and released my magic, sagging as golden spots danced across my vision.

"Do you understand how a Blood Pact works?" Selena asked, her tone gaining that clinical familiarity.

Harbinger's lip curled in abhorrence. "I care little about your personal pleasures—"

"If you think a Blood Pact is just about sex, we shouldn't be having this conversation." She breezed past Quakelord and Gale without a glance back.

"This is getting interesting," Quakelord quipped, but Terraknight silenced him with a fist to his chest.

"You have my attention, Lieutenant," Harbinger said.

Selena's eyes sought mine, asking permission. I nodded, grateful they'd stopped prying into my life.

Harbinger studied me with an agile gaze. I met it head-on, refusing to shrink away despite the memories this discussion would inevitably dredge up.

"Think of it as a consensual blood exchange, with emotional baggage," Selena explained, interlocking her fingers. "Your partner gains unrestricted access to your thoughts. The longer they feed, the deeper they go. No hiding, no holding back—only blind trust and vulnerability. A temporary, but intense bond forms, linking two beings in ways beyond the physical.

"Now," she turned to Harbinger, "this connection often ignites intense feelings. Lust, for example." A suggestive grin appeared on her face. "It's not solely dependent on the feeding, but it's one hell of an advantage.

"When two originals feed off each other..." she puffed out a breath, her hands mimicking an explosion, "things don't just escalate. They detonate. I'm sure you can provide more... intimate details. You've experienced it firsthand, haven't you, Harbinger?"

Ember's foot slammed against the floor. "She forced herself on him!"

My forehead burned as if branded with a neon 'villain' sign. I met Harbinger's gaze and froze. A hot, predatory fire played in his sunlit eyes.

"Oh, but she did not." Selena laughed, a sharp edge seeping into her voice. "He consented during the Initiation."

"What if it's not consensual?" Terraknight asked.

"If a willing Blood Pact brings bliss, then a forced one..." Selena's eyes flicked to me, worry etching her features. "Simply put, a quick death would be more merciful."

The ground gave way beneath me, plunging me into thick darkness. Lev's face flashed before my eyes, his cruel smile as sharp as the fangs that had torn into my flesh. The phantom scent of cyanide—his scent—filled my nostrils. My silk scarf morphed into his hand, tightening, choking, controlling as air refused to escape.

Pearl's voice wavered, distant and distorted. "And if an original feels more than a pureblood—"

"You've nailed it."

I wanted to scream, to claw at my ears, to silence the voices blurring past and present. But I couldn't move, couldn't breathe. The flashback threatened to pull me under, ready to drag me back into that cursed night. No. I gritted my teeth, shaking my head. I wouldn't let it win. Not now. Never again.

"That's how you got your scars." Harbinger's growl jolted me from my downward spiral. He took a halting step toward me, arm half-raised, before he caught himself.

My secret lay bare, stripped raw for all to see. I blinked hard, willing away tears, and fixed my gaze on a water stain on the ceiling.

Gale's sharp inhale cut the silence. "Who did this to you?"

I couldn't meet their eyes, couldn't stand to witness the pity, horror, or worse—judgment. But with my wounds now on display, what was the point of hiding?

Drawing a deep breath, I mentally prepared myself. They *deserved* the truth. Maybe they'd understand our situation better. And perhaps, unburdening myself would loosen the stranglehold of anxiety around my throat.

"When my superior appointed me as your projector, I assured him I'd get to know you to the best of my abilities." I clasped my trembling hands behind my back. "He opposed the idea, insisting I prioritize my survival. My behavior has nothing to do with the Republic, Total Rendition, or Russkaya. I apologize for my poor conduct. How I treated you reflects on me, Aurora Tepes, without the titles and rank."

Silence dried my throat. "I haven't been completely honest with you. To explain, I need to tell you how our politics work." No interruptions, so I continued. "Until Derzelas chooses otherwise, his eldest son, Dracula, rules the Republic. I'm next in line to inherit his magic, making me heir to the throne. It's my birthright."

Terraknight crossed his arms over his chest. "Hasn't someone else taken your seat?"

"They have, for the next fifty years, or until I grow strong enough to take it back," I replied, gulping down bitterness. "After Father's passing, our coven fell into ruin. We lost half our people in the war. Allies betrayed us, subjects broke their loyalties. Later, we discovered the Wurdulaks had created dissent to remove us from power. They succeeded."

I glanced at Selena.

Her nod encouraged me to go on.

I sighed. "Mother feared Lucian and Marcus would fight for the crown. She said it had been too long since Derzelas favored our Creator. I became our last hope. She arranged my marriage to Lev Wurdulak, Lucian's heir, to secure an alliance, regardless of our Dark Father's decision."

"She promised you to the people who plotted against her? That's seriously messed up," Quakelord retorted, disdain sharp in his voice.

"You can say that again," Selena hissed. "Elena Tepes is a cold-hearted bitch."

"I fought her decision," I admitted, my voice growing faint. "But when he..." My throat constricted. The room started to spin. I shut my eyes, fighting sudden nausea.

"Lev gifted Aurora a halfblood-massacre on her birthday," Selena seethed.

Terraknight and Hummingbird's simultaneous roar shook the house. "He what?"

Swallowing bile, I forced the words out despite the wails echoing in my mind. "Lev sealed their fate when he brought them to court. I confronted him, but he'd already inherited Lucian's power. My weakness..." I choked on my words, shame heating my cheeks. "He was too strong. I could do nothing."

"Why not report him?" Pearl startled.

Selena, sensing my racing pulse, stepped in. "Forced Blood Pacts mean immediate execution, except for the prince. The Wurdulaks control everyone, even Aurora's brother, the governor."

"You're joking," Quakelord sneered.

Gale's eyes narrowed. "What about your mother?"

I shook my head. Her brows furrowed into a scowl.

"She's heartless," Selena hissed. "Ready to sacrifice her own daughter for the coven's benefit."

The room filled with seawater and brine as Pearl's eyes started to blaze white. "She'd give you to that monster?"

"We aren't known for our compassion," I murmured. We treated them like animals, after all.

Silence fell, thick and suffocating. The varva's mouth slackened, sharing a furtive glance with the captain. Terraknight leaned against the wall, hands in pockets.

His piercing hazel eyes studied Selena. "And yet here you are, leaving behind a life of riches to protect your friend."

"I haven't abandoned anything," she retorted. "Not that I see why it should concern you if I had."

Their stare-off stretched for an uncomfortably long time.

"I never wanted this for her," I intervened, before they could come to blows. "But she's stubborn. Once she makes up her mind, there's no changing it."

Ember elbowed her way forward. "You still haven't told us what a Blood Pact has to do with the Red Moon." Her hateful gaze felt like a noose tightening around my throat.

I stiffened.

"Let me," Selena said with a gentle squeeze of my arm. "The Blood Pact performed during the Red Moon is a marriage contract—an eternal bond. It's an archaic court ritual requiring pure, undiluted blood. That's what Elena Tepes had in mind for her daughter."

"That vile woman!" Gale spat.

Selena's glare zeroed in on Harbinger. "Now you understand my reaction. Once complete, this bond can't be undone."

The air around Harbinger morphed, darkness and lightning swirling as if hunting each other. Coffee and roses perfumed the air. His brawny arm popped out of nowhere, curling around my waist.

"Hold your breath," he commanded.

Before I could react, the ground vanished. He yanked me backward into an abyss crackling with golden vines, my hair flying in front of my face, blocking out the room and the gaping outliers as we plunged into nothingness.

Aurora

One second I was standing in the war room, the next—hell. Pure, unadulterated hell.

Teleporting with Harbinger felt like being shoved through a meat grinder made of ice and crushing pressure. Darkness squeezed the air from my lungs. Freezing walls scraped my shoulders, the chill burrowing deep into my bones, making them ache as if they might splinter.

The air was dense, oppressive. An arctic weight pressed from all sides, turning every twitch into a herculean effort.

I began to scream, too late remembering Harbinger's warning. The instinctive inhale filled my throat with crystallizing shards. Terror clawed at me.

Was this how I'd die? A pureblood popsicle in Harbinger's godforsaken portal?

My numb fingers tightened around his hand—my only lifeline in this frozen hell. I commanded my legs to move, but they may as well have been concrete. Every inch forward was a battle against an invisible riptide of tar.

Just when I thought I couldn't take another second, Harbinger stopped.

I slammed into the brick wall of his back, my insides lurching sideways, and stumbled, but his iron grip kept me upright.

Frost melted from my lashes, blurring my vision. I blinked rapidly, desperate to confirm we'd escaped that nightmare.

"What in Derzelas' name was that?" I croaked.

"That, princess, was Chronoportal," Harbinger replied, casual as a Sunday stroll on Aviators Boulevard.

"I almost died!"

He snorted. "Not even close. You'll get used to it."

I glared, teeth chattering. "I'd rather walk barefoot through lava."

Harbinger's lips twitched, crimson flaring in his eyes. "You continue to surprise me."

The chill dissipated, replaced by an intense heat blooming deep inside me. My eyes darted around, taking in our surroundings.

Neat. Tidy. He'd brought us to his bedroom.

The floorboards vibrated with Selena's shouts. Her hysterical voice faded under the baritone of Terraknight's voice, probably explaining that everything was alright. *Good luck with that.*

All around us, a dozen candles flickered, their flames painting the olive-green walls with playful shadows. The warm light caught on the polished surface of the cherry wood bookshelf, sending sporadic glints of orange across the room. Books lined the shelves, some jutting out at odd angles, as if hastily shoved back into place after a late-night reading session.

My skin prickled. The intimacy of the space, of our proximity, was jarring. It wasn't just his physical size but the power radiating from him, leaving me both giddy and on edge.

"Harbinger," I wheezed. "Why are we here?"

He raked a hand through his silver hair, his gaze never leaving mine. "You've piqued my curiosity. I find myself... intrigued."

"If this is about pity—"

"No such thing, princess," he cut in, prowling closer. "Pity's not in my vocabulary."

I didn't move. We faced off like two apex predators.

"Those scars," he said. "Why keep them hidden?"

I shrugged, feigning nonchalance despite my raging pulse. "Didn't think it'd matter to you."

He smiled like a wolf baring its fangs in a dark forest. His dimples made an appearance, too, and my heart backflipped. It'd made a lot of unexpected jumps lately.

"Maybe it doesn't."

"Then we agree."

His husky laugh slid down my spine like warm honey. "Is that all you've got? I expected more fire."

"Yep." When in trouble, keep it monosyllabic.

I tried to convince myself he was nothing special. Just a guy in worn leather pants and—of all things—a dark blue polo shirt. It should be impossible to look deadly in a polo shirt, but Harbinger defied logic. The fabric molded to his form, outlining every ridge and valley of his chest. His hard shoulders stretched the seams to their breaking point. I half expected to hear stitches popping if he so much as flexed.

I'd felt what lay beneath. His body wasn't just hard; it was forged steel.

Perhaps it wasn't his physique, but his insufferable confidence that put me on high alert.

I backed up, but not quickly enough. My breath hitched as we collided, the force of it making my heart jackhammer against my ribs. A painful, rapid beat. The steady thrum of blood in his neck seduced me like nectar—obsessively, compulsively.

"The other day..." he murmured. His breath caressed my cheek. "Did you mean it? About not getting hurt if I'd bitten you?"

Heat flooded my face. "I told you, I got carried away."

"Hmm." He crowded me backward until my spine met the door with a soft thud.

A pathetic whimper escaped my throat.

"You're dodging the question, princess."

He dipped his head, silky hair tickling my skin as he nuzzled the hollow of my neck. The *exposed* flesh I'd fought so hard to keep covered. My hand flew up, fingers grasping at nothing—the scarf was gone, lost somewhere in Harbinger's cursed portal. My breath hitched. His tongue traced my pulse, just above my scars, and I swore I felt an echo of it between my thighs.

I bit back a moan, desperately searching for a distraction. Maybe I should lock myself in the bathroom before I succumbed to the urge to climb him like a tree and finish what we'd started in my room.

"Since when do you care about my well-being?" I forced out, ignoring those sinful lips hovering over my skin. "We don't get along, remember? You lie. You order me around. I fantasize about murdering you. I'm stubborn. You're infuriating. We drive each other mad, and you want to throttle me."

"That was one time."

"One time too many. We can't stand each other. We—"

He cupped the back of my neck and crashed his mouth to mine.

Heat rolled through me as his tongue teased the seam of my lips.

I couldn't help it. I arched into him, grinding against his hardness. His fingers twisted in my hair, tugging just shy of painful. The sting cleared my head.

I shoved his chest, but he pulled back, his heart thundering beneath my palm. The look in his hooded eyes could've melted the snow on the Carpathians.

"Harbinger," I panted, "what are you doing?"

"Kissing you." The way his lips curved around those words was positively indecent. Realization dawned on his face, one dark-blond eyebrow arching skyward. "Hold on. Someone has kissed you before, right?"

I scoffed. "Of course I've been kissed." Like, eighty years ago. But he didn't need to know that. Or that kissing took a backseat during a Blood Pact.

Mirth danced in his gaze. "Oh, princess, you're a terrible liar. No one? Really? "

My cheeks burned. "Fine. There was a guy at the Academy obsessed with mortal acts of affection. We experimented a few times before my rival stole him. I don't see the appeal. Satisfied?" I snapped, pushing him again.

His smile widened, showing the sharp tips of his fangs. My toes curled in my boots. "Well, princess," he leaned in, "let's fix that, shall we?"

I tried to retreat, but the door blocked my escape. "We really shouldn't—"

His scorching lips claimed mine, and my reason evaporated. Exhilaration surged through me, every nerve ending singing. His tongue caressed and teased—not conquering but enticing; confident, yet tender.

I craved his taste more than my next breath. Maybe I should kiss him back and exorcise this curiosity so I never think of it again.

I surrendered and let him in.

Sweet. Holy. Darkness.

The world exploded into a kaleidoscope of sensations.

He tasted divine—smoky and masculine, like a forbidden elixir. My body roared to life, as if emerging from a century-long slumber, guided by his tongue.

A deep, hungry growl rumbled in his chest as he nipped at my lips, his hand fisting in my hair. I reveled in the feeling of his arms around me, the heat of his body pressing against mine. His tongue thrust into my mouth, possessing, seducing, and I matched his fervor. Time lost all meaning as we moved in perfect harmony. When we finally parted, we were both gasping for air.

An arrogant smirk traced his lips. "Well?" he asked, voice husky. "How did that measure up? Do I *appeal*?"

This insufferable man.

"Underwhelming. No fireworks. Nothing. Like kissing my own reflection." My head still spun. He could be as smug as he wanted, but I knew he'd felt it too. The evidence of his desire pressed against me, leaving no room for doubt.

He didn't even try to hide it.

"Lie to yourself all you want, princess, but we both know the truth."

"And what's that?"

If he flexed one more time, I'd need to take drastic action. Maybe jab him in the eyes. Hard to look seductive while tearing up.

"You want me."

Oh hell.

"You're captivated by my irresistible charm, and you're afraid to admit it."

I gaped at him. "Doesn't your neck hurt from holding up that massive ego?"

He laughed, the sound sending my traitorous heart into somersaults. I opened my mouth to deliver another smart retort, but something in his demeanor changed. A glimmer of vulnerability flickered in his gaze.

"Come here," he said and tugged me toward his desk. "There's something I want you to see."

Releasing my hand, Harbinger pulled open the top drawer. His movements were careful, almost reverent, as he retrieved a metal box, not much larger than the one I held my Nexus and Astral Visor. Recognition flashed through me.

That box. I'd seen it before, sitting on his nightstand the night I'd come to discuss the shipment. The dim candlelight caught its edges, revealing a patina that spoke of years of handling.

He set the box on the desk and lifted the lid. I leaned in to have a better look and couldn't stifle my gasp.

A treasure trove of trinkets spilled forth. Delicate jewels nestled against rough-hewn wooden figurines, stones, polished to a gleam, soft feathers. A tiny compass, its needle wavering slightly, sat atop fragments of yellowed letters, their edges crisp with age.

Harbinger's expression turned somber. The cocky, exasperating captain vanished, replaced by a man who'd seen too much death—and had lost all hope.

A sudden tightness gripped my chest. I massaged it with the pad of my hand, trying to ease the unexpected ache.

He procured a small pocket knife from his back pocket, plucked a silver necklace from the pile, and sank into his chair. The silver medallion gleamed gold as he laid it flat before him.

"When I was with my first guild, we made a pact." His voice was flat, but the sorrow in his eyes betrayed a deep-seated pain. "We'd engrave the names of our fallen on their favorite belongings. The last survivor would carry them to freedom, ensuring everyone found peace."

He paused, a heavy sigh escaping his lips. The candle stump sitting in the saucer cast shadows on his face that seemed to age him decades. "I try to retrieve their personal items, but it's often impossible. It's not much, but it's... tangible proof they existed."

The scrape of metal on metal filled the silence as he etched two letters into the medallion: DF. My stomach twisted into knots.

"Her name," I murmured, comprehension sinking in. "You're carving Phoenix's name..."

Dark Father.

The weight of his burden crashed over me. How long had he been carrying these mementos, honoring a promise to ghosts? My vision blurred, pressure building behind my eyes. I blinked, fighting back the tears.

He leaned back, the chair groaning beneath him. "Ditoa Firestarter," he said in a hoarse whisper. "That's Phoenix's real name."

A pair of jade-green eyes flashed in my mind, fierce and agile.

A sob tore from my throat before I could stop it. I swiped at my cheeks, forcing a smile that felt more like a grimace. I didn't want to add to Harbinger's sorrow. They were family. The gnawing emptiness in my chest couldn't compare to his loss.

He placed the necklace inside the box and closed the lid with a soft click, tapping it gently. For several heartbeats, he sat in silence, head bowed. I held my breath, feeling like an intruder in a private eulogy.

"It's only the five of us left—Terraknight, Hummingbird, Gale, Pearl, and me," he finally spoke, his tone heavy with resignation. "That's why I must take them with me. Every soul that fought and fell... they'll stay with me, protected, until I die."

Harbinger's words carved into my chest. A deep ache settled in my heart. How did he bear it? This mountain of grief that no one could see?

"How many?" I whispered, dreading the answer.

"Four hundred and fifty-three, including Phoenix."

The number knocked the breath right out of me. I'd lost outliers during my service, but I couldn't recall the exact count. That he knew precisely spoke volumes of the weight he carried.

"Is that... why they call you Harbinger?" My voice cracked. "Because you shepherd them to their final rest?"

"That's part of it, yes."

The Republic had denied them proper graves. Harbinger's devotion to preserving their memories suddenly illuminated why he commanded such respect. A profound urge to comfort him, to shoulder even a fraction of his burden, flooded me.

I reached out and gently swept the hair from his forehead. The candle flame highlighted the moisture in his eyes, and in that moment, I saw not the formidable Harbinger, but a man drowning in an ocean of loss.

It broke me to see him like this. The invincible hybrid, laid bare by grief and duty. I wanted to wrap my arms around him, to offer some small respite, but I hesitated, unsure if such intimacy would be welcome.

Why not? Worst case, he gets angry. Still better than that defeated expression on his face.

Before I could second-guess myself, I straddled his lap, sliding my hand up his chest and scraping my nails through the short hair at the back of his neck.

He let out a masculine groan, tilting his head back. Those mesmerizing dual-colored irises focused on me. "What are you doing, princess?"

"Provoking Death," I breathed.

An irresistible pull tugged at my core—not just physical, but emotional. Spiritual. We became magnets, drawn closer until no space remained between us. Our lips hovered inches apart, breaths mingling, hearts synchronizing. The intensity, the surging heat and raw emotion, ripped a moan from my throat.

"Tell me what you want," he murmured, low and rough.

Leaning into him, I absorbed the vibration of his words. "You. I want you."

He gripped my hips and pulled me flush against him, his arousal pressing hard against me. We lunged for each other, colliding like stars.

Then our mouths met. His tongue delved deep, exploring, making my world tilt on its axis.

Pure ecstasy.

I was lost, utterly and completely.

He tasted like heaven and sin combined.

I matched his passion, grazing his lower lip, studying with my tongue, melding my body into his. He groaned in pleasure as his mouth blazed a trail of fire along my jawline, licking the sensitive spot below my ear. The gentle suction sent shockwaves through me, molten and electric, short-circuiting my brain.

I craved his touch as desperately as I craved his blood.

"If you want me to stop, say no," he whispered raggedly, gripping my thighs as he rose to his feet.

I nodded, that inexplicable feeling of safety I always felt with him washing over me, emboldening me to continue.

It was strange. I'd known almost nothing about him, except that he was the most dangerous man I'd ever met, and I felt secure. Protected.

Wrapping my legs around him, I shifted to get a better hold—and elicited another delicious grunt from him. My eyes fluttered closed in anticipation of his kiss. But instead of his lips on mine, his grip suddenly vanished. I was airborne for a heartbeat, gasping as I hit the mattress.

Oomph.

My eyes flew open just in time to watch him remove his shirt. The sight took my breath away—the robust strength of his shoulders, the powerful chest, the flat planes of his stomach. A black rectangular stone pendant nestled between his pectorals, hanging from a silver chain. Harbinger, shirtless and barefoot in only his leather pants, was a vision of masculine perfection.

The sheer physical power of him was staggering. He had the kind of body that made women sigh knowing they could never touch it. Yet here he was, flexing before me—no longer a fantasy but *mine*.

The old springs groaned as he propped himself on his elbows, pinning my arms above me. His eyes, guarded and hollow moments ago, now blazed with a crimson glow that made my heart gallop. "Pay attention, princess, because I'm about to kiss every inch of you."

He tore my silk shirt open, buttons scattering across the floor. The front clasp of my black lacy bra popped, and my breasts sprang free. Harbinger dipped his head, sucking at one nipple, grazing it with his teeth. I fisted his hair as a wave of pleasure radiated downward, burning through me.

I moaned, arching my back to give him better access. "Harbinger..."

"So sensitive..." he murmured against my skin.

He blew cool air over the sensitized peak, sending my body into overdrive. Every cell in me focused on his touch as he rolled it between his fingertips. Harbinger's torturous assault continued, his mouth claiming my other breast—sucking, licking, teasing. When he nipped just hard enough, a galaxy of stars exploded behind my eyelids.

He rose to his knees, and my gaze lingered on the sculpted planes of his body, following the tapering muscles that led to his narrow waist. The prominent bulge in his leather pants was catastrophically distracting. My mouth went dry, and I gulped, conscious of how parched I felt—and not just for blood.

"Come, princess," he invited, arms spread wide, presenting the world's most perfect chest. "Have a bite."

How could I resist when he looked at me like that? As if I were something precious, offering what I craved most. I licked my lips, savoring the lingering taste of him, and swallowed hard.

I climbed onto his thighs, straddling him, and trailed kisses along his neck. A rough growl rumbled from his chest as he tilted his head back, offering me his throat. I sank my fangs into his vein, and the gates to the Underworld burst open. His blood mixed with his scent—smoky, floral, intoxicating.

His fingers tangled in my hair, alternating between gentle tugs and caresses. Fire ignited low in my belly. My hands roamed greedily, tracing every ridge, reveling in each muscle spasm beneath my touch. I pulled away from his neck, fumbling with his waistband, desperate to feel all of him.

He caught my hand, pressing a gentle kiss to my palm. "Not tonight, princess."

Heated, tightly controlled want burned in his gaze as he guided my arms around his neck. His hands slipped under my skirt, teasing, before tearing away the thin fabric of my underwear.

I gasped, the sound lost to the crackling portal behind him. "No, you don't," I protested, reaching for the scrap of lace dangling from his fingers.

He stretched out of reach, his self-assured grin making me shudder. With a flick of his wrist, he hurled the ruined garment into another dimension.

Gripping my hips, he pressed every hard inch of himself against me and leisurely lowered me to the bed, his tongue blazing a trail between my breasts.

Oh, stars and Moon.

The muscles in his back flexed beneath my fingers, firm as steel. He paused at my navel, lifting his head, giving me a chance to stop him.

I wouldn't. This felt too good... too *right*.

His eyes glowed with raw, honest need, and the wildfire inside me spread through my veins. He nipped at my skin, stoking the fire, before pushing up my skirt and settling between my thighs.

The first touch of his mouth tore a scream from my throat.

Harbinger devoured me like a man dying of thirst, and I was his oasis. His tongue explored, lips sucking, drawing out sensations I never knew existed. Everything faded until all that remained was the hot knot of pleasure blooming between my legs. Each heated stroke intensified the pressure, lifting me to unbearable, wonderful heights.

"Mmm, you're the best thing I've tasted in a very long time, princess," he purred, the thrum of his voice nearly sending me over the edge.

He slid a finger inside, setting a slow, tantalizing rhythm.

My hips rose to meet each stroke, chasing the maddening pleasure. Another finger joined, curling slightly as his pace quickened. My world narrowed to the sound of my frantic heartbeats and the exquisite sensations he drew from me.

His teeth grazed my inner thigh, not quite breaking the skin. "You like that?" he whispered, his breath hot against me. "Give yourself to me, Aurora."

The sweet pressure built to a crescendo then erupted. I cried out his name, electric shockwaves rolling through my body. If he could shatter my world like this, I doubted I'd survive a true Blood Pact.

Harbinger released me, and I lay limp, a blissful exhaustion weighing down my limbs.

The mattress dipped, his body heat seeping into my side. His fingertip traced a path from my hip to my waist, grazing the side of my breast. A shiver rippled through me as he gripped my chin, claiming my mouth once more.

I responded to his kiss with unbridled hunger, moaning in satisfaction. A primal, possessive need overtook me, the predator in me claiming its stake, refusing to let go. *Would I ever be able to let this man go?*

"It's Radolf," he whispered against my lips.

"Mm-hmm, what is?"

"My name. You called me Harbinger earlier, but I'd prefer hearing my real name when you're squirming underneath me." He propped himself up, his smoldering gaze trailing over my body. That smirk could melt a trail of Stalkers straight to their territory. "You can call me Radu. It's shorter."

Shame and guilt pounded through me as I lay frozen, ensnared by his gaze. What had I done? Becoming intimate with the very outlier I was sent to investigate—a half-varcolac who'd cared for me during my bloodlust, whose name I'd never bothered to learn.

I was so furious with myself that I could cry.

"Hummingbird was right. I am a hypocrite," I groaned, slamming my forearm over my eyes.

"It's just a name. Don't overthink it," Radu said, gently uncovering my eyes.

But it wasn't *just* a name. It was everything.

"If what Hummingbird said still bothers you," he sighed, "it shouldn't. Not everyone shares his opinion. This situation isn't your fault, and you can't change it. Don't feel guilty over things beyond your control."

"That's not the point," I countered, my voice thick. "I was terribly inconsiderate, not even trying to learn your real names."

He brushed a lock of hair behind my ear. "Our identities are irrelevant. Ever wonder why we use call signs when Stalkers can't breach the Harmonization? Or why the Republic destroyed our records?"

"So projectors wouldn't know who they're harmonizing with..."

"Exactly. Most of us don't survive a year after drafting. The higher-ups probably thought the death toll would overwhelm a projector."

"But that makes us cowards," I murmured. "I wronged you and your guild. I need to make it right." I'd do whatever it took to make amends, starting with him.

"Radu," I tested his name, its exotic sound unique on my tongue. Meeting his gaze, I felt a blush warm my cheeks. "Radu, where did you send my underwear?"

His head fell back, rich laughter echoing through the room. It was the most beautiful sound I'd heard from him yet, making my heart flutter and then soar.

He sobered, grinning. "I hope they weren't your favorite because they're gone, princess."

I chuckled and scooted closer. "They were already shredded, anyway."

Radu pulled me into his arms, and for the first time since Father's passing, I felt safe and wanted. Something no one else had done for me.

AURORA

I TWISTED THE TARNISHED brass doorknob, palms damp. "Sel!" I called out and burst into her room.

The embarrassing amount of groveling I'd have to do just to get her to talk to me again made me oddly giddy. She'd been cold toward me since Sighisoara, and I'd had enough. The apology for leaving her behind was already forming on my lips when a wall of scents hit me, so potent my eyes watered.

Selena and Terraknight's mingled blood hung thick in the air, almost tangible. But there were other, more primal *clues* that my slow brain failed to process. The musky smell of a recent coupling, the sound of breathless, soft moans. *Oh, shit.*

My mind finally caught up with my senses, and I realized I'd barged in at the worst possible moment.

"Go away," Selena groaned, her voice muffled by the pillow she'd buried her face in. "I'm still pissed at you."

Terraknight rolled to the edge of the four-poster bed and rose with the fluid grace of a panther, wrapping a silk sheet around his waist. The fabric slipped a little, presenting a perfectly sculpted buttock gleaming in the dancing light.

"I'll leave you ladies to work through your issues," he said, his voice a melody of gravel and honey. He never sang, or at least I'd never heard him, but if he ever did, I was certain women from every corner of the Outer Wards would trip over themselves just to catch a note.

"Traitor!" Sel hissed at him, but her tone melted into a purr when he shot her a wink.

Terraknight and I hadn't talked about his harsh dismissal at Phoenix's wake, but we usually sorted out our differences with silent nods. He navigated around the room's dark wood furniture—a heavy mahogany wardrobe, a velvet-cushioned chaise lounge, and a writing desk with intricate carvings—and I couldn't stop myself from staring.

He wasn't handsome or sexy in the traditional sense—he was sizzling hot. His features were all rough angles, but his autumn-toned eyes, intense and lit from within, immediately conjured thoughts of tangled sheets and passionate Blood Pacts. Add to that his skin—the rich, deep brown of the finest dark chocolate—and a physique that looked like it was chiseled from living stone, and you had a combination that was downright lethal.

"Hey!" Selena clicked her fingers, the sound sharp in the vaulted room. "Eyes up here, missy. He's taken. Find your own blood source."

Heat flushed my cheeks as Terraknight's low, husky laugh echoed from beyond the bathroom door. The old pipes groaned as the shower started and cloaked his movements.

"I should have knocked," I mumbled, shifting awkwardly on the creaky floorboards.

She sat up, letting the cover fall away, and fixed me with a glare fit to singe hair. "You think?"

I scrubbed my face, hoping to wipe away the layer of fatigue. We'd never fought like this before, and it was keeping me up during the day. "About the last mission…" I began, but Selena's expression turned glacial, and I stopped speaking.

"You mean about you leaving me behind and nearly getting yourself killed? Again?" The bite in her tone made me wince.

Guilt burrowed deep inside me. "I'm sorry. I know I screwed up."

"Screwed up?" Her voice rose to a near shout. "Your guts were mush, your bones ground to dust! Nothing inside your body was solid anymore. You didn't have enough blood left for me to heal you. If Harbinger hadn't stepped in to offer his blood, you'd be a skin bag!"

Harbinger offered? I'd assumed Selena had instructed him what to do. The contradiction made my head spin, especially because she hadn't been the only one treating me with a cold shoulder. I hadn't seen Harbinger since we spent the night together—and that was more than forty-eight hours ago.

I stepped further into the room, palms raised in a gesture of peace. "I know, Sel. I felt every bone shatter inside me. The last thing I wanted was for you to go through that again, trust me, please. But you have to understand, I did it to save Phoenix. There wasn't time to—"

"To what? To trust me?" Her scathing look tightened my stomach. She stood, crossing the oriental rug to her dresser, unbothered by her nudity. "I know I was close to bloodlust, but I still could've managed myself."

"You were in far worse shape than I was," I countered. "The risk was too high. If you'd lost control…"

Selena yanked on an oversized t-shirt, then whirled to face me. "That wasn't your call to make, A. We're partners. We face these things *together*. We came here together. Separating was idiotic. I could've helped with that Nebula, held off the Ignises myself. Phoenix…"

The unsaid words floated in the air: Phoenix could've still been alive.

The world spun and kicked me in the face. "You're right," I whispered. "I was trying to protect you, the guild, but I ended up hurting everyone. Myself included. I'm sorry."

Selena's expression softened, her anger giving way to worry. "I get why you did it," she said quietly. "But I hate being left behind, especially when you're in danger. Promise me, no more solo heroics?"

"I promise," I said, closing the distance between us. "From now on, we stick together no matter what."

Selena studied me, her dark eyes searching my face. Then, with a small nod, she opened her arms. "Come here, you idiot."

I fell into her embrace, but her floral scent mixed with Terraknight's musk was almost overwhelming in the close quarters. My gums started itching, reminding me I needed to feed.

"Don't ever scare me like that again," Selena murmured. "I can't lose you, A."

"You won't," I promised, squeezing her tight.

She groaned, tapping my shoulders to release her, and as she backtracked to the bed, a devious glint entered her eyes. "So, spill—how was it?"

"How was what?"

She rolled her eyes. "The Blood Pact, you dolt."

My heart stumbled, then sped up. I turned away, fixing my gaze on the mirror in the corner. Memories flooded my mind: Radu's lips on mine, his teeth gently nipping my bottom lip, our shared breath more intimate than anything I'd done before. A quiver danced through my muscles, a delightful burn pooling in my belly.

Dear heart, why him?

It wasn't just the physical pleasure or his intoxicating blood. What drew me in was that overwhelming, single-minded focus he radiated when he concentrated. Call it feminine intuition, but I sensed that, in a Blood Pact, he'd be wholly committed. He'd approach intimacy like other men waged war.

Part of me—a dangerous, reckless part—wanted to be the center of his world, even if just for a few precious moments. I craved every part of him, mind and body. And that frightened me even more than the prospect of building an addiction to his blood.

I slumped against the wall, feeling the peeling wallpaper catch on my silk dress. "There was no Blood Pact," I said.

"Seriously?" Selena scoffed. The rusted springs in her mattress creaked as she leaned forward. "You have the balls to deny it when you reek of him?" She stretched her neck and inhaled the air, like a bloodhound on a scent.

"It was him," I admitted, striving for calm but failing miserably. "He didn't bite me. Happy now?"

Her approving nod twisted the knife in my stomach. "So he does have a brain, after all."

I leveled her with my glare of doom. "How would you feel if Terraknight did that to you?" I snarled, but my voice sounded quiet and cold. "Wouldn't it make you feel... I don't know—undeserving? Like you're not *enough*?"

"Well, if you put it like that, I'd be pissed. Obviously."

Obviously.

"But he's not my outlier," she continued, raising a finger to silence my protest. "And I'm not his commanding officer. There's a reason for these rules, A. It's not just about him, or his varcolac heritage. If you grow too attached, you endanger not just yourself, but everyone around you."

Gah. I pushed off the wall, pacing the length of the rug. The rational part of my brain knew she was right, but every other part of me rebelled against her logic.

"I know," I said, brushing my fingers through my hair. "I know all of that. But Sel, I can't stop thinking about him. It's driving me crazy." His scent clung to me; I couldn't get rid of it.

Concern twisted her face, her brows furrowing. "Is it the blood? Are you craving it?"

"No more than I did after the Initiation." I shook my head. "It was... the kiss. He kissed me instead of biting me."

"He refused your blood for a kiss?" she demanded, aversion curling her lip.

"It was more than a simple kiss," I defended, then bit my tongue. "That's beside the point. You're giving our 'relationship' too much credit. He's confusing the hell out of me, yes. But there's nothing more to worry about. I'm pretty sure it was a one-off thing, since he's been avoiding me like I'm carrying the plague."

I tried to rationalize it. He knew I was attracted to him. For him, this was probably just a game. I was a pureblood, his natural enemy. Not exactly the type of woman he'd settle down with. And I... I wasn't the kind of woman who *could* settle down with him.

"I'm going to be a queen, Sel. Court life is all I know. Any relationship with Harbinger would be reputation suicide. I'd have to abdicate, leave my coven." I pressed my fingers to my temples, trying to stave off the mounting pressure. "The throne would remain in the Wurdulaks' clutches. I'd be a traitor to my country, a pariah. And I would have no power to help end this."

"A, you're getting way ahead of yourself—"

"Am I?" I spun to face her. "Even as we are now, if the Council ever finds out about him—about us not reporting him—they could put us on trial. They'd likely organize a Nightwatch hunt to kill him." A growl rattled deep within. "By the Moon, what was I even thinking getting involved with him?"

Selena stood and crossed the room to place a steadying hand on my shoulder. "You're right," she said softly. "Using Harbinger as a blood source is one thing, but you and him together... it's not a good idea."

I had every reason to stay away, yet I craved him. Harbinger pulled me in like a black hole. I wanted him more than I'd ever wanted anyone in my life.

But no. This couldn't happen. I knew my heart too well. If I let myself get close to him, attachment would be inevitable. It would be so hard not to fall for him. And once he tired of me, he'd shatter my heart into a million pieces, leaving me to pick up the jagged shards alone.

Giving in to this feeling would be like diving into a stormy sea. I'd be swept away, lost in the current. I would drown.

I didn't want to drown.

I couldn't afford to drown.

During those fleeting moments with him, he'd made me feel safe, cherished, desired, essential. But it was all smoke and mirrors.

I needed to snap out of this fantasy. The more I dwelled on it, the more furious I became—at him, at myself, at the whole damn situation.

"He needs someone to fawn over him anyway. And that's definitely not me," I said, rolling my eyes.

The bathroom door opened, and Terraknight emerged, looking... Underworld's balls. His dark skin gleamed, still damp from the shower, and he'd donned an all-leather ensemble: shiny black boots, leather pants that hugged his sculpted thighs, and a black leather cuirass strapped across his ribs. An oversized sword, rusted and blunt, dangled from his back.

What the hell had I interrupted?

I arched a brow. "Should I even bother to ask?"

"Burebista," Terraknight provided with a smug grin, "the greatest king of Solanthia."

Selena's hungry eyes roamed over him. "We had different views about mortal prowess, and he was working *hard* to prove me wrong," she explained as her voice grew throaty. "We're still debating."

Terraknight prowled toward her, scooped her up, and slumped on the bed with her sideways on his lap. She let out an uncharacteristically girlish shriek.

"I'm sure you'll reach a conclusion eventually," I muttered, unable to keep the bitterness from my voice.

Envy ate away at me—envy of my best friend, of her ability to separate her heart from the simple pleasure of a Blood Pact, of her life. For once, I wished it was her bloodright to rule over the Republic and mine to head a department of magical geniuses.

Terraknight's smirk was slier than a fox's. "So, who's fawning over whom?"

Great. He'd been eavesdropping.

"Aurora was just saying that Harbinger needs a pleaser-babe, instead of a strong, independent woman," Selena oh-so-helpfully supplied.

"A pleaser-babe?" He frowned.

"Oh, you know. Someone to cater to his every whim." I placed a hand on my chest and lowered my voice. "Oh, exalted captain, shall I fetch your slippers? Would you like me to fan you with palm leaves while feeding you grapes? Perhaps I could write a sonnet about your mastery in battle? Or maybe you'd prefer I just grovel at your feet and praise your infinite wisdom?"

It wasn't until I finished my tirade that I noticed Selena had gone eerily still. She sat frozen, her eyes fixed on a point just above my head.

A draft fluttered my dress. The hairs at my nape stood on end. "He's right behind me, isn't he?"

Selena's slow nod confirmed my worst fear. Terraknight pressed his lips together, clearly fighting back laughter.

Damn it. How had I not heard him open the door? And where was that intoxicating scent of his when I needed an early warning?

"I believe the correct phrasing would be 'May I grovel at your feet, sir?'" Harbinger's deep voice sent an involuntary shiver through my body. "If you're going to mock me, at least do it with proper grammar."

He moved into my line of sight, his arms folded across his chest in a way that made his biceps swell. As if that wasn't enough, he was wearing loose-fitting gray sweats and a shirt that had seen better days, torn in all the right places. It was totally unfair. By all rights, he should've developed a terrible case of acne, lost his perfect hair, or at least gotten a bit pudgy in the last couple of days. But no, he looked good—like this time apart had been the best thing that had happened to him.

Just breathe. Don't let him see how affected you are.

He produced a small vial of blood and offered it to me. I reached for it, and our fingers brushed. His touch lingered, sending a spark of electricity up my arm. Golden feathers swirled around his pupils, dancing among tiny flecks of crimson.

My heart skipped a beat and rose to my throat. His lips parted to reveal the edge of his teeth.

"I left this for you in the icebox, Projector," he rasped, a growl emerging from his throat. "Terraknight should've given it to you yesterday."

At the mention of his name, Terraknight bolted upright, catapulting Selena from his lap. She stumbled to her feet, her wide eyes darting between us.

"Shit! I forgot," Terraknight said, running his hands over his short-cropped hair.

A flash of gold rolled across Harbinger's irises. I snatched the bottle and retreated backward. His face showed no emotion. No triumph or rage, nothing at all.

Terraknight's gaze flicked from me to Harbinger, then back to me again, his brow furrowed in confusion or concern—I couldn't tell which.

"I'm sorry, Projector." He tapped Harbinger on the chest and said, "You. Sparring room. Now," before stepping out into the hallway.

Harbinger followed without another word.

I slammed the door shut and leaned against it, my heart pounding as I tried to make sense of what had just happened.

Harbinger. Radu. The hybrid. The legendary outlier. A maddening, exasperating, perilous man who pushed me to the edge of sanity and made my thoughts race and my mouth run wild.

He'd kissed me. Done more than that... so much more. He'd let his guard down, revealed a gentler side I hadn't known existed.

And then he'd bled into a bottle instead of touching me again.

I slid down the door, clutching the vial to my chest. I understood his reasoning—keeping me fed, protecting his team. But was that all there was to it?

Was any of it real? This... whatever it was between him and me.

No. Probably not.

With my palms pressed to my eyes, I fought back the sting of tears. I was fooling myself. This desperate yearning for someone to accept me, love me for who I was—it was clouding my judgment. It's easy to see what you want to see when you're starved for affection. I'd fallen into that trap before and gotten burned. Never again.

To Harbinger, I was likely nothing more than a puzzle to solve, a challenge to overcome. He'd played his part perfectly, drawing me in with sweet gestures and smooth words. And I'd fallen for it hook, line, and sinker.

That was the cold, harsh truth. Ugly and inescapable as it was.

Now I had to accept it and move on.

AURORA

"WELL, THAT WAS INTENSE." Selena's whistle cleaved through the quiet. "You okay, A?"

I raised my head, meeting her gaze. "I'm fine." The words tasted slimy, as if I'd drunk a bottle of rotten blood. *Liar.*

She narrowed her eyes, unconvinced. "Look, I know I've said this before, but I'm going to say it again because I love you. Whatever's going on between you and Harbinger... is dangerous. And I'm not just talking about the political ramifications. That man—"

"Radu." His name slipped through clenched teeth.

Selena's eyebrows shot up. "Oh, so you're on a first-name basis now?"

"That's only me. To him, I'm still 'Projector.'" I rolled the vial between my fingers, watching it catch the candlelight. My stomach knotted.

"A," Selena said softly, "you're playing with fire. The way he looked at you..."

Something fierce and violent boiled inside me, straining against my control. I rose to my feet, smoothing out nonexistent creases in my dress while I counted to five in my head.

It didn't help. Resentment seeped into my voice like poison. "And how exactly did he look at me? Like I'm dirt? Like I'm no better than the people who killed his parents?"

Selena took a step back, surprise flashing in her eyes. "That's not what I—"

"No, you're right," I pressed, straightening my spine. "Because from where I'm standing, all I see is a man who tested the waters and now regrets it. I probably repulse him. You know, since he'd rather bleed into a bottle than let me touch..." I bit down so hard that my jaw started to throb.

A fire spread through my chest, scorching my throat. *So what if I thought it was more?* I crushed the thought and scattered the pieces. I could do this. Use him purely for his blood. *Just stay cool. Wait for this infatuation to burn out.*

Selena gripped my shoulders and gave them a light shake. "A, wait. You've got it all wrong."

I shook my head, turning toward the door. "It doesn't matter. I need to go make amends with the others. I really messed up things with them."

Pounding footfalls on the stairs stopped me in my tracks. For a split second, my weak heart hoped it was Harbinger.

But of course it wasn't. He had no reason to come back. To him, I was just a *Projector*. Nothing more.

And it was time I accepted that.

"Ember... Wait a second," Quakelord's voice rumbled in the hallway.

A wave of rosemary and honey wafted through the door, followed by hurried steps halting two doors down. Ember's mortal heart thundered like a war march, her breathing short and fast.

I released the doorknob, taking a step back.

"Why? Why does Harbinger always take her side?" she snapped. The resentment in her tone sharpened her scent, wedging it in my sinuses like a serrated blade.

Quakelord's soft *pat-pat* did little to soothe her. If anything, her pulse quickened. "Come on, Ember... She won't last. What projector has ever tolerated harmonizing with him for more than a couple of months?"

My stomach twisted, anger boiling inside me. More lies, more secrets. The bitter taste of betrayal flooded my mouth.

"You're right..." Her voice softened slightly. "But we barely have any time together, and now... Phoenix's gone, and I-I hate that she's stolen our peaceful mornings."

The desert in my mouth grew, each swallow a grain of sand scraping my throat raw. I stood frozen, caught between the urge to confront them and the shame of eavesdropping.

"She's lucky we haven't met any Black Sheep or the Shepherd yet, but luck like that won't last."

"I hope, the next time we face them, Harbinger ends her!" Ember spat. "Why is he so concerned about one wretched immortal?"

Selena's eyes widened in shock, her mouth forming a silent 'what the fuck?'

Ember's loathing struck me like a venom-tipped arrow, piercing straight through my heart and feeding the inferno raging inside. My fingers curled into fists, nails cutting into my palms.

"Captain doesn't hurt projectors because he wants to," Quakelord reasoned. "Could you say that to his face? 'I don't like the princess, so just destroy her.' Could you ask him to do that?"

Ember's breath grew heavy, her heartbeats slowing. "You know I couldn't. He's family. I can't ask that from him. Even though he's used to hearing those monsters scream before they break, I still can't bring myself to do it."

I buried my fingernails deeper into my palms, drawing blood. The pain grounded me, reminded me of my self-control, and kept me from bursting out of the room and demanding answers.

"Come here," Quakelord murmured, followed by the rustle of an embrace.

"I can't forgive her," Her voice cracked. "They killed my family. They toyed with them like targets at a shooting range. The purebloods are all scum... I'll never forgive them."

On a scale of one to ten, Embers' hatred was a twenty. It crushed my chest like an anvil. Fury and remorse waged war inside me—not at Ember, but at the unjust past and its repercussions.

"I know, and you don't have to," he soothed. "Take what you need, and let's get back before Terra and Cap finish sparring."

Ember's door creaked open, lost in the high-pitched ringing in my ears. I unclenched my jaw, tasting blood where I'd bitten my cheek.

Once their voices faded down the stairs, Selena whispered, her voice tight, "She fucking hates your guts."

"Can you blame her? You heard what they did to her family." I gripped the doorknob, snapping it off. With a grunt, I shoved the useless chunk of metal onto the floor, leaving a dent.

"I must apologize to them, Sel. I need to go."

The purebloods are all scum... The chasm I had to bridge after reclaiming my crown grew wider by the second.

"Go. I'm right behind you, just let me freshen up," she said, slamming the bathroom door behind her.

I stepped into the corridor and drew a deep breath. The scent of rosemary, honey, and Quakelord's moss still lingered in the air. A fire inside me raged from two sides: the prospect of facing Harbinger again, and the echo of Ember's hateful words. Time to confront this mess head-on.

Because that's what a future queen would do.

I slipped the vial of Harbinger's blood into my cleavage and descended the stairs with calculated slowness while I crafted my strategy. The key to dealing with him was indifference. I'd be cool, calm, collected—a mountain lake unruffled by storms. Harbinger didn't deserve my attention anymore.

No violence. No matter how satisfying it might be. You're above such impulses.

Breathe in peace, breathe out frustration. You're Aurora Tepes. You don't lose your composure over a man.

Hummingbird's boyish voice drifted up from the foyer. The stairs ended far too soon, leaving me cursing the bastard who'd designed them so short. I imagined introducing him to each step personally, and making him count them with his head.

Breathe in, breathe out.

I headed for the double doors, which stood ajar. Ceramic clinks and Quakelord's hacking coughs spilled through the narrow crack.

"This is terrible. Why did you let me drink it?"

Gale's laughter rang out. "Someone had to try Terra's new mead recipe, and it surely wasn't gonna be me."

Squaring my shoulders, I swung the doors open. The room that greeted me was a shell of a Victorian salon, stripped down to its bare bones. Tattered wallpaper revealed raw plaster, severed cables hung where chandeliers once sparkled, and the scarred wooden floor told tales of countless sparring matches.

Quakelord and Gale shared a murky bottle at a corner table. Hummingbird perched on a chest, cocooned in his dusty-white wings, cheering the fighters. Ember lounged on a threadbare sofa, watching Harbinger hold Terraknight in a guillotine choke.

At my entrance, Harbinger's grip loosened, and Terraknight escaped, rolling backward.

"Do you need something, Projector?" Harbinger's tone was ice. His dismissiveness fueled the wildfire inside me. I saw his face out of the corner of my eye—like staring into a sheer stone cliff.

Plastering on a cordial smile, I addressed the vice-captain, "Terraknight. Please tell your captain the world doesn't revolve around him."

Pearl appeared at my side, offered me a cup of kafea, and winced at my expression. Catching my reflection in the metallic mug, I saw why—the face staring back was less 'composed royal' and more 'deranged killer'. I quickly schooled my features and accepted the drink.

A tidbit from a psychology text came to mind while I stirred. Repetitive motions like this, or the twisting of a ring on a finger, could calm the mind. Right now, I needed all the calm I could get, lest my pent-up anger explode all over Harbinger.

Round and round goes the spoon. Don't look at him. Don't think about punching that infuriatingly stoic face.

It wasn't meditation, but if it prevented an inter-guild incident, I'd call it a win.

Terraknight's gaze ping-ponged between Harbinger and me, the corner of his mouth twitching upward. "Projector says—"

"I heard what she said."

I didn't need to look at Harbinger to feel the heat of his glare burning into me. The spoon warped under the pressure of my fingers. Needing an outlet to vent my frustration, I pulled it out and began working it back and forth between my hands.

I deliberately turned my back on him, addressing the rest of the guild. "I realize this is long overdue, but I owe you an apology. What I did is unforgivable, and your resentment is justified. It's only natural, given my actions and who I am—"

"Damn right," Hummingbird yelled, his feathers bristling.

The spoon snapped in my grip. I tossed it onto Pearl's tray and held Hummingbird's fawn-brown eyes, choking down the clump in my throat. "I didn't leave the Republic to save you, but myself. Circumstances have changed, and now that I'm here, I would never forgive myself if I let you fight alone. So, regardless of how much you may hate me, please allow me to help you."

The room fell silent. I could feel their eyes on me, assessing, judging. My pulse quickened and my skin crawled under their scrutiny.

Ember sat up, her voice edged with frost. "You've joined us in battle. What more could you possibly want?"

I swallowed hard but kept my chin high. "I would like to know your real names," I said, then quickly added, "if you're willing to share them. I understand if you aren't."

Quakelord raised the bottle to his mouth and took a long gulp. He grimaced, his whole body shaking with disgust. "I remember this projector from my early days out of the camp," he started, a touch of reluctance showing in his voice. "He'd inspect our quarters, always wearing this stupid smile. But like us, he believed it was messed up that only the halfbloods were on the front lines. So, he returned to the battlefield on his own. Sound familiar?"

My hands trembled, and I clasped them around the cup, trying to hide my nervousness.

"Anyway," he sighed, leaning on his elbows, "we couldn't say anything to his face, but the whole guild trash-talked him behind his back. We all hated his guts. I mean, how couldn't we? He called himself an outlier like us... but then he chose to be here. We never got that choice."

He took another gulp, then breathed fire. "We'd place bets on when we thought he'd tire of his pity game and hightail it back home. But we were wrong. The projector never made it back. He stayed to defend us and got himself killed." His dark eyes met mine, filled with grudging respect. "I'm Horia Bratu, by the way. Call me Horia, little brat, or whatever you want. I'm fine with anything."

I managed a nod and a weak smile, afraid my voice would crack if I spoke.

Terraknight stalked over to Quakelord and snatched the bottle.

"The name's Sabin Cantemir," he said, his voice gruff but not unkind. "But I should apologize before anything else. When you arrived, we mocked you, thinking you were just another patronizing scum, just like all those before you. I'm sorry about that."

Before I could respond, Gale cut in. "Speak for yourself, asshole. I liked her from the start." She winked at me. "I'm Alina Wyrm."

Pearl wrapped an arm around me, pulling me into her side. "Yeah, don't listen to him, Projector. He's full of shit." She clinked her cup to mine, her smile warm. "My name is Karina Bulwark."

"Tudor Steros," Hummingbird leaped from his perch and shoved his hands in his pockets. His brows sloped down, shadowing his eyes. "I'm sorry too. I shouldn't have called you a hypocrite or accused you. You didn't throw us into this hellhole. I know that. I'm sorry for the way I talked to you."

A strange, gratifying fatigue settled into my bones. My eyes welled up, but for once, they were happy tears. I felt a glimmer of hope, fragile but real.

Ember's scoff broke the moment, and Hummingbird rounded on her. "Why are you looking away, as if you've got nothing to do with this? You were just as pissed off as I was. If I hadn't snapped at the projector, you'd have been yelling at her instead!"

Her face flushed a deep red, and I quickly stepped in, trying to diffuse the situation. "It's alright, Ember. You don't have to say anything—"

"No, he's right." She sighed, lifting her gaze from the floor to look at me. "It's not your fault what happened to us, to our families. We can see that you're trying. You put your life in danger for Ph-Phoenix..." Her voice cracked on the name.

My chest tightened, crushing my lungs. "Ditoa Firestarter," I murmured. "Her name will live with me for the rest of my life."

Ember's green eyes glistened, but she worked to steady her voice. "Lena. My name. It's Lena Longtail."

I bit my lip, tasting the salt of my own tears. "And I'm Aurora Rada Tepes. But everyone calls me Aurora." My voice came out thick as I wiped my eyes, smiling through my tears. "Thank you. I'll cherish and carry your names with me forever."

A rush of warmth spread through me. This was monumental progress. I felt light, almost giddy.

Then, Quakelord's ill-timed question shattered my euphoria. "What about Captain? Aren't you going to ask his name?"

Gale groaned. "Oh, you idiot..."

I turned, locking eyes with Harbinger's scalding hot gaze. The amber in his eyes glowed like the wrath of a vengeful god.

My muscles coiled, fine hairs rising on my nape. Every instinct snarled 'don't antagonize him,' but when had I ever listened to reason around him?

Cocking an eyebrow, I drawled, "Your death glare doesn't intimidate me." My fingers flexed at my sides, betraying the tension I tried to hide.

"Oh, so you're talking to me now," he rumbled.

His throaty voice sent an unwanted shiver throughout my body, but I stepped closer, drawn in despite myself. "I never stopped. Just saved my breath on you."

"Careful, Projector. Someone might think you care."

"Care? About you?" I scoffed. "You're not that special."

The room sucked a collective inhale.

Terraknight shook his head, amused. Hummingbird and Pearl exchanged wide-eyed glances. Quakelord's jaw dropped, while Gale bit her lip to stifle a laugh. Ember looked utterly bewildered, her gaze flitting between us.

Harbinger's eyes narrowed to slits. "Oh, but I think I am, *Your Majesty*. Otherwise, why get *involved* when all I'm good for is jeopardizing your precious reputation?"

Underworld's pits and balls. He'd heard my conversation with Selena.

I pressed the Nexus, initiating the Harmonization. *"You vanished,"* I projected, raw hurt bleeding through. *"Left your blood in a vial like I was diseased. What was I supposed to think?"*

His mental voice snapped with anger. *"I had urgent business. The blood was to keep you strong. If you didn't want that kiss, you should've said so, not act like a teenager with excuses."*

"Don't insult me," I snarled. *"Urgent business? In this wasteland? Enlighten me, where did you have to go?"*

"Uh, guys?" Terraknight interrupted.

"What?" we snapped in unison.

He looked between us, confused. "Should we... give you some privacy?"

"Yes," Harbinger said, just as I countered, "Absolutely not. We're done here."

Harbinger's jaw muscles ticked. "We're not finished yet. You're going to listen, and then we're going to have a civil conversation. If you've forgotten how, I'm sure someone here can remind you."

A laugh rose from my throat. "Always so *commanding*. Has anyone ever told you that's not attractive?"

"You seemed to find it attractive enough the other night," he shot back through our link.

I stalked toward him. *"Let me spell it out for you. You disappeared without explanation. Avoided me. Bottled your blood instead of letting me feed from you. You made me feel things I thought I could never feel again, then froze me out. Didn't even bite back. Face it, Radu. Whatever this was, it was over before it started."*

We stood toe to toe, charged air raising goosebumps on my skin. The room faded away, leaving just us and the magnetic pull between our bodies.

I wasn't sure if I wanted to slap him or kiss him senseless—and from the hunger in his eyes, he battled the same dilemma.

"Is that what you really want, Aurora?" he murmured, low and intimate.

The sound of my name on his lips nearly crumbled my walls. What I wanted was for him to stop playing games with my heart—

BOOM!

The grandfather clock crashed down. Wood splintered, glass shattered, and Selena's gut-wrenching screams mingled with the swinging pendulum.

"Selena!" I yelled, bolting to the exit, my pulse racing like thunder.

AURORA

I BURST OUT OF the sparring room just as Selena leaped over the railing and crashed onto the marble coffee table. Pink primroses, delicate figurines, and crystal shards exploded across the polished floor and velvet settees.

She dove behind me, using me as a pureblood shield, her eyes scanning the upper level. "There's a-a *thing*!"

Before I could ask what 'thing', a blur of charcoal wings and gangly limbs came hurtling over the banister. It hit the floor with a squeak, rolled, and let out a shrill wail from its beaked mouth. Yellow eyes blinked owlishly, scanning the foyer.

The doors slammed open, and Terraknight rushed past. "Sugar!" he called out, his voice rising to a pitch but filled with affection. "Where have you been, you little troublemaker?"

The rest of the Black Guild poured into the hallway.

Selena, still clinging to my shoulders, demanded, "What the hell is that?"

Terraknight chuckled, kneeling to welcome the creature. "So, there is something that scares you, huh?"

The creature had other ideas. It soared over Terraknight's head, bypassing us all to land squarely in Harbinger's arms.

My breath caught. "Is that a… zmeu?" I whispered as Harbinger sat on the burgundy settee.

Zmei belonged in the snowy peaks of the Carpathian Mountains, not here in the Outer Wards. And certainly not as a pet.

Gale sidled up, cooing as she stroked the rough skin between its eyes. "Oh yeah, he's our little mascot. Likes to play hide and seek, though." She grinned at Harbinger. "Captain picked him up. Tiny thing's been following him around since hatching."

I frowned, recalling the illustrations in Sonya's atlas. An adult zmeu was massive, twice the size of a pureblood, with wings spanning three times an iele's and scales as hard as forged iron. The zmeu in Harbinger's lap couldn't be more than a few months old.

It pawed at his gleaming white hair, and my heart swelled. Despite our issues, I couldn't help but soften at the gentleness with which he cradled the little dragon. It was the same side of him he showed me in his room, and it stirred feelings I wished gone.

Pearl rolled her azure eyes. "I don't know what it sees in him. The captain doesn't even pay attention to it."

"Maybe it just likes him for a comfy perch," Hummingbird quipped. "Cap never moves when he's reading. Perfect nap spot."

"Unlike you," Pearl shot back. "You're too loud. That's why it doesn't like you."

Hummingbird clutched his chest in mock offense. "Wow, rude! And totally unfair! I demand a formal apology and snacks as compensation."

Their banter faded into the background, but my eyes remained fixed on Harbinger. It was moments like these, I realized, that kept them going. Radu was the calm eye of their storm. He was the protector between them and the grim world outside.

"So," I said, smiling when the zmeu purred contentedly, "what's his name?"

Everyone chimed in at once.

"Ash!"

"Sugar!"

"Birdie!"

"Boy!"

"Chubby!"

They all turned to Harbinger. He looked up at them, one dark-blond eyebrow raised. "Zmeu," he said.

Our eyes met over the creature's head, and the scarlet ring flickered in his gaze before he blinked it away—warmth, calmness, perhaps, a silent apology. I couldn't know for sure.

The zmeu chirped, and Terraknight swatted at Quakelord. "For the hundredth time, stop calling him fat. He's just a baby!"

"Wait... Have you all named it?" I asked, puzzled.

Gale chuckled. "It's an ash-colored baby boy who loves cakes and sings like a crow when hungry. We haven't settled on a specific name, so we just call him whatever we feel like. Lately, he's learned to come when we glance his way."

"But why not just decide on a name?" Selena asked over my shoulder.

Sabin was quick to defend, "His name is Sugar!"

"It's not," Gale rolled her eyes. "We all have our own attachments to him—"

Harbinger jumped to his feet, his tattered shirt stretching over coiled muscles. The baby zmeu whimpered, soaring toward the chandelier.

My pulse stuttered.

He fixed his piercing amber gaze on the diamond entrance doors, but it was the stillness in his gaze that betrayed a wandering mind. He was listening intently to something only he could hear. The others followed his line of sight, awaiting orders.

An icy breath swept over my spine. "Did something happen?" I asked, noticing the tight muscles jumping along his jaw.

I'd learned to read his body language. When he squared his shoulders and crossed his arms like that, it mirrored a cobra poised to strike. A prickly rush of adrenaline swept over me.

I stretched out my magic, mapping our surroundings. I pushed my limits until my head throbbed with pain, extending my senses to the glade where the zeppelin had dropped Selena and me. But I detected nothing unusual.

"Projector Tepes," Harbinger's gravelly voice cut through the air like a knife on stone. "Please get ready for battle. Stalkers are coming."

TRANSYLVANIAN SPRINGS SEEMED DETERMINED to outdo themselves in unpleasantness. Typically, we could count on a steady diet of rain and gloom. Sometimes a light dusting of snow would make an appearance, melting almost as soon as it touched the ground. But in recent years, the season had taken on a more capricious nature.

Three times out of four, we'd get the usual dreary mix. But that fourth time? Winter would return with a vengeance, bringing heavy snowfall and bone-chilling cold. Some blamed the Gloom, which I now knew as the insidious Limus-sand mist. Others saw it as divine retribution for the ongoing war. Whatever the cause, I longed for the predictable misery of springs past.

By the time we reached Brasov, I was chilled to the marrow.

The city stood silent, a ghost of what it once was. Where bustling markets thrived a century ago, now only ruins remained.

Selena and I huddled by a brick chimney, surveying the desolate landscape of collapsed rooftops and moss-covered turrets. Nature had reclaimed its territory, vines snaking up weathered walls. In the central square, Derzelas' fallen statue rested among shattered cobblestones half buried in snow. A lone black marble wall, all that remained of the old temple, gleamed in the moonlight.

Stalkers prowled the ruins, eyes glinting with bloodlust. A frosty whisper that had nothing to do with the weather slithered down my back and settled in my bones. Their numbers far exceeded our expectations.

Harbinger's words from our strategy meeting bounced around in my mind, raising my blood pressure. *'Three legions, approximately fifty each. Mixed types.'* His precision had nagged at me then, and still did now.

How was Harbinger so certain without Blood Manipulation or scanners?

Now, as moonlight silvered Brasov's ruins, that question burned anew. Harbinger's eyes darted across the square through the Astral Visor.

"This place... it feels different today," his voice streamed in my mind.

Terraknight countered, *"Just the calm before the storm. We've been through this before."*

"If you're making it sound like a piece of cake, I might strangle you." Harbinger growled, his tone darkening. *"Something's off. It's too quiet—never this quiet."*

Selena shot me a questioning glance as uneasy silence spread through the Harmonization.

"But that's a good sign, right?" Hummingbird's light words relieved some of the tension. *"No Black Sheep in sight."*

"Can't sense any," Harbinger confirmed.

"So, what's the call? We proceed?" Terraknight asked.

Harbinger didn't reply straightaway, likely weighing options, then said, *"Yes, but be careful."*

We leaped from the rooftop and crept down the alley. My magic thrummed beneath my skin, ready to explode at the first sign of a Stalker.

I was about to report on the enemy's composition when I sensed a shift. The Stalkers regrouped, forming tight formations.

An unsettling hush fell over the city, like that ill-fated mission with the Sparrows. Dread coiled in my gut.

"Harbinger," I said, recalling his past battles, searching for patterns, "their formation's changed. It's more precise. Have you seen this before?"

"You're right, Projector. They are... more compact." His evasive tone made my blood boil. He was hiding something—something bigger than his usual lies or even his ability to predict Stalker attacks.

"Based on your reports, if they've developed self-preservation, Ignises wouldn't be at the vanguard," I pressed on, voice sharp. *Let him hear I was onto him.* "We should separate them, target the Ignises before they combine powers."

"You keep talking about preservation and tactics... Do you even sleep, woman?" Terraknight chuckled.

"I don't have time for that," I muttered, thinking about the mountain of reports Harbinger had 'found' last week. Another lie to add to the pile.

"Projector," Harbinger cut in, a harsh note seeping into his tone. *"I need you to shut down your Nexus for this mission."*

His command stabbed deep, penetrating the mental armor I had donned for him. Without the Nexus, I'd be blind. I couldn't believe he'd sideline me to satisfy his petty revenge. My chest constricted. After everything, he still thought so little of me.

"If you want an explanation, I'll provide one later. Cut the link!" he yelled.

I'd been a fool to think he'd trust me in battle. Tears burned my eyes, pain curdling into rage.

"With all due respect, *Captain*," I said, injecting as much frost into my voice as I could muster, "I fail to see how cutting off my primary means of communication and tactical awareness benefits this mission. Unless you have a damn good reason, my Nexus stays on. The guild's safety comes first, regardless of... personal issues."

"Projector, do as I say. You'll thank me later."

"Transmitters might jam in the Gloom. I'm not cutting my connection."

The Stalkers' sudden movement swallowed his growl.

"For what it's worth, I warned you."

His bitterness stung more than I cared to admit. I whirled to Selena. "When this is over, I'm going to kill him."

She nodded. "You've put up with enough of his bullshit. I'll hold him down for you."

The air soured. Two Glacies landed before us, massive ebony wings blotting out the moon. At the alley's other end, a Limus appeared from the Gloom, claws scoring deep furrows in the stone. Its howl froze my blood, but rage kept me burning.

The hellhound charged, eyes blazing crimson in the darkness. I moved, shoved Selena to safety, and plunged my fist through the first Glacie's throat. Bones and vocal cords shredded beneath my fingers. It collapsed, ice shards exploding into a glittering mist.

I pivoted. My leg hooked the second Glacie's as I ripped its heart out before it hit the ground. The crunch of ribs seemed distant as I fumbled for my needles.

It cost me a fraction of a second. The Limus ascended, jaws gaping. I caught it mid-air, driving a needle deep into its rabid eye. Twisting past, I unleashed a savage kick into the first Glacie's abdomen.

Stay down.

Bones splintered under my heel as it gurgled on its own tainted blood.

It staggered, and I seized its head in both hands. With a furious roar, I wrenched, feeling vertebrae snap and tendons tear. The Glacie's head came free in a spray of ichor.

Silence fell. The Limus gave one final, pitiful whine before collapsing.

Selena gaped at me, awe etched on her face. "Remind me never to get on your bad side," she said, eyeing the carnage. "I almost feel sorry for Harbinger. Almost."

My chest heaved, each breath tasting of rot and bitter anger. "I'm so furious I can barely see straight," I snarled.

Black Guild herded the Stalkers into the square, and the threads in my head grew tense. Wails and explosions fractured the night, injecting more adrenaline into my muscles. It was all going how it had before, so why did I feel so on edge?

"Where do you want me?" Selena asked.

"Take the south," I ordered, already scaling the sandstone facade. "I'll handle the north."

She nodded and disappeared into the shadows, touching her forehead with a quick tap.

From my perch near the eave, I surveyed the battlefield, my hands still slick with Stalker blood. But it wasn't enough to quench the firestorm of betrayal in my chest.

Terraknight and Ember emerged from the east, flanking over fifty Stalkers. Ember's veins lit up as she summoned her magic. A ghostly pinwheel of flames formed between her fingers, growing into a blinding ten-foot fireball. She hurled it at the rear guard. Limuses, Nebulas, and Glacies ignited, their cries choked by thickening sand.

I lashed out with my magic, seizing the vanguard. A sharp pang coursed through my skull, but I channeled it into my assault. The Gloom thinned, and I saw Terraknight raise his hand. Dark, thorny roots erupted from the ground, impaling Ignises. Ember's twin-flame jets engulfed the flanks.

To the south, the ieles provided aerial support to Pearl and Quakelord.

Pearl's water blast sliced through Stalkers while Quakelord cleaved the earth open. It looked as if a giant had driven a sword into it. Winds howled, sweeping monsters into the abyss.

Harbinger flickered across the square, a blur of platinum strands and his flashing blade. Corpses littered his wake. The stench of death thickened the air.

The remaining Stalkers regrouped, advancing in a tight column. The Gloom spread before them like a living shroud.

A piercing scream broke my concentration. I gritted my teeth, tracing the threads to find its source. One outlier was at the receiving end of that terrible sound.

The Stalkers froze as if hitting an invisible wall—Selena's handiwork, no doubt. But one Nebula broke free, approaching Harbinger with sinister purpose.

Move, you idiot, I thought, fists clenched as he remained motionless.

The Nebula stopped just out of reach, raising all four arms in a grotesque embrace.

A single word rang through the Harmonization.

"Brother." The voice thundered in my head with bloodcurdling clarity.

At that moment, everything—Harbinger's uncanny knowledge, his secretive behavior, the Stalkers' bizarre tactics—crystallized into a horrifying truth.

Rage, hot and vicious, surged through me. I'd trusted him, defended him, even started to care for him. And all this time...

He could *communicate* with them. With the enemy.

"Harbinger," I snarled, my voice quivering with fury, "when this is over, you and I are going to have a very long, very painful conversation."

The Nebula's voice rasped again, hollow as a dying child's final gasp. Warmth trickled down my neck—blood, I realized with mounting horror.

"Brother, Brother, Brother—"

Each whispered repetition was a dagger to my skull.

I whimpered, muscles seizing. Roof tiles shattered beneath me as I collapsed, every fiber in my body rigid with terror. The haunting cries shredded my mind like paper in a storm, flaying me alive from the inside out.

"Brother."

Desperate, I clapped my hands over my ears, though I knew it was futile. The assault came from everywhere—my head, my bones, my very blood. The wail stabbed, shredded, scorched, its call to Harbinger relentless. Language dissolved into pure, excruciating noise.

Finally, I broke.

A scream tore from my core.

My veins turned to lava, searing me from within. More voices invaded, a tsunami of agony crashing over me. I choked on my own blood, hot and metallic, as it streamed from my eyes and nose.

"Help me! Help me! Help me—" a shrill plea echoed.

Another joined the hellish chorus. *"It's hot! It's hot! It's hot."*

"No... No... No!"

A dozen echoes clamored in my head, tormenting me.

The world tilted, and air rushed past as I plummeted and crashed into the cobbled alley, the impact sending shockwaves of fresh pain through my body. Darkness encroached. Blood bubbled in my throat. I was drowning, suffocating, dying—and still, the voices wouldn't stop.

"It hurts! It hurts! It hurts!"

"I don't want to die! I don't want to die! I don't want to die!" Ditoa's—Phoenix's—voice, horrifyingly familiar, pierced through the chaos, but agony consumed any chance of response.

I could hear them all.

All sensation left my body, and I felt myself slipping away.

Harbinger's angry growl rose above the maelstrom of moans, whispers, and wails. *"Projector, cut the link! Cut the fucking link!"*

To be continued

✦ ✦ ✦ ○ ◐ ◑ ✦ ◐ ◑ ○ ✦ ✦ ✦

AHHH, I know - that ending was quite the shocker!
The good news is, you won't have to wait too long for the next install-
ment in the Beyond the Gloom series.
Want to get an early look? If you sign up for my <u>newsletter</u>, you'll get
exclusive access to the Prologue of Book 2! Plus, <u>ebook preorders are now
live</u> if you want to secure your copy.

Acknowledgements

Writing a manuscript is a solitary endeavor, but creating a book is a collaborative journey. Introducing my world of the Crowned Republic of Transylvania to you has been an incredible adventure, and I'm indebted to many who've been part of my creative and support team. Without each of them, this book would not have come to fruition.

To my beta readers—Alexandra Camarasan, Jayd Burns, and Julieonna Brewer—thank you for seeing through the unpolished scenes and not-yet-fully-developed characters, providing critical feedback and words of encouragement.

To my writer friend, Aura Tudor, who read every version of this book and challenged me at every step. Your input has been invaluable, and I'm forever grateful.

Lauren Carpenter, my book-sensei, your firm developmental editorial guidance was crucial. Thank you for fearlessly slashing through my manuscript and pushing me to refine various scenes. Aurora is a stronger, more well-rounded character because of you. I'm grateful for your vast experience in English literature, your professionalism, and the friendship we've developed through odd messages and long chats.

To my extraordinary copy-line editor, Ellie Race: I thank my lucky stars for you. Your edits and suggestions were invaluable, your encouragement inspiring, and your dedication admirable. You've transformed this book from a rough diamond into a precious stone with your professionalism and above-and-beyond efforts.

My gratitude extends to the talented cover designer at Miblart for their fantastic work, and to Tania for her invaluable role as intermediary.

A heartfelt thanks to my street team, my biggest supporters. Your enthusiasm and dedication have been a constant source of motivation and inspiration throughout this journey.

A special thanks to my husband, Gabriel, for the countless discussions about this book over the years and for shouldering the housework to help me see it through.

Finally, and perhaps most importantly, to my readers: thank you from the bottom of my heart for choosing to embark on this journey through the Crowned Republic of Transylvania. This is only the beginning, and I hope you'll join Aurora, Harbinger, the outliers, and the many other characters to come in their trials and tribulations. Here's to you!

About the author

Denisa Mih always knew creative arts were her calling, but becoming an author was an unexpected turn. With a background in Landscape Architecture, she stumbled into writing when an idea refused to let go. One page turned into ten pages, ten pages turned into chapters, and before she knew it, her first novel, *Blood Sings*, drew breath and came to life.

Born and raised in post-Communist Transylvania, Denisa grew up surrounded by stories of resistance and change. These experiences, along with Romanian folklore and Dacian mythology, heavily influence her writing. With inspiration from her time in Australia, she blends these elements and creates unique, paranormal tales.

Denisa currently lives in Transylvania with her husband, eagerly awaiting the arrival of their twins. When she's not writing or preparing for parenthood, she can be found exploring the mystical landscapes that fuel her imagination.

Sign-up for Denisa Mih's Newsletter:

For More Information:
www.denisamih.com